They Made The Rules

There was Roger Megan, fading movie star and MC of the Contest, determined to hold on to his own title as showbiz's greatest stud . . . J. F. Fleming, the Mr. Big of the Contest, who supposedly was immune to any human touch . . . Sue Rossiter, the first winner of the Contest, and now a woman whom every new winner had to please . . . Dr. Lydecker, who conducted his own very special physical examinations . . . Max Gerber, famous for his photographs in the big magazines, and notorious for his private collection . . .

They ran the giant beauty game known as the Contest—and every girl who wanted to come out on top had to play it their way. It was hard to know whom to pity more, the losers or the winner of—

THE CONTEST

"Strips the reader of all illusions . . . a natural for a Hollywood smash!"

—*Saturday Review*

The Contest

Mort Weisinger

Library of Congress Catalog Card Number: 72-128482

This is a reprint of a hardcover edition published by The New American Library, Inc., in association with The World Publishing Company. The hardcover edition was published simultaneously in Canada by Nelson, Foster & Scott Ltd.

SIGNET TRADEMARK REG. U.S. PAT. OFF. AND FOREIGN COUNTRIES
REGISTERED TRADEMARK—MARCA REGISTRADA
HECHO EN CHICAGO, U.S.A.

SIGNET, SIGNET CLASSICS, SIGNETTE, MENTOR AND PLUME BOOKS
are published by The New American Library, Inc.,
1301 Avenue of the Americas, New York, New York 10019

FIRST PRINTING, AUGUST, 1971

PRINTED IN THE UNITED STATES OF AMERICA

To my wife,

Thelma,

the fairest of them all.

BOOK ONE *Sunday*

1 · PRINCESS AMERICA

VIRGINIA LOUISE KERR walked out of the door of Surf City's oldest Baptist church just as the bells tolled eleven o'clock. Behind her she could hear the Sunday worshipers asking her female chaperone, "Is it really her? Can I get her autograph?" She shook hands with the minister, smiled radiantly as she praised his sermon, then headed for the forest-green limousine parked at the curb.

"Yes, that's Ginny Kerr, formerly Miss California, now Princess America," her chaperone informed the awed group. "But she never gives autographs in front of a church."

The identification was entirely superfluous. There was no mistaking the classic features.

Even her stride was regal, in sharp contrast to the lumbering gait of the vigilant matron who trailed her. To the enchanted onlookers the scene was a fairy tale come true. The beautiful princess was being whisked away in her royal coach.

Inside the luxurious car, Mrs. Amanda Clarke, Ginny's inseparable companion, leaned forward toward the chauffeur.

"Please turn down the air-conditioning a bit, Henry. Miss Kerr always gets the sniffles when it's too strong." She settled back in her seat and faced Ginny. "Besides, dear, it was blowing straight down on your head. You don't want to appear at your last press conference with your hair a mess."

"Thank you, house mother," said Ginny. She was busy mentally recapping the material Norm Prescott had reviewed with her for two grueling hours yesterday afternoon.

For fifty-one weeks, eleven hours and six minutes, Ginny Kerr had reigned as the twelfth Princess America, the nation's undisputed symbol of beauty, charm and talent. Wherever she had gone, she had been admired, applauded, congratulated, envied, photographed, listened to and looked at, taped and quoted.

But this coming Saturday night, at approximately a quarter to twelve, she would relinquish her scepter to the thirteenth Princess America. More than sixty million viewers would witness her gracious abdication. By midnight, stripped of title, mantle and crown, she would join the circle of Cinderellas who had won the previous contests.

Only three of her predecessors were remembered. The names of the others were in limbo, recorded only in the *petites histoires* published for devotees of the trivia game.

Amanda Clarke glanced at her watch. "We've got time to kill," she announced. "There's something I'd like to show you just outside the city limits."

"Surprise me," said Ginny, noting the twinkle in her eyes.

Mrs. Clarke issued directions to the driver. Gently he applied his brakes, made an expert U-turn, and the car purred smoothly as he headed west on the main concourse. Finally, on the outskirts of the city, Amanda told him to slow down.

"Well, Ginny, what do you think? If you like it, get out and I'll take a picture of you standing under it."

On the left side of the road was a huge billboard. Ginny's eyes sparkled with pride as she read the words.

WELCOME TO SURF CITY
HOME OF THE PRINCESS AMERICA PAGEANT
WE KEEP AMERICA BEAUTIFUL

Ginny opened the door of the car.

After a while Roger Megan decided that the doorbell wasn't going to quit, so he surrendered and propped himself up against the headboard of his double bed. When he opened his eyes, ceiling and floor were spinning. Sunlight came glinting through the blinds to stab him in the back of his skull.

Then he smelled the salt in the air and remembered. It's beginning, he thought, here it is again, the precious week on which everything depended, beginning again.

The doorbell became imperious. Drop dead, Felix, he thought, and he let out a bitter curse. Somehow the resonance of his voice made him feel better, that glorious resonance forever his, and only his.

Once, a decade ago, when his variety show had led the

Nielsens and mocked the critics, that same voice had been as familiar to the public as the MGM lion's roar.

He got out of bed, finally located both halves of his pajamas and clumsily put them on. Barefoot, he staggered out of the bedroom through the mess in the sitting room and unlatched the door to his hotel suite.

To his relief, instead of Felix, there stood Lou Cates, his personal secretary and "take charge" aide. Lou faced him, properly expressionless, with a briefcase in one hand and a slim typewriter case in the other. Good old Lou. Slavishly devoted, yet honest and self-respecting enough never to be obsequious. Megan studied him silently, his glazed brown eyes semaphoring the agony of his hangover, then tottered back to his bed.

In the next room he could hear his secretary righting furniture, gathering the lipstick-rimmed glasses and getting rid of bottles. Then Cates came in and replaced the bedroom phone in its cradle. He had brought the typewriter case with him. Now he laid it on the bed next to Megan and opened it, the beginning of an oft-repeated ritual. Inside was a small tank of oxygen and a face mask. Cautiously sweeping the room with his eyes to make certain there was no smoldering cigarette in the area, he handed Megan the mask and turned the dispensing knob on the cylinder. There was a faint hissing and, almost by reflex, Megan pressed his face into the mask and began to inhale deeply, slowly.

Cates stood by indulgently and watched the transformation. With each pull of the gas, Megan's sodden lifelessness diminished visibly until, after half a dozen inhalations, he yielded the mask. Cates packed it back in the case and took out a small box. From it he removed a hypodermic syringe and an ampule of vitamin B-12. Megan turned over on the crumpled bed sheets and, without being cued, pulled down his pajama bottoms. Cates dipped a cotton swab into alcohol, prepared Megan's right buttock for the shot and probed the needle home with dexterity. Then he went into the bathroom, started the shower and came out to say, "Good morning, great one. We're running half an hour late."

Moments later in the sitting room, Lou Cates went through his briefcase and began laying out its contents on a ridiculously long marble-topped coffee table. In neat stacks he arranged a plethora of memos, releases, clippings, telegrams and letters. Finally he took out a handsome, brand-new red leather spiral-bound notebook. On its cover, embossed in gold, was the legend "13TH ANNUAL

NATIONAL PRINCESS AMERICA PAGEANT, SURF CITY" and under it "ROGER MEGAN, MASTER OF CEREMONIES."

Cates flipped open the notebook and turned to a page studded with a list of appointments that would start in an hour and go on until past midnight.

It was the second Sunday of September, a sunny, windless day, and bright with auspice for Surf City's approaching week of sex and splendor. Tomorrow would mark the opening ceremonies of its claim to the national limelight. Today they were on their way to Surf City from all over America—fifty of the fairest females from the fifty states, each winnowed from thousands, the sweethearts of Sigma Chi and the chosen of the chambers of commerce, with donated sets of matched luggage full of soaring hopes and troubled dreams—converging in a great pilgrimage to the site of the coronation for the annual Princess America.

It was an extraordinary event, a magnificent spectacle and a drama, and also, almost subliminally, a quiet testimony to the commercial benefits often generated by chartered, civic non-profit organizations. For most of the shore resort towns along the coast the season was already over, their bungalow colonies shuttered, motels flashing Vacancy, shops with a sign in the window proclaiming "See You Next Spring." Only a few of the larger towns survived after summer with some semblance of their economy intact. Of these only one—the largest, easily the most eminent, and the only one with a national reputation, Surf City—managed to thrive the year round.

Surf City had long ago learned how to ease the discontent of winter. From one end of the year to the other it played host to an endless series of assemblies, exhibitions, alumni reunions, celebrations, centennials, conventions and contests ("Home of the National Baton Twirling Finals"). All of these, assiduously ballyhooed, were magnetized to Surf City by the most fabulous promotion of all, the lodestone of its prosperity, the Princess America Beauty Pageant.

For fifty-one weeks the Pageant had been in preparation on a vast scale. It had enlisted (its highly paid public-relations chief had proudly told the press) the cooperation of a hundred thousand civic leaders, three thousand communities and more than three hundred colleges. Their collective labors were estimated to have consumed more than a million man-and-woman hours of time.

On this Sunday morning, the exhilarating results of such devotion to beauty were in evidence all over town.

Elsewhere along the coast the boardwalks were deserted, legal terrain again for bicycles and skate boards. But in Surf City the rolling chairs were out in force, wending cautiously past hand-holding couples. The souvenir shops were stocked with bamboo canes, stuffed animals and satin pillows, the taffy kitchens piled high with boxes for mailing to the hinterland, and the penny arcades and hot-dog stands and pizza parlors kept the air ringing with their cash registers. All along the planked promenade, in massive, ornate hotels named after French chateaux and English manor houses, the vanguard of a host was arriving, and in scattered sheds and garages the finishing touches were being applied to the floats for the torchlight parade.

Down on Michigan Avenue, at the armory where twelve thousand would assemble on Saturday night for the zenith hour of the crowning, the Pageant banner floated in the sea air a respectful few feet under the American flag. From its bastions workers arranged the last of its bunting. Below, in the armory parking lot, trucks from the TV network which owned the exclusive rights to telecast the Pageant were unloading python-thick cables for the color cameras. Nearby, perfectly aligned, a fleet of fifty white convertible Pontiacs waited. Inside the armory itself, the men who would drive them—a complement of fifty escort-chauffeurs, all of them police, immaculately clad in dress blues, on official loan from the city's ten precincts—were gathered for a final briefing that would end when Roger Megan came out on the newly erected stage to give them his private pep talk.

Megan had been in the shower less than six minutes when Felix Wolfe was at the door. "Good morning, Lou," he said warily. "How is he?"

"Semi-sensational," said Lou Cates, letting him in.

Wolfe glanced around the room suspiciously, noting how tidy it was. Then his built-in radar guided him to behind a screen, where he found the wastebasket with the betraying empties in them. He sighed unhappily and sank into a chair, simultaneously unbuttoning the cashmere sports jacket he had picked up in Hong Kong three weeks ago.

From the bathroom he could hear Megan singing.

"You do a good job, Lou," he said.

Lou Cates nodded. "Listen to him."

"Why not?" said Wolfe. "It's for my benefit. I'm not supposed to know you just brought him back from the dead. They tell me you've shot enough B-Twelve into his ass during the past years to stock a drugstore."

Cates ignored the hyperbole, fleetingly wondered who was the Big Brother giving Wolfe his information.

"Please listen," he persisted. "He's really vocalizing. You know, he started taking lessons again. He's serious."

Wolfe clicked a gold-plated lighter and puffed on a non-filter cigarette as he listened to Megan sing "My cup runneth over with . . ." then hold the note as he hit "lov-v-ve."

"Not bad," said Cates.

Wolfe exhaled twin streams of smoke from his nostrils and nodded approvingly. "In a toilet he's as good as Robert Merrill."

It was not the first time he had said it, but this time he added, "And the toilet is where he's going."

"Ah-so?" said Lou quietly, raising his eyebrows, suddenly realizing that Felix was far more disturbed than usual, dangerously disturbed, in fact, to be talking out loud like that.

Felix Wolfe, although half a century old, was the junior member of Blassingame, Mangon and Wolfe, the theatrical management agency into whose hands Roger Megan had entrusted his career and his destiny some eight months earlier. At that time Megan's career was approaching a standstill, and his destiny seemed increasingly murky. When Roger Megan had come to their agency—not that *he* came to them; things weren't done that way in the show-business establishment, where who called who was a ploy. Actually, a friend had suggested they sound him. The firm knew he was in trouble. They took him on only because Felix Wolfe stuck his neck out, not for friendship, he made clear, but because he thought there might still be five good years of commissions left in Megan if someone handled him right. And Wolfe had personally undertaken to do the handling. From that day on Wolfe cursed the original friendly impulse—it really *was* friendship at the bottom and thus more unforgivable—that had prompted him to volunteer.

The singing had stopped, and a moment later Roger Megan came into the sitting room wearing a pastel-blue terry robe. "Felix, baby, how nice to see you," he said loudly, smiling brightly through his superbly capped teeth. They shook hands and Megan looked around the spacious room. "No breakfast, Lou? Why no breakfast?"

"I'll order it," said Lou, picking up a phone.

"He didn't know if you could eat," said Wolfe.

Megan looked at his manager quizzically, the smile fading from his face. "Please, Felix," he said, "try not to be unpleasant."

Wolfe said evenly, "Friday night I called you in Beverly Hills. You promised me you'd make no waves."

Megan sat down on the arm of a chair and shook his head at Wolfe, taking advantage of Lou's talking to room service to postpone answering.

"I don't want to spoil your day," said Wolfe, "but they heard you in the courtyard. The whole hotel heard you. And the broad, too."

"Sorry about that, Chief," said Megan. "You know I always leave the windows open. The air-conditioning does something to my voice."

Felix Wolfe laughed softly and crushed his cigarette. Then he reached into the breast pocket of his jacket and came out with a folded sheet. It was a faintly smudged Xerox copy of a newspaper column. He held it up for display in front of Megan's face and said, "Isn't it enough what Ed Sullivan wrote last week? Do you know what it takes for a nice guy like Ed to print a blind item like that, without even using your initials? You want more? Just go on like this. You'll go all the way back to announcing specials in a supermarket."

"Smart guys don't worry about pimples," Megan snapped. "When the day comes when I have to worry about columnists, I'll turn in my Teleprompter."

Wolfe shifted his frail form in his chair. Physically, he was a gnome. When seated, as now, he seemed more dwarfish than usual.

"Roger, I'm pleading with you," he said. "They're paying you twenty-five grand to handle the Pageant for five days. Can't you get your mind off pussy for five days?"

"What do you want me to do, live in a monastic cell? Or would you rather weld a chastity belt around my hardware? Wise up, Felix. I've MC'd a dozen of these Pageants, kissed five hundred and eighty of the contestants on the cheek, sometimes even patted their rumps. But I swear to you by all that's holy I never pronged any of them, never even squeezed one tit."

"I'll buy that," said Felix, reaching for another cigarette. "Your batting average with the contenders is zero. But they say you score pretty good with the winners."

Megan gave him a baleful glare. "Just *one* of the winners, Felix. You know who she is. We've had a thing going ever since her marriage broke up ten years ago. We may even get married if she ever completes her psychoanalysis."

Wolfe shook his head, frowned. "But Sue is still associated with the Pageant. She briefs the hostesses who chaperone the girls, announces most of the commercials for the TV special. Take my word for it, Roger, the front office would flip if they knew about this affair. They'd have to give you the ax. It would tarnish the Pageant's image."

"Tarnish the Pageant's image?" Megan echoed. "*I'm* the image. Without me the Pageant would be just another beauty contest, a parade of flesh on the hoof no different from more than seventy others."

Megan stood up, dug into the pile of papers Lou Cates had assembled on the coffee table, shuffled through them until he located a blue folder.

"Shall I reel off the list of carbon copies, Felix? Forgive me if I don't read them alphabetically, but there's the Miss World contest, Miss Universe, Miss America, Mrs. America, Miss Venus, Miss U.S.A., Miss Teen-Age America, Miss Campus Queen, Miss International, the All-American Girl Contest and, oh, hell, I see they even have a Miss Catskill Pageant."

Megan paused for breath, his eyes flashing anger. He was winding up for his Sunday punch.

"Of all these contests, the only one that counts, the big blockbuster in revenue and ratings, is the Princess America Pageant. What has it got that none of the imitators has? *Me.* Yes, Roger Megan and his phony capped porcelain teeth and his ham personality and the corny way he sings the corny theme song, 'Good Luck, Sweet Princess, Whoever You Are.' Let them drop me, and overnight the Pageant loses its continuity. Remember what happened when the Academy Award brains let Bob Hope skip one of the Oscar shows? It bombed. Tell that to your pals in the front office."

The doorbell rang sharply before Wolfe could answer. It was a bellboy with a telegram. Cates fumbled in his pocket for some change, ransomed the glassine envelope.

"It's for you, Roger," he said, tearing open the flap. He withdrew the message inside, handed it over, unread, to his boss.

Megan scanned the strip of tape. "Man, oh man," he groaned, waving it at the others. "The fettucini has hit the fan!"

Wolfe grabbed for the wire. As he studied the contents,

his eyes widened in disbelief. He read it aloud, his voice registering shock.

ROGER MEGAN
HILTON BY THE SEA
SURF CITY

WE ARE NOTIFYING ALL PERSONNEL AND SPONSORS CONNECTED WITH THE 13TH ANNUAL PRINCESS AMERICA PAGEANT THAT UNLESS THE PAGEANT MEETS OUR DEMANDS FOR RACIAL INTEGRATION, WE WILL PICKET THE CONTEST, MARCH IN PROTEST, DEMONSTRATE, AND TAKE WHATEVER OTHER ACTION MAY BE NECESSARY. WE WILL ALSO URGE ALL CIVIL RIGHTS AND PROGRESSIVE ORGANIZATIONS TO BOYCOTT SPONSORS' PRODUCTS.

THOMAS WORTHINGTON WALSH
DIRECTOR, NATIONAL FREEDOM LEAGUE
30 ROCKEFELLER PLAZA
NEW YORK CITY, N.Y.

Wolfe let the telegram flutter to the carpet. "A thing like this could put the network on the hot seat," he said grimly. "And if they fry enough, they could cancel the show."

There was another interruption as a waiter appeared, rolling in Megan's breakfast and pots of coffee for the others. After he had gone, Megan picked up the silver cover, regarded the bacon and eggs with distaste, then replaced the lid.

Wolfe sat down by the food cart, tucked a napkin under his chin. He removed the cover and speared a rasher of bacon with his fork. "No point in wasting a five-dollar breakfast just because of a few dark clouds," he punned. "I'm sure the front office will be able to work out some deal with this freedom bunch."

"Don't bet any of your commissions on it," said Megan. "I know Thomas Walsh. He's no Uncle Tom."

After Megan had disappeared into the bedroom to get dressed, Lou Cates poured himself some coffee and dropped two cubes of sugar in his cup. As he stirred them, his eyes met Wolfe's.

"At least, Lou, you should have closed the windows," admonished Wolfe. "All those ears."

"I know," said Cates. "But he wouldn't let me in. I'd begged him not to take a suite below the fifteenth floor."

2 · PRINCESS AMERICA

NORM PRESCOTT, public-relations chief for the Princess America Pageant, looked around the VIP lounge of the St. George Hotel and liked what he saw. A healthy turnout. Obviously, Ginny Kerr still had the power and the glory to draw a full house.

His photographer, Max Gerber, followed Ginny like her shadow as she chatted briefly with the reporters. Ingenuously, never too obvious, she would smile at each one, a signal for Max to click his shutter. Later he would blow up the prints and send each reporter a set of large glossies. It always inflated a man's ego when he could show his pals a picture of Princess America gazing at him with adoration.

After Ginny had made her dutiful rounds, Prescott motioned her to the slightly elevated stage, normally reserved for a combo trio. As befitted the occasion, Ginny's seat was the throne identified with each of the Pageants. To the nation, it was as familiar a prop as the late President Kennedy's rocking chair. After the press conference the velvet-upholstered royal seat would be carefully shipped back to the Armory on Michigan Avenue, to be occupied Saturday midnight by Ginny's successor. Meanwhile, Ginny decorated the throne majestically.

There was a bustle of activity, the sounds of chairs scraping, as the reporters took their places in rows of seats before the miniature dais. On each chair lay a compact press kit contained in a large white envelope. Each kit contained the usual releases, plus a variety of pictures showing Ginny with the mayor of Surf City; opening up a bank in her home state, California; appearing on a television panel show.

Prescott waved his hand to capture their attention. "Ladies and gentlemen," he began, "I know most of you have met Ginny before. For those who haven't, we've included a fact sheet inside each kit to cue you in on her vital statistics."

There was a rustle of papers as all the reporters searched through their kits for the fact sheet. "I suggest you read it swiftly," he resumed, "so we can all get out of here fast and back to our families."

They laughed. Norm Prescott was noted for his sense of humor; his light touch was always sought for at every Surf City convention and event. As he moved toward the rear of the room every pair of eyes in the audience studied Ginny's dossier.

Official Fact Sheet *Miss California*—1969

NAME & ADDRESS	Virginia Louise Kerr (Ginny) AGE—20 1894 Arthur Avenue Westwood, California
WHERE BORN	Westwood, California Date of Birth—4/25/50
PARENTS' NAME	Judge and Mrs. L. B. Kerr (Same address)
EDUCATION	High School—Westwood High School —1967 College—Auburn University—Junior Social Sorority—Delta Zeta Special Training—Voice—2 years; and Art
TALENT	Folk Singing—accompanying self on Guitar
MEASUREMENTS	Height 5 9 Weight 128 Bust 36 Hips 37 Waist 26

Shoe size—7A Dress Size—10 Color Eyes—Blue

FAVORITE HOBBY	Folk singing, politics and painting
FAVORITE SPORTS	Tennis, swimming, horseback riding

AMBITION FOR THE FUTURE—To become a corporation lawyer or a judge.

Other Facts: President of her sorority and a member of Pan-Hellenic Council; traveled with Auburn University Showcase; and toured Europe as soloist with the University Choir. Member of Auburn Chapter of American Institute of Design.

Miss California was the recipient of a $5,000 Scholarship

from the California Merri-Cola Bottlers Association and an annual $2,000 Lane Bryant Fashion Award.

The Miss California Pageant was directed by the Los Angeles *Herald.*

Crowned Princess America, September 13, 1969.

A clean-shaven young man who looked over draft age raised his hand.

"Tim Hartley, correspondent for the *Wall Street Journal,*" he introduced himself. "Last year's winner, Miss Ohio, earned more than ninety thousand dollars for endorsements, TV commercials, public appearances, et cetera. Did you do as well financially?"

Ginny gave her prepared answer. "Oh, yes. Of course, I have to give more than half of it back to the government," she went on demurely, "but I don't begrudge it. And best of all are the scholarships. They're tax-free, and what with my Miss California scholarship and my Princess America scholarship, they'll pay for my next two years in college and two years in law school."

The thunderous roar of a 747 jet flying over the hotel discouraged further conversation. Ginny paused, waiting for the roar to fade. She wondered how the Wall Street community would have reacted if she had given them the true fiscal picture. An A student in finance, she was adept at reading a profit-and-loss statement.

Total income so far this year, $210,000, more than the salary of the President of the United States. This does not include $60,000 in royalties Licensing Corporation of America is holding in escrow on Princess dolls, miniskirts and swim suits. Daddy hired a smart Washington lawyer who specializes in tax shelters for clients in the superbrackets. He invested more than half my money in an oil-well-drilling syndicate that gives me a fat depletion tax benefit. Right now I own part of an oil well that brings in 2,000 barrels a day of beautiful black gold—and all the profits are capital gains. That's more than Lynda Bird ever made working at McCall's!

The next question came from a chain-smoking and spinsterish female who wore a Robin Hood hat and blinked her eyes unceasingly.

"Maggie Hollis, *Time* magazine. Miss Kerr, has your year of public appearances given you a taste for performing? Would you be interested in a good movie contract or a television series of your own?"

Ginny hesitated for just the proper interval, inferring deliberation. Finally she said, "Well, I don't know. I don't think so. I'd be awfully tempted. But I'd want it to be temporary. I don't think there would be any permanent satisfaction in it. I still want to be a lawyer, maybe a judge, like my father."

From the rear of the room, Prescott raised his right hand, thumb and middle finger forming the familiar O of approval. Two questions, two hits. She was remembering her lines like a trouper.

Next was a planted question, delivered by a friendly local reporter.

"Clem Bumberg, Surf City *Press*. Now that the year is over, Ginny, and you can do whatever you please without being chaperoned, what do you look forward to the most?"

Again the canned response. "The chance to be myself whenever I feel like, not worrying about my hair or make-up, wearing slacks, sweaters and loafers on weekends. I'm also looking forward to staying in one place."

Suddenly Ginny bent forward confidentially. "I know I'm among friends, so I'll tell you what I'll miss the least." She opened her lips wide to expose her flawless, gleaming teeth. "I'll be just so happy I don't have to put that blankety-blank Vaseline on my teeth every day so that they show up shiny in all the photographs.

The audience laughed, and there was a warm round of applause. Norm Prescott sipped the Scotch in his glass. A great quote, he told himself, even if Ginny had ad-libbed the last bit. Surefire stuff for the wire services.

Behind her innocent smile, Ginny chided herself, overcome by a torrent of guilt.

Fake ... impostor ... hypocrite.... Ginny girl, you know what you're really looking forward to . . . the things you've missed for the last year . . . Cigarettes . . . Scotch-sours ... and sex ... glorious, wonderful s-e-x.... For one year you've been embalmed as Virginia the virgin.... Now . . .

A few more questions, none of them too hot to handle, and Prescott decided to quit while they were still ahead.

"Thank you, Your Highness," he called out loudly from the back of the room.

The reporters chuckled at the gag, got the message. They got up from their chairs, some to refill their glasses, others to head for the door.

The curtain had come down on the twelfth Princess America's last press conference.

Later, when everyone had departed from the lounge, with the exception of Amanda Clarke and the bartender, Ginny walked over to the bar and sat down on a red-leather stool.

"Now, honey," said Mrs. Clarke, "you know I can't let you order a drink. Just be patient one week more and next Sunday I'll treat you to champagne."

Ginny smiled disarmingly at her warden. "You know I don't drink, Mrs. Clarke. I just want some ginger ale so that I can take an aspirin. All that smoke in the room gave me a slight headache."

The bartender uncapped a bottle of Canada Dry, poured the effervescent liquid into a glass over an ice cube. Ginny took a sip, simultaneously popping a tablet into her mouth.

It was the oral contraceptive pill she had forgotten to swallow before breakfast.

3 · ROGER MEGAN

THEY were ready for him out there, waiting, and Megan could feel their excitement, sharing it, buoyed up by it.

"And now," a voice boomed from the Armory PA system and paused long enough to produce an expectant hush, "a man who needs no introduction, the great introducer himself, our pageant's master of ceremonies—Mr. Roger Megan!"

Out came Megan, striding on the armory stage with his characteristic bounce, flashing a huge, delighted grin and bobbing his head to acknowledge the applause. Down below on the floor, in a roped-off section, the police complement of Pageant chauffeurs had risen from their folding chairs to greet him with a standing ovation. At that moment Megan loved them. What a fine bunch of men, he thought, looking down at them, spruce in their best blues, reeking of virility and after-shave lotion. The applause continued and Megan did nothing to hinder it.

He shot a quick glance toward the wings, looking for Felix Wolfe. There he was, the little bastard; now Wolfe would have a chance to see how beautifully Megan handled just one of his chores. It hadn't even really been part of his job originally, but Megan had included it, some years ago, among the extra little services he rendered the Pageant, to the enormous satisfaction of everyone concerned.

Now, with quiet almost restored and the audience seated, Megan looked around conspiratorially and spoke into the mike with a mock whisper. "Are we alone, fellers? Nobody here but us men? Listen to this—a friend of mine in the Los Angeles police department told it to me. They had a promotion examination out there a couple of weeks ago, and they had a question that went like this: 'Late one night, while you're patrolling your beat in a local park, a young lady runs up to you. She tells you that a few minutes ago a strange man grabbed her, pulled her into the bushes and raped her. What would you do?' " He gave them a moment to think, to heighten their anticipation. Then he said, "I don't know how you fellers would answer that, but one guy answered, 'I would immediately take the young lady back to the scene of the crime and try to re-enact it.' "

Bang went the laugh, up to Megan's expectations and beyond it. He let it roll around the cavernous armory, savoring it to the end. Then, as the echoes died away with a smooth, practiced change of pace, Megan said, "Gentlemen, let's be serious for a moment. We all have a big job to do these next few days for a lot of lovely girls who came here to be looked at for the next week.

"They want to be seen, and we want you to let people see them. That means driving slowly, probably slower than you like, about thirty miles an hour. Furthermore, no matter where you're going, take the long way round whenever and wherever possible. And that means you'll have to figure your time carefully.

"Another thing—personal use of your vehicles. There ain't no such thing. Anyone who gets caught joy-riding an official car will get a ticket—by which I mean a bus ticket to some other town, where he can start a whole new life."

There was a laugh, embarrassed but good-natured, and Megan laughed with them. Then he said, "Next, booze. Need I say anything about that? I'll say it anyway. No booze. And no beer. This doesn't mean avoiding getting loaded, or not looking or acting loaded. It means not the slightest hint of it on your breath. And that doesn't mean walking around smelling of Sen-Sen or Binaca or Chlorets. No booze. And no beer."

And now, sensing the slight unhappiness settling on his audience, Megan changed gait again. "There was a story that made the rounds last year that tells it all. A drunk came staggering over to one of our police escorts and asked, 'Is this the way to go to the Pageant?' And the officer answered, 'It sure is, and if I wasn't a cop on duty, I'd go the same way.' And that's all there is to it."

The laugh was a relief, and Megan decided he was ready to launch into the main subject of his talk.

Walking slowly back and forth across the stage, carrying the mike with him, Megan spoke quietly. "Just one more thing," he said. "We're proud of the fact that in all the years of the Pageant there has never been a breath of scandal, or any occurrence of which all of us couldn't be proud. You men who have been chosen as escorts to our contestants are the cream of the department. We know all about you—that you all have fine records, that you're alert, competent, civic-minded, and, most of all, married." He allowed himself a little smile and saw it mirrored on their faces. "Those of you who have served on our escort committee in past years know what kind of fun it can be." He cleared his throat and added, "And what kind of fun it can't be. You men are not merely ceremonial chauffeurs and escorts, but in a very real sense you are bodyguards. That means just what it says—you have a body to guard. It is sure to be a lovely body. You will enjoy looking at the body, and you may do so, but only very discreetly. You may like to dream about the body, and you may do so, but confine your dreaming to off-duty hours. The main thing to remember is that you must not do anything about the body except guard it.

"Gentlemen, let me put it to you straight. If you have a hot nut, do yourself a favor and resign right now. Anybody who can't keep his pecker in its holster will be sent to Denmark for an operation, all expenses paid by the Pageant."

Megan bowed and they were on their feet, applauding, whistling, stamping. He stood there nodding, smiling, waving to them. Then with a flourish he restored the mike head to its stand and walked off the stage.

In the wings he made his way through the crowd of minor officials and well-wishers, shaking hands, accepting compliments, taking the triumph with studied modesty.

"Loved it," said Felix. "Great. Just great."

"Where's Lou?" asked Megan, looking around.

"In your dressing room. There was an important phone call for you a few minutes ago, and he went to answer it."

"Important? From whom?"

"The page said it was Sue Rossiter."

Megan frowned slightly. "Why should that be important?"

"I'm only quoting the page. He said Sue Rossiter was on the phone and it was very important."

"Come on," said Megan, leading the way.

They went deeper backstage and climbed an ironwork stairway to the floor above and from there along a catwalk to that part of the armory given over to various rooms. On the door of one of them there was a large gold star and under it, in gold letters, Megan's name. He opened the door and went in, Felix Wolfe following.

Lou Cates was inside sitting on Megan's desk, the phone

still in his lap but no longer in use. "Sue Rossiter," he said. "I just hung up."

"What is it?" said Megan.

Cates hesitated. He seemed reluctant to talk. Megan looked from him to Wolfe, then back again. "It's all right," Megan reassured him. "What did she want?"

"She was over at headquarters a little while ago," said Cates slowly. "She was talking to Mr. Fleming. He told her he's preparing a wonderful surprise for you."

"Yes?" said Megan. He didn't like the way Cates sounded.

"Mr. Fleming called Beverly Hills this morning. He invited your wife to come and spend the week here with you."

"He did *what*?" said Megan incredulously.

"She's to be a guest of the Pageant. They'll pick up the whole check."

Megan stood there utterly confused, staring around the small room. John Fleming was the president of the Pageant, and when Fleming made a move it was worth thinking about. Unquestionably he had made a move.

Felix broke the silence. "Nice of her to call, wasn't it?"

Megan regarded him with cold anger. "Are you trying to say something, Felix?"

"Not at all," said Wolfe, and then in tones of mildest interest he asked, "You really serious about divorcing your wife for Rossiter?"

"Why?"

"Just asking."

"Go fuck yourself," said Megan. "Lou, get my wife on the phone."

"What are you going to do?" said Felix.

"I'm going to tell her not to come."

"After Fleming invited her?"

"Fuck Fleming."

"All right," said Felix, "fuck Fleming." He was completely calm, seemingly almost disinterested. "Meanwhile, let me tell you this. You and I know that John Fleming has a lot on his mind this morning. I also happen to know—I knew yesterday—there are rumors all through the business of a rival network show—something big planned to come on opposite the Pageant Saturday night. Then this thing with the blacks, the National Freedom bunch, threatening to bust up everything. And in spite of all this, Fleming takes the trouble, the time, to phone your wife and issue a personal invitation—"

"Why?" Megan shouted. "Because he's a sweetheart? Is that what you think?"

"No," said Felix quietly, "that's not what I think. I think you're bugging him. He's figured out a way to keep you out of mischief."

"Nobody takes charge of my balls!" Megan said savagely. "Not you, not Fleming, nobody!" He reached for the phone. Cates handed it to him and got off the desk in a hurry.

"Don't call," said Felix. "Make the best of it."

But Roger Megan was already dialing.

4 · MISS FLORIDA

ROBIN GERVAIS was lost in that special thought again, off somewhere in a secret dimension, lulled by the steady motion of the big Army transport and the whispering jets outside.

From his adjacent seat, Art Waldo nudged her in gentle reproof. "Doll, you're not paying attention."

"Yes, I am." said Robin. Her eyes were closed. "Greenhouse flowers. Especially peonies."

"Good girl." He blottered his moist brow with a soggy handkerchief. The Lockheed Electra was air-conditioned, but Mr. Waldo's girth, his official responsibilities, and his personal tensions combined to produce a talent for perspiring. "I know it's tiresome, boning up on all these little things, but believe me, Robin, this is my sixth year with the Pageant, and I've seen these little things add up to a big payoff."

He nodded at her wisely, an overweight sage in white linens, and added, "Right now that's all you should be worrying about."

They're even prepared to tell me what to worry about, she thought. And doubtless they were right. For these next few days, there was only the Pageant. Everything else was meaningless, even the one problem that had preoccupied her for weeks, that she had been unable to obliterate from her mind.

But how did one stop thinking about it? she wondered. It reminded her of something she had once read—an old colonial remedy for curing a headache, which was to run around the house three times without thinking of a fox. The remedy never worked, because it was impossible to forget the fox.

Robin move restlessly in her upholstered seat, inadvertently touching Waldo's thigh with her own. He was relieved when shortly she shifted her position and broke the delicious circuit. A minute's more physical linkage with this exquisite girl and he'd be ready to talk to himself.

As public-relations man for the Florida Jaycees, Waldo was along to catalyze publicity for their esteemed state and to shepherd and coach Robin, their chosen entrant. He had been running such interference, he made it a point to remind everyone, for six years, and he had mentored the five previous Miss Floridas.

None of the girls he had handled had ever won the coveted crown, but Waldo was far from discouraged. This year, his expertise told him, he was backing a winner. Robin had talent, personality, looks—and other ammunition. The pink woolen pullover she was wearing gave ample evidence that she would be a hell of a bet in the swimsuit competition, he thought, and tried to keep his mind from wandering.

"Now lend me your pretty pink ear, doll," Waldo resumed. "I'm building up to something. Does the name Deborah Bryant ring a bell?"

Robin toyed with the one-ounce golden Eiffel Tower charm on her bracelet. "Didn't she win the Miss America title a few years ago?"

"Right. Nineteen sixty-six, to be exact. The judges loved her, particularly Joan Crawford. Can you guess why?"

Waldo scowled at a streak of dirt he had just spotted on the right cuff of his jacket, went on as though he had never asked the question.

"Debbie had read up on the background of all the judges. When she learned that Joan Crawford had grown up in Kansas City, she made sure, during the interview, to let her know that she, too, had been raised there. Of course, Debbie had lots going for her in the other departments. But taking advantage of this bit of intelligence certainly didn't cost her any demerits."

Robin relinquished the tiny Eiffel Tower to favor the miniature Taj Mahal on her wrist.

"Now here's my point," said Waldo, casting himself in the role of an omniscient Buddha. "I've just found out that one of the judges, Eames Bentley, the movie producer, raises flowers in a greenhouse. Very big on peonies, wins prizes and so on. Now suppose you're contemplating the same hobby? Not exactly the same, more exotic, really tropical, African violets or orchids or something. Just put in an hour or so with this book, and pick one or two flowers you like. He's bound to be impressed if you mention it during the judges' interview." Her eyelids flickered open long enough for her to read the title on the paperback, *Gardens Under Glass*, and closed again.

Maybe, she thought, there was a chapter in the book on fertilizer and its presence in the discourses of Mr. Art Waldo. Everything about the plane conspired to put her to sleep—the serenity of the big ship, humming a lullaby; Aunt Charlotte, her appointed chaperone, sitting behind her across the aisle, riffling cards on a solitaire board on her lap; her father, up front at his desk, energetically dictating to a tape recorder.

Up forward in the hurtling plane, in the somewhat partitioned cubicle that was his office aboard the craft—his flying desk, he called it—Brigadier General Clinton Gervais paused in his dictation and lit a long panatela from the copper grenade that served as a paperweight and cigar lighter. The clearance roster he must check for Emmett at the CIA would wait until he returned to Washington from Surf City.

He had been listening to Art Waldo talking to Robin, thinking how strange it was to hear someone else calling her "doll." It would be different now, a vanished intimacy, and if he had lost something of her, he would lose more. The inevitable day must come when he would surrender her at the altar. And that was as it should be. But in time, all in good time. There was so much ahead for her yet, so much that he wanted for her. A current of fear raced through him, and for the second time that morning the general was frightened.

It was part of a feeling that had obsessed him for days, a vague apprehension, but it had begun to take form. Earlier that morning, as the plane took off from Orlando, it had occurred to the general that once again he was embarking upon the realization of a lifelong dream. The thought had terrified him.

So many times he had reached out for something he fiercely wanted from life. But always, when it came within his grasp, it died in his hands, as if his touch were fatal. And this lay close to the root of his fright. He was a jinx. A Jonah. An evil eye. It was as if by his very hoping for her, he insured that nothing would come of it.

Why did Robin's winning the Pageant mean so much to him? It was as if he were guilty for her being motherless from the age of five, and he had set out to prove how rich and full her life had nevertheless been. By winning this contest she would demonstrate how remarkably well her father had done by her. The crown they would place on her head would be the symbol of his honorable acquittal.

They had been living in Bonn, where he was then stationed, when his wife had died. For the next eight years Robin had gypsied with him wherever he was assigned—England, Japan, France, Korea—educated in foreign schools and by private tutors, mothered by a succession of governesses and housekeepers.

And at the end of that time, as Robin had entered her teens, her Aunt Charlotte had said, "Well, Clinton, it looks like you're not going to get married again, and I hardly imagine you're celibate. So don't you think, all things considered, she'd be better off now with me?"

The insinuation had angered him. "I have never once brought a strange woman into my home," he told his sister-in-law.

"That's only part of it," Charlotte had said. "It's time Robin stopped living out of a footlocker. Two years in this place, three years in that place—is that a home? No, you let me have her. A few years of finishing school, maybe a good junior college, and after that we can leave it up to her."

Leave it to her? What nonsense, he had thought. Nothing ever worked out right unless people took orders. How difficult it was to be in command of the events in one's life. But he had gone along with it, enforcing his will and his decisions as best he could from a distance, and everything had worked out beautifully.

In the half dozen years that followed, they had been separated for long periods, sometimes oceans and continents apart. But always they had managed to unite for an occasional visit, a trip together somewhere, and last year a vacation for two weeks in Nassau, when he began to wonder whether they hadn't become strangers to each other.

It was all the more poignant because of the deep and intimate relationship he saw had developed between Robin and her aunt. It had evoked a profound jealousy in him, but stronger still was the satisfaction, the confidence it gave him that all was well with Robin. All through the years he had watched her growing up, blooming into a lovely young woman, until now she stood at the threshold of bringing his hopes and plans to fruition.

And yet, especially these last few days, there had been this nameless anxiety, as though this instinct was trying to warn him.

Finally he had dared mention it to Charlotte during

cocktails one evening, after his third round of Gibsons. The gin fumes had seeped from behind his eyes and into his brain, liberating his tongue.

"It's this Paul Brioni," he had told her. "I can't help wondering whether there's something between them."

Charlotte had gulped down her onion, half chewed.

"You're not serious?" The thought was utterly alien to her. "You don't suspect Robin's having an affair with him?"

"No, not really. But it did cross my mind."

"But why? Do you know anything? Have you seen anything?"

"Nothing much," he had admitted. "I've seen them touch hands 'accidentally' once or twice. But mainly it's the way they look at each other."

"It isn't possible," Charlotte had declared with conviction. "They've never dated. Why, they've hardly ever met, except in your presence."

"They could have met every time Robin came to visit me in Washington. It's quite possible."

"And I wouldn't know? Robin wouldn't confide in me?"

Charlotte's firmness should have reassured him, but this time the uneasiness had persisted, and it had resulted in his making plans to find out. To find out what? That he was wrong, he told his conscience. But this very plan had produced new misgivings. Was he justified in invading Robin's privacy? Was he helpless in the face of this irresistible compulsion to pry and trap, to search and destroy?

In the end, as he had known all along, from the first moment of doubt, he would have to go through with it. Not from a lack of faith but out of superstition, out of the feeling that life conspired against him and therefore against those he loved. He would carry out his plan, and the time for implementing it was now, while the plane was still in flight, six miles above land and sea.

General Gervais turned off his tape recorder, which had been spinning wastefully, and listened to what Art Waldo was saying.

"Now here's something I wanted to show you, Robin. Remember that official form you filled out for the judges? Vital statistics and so on? You'll notice I made a few changes, just minor ones, like here I've added gardening among your hobbies so we'll sound legit if it comes up."

Robin studied the revised sheet. "What's this about water skiing?"

"It gives you a more rounded picture. The tennis is fine, but I wanted something more daring, up to date. Kind of balances the gardening and piano. I mean, we're creating a mystique here, an idea, the all-American girl. Does it bother you, doll?"

There was no audible answer, and the general got up and looked toward the rear. "No, I suppose not," she said finally. "I'm getting used to it. I'm just glad you didn't put me down as a sky diver. The judges might have asked for a demonstration. Anyway, what difference does it make?" Then, looking up, she saw her father standing. Their eyes met and she smiled faintly at him, enjoying, as she always did, his distinguished posture.

"Were you listening, Dad?" she asked.

"A little," said the general. "Couldn't help hearing some."

"What do you think of it?"

"It?"

"All this—" she hesitated briefly, searching out the word—"this chicanery."

"Please, Robin." Art Waldo's voice registered deep hurt. "We're only creating an image."

"See how wrong you've been about me, Dad? All this time you've thought I was the perfect all-American girl, and I'm not. I have to be created. I'll be a paper princess."

The general regarded his daughter in silence for a moment. He was proud of her for speaking so frankly about what she considered dishonest, even though she was a party to it. But there was such a thing as being realistic as well as polite. The image was extremely important.

"You want to win, don't you?" he asked.

She nodded slowly, pursing her lips a little, the way she always did when she became serious. He thought, How much like her mother she looks at such times. The oval face, the direct eyes deep and dark and lustrous as black olives, a turned-up nose delicately carved from marble, and a good-humored mouth from which flowed, these days, statements and observations and opinions that often surprised him.

And this truly lovely face, surmounted by gleaming dark brown hair, braided and worn like a tiara, already suggesting the Princess America to be. Wherever she had appeared in earlier elimination contests, the initial gasp and murmur that followed had always foretold her as the winner.

But now it would take more than her beauty to win. This was it, the culmination of the campaign, and victory would call on her every resource, on her mother wit, and talent. Whatever else it would require, he would endeavor to supply. Background dope about the judges, for example, like the flower bit Waldo had dug up about Bentley. With his pipelines in the Pentagon, he could find out what each judge ate for breakfast.

"You've worked hard for this, Robin," he said at last. "Unless you want to throw it all away, you'll concentrate only on winning. That means paying the strictest attention to Mr. Waldo."

"Can't argue with a command decision," she said, half blithely, half mockingly.

"She's tired, Clinton," Charlotte interjected, as though it was necessary to ask for a cease-fire. She smiled at Robin. "What about some coffee, dear?"

"Not really, thank you."

And now the general quickly saw the golden chance for which he had been waiting patiently. This was the precise moment to entice his daughter with the airborne bait that was less than thirty feet away.

His tone parental, yet unmistakably authoritative, he issued the order veiled as a suggestion: "Robin, why don't you go forward and sit in the control cabin for a while? I have to discuss some details with Major Spofford out here, so you can take his seat. It'll be a nice change, and the major's co-pilot can point out the view."

He saw her hesitate, and he felt the blood suddenly rush to his face. Quickly he turned his head. "A ride in the cabin," said Robin finally. "It sounds groovy. But first I want to powder my nose."

General Gervais watched his daughter head for the rear of the plane. Guilt had dried his lips and parched his mouth. He took a cup of ice water from the chrome tap nearby. Returning to his desk, he pressed the black intercom button. A Southern drawl responded immediately. "Major Spofford, sir."

"Can you come out here for a few moments, Major?"

"Yes, sir. Captain Brioni will take over."

A moment later, Spofford, the chief pilot, emerged.

"Sit down, Major," said Gervais, indicating a chair inside the cubicle, then called back, "Mr. Waldo, will you join us, please?"

Art Waldo waddled forward and eased himself into the chair beside Spofford, facing the general. "You gentlemen have met?" asked Gervais, and when they nodded: "Take a look at this, Major." He handed Spofford a news clipping. "It's from yesterday's Orlando *Post Herald*."

The major glanced at the headline—GENERAL FLIES

DAUGHTER TO PRINCESS AMERICA PAGEANT IN REGAL STYLE.

"I've seen it, sir."

"Mr. Waldo seems to feel there's something here he wants to take up with us."

"Yes, sir," said Spofford, trying not to look surprised and not succeeding.

Robin was coming down the aisle, on her way to the control cabin. She smiled at the trio as she went by. "Council of war?"

"Board of strategy," the general said lightly. She opened the door to the control cabin and disappeared inside, and the general said to Waldo, "That's what this is about, isn't it?"

"Yes indeed," said Waldo. "Of course, General, this may strike you as a minor consideration, a detail, but we want to give your girl her best shot, right?" He paused, waiting for some sort of affirmation, a nod, even a grunt, but there was none. "Well," he went on uneasily, "we have to watch every detail." He pointed at the newspaper. "For instance, this news item. Now, during the next few days, all the girls in this Pageant are going to get publicity—interviews, photos, newspapers, television. It can help, but it can hurt.

"For instance, three years ago we had a Miss Florida who was a top favorite, all the attributes, looks, figure, brains, charm, and a rare, radiant smile, a dazzler, the best thing about her. So? So some s.o.b. from a wire service filed a story that gave the impression our girl's teeth were all capped. Supposed to have had them capped just for the Pageant, like Roger Megan. It wasn't true, but we couldn't fight it. Everybody kept staring at her teeth. Made me cringe every time the poor girl smiled, which was less and less. Came the judges' interview, the personality test, where our girl should have wowed them. Nothing. Flat. She could hardly open her mouth to talk." He sighed at the recollection. "Might have been the big winner."

"Very interesting," said the general, "but what has it got to do with this news item?"

Waldo cleared his throat. "The point is," he said silkily, "an adverse story—and the talk that follows it—can wreck a contestant's morale."

"What is it that bothers you, Mr. Waldo? Come to the point."

Waldo took a moment for another brow-mopping operation, then said resolutely, "This 'regal style' business. This flying to the Pageant because Miss Florida's father is a general, with an Army jet at his disposal, that's not good for us. Some columnist like Jack Anderson might just decide to work up a little indignation, government property being misused." Waldo paused, relishing the shaft he was about to deliver. "Or isn't it wonderful what rank and privilege can do, and was the general really in Florida on official business?"

"We're perfectly safe. I was on official business when we picked up Robin in Orlando. And are you forgetting that my mission to Surf City is to interrogate convalescing personnel at the veterans' hospital there?"

"Good, very good indeed. But the truth of the matter has little to do with what people think. Suppose somebody does snoop and finds out that everything was legit and prints it. What happens? Half the people who read it think it's a cover-up. Hokum. True or false, you've got the makings of a debate. Our objective is to try and see to it that the subject does not come up again in any way."

"And you think it may?"

Art Waldo shrugged. "Who knows? It's not altogether unlikely that someone may try to interview the crew of this plane." For the first time, Major Spofford looked interested. "Or you, General. And that's not easy to handle."

"I fail to see why. The interview is simply refused."

"That can be worse than going through with it. But in either case, we're in trouble, we're keeping the issue alive. So there really is only one way to proceed."

"Yes?"

"I would suggest that the crew of this plane remain off the scene."

"How far off?"

"Away from Surf City. Just to play safe." Waldo turned to the major and added apologetically, "I understand you and Captain Brioni are on leave until next Monday. Possibly you've planned to spend some time in Surf City. But I wouldn't advise it. No, sir. I have this recurring nightmare in which I see Robin in a photograph showing her surrounded by a general, a major and a captain, with a government-owned Army jet in the background."

The major looked from Waldo to the general.

"It's that serious?" Gervais asked Waldo.

Waldo nodded. "I'm just expressing my mind. That's my job. The main thing is not to give anybody a chance to hurt us. Rank and privilege. They can hate Robin for it."

"All right," said the major. "So Surf City is off limits.

I'll disguise myself and hide in New York until after the contest."

Waldo managed a feeble smile at his sarcasm. "It doesn't necessarily mean all week. Let's get to Thursday, say, and see if there's anything to worry about. After that, if we're clear, if you and the captain want to come to Surf City quietly, in your civvies, fine. But no fanfare, no publicity."

"Is that all?" the general asked.

"That's all," said Waldo. But the hell it was, he thought. What he really wanted to say was "Listen, General, why don't you get your ass about a thousand miles from here and stay there?"

He could imagine the effect such a suggestion might have on this granitic, self-centered man. In his daydream, Waldo could hear himself saying, "General, you're bad news. You stink up your daughter's atmosphere. You're used to talking to people who can't talk back. You look at them as though they had crawled out from under a rock. You're sure to antagonize people. And you have a lousy influence on Robin. She isn't the same when you're around. She's a bright, witty, friendly girl, a ton of laughs. But when you show up, undertaker time."

At the conclusion of which, Waldo could also imagine himself hunting a new job.

The major rose to go and Gervais said, "You'll explain this to Captain Brioni?"

"Yes, sir." He started back to the control cabin.

"Phone me Thursday, Major," said Waldo. "I'll be at the Sea Turtle Motel."

The control cabin door opened, the major went in, and a moment later Robin came out. She stopped at the cubicle and leaned on the partition, face cupped in her hands, an elfin smile on her face. "Everything settled?"

"Everything," said her father. "Feeling better?"

"Much. The view of the coastline was terrific."

Art Waldo got up. "In that case, doll, back to business. We've still got a couple of things to go over."

"Oh, I was sure of that," said Robin.

"General," Waldo said as an afterthought, "I hope you don't think I'm being overcautious about the publicity."

"Not at all. In fact, if I'd had any idea of all this, of all the considerations, I don't think I'd have used the plane."

"W-e-ll," said Waldo, and let it lay there.

The general watched him until he had rejoined Robin, thinking of what he had just told Waldo. Part of it was true—he had indeed, on his own, considered not using the plane after he had seen the news item. He had smelled the trouble himself, the uneasy potential for damage. A simple announcement could have said that General Gervais had suddenly been called away on Army matters and been forced to cancel the flight to Surf City.

But there was a reason why he had dismissed the thought, a powerful and overriding reason for keeping to his plan to use the plane.

He had some days earlier bugged the control cabin. Neither of the two pilots knew it, but there was at this moment a tiny hidden microphone safely secreted amidst the banks of instruments that surrounded them. It led through a concealed line to the general's tape recorder, and with a simple flick of a switch he could tape whatever was being said behind the cabin door.

A few minutes earlier he had used it. He had turned that switch when Robin had entered the cabin, and the tape machine had been spinning silently, the lid covering the mechanism, since then.

When Robin came out, he had stopped the machine. He now had a record of everything audible that had transpired up forward while Robin had been inside. All he had to do now was turn the switch again, and he could hear everything.

But he hesitated. Once, a long time ago, the general had undertaken a monitoring action almost similar to this one. The result still haunted him. Now he sat there thinking, weighing the risks over again and again, considering every facet.

At length, he opened the plastic cover of the tape machine, pressed the switch that readied the tape for replay. There was a barely perceptible whine as the spool rewound itself. When it had fed back sufficiently he halted its revolution by pressing another lever. He put on his headphone. Then his finger touched the replay switch, held there a brief instant.

Suddenly he turned it, and he listened.

The first voice was Captain Brioni's: "Holy smoke, what are *you* doing here?"

Then Robin's voice: "I'm hijacking the plane. Turn around and head for Cuba."

"Robin, I'm serious, what the hell are you doing here?"

"I'm bored, Paul. I thought maybe I'd come in here and we could make love."

Brioni's voice, exasperated: "Robin—"

Interrupted: "It's all right, darling. Daddy sent me in here to relax. It's his idea, not mine."

A momentary silence, then Brioni: "What are you doing? Are you crazy?"

"Just one. Just one teeny weeny little one."

"Robin, what's the matter with you? Don't you realize I'm flying this goddam ship?"

"Don't you realize I haven't kissed you in two goddam days?"

"Robin!"

Silence again, then Robin: "And I probably won't get another chance until God knows when?"

"Why not? Tonight, tomorrow, we'll see each other."

"Are you kidding? Don't you know how strict they are? I'm in Coventry from here on in. Coventry, hon. Now hold still."

Silence, longer this time. Then: "Are you getting lipstick on me? That's all I need."

"I'll lick it off."

"For chrissake, will you sit down? Sit down. I want to talk to you. This is important."

"Yes, dear. What is it?"

"I'm not even sure I know. It's just a feeling."

"Yes, dear? What kind of a feeling? I love feeling."

A pause, then Brioni: "I keep thinking what could happen if your father ever starts wondering."

"About what? Us?"

"Yes, us. Something is wrong. His attitude, something."

"Impossible."

"Why impossible?"

"Not that Dad isn't perfectly capable of having me followed."

"Or me. What's to stop him from having his Pentagon fuzz tail me?"

"I just don't think so, that's all. He has no reason. We've hardly been together for weeks. We haven't taken any chances."

"I don't know. He seems different. The way he looks at me, I have a hunch he'd like to cut orders shipping me out to Antarctica."

"You just feel guilty, that's all. You're just an old-fashioned square underneath."

"All right, forget it." Another pause, then Brioni again: "I wish this whole miserable Pageant was over with."

"So do I."

"Robin, sit down! What if Spofford walked in?"

"You mean he wouldn't knock?"

"Robin!"

"Just one more, Paul. I need it." Silence again, then

Robin softly: "Touch me, darling. Don't be afraid to touch me." And silence again.

General Gervais reached out savagely and stopped the machine. For a moment he sat there barely breathing, his eyes closed. Then he took off the headset and put it down. Fumbling on his desk, he found a cigar. He lit it with trembling hands. For a long interval he sat staring numbly at the floor, like one of the shell-shocked soldiers he had seen at Walter Reed.

"Now here's the way I've got it set up," Art Waldo was saying to Robin. "We enter the hotel and cross the lobby slowly. I'll set the pace. I don't want you running ahead of me like you usually do."

"Yes, yes, yes," said Robin wearily.

"You know, doll, there's usually a reason when I suggest something. The Pageant doesn't want anyone to solicit individual publicity, but they can't say anything if it happens by itself, if somebody starts taking pictures of you in the lobby. Now, when we get to the desk, there'll be a huge basket of flowers there—orange blossoms."

"Why orange blossoms?"

"Our state flower. Don't you know that?"

"I'm sorry. Of course. Orange blossoms from the Sunshine State. And the state bird is the mockingbird, and the tree is—"

"Never mind that now. The flowers'll be from the Governor. And there'll be a big stack of telegrams. So when you get to the desk, you'll pick up your flowers and your telegrams, and you'll turn around, facing the lobby, looking happy as a bride and smiling a big, big smile—and that'll give the two photographers I've got waiting in the lobby a chance to get a few good shots of you, all laden with flowers and congratulations, and maybe even giving a few autographs to some of your many well-wishers. How does that sound? You like it?"

"I love it," said Robin. "I absolutely love it, and I love you too, Mr. Waldo."

"All right," said Waldo, resigned. "Just get back to that flower book and do your homework. We should be landing in the next twenty minutes."

Robin Gervais opened *Gardens Under Glass* and laid it in her lap. The words and the illustrations swam before her eyes. Orange blossoms, she thought, and wondered how she could have forgotten the irony even for a moment. Orange blossoms and Paul Brioni. And then she thought what the mockingbird could possibly signify, as long as she was searching for omens.

Here in the plane with her were the two men who meant most in her life, and neither one had the slightest notion of what was going on in her life, in her secret life. After next week there would be time to deal with it.

Until then, she thought, if all went well, if all went splendidly, by next Saturday night it was possible she might achieve the novel distinction of being the first Princess America who was pregnant the night she won the crown.

5 · MISS CALIFORNIA

STACY DEGRAY stood by the open window, looking out at the dun expanse of Surf City ten stories below, watching it recede in the soft September twilight. The cigarette she had rolled minutes earlier was almost gone; already she was beginning to feel relaxed. That was the wonderful thing about grass. It always worked. It always came through. Soon she would be equal to the demands of the evening ahead and aware of all the nuances, all the vibrations. Dear, sweet grass, how compassionate to do this for Stacy.

But meanwhile it was important to keep an attentive ear on sounds from the bathroon, where Mama was performing her formidable toilette. Her off-key snatches of "Someday I'll Find You" trailed off, probably indicating the application of lipstick. Who the hell was Mama doing now? Maybe Jeanette MacDonald?

The day had been all noise and fatigue. They had arrived at the Hilton at noon, and the phone was already ringing when the hotel manager ceremoniously ushered them into their room, pointing out that the celebrated Roger Megan's suite was a mere four doors away. Then the unpacking, the tedious laying out of wardrobes, the innumerable decisions: What required room service and what they could do alone; was tonight too soon for the organza gown, or ought she to wear the *peau de soie?* A late lunch in their room, hurried and tasteless.

And all afternoon a parade of bellhops delivering telegrams, flowers, and stuffed animals, chocolates, burying the room in clutter. When the phone let up a moment, Mama seized it to make calls from a list she had been weeks compiling. Where did she get them all? Who were they all? "They're people you need, honey. People who can do things for you. Now just close your eyes and take a little nap."

She had stretched out in bed, trying to rest while Mama

chattered away. But it was impossible. Not that it was Mama's fault. She was only too familiar with Stacy's talent for achieving detachment and withdrawal. And usually Stacy knew just how to tune things out. She knew how to get all the quiet she wanted. *She had only to bring back a memory, and she was there again, in another time in her life, in that complete and never-ending silence.*

Now for the first time all day, briefly safe from surveillance, she had found the interval she needed to compose herself. It took only a few minutes. The buzz was there; peace was on the way. A freshet of wind billowed the curtains, bringing the cry of sea birds. She thought the sound they made was gray and lavender. Closing her eyes, she could see them and was delighted.

The click of a lock across the room jolted her. Stacy was instantly alert. She flipped the last half inch of the butt out the window and turned around. The bathroom door was only slightly ajar, enough to let her mother's voice out.

"Almost ready, darling. Now what was it you were saying about the invitation?"

How excited Mama sounded. There was a high edge to her voice, a sort of cuckoo hysteria when life was living up to her expectations and she was really flying.

A shudder of misgiving went through Stacy. Who did Mama sound like now? Was it Billie Burke, waving her arms, fluttering her eyelids, emitting birdlike noises? Mama had a whole gallery of them—actresses from her generation who Mama had always thought she was just as good as. Stacy had learned to identify them through the years, one by one, from TV late movies. If you knew who Mama was doing, it helped you know what to expect and how to handle her.

"I said I'm dying to keep it, Mother, but we can't."

"And why not?"

"Because it says so, right on it."

"What?"

"It says so, Mother."

"Nonsense."

Stacy shrugged. That's my Mama. Starting an argument with her was like taking your finger out of the hole in the dike. She may not be right, but she's never wrong. Unaccustomed as I am to arguing with bathroom doors, dear Mama, to say that you are full of shit is merely scratching the surface.

Purposefully, she went to a writing table that separated twin beds. There, atop a pile of oversized picture postcards, was a square envelope bordered in purple and gold. Across the face of it, a decorative hand had written "Miss California—*Hilton-by-the-Sea.*" Inside, on a card embossed with the Pageant seal, was a note by the same hand.

> Dear Stacy:
> Won't you and your mother, Mrs. Robert DeGray, join me this evening for an informal get-together with some of the other contestants? We're gathering at La Grenouille at eight-thirty, and I look forward to meeting you both.
>
> Sincerely,
> Sue Rossiter
>
> P.S. Please turn in this note to the receptionist at the door.

Her eyes were swimming a little, finding it more difficult to focus, but all she needed was the last line.

"Mother?" she called. "May I quote? 'P.S. Please turn in this note to the receptionist at the door.' Unquote."

"I know, sweetheart," came the cheerful answer. "Never mind what it says. They'll let us in without it."

How wonderful. Mama was wrong, but of course she was right. Mama didn't think the way other people did. She never let the rules hang her up. How simple things were if only part of your head was missing.

Delicately, Stacy rubbed her fingertips across the embossing on the card. "It's just perfect for my Pageant scrapbook."

"Of course it is, and that's where it belongs. Now don't interrupt, sweetheart. I'm starting on my lashes."

Slowly Stacy slid the card back in its envelope, endowing the act with a certain reverence. Was it not, in its own way, quite possibly an historical document? It would take its place inconspicuously among the trophies and mementoes that marked the progress of her career. But in retrospect its prophetic importance would be clear:

> This document was the first communication between Sue Rossiter and Stacy DeGray. It arrived at the Hilton at 3 P.M. on the Sunday preceding the official opening of the Pageant. That evening, Rossiter and DeGray met for the first time, beginning a friendship that has continued ever since.

It was not unusual for Stacy to think of herself in historical perspective, as an illustrious figure whose biographer she was. These occasions were more likely to occur when she felt as she did at this moment—buoyant, vibrantly optimistic—and often they seemed to lend her mysterious insight into the future. Viewed from the protected vantage of years, almost all things took on new meanings and revealed what had been latent in them.

To someone so gifted, this room was not an anonymous cubicle with anonymous furnishings, anonymously inhabited. It was a room whose door was destined to be graced with a bronze plaque commemorating the celebrated place where Stacy DeGray had lived when she became Princess America. Here was the very bed where Stacy had slept. Here she sat. Here the rug on which she walked. And here she stood before this window, looking out at the city whose heart she was soon to win.

The light was gone, the sky opaque and horizonless. All was still. Immobile, entranced, she searched the heavens, waiting. And suddenly there it was—the first star of evening. Still holding the precious invitation, she pressed it to her bosom with both hands. Then, catching up her breath, she hesitated, because the trick was not to ask too much, so it could be contained. Then she whispered, "Let tonight be wonderful."

She was no longer in the room, but out there somewhere, without form or substance. She was an abstraction, soaring in space. She was a single unwavering thought.

An infinite time passed. She was observing herself. Stacy DeGray, wishing on a star. Could anything be more hilarious? But why not? The world was made of magic. It was everywhere, pervading everything, magic of every kind, waiting only to be invoked. *Come to Stacy, all you spirits and shades, you genies and demons. Help Stacy tonight . . .*

"What on earth are you laughing at?"

It was her mother, behind her. Startled for an instant, Stacy was calm as she turned around.

"Was I laughing?"

"What kind of a question is that?" Mama was staring at her. Her green feather boa seemed to be standing on end, like the neck of a ruffled bird.

Stacy had no answer. All she could do was grin. "I'm just feeling good, Mother. I didn't think I was actually laughing."

"Whatever it is, that sound you make. I've heard you do it before. It frightens me."

"I'm sorry," said Stacy and added soothingly, "You look absolutely scrumptious."

Mama brightened a bit. "Do I really? Thank you, dear," she murmured, turning to inspect herself in a full length mirror. The meticulous care with which she had dressed was evident from her platinum coiffeur to her silver shoes. Her silver brocade gown gleamed along the more than ample curves of her figure. An emerald pendant showed among the green feathers around her throat. A blinding diamond bracelet encircled one wrist, a diamond-studded watch the other. "I was thinking," she said, addressing both her image and Stacy, "maybe my chiffon handkerchief?"

"Not with the boa."

"Which do you prefer?"

Stacy shook her head. "Either one," she said. The dialogue was meaningless. Its only purpose was to cover the time Mama was capable of spending before the mirror.

Presently, apparently satisfied with the inspection, Mama tried on a smile. Stacy watched her with fascination. She was seeing her mother as though looking down from a height great enough to have turned her face into a relief map. Mama's smile was a phenomenon when she was all made up. It began with a narrowing of the eyes, producing a delta of wrinkles on both sides. Her nostrils dilated like the air sacs on a cobra displaying emotion. Then the heavy red lips parted and the smile became fully operational.

When the effort attained its peak, several ounces of assorted creams, powders and emulsions had been shifted and rearranged. Then slowly she brought the smile down to a size more practical for long exposure, something she could attempt to maintain through the evening, and said, "Shall we, dear?"

"Yes, Mother." By then Stacy had decided that Mama was trying to do Greer Garson, or maybe even Ann Harding. It was unfortunate, she thought, that the actual effect was somewhere between Marjorie Main and Count Dracula.

6 · SUE ROSSITER

BY 8 P.M. the crowd was hanging on sawhorse barricades, packed ten deep along both sides of the canopied entrance to La Grenouille. They were waiting for something to happen, though exactly what no one there seemed to know; this only sweetened the suspense.

They had started collecting from the instant a large truck emblazoned with the letters WPAG-TV had parked directly across the street. Shortly afterward, when a platoon of police mustered on the scene, it was clear that something momentous was in the works.

For those to whom happiness was a glimpse of a celebrity, Surf City during Pageant time would be a grab bag of treats and surprises. So they jostled and jollied, sharing peanut crunch, sustained by hopeful rumors spread by pickpockets and mashers. (Jackie Onassis was coming; no, it was Barbra Streisand; it was Frank Sinatra; it was Shirley Temple.) Whenever the TV crew tested a light, they were given an ovation and a sea of arms waved madly at the dead cameras.

But finally faith and patience were rewarded. Police whistles began blowing importantly down the block. The brilliant TV lights all came on together, cheers resounded and a limousine turned the near corner and slowly rolled up to the dazzle. Two doormen uniformed as Parisian gendarmes opened the car door and saluted. A small, wizened man in a plaid evening jacket emerged nimbly. Turning, he reached into the car and helped out its other occupant. It was an elegant and Junoesque young woman with dark upswept hair and a smile of surpassing radiance.

At the sight of her the crowd whooped and squealed and broke into applause. The clamor rose as she and her escort walked the twenty feet of red carpet to a waiting microphone where an announcer was making the identification, half of which was obviously unneeded.

". . . lovely as always, Sue Rossiter, the hostess of the Princess America Pageant, and Dr. Frank Lydecker, the official physician for the Pageant, popularly known as the Surgeon General of Surf City."

But it was impossible to continue against the uproar. The crowd, having found at last a reason for its existence, fed joyously on its own ebullience. Flashbulbs were popping from all sides, not only from news photographers but from eager amateurs. In Surf City this week half the population would be armed day and night with cameras, stalking the town. They shouted instructions at Sue and she obliged, turning for them this way, that way, laughing, waving, blowing kisses, paying her dues with modesty and grace.

Sue Rossiter was the embodiment of the dream that was at the foundation of the Pageant—the dream wherein a beautiful, charming, talented, pure, nubile, unknown American maiden wins a beauty contest and launches a glittering career. She had come to the Pageant in its third year, a Pageant still striving for major recognition, and they had made it together. Sue Rossiter became the third Princess America, and the Pageant crashed through on the national scene. Possibly it was coincidence; they were ready for each other. Certainly they had done a great deal for each other.

She had been Miss Massachusetts, twenty years old, a senior at Radcliffe studying journalism. "Her credentials," wrote *Life* in a cover story, "were impressive—Phi Beta Kappa, editor of the literary magazine, varsity field hockey—and her physical attributes likewise. Though she apparently scored high in every department, her performance in the Pageant's talent competition was unusually notable. She had been preceded earlier in the evening by a ballet dancer, a tap dancer, a harpist, a pianist, a soprano, an acrobat and a comedy magician. For her specialty she simply came on stage and introduced herself as a New Englander born in Concord and the admirer of a quondam neighbor whose writings she intended to quote. Miss Rossiter then proceeded to recite from Thoreau's *Walden* in a finely modulated and expressive voice, her diction impeccable, her bearing superb. By all standards, this Princess America is a knockout."

In the months that followed, the popular Princess brought new dimension and dignity to the crown. Whereever she went they loved her. She fashioned a string of triumphs all over the country. The Pageant booking office couldn't satisfy the demand for her, and the publicity office had a ball. People wanted to hear about her, and she had a knack for involving herself with pleasant, interesting news.

When her reigning year ended, it was a foregone conclusion that the Pageant hierarchy would find a way to retain her in some capacity. This they had accomplished by creating for her the title of "Official Hostess," and she had been with them ever since.

And she had thrived. She had written two well-received books on travel (Mexico, Japan) and contributed to a wide range of periodicals. She played silly games on afternoon TV and discoursed with intelligence and wit on her own panel show. She appeared at scores of expositions, parades, football bowls and jubilees in addition to her duties all through the year at numerous shindigs connected with the Pageant.

Secure in the public's affection, she seemed one of those golden people whose careers flourish forever. Here, tonight, she was in her element. She basked in the effulgence of the lights, her dark luminous eyes sparkling with excitement, drawing energy from the adoring crowd. There was a galvanic affinity between them.

When she and Dr. Lydecker entered La Grenouille, the maître d', flanked by several lesser stewards, sped across the foyer to greet her. Behind them she saw Norm Prescott surreptitiously waggling an urgent forefinger at her. Disengaging herself, she took Prescott aside with a look of pleasure and surprise, as though finding a friend with whom she must spend a moment. They talked quietly, maintaining an air of mild joviality.

"Sue, there's a situation inside."

"Yes?"

"Three of our judges are in the dining room, all at the same table."

"Three? Glenda Dowling? And who else?"

"Bentley and Mrs. Smith. You knew about Glenda?"

"Not really, but it's no great surprise. I'll tell you later." She reflected a moment. "I don't suppose there's anything we can do."

"Like what? Explain they practically crashed the party and are unwelcome or something? Can you imagine telling that to Glenda Dowling?" He chuckled, but it had a wry sound. "Who knows? They finished dinner a little while ago. Maybe they'll be leaving soon."

"Want to bet?"

From inside the restaurant proper there was a roll of drums and an orchestra broke into music. Sue touched

Prescott's arm in commiseration and said gaily, "They're playing my entrance, dear. I must be off."

On Dr. Lydecker's arm again, she swept grandly down the foyer and into the main room. There at the head of a short flight of stairs they stopped for the duration of the music, bathed in rose and blue and amber light, as though on a stage. Applause immediately welled up from the relative darkness beyond as the orchestra endeavored to thrill with their rendition of the Pageant's anthem, "Good Luck, Sweet Princess, Whoever You Are."

To look at Sue Rossiter it would have been an absurdity to imagine that this sublime creature, so tranquil, so poised, standing at the threshold of the felicitous evening about to unfold, was carefully weighing her chances for disaster.

But she had much to think about. The hours ahead abounded with pitfalls. Some of them were marked, but others—such as the unfortunate and galling presence of the three Pageant judges—defied anticipation. Well, she would try to make the best of it. Tonight was an experiment, and despite its uncertainties there were ample reasons for trying it. Each year there was an increasing tendency among the contestants to arrive in Surf City a day or two before the Pageant opened. The idea was to get a little jump on the others, a little extra notice and possibly publicity—before so many poured in that they all became anonymous.

Of course, they weren't officially here yet, not until they checked in tomorrow morning. But their presence was nonetheless real and gave rise to certain problems. One of the basic tenets of the Pageant was never to allow the girls any sort of unsupervised activity. Such matters as posing poolside in swimsuits or granting unauthorized interviews or attending private parties were fraught with danger.

To be sure, there were Pageant rules for every eventuality, effective the moment the girls set foot in Surf City, officially or not, and it was assumed that the state chaperones accompanying contestants would see to their enforcement. Sadly, however, it had been observed that state chaperones were often more competitive and guileful than their wards, not only willing to wink at an infraction but to instigate it. Until the Pageant's own loyal chaperones, ably schooled and screened, were in charge, monitorial precautions seemed in order.

The Pageant brass was aware of these circumstances and to some extent disturbed, but it had remained for Sue

Rossiter to propose tonight's soirée as the beginning of a possible remedy.

Ordinarily, John Fleming, the president of the Pageant, was somewhat less accessible than the Dalai Lama. But not to Sue. Others might cool their behinds in his outer-outer office for days, waiting for an audience. But she had marched in unannounced, planted a kiss on his bald dome and told him about her idea. Subsequently the Executive Planning Committee had met, meditated, and given her a green light.

She had tackled the job with energy and competence, overseeing every detail, thoroughly sensitive to the ticklish problems involved—the guest list; the costs; security; refreshments (a potentially explosive business); even the choice of ornamental flowers, which either had to avoid or include all the state flowers of those attending; and the publicity (to be kept within bounds, to support the ostensible informality).

Basic to these had been her decision to use La Grenouille for the event. It was a prominent and impressive establishment, a landmark. Equally important, it was independent of any of Surf City's hotels. The award of such a function to one of them—without the guarantee of an eventual round robin—would have given rival innkeepers paroxysms. Each was jealously attuned to the juicy rewards his competitors derived from the Pageant. Her selection of La Grenouille therefore, the undisputed leader in its class, had aborted any dissension.

La Grenouille had formerly been a commercial bank and you could still smell the money, its fragrance rising with fluted marble columns to a vaunted ceiling. It was a place where people came to look and to be seen. To provide this maximum exposure, it was arranged like an amphitheater, with three tiers separated by ironwork balustrades and a central area for dancing.

Rank was denoted by proximity to the arena. Those tables bordering on it were withheld for the elite. But not tonight, where the occasion urgently required certain departures from custom. For tonight, half of the uppermost tier had been roped off, and the lighting, which was everywhere else sufficiently dim to be kind without obscuring, had been specially augmented. Here the party could be on display but safe from intrusion.

Most significant of all, it offered a solution to one of the evening's thorniest problems—the availability of liquor on premises where Pageant girls were to be found. This was among the Pageant's most ironclad taboos. It operated on the theory that the mere presence of alcohol rendered the ground unholy for its innocents. Under no conditions were contestants permitted to be in a place where hard liquor was served. But La Grenouille's tiers provided a makeshift means for isolation. Two bold-lettered signs hung conspicuously from the railing on either side of the reserved forbidden area.

PLEASE NOTICE: ALCOHOLIC BEVERAGES ARE NOT
PERMITTED WITHIN THIS ENCLOSURE
AND WILL NOT BE SERVED.

This improvised disclaimer was expected to do the trick, at least for tonight—which was, as one had to remember, presumably a private affair of Sue Rossiter's.

And so were the headaches, of which this was only one. In all, she had invited some sixty guests. These included Pageant functionaries, distinguished Surf City burghers, and fifteen contestants and their state chaperones. Would all the girls show up? Was it plain enough in the way she had worded their invitations that appearance was practically obligatory? Had she been too subtle in hinting at an attendance check with her postscript requesting them to present the invitations at the door?

And what of the three judges somewhere in the room? Could this unfortunate development be kept under control? Her eyes, by now acclimatized to the light, casually searched the room around the reserved tier without spying them. At least, she comforted herself, they were not sitting too close.

And there was more to think about. There was Roger Megan, who in some ways was the biggest headache of all, and not only for reasons connected with the importance of this evening.

The orchestra concluded its serenade. Dr. Lydecker came out from the shadows again and followed Sue behind a captain who led the way down the stairs, across the arena, and up to the partitioned enclave. A few of the Pageant confreres were already there: Jay Mallett, the staging director; Grimston, from Transportation; Akins, from Housing; and Mrs. Phoebe Lockwood, supervisor of chaperones. She greeted them pleasantly and went to the far end of the long table where Olga Loomis, her social secretary, was waiting. Olga, a pert, buxom girl in black, began unzipping a small portfolio.

Before she could speak, Sue cut her off. She sank into a chair, shaking her head. "Not just yet, Olga. Please get me a phone." When a waiter delivered the phone, Olga perceptively removed herself from the vicinity.

Sue dialed. Then, when a voice responded, "Eight eleven, please," she said, "I'm calling Mr. Roger Megan." Again she waited. "Thank you." She hung up, then dialed again. "The desk, please? . . . Hello, this is Miss Rossiter. Do I have any messages? . . . Are any of them from Mr. Megan? . . . No, thank you, Miss Loomis will call you about the rest."

This time she replaced the phone more slowly, with a frown of disappointment that seemed utterly anomalous on that well-favored, vivacious face. She raised her eyes, looking off into the club at nothing in particular, and was startled suddenly to realize that she was staring directly at the table with the three Pageant judges. They were halfway across the room, on the lowest tier, just off the arena, facing in her direction and returning her gaze. She waved a glove at them, with the friendliest smile she could manage.

"There, you see?" said Eames Bentley to the female judges between whom he sat. "She does know we're here. She's waving at us."

Glenda Dowling, on his right, took her drink away from her mouth long enough to say, "Imagine being waved at by Sue Rossiter." She lifted her free hand and dangled it limply, joining her companions in a return salute, adding in a mutter, "I can't tell you how thrilled I am."

The other woman, Mrs. Lois Potter Smith, glanced at her with a quizzical smile, as though to inquire about the astringent quality of her remark, but Bentley spoke.

"Do you think perhaps she wants us to join them?" he asked. "I don't see how we can avoid it, if just for a bit, before we leave."

Glenda Dowling's laugh was derisive and rowdy. "You needn't worry, Mr. Bentley. We won't be invited."

"Really? How do you know that?"

"Oh, it's some damnfool nonsensical rule they have about the judges not mingling socially with the contestants. They claim fraternization might give some of the girls an unfair advantage."

"I didn't know there was such a rule," said Mrs. Smith.

"Neither did I," said Glenda Dowling. "But I was informed about it when I called Miss Rossiter and asked—actually went so far as to ask, mind you—*asked* if I could join the party."

"Then you knew about this party," asked Bentley, "before we came here tonight?"

Glenda Dowling nodded. "Not much is going to happen around here this week that I won't know about."

"I feel very awkward," said Mrs. Smith quietly. "Frankly, had I known the circumstances, I'd have stayed away from here."

"Oh, come now," said Glenda Dowling, "you're not going to let Sue Rossiter bother you. Who the hell does she think she is?"

Mrs. Smith was having her cigarette lit by Bentley. She inhaled and blew out smoke, and then she said, "What I meant was, Sue and I are old friends. I wouldn't want her to misunderstand."

"Ohhhh, no," said Glenda Dowling with a loud groan that turned into a loud hiccup. "In that case, I better keep my mouth shut." And she picked up her drink and tossed it down.

Bentley blinked behind his glasses and cocked his somewhat hydrocephaloid head, about to launch some saving witticism. But at that moment the orchestra suddenly came to life and plunged into "The Jersey Bounce." The song heralded the entrance of Miss New Jersey. Responding to the tempo of the music, she strutted into the baby spots at the head of the stairs and lapped up the applause. The three judges seemed thankful for the interruption as they leaned back in their chairs to look her over.

Though they were perhaps no more than vaguely aware of it, these three had been through a contest of their own, months before, when the Pageant's board of governors had chosen this year's panel from over two hundred candidates available for the honor.

The final dozen was a widely varied assortment, but they had much in common. They were, to quote Pageant literature, "notable representatives of the arts and sciences, of commerce and industry." All were pretty much in the public eye, either celebrities or close enough to make a run for it.

Glenda Dowling was a Hollywood columnist, syndicated in over a hundred third-rate newspapers, which made her a power. Though her scribblings persuaded her that she was a writer, she was happiest as a talker. She had run into Mrs. Smith in the lobby of the Wellington Manor, where they both were staying. On impulse—she hated dining alone, with no one to harangue—she had proposed they have dinner together, and Mrs. Smith had accepted.

In Eames Bentley, the Pageant had secured a venireman whose latest motion picture was already being touted for an Oscar. He had achieved artistic eminence and financial solvency by writing, directing and producing a biting melodrama with an all-Negro cast. Prodded by his studio's press department, Bentley had finally, at 6 P.M. that day, invited the Dowling woman to dinner, and considered himself fortunate when she told him about her earlier commitment and asked if Mrs. Smith might be included. Seated there, daintily sipping a champagne cocktail, he pretended to be scrutinizing Miss New Jersey, training his large spectacles with their powerful lenses in her direction. Meanwhile he tried to sneak a glance at his watch, and Mrs. Smith caught him at it. They both smiled and Bentley said, "Not so, my dear. I'm just beginning to enjoy it."

"I'm glad," said Mrs. Smith amiably. Looking into those spectacles, she thought, was like looking into two miniature aquaria where eyeballs swam like baby Black Tetra fish.

But Lois Potter Smith was not unaccustomed to exotics, and she rather liked him. She admired success in others no less than she prized her own. In her middle thirties, executive editor of the fashionable and influential woman's magazine *Smart*, she suited the part admirably, ultra chic but unostentatious, spirited but dignified, with a status that made her highly desirable to the Pageant.

She hadn't wanted to serve as a judge but had finally yielded because of Sue Rossiter's persuasion. Their friendship had begun the year Sue was Princess America and she was Lois Potter, a junior editor from a trade gazette, supervising a picture story. She had been more than helpful, and the story came off so well it got Lois a chance with a major publisher; and she was on her way.

In the years that followed, they had grown to know each other with increasing respect and affection. It annoyed her to find herself tonight trapped in an embarrassing situation, an unwitting trespasser, and she wondered whether to send Sue a note of explanation.

Sue Rossiter was feeling encouraged. It was not yet eight-twenty and already six contestants had made their appearance. The evening looked good, at least in that regard. She'd barely had time to exchange a few words with Miss Texas and her chaperone when the orchestra started welcoming Miss Hawaii. As she fixed her attention on the new arrival standing motionless in the spotlights across the room, Bert Blye, of the Executive Planning Board, sidled up confidentially.

"Well, Sue, what do you think? Spot the winner yet?"

She laughed. "Not *that* fast, Bert. I have to meet them."

It was a private game that Sue and others intimately involved with the Pageant played—appraising the contestants, guessing how far up the ladder they'd go—and Sue was an acknowledged marvel at it. Now, as she studied Miss Hawaii, the subliminal impressions were registering, and she tried to analyze her reactions.

The girl's smile was relentless, drained of merriment. Her breathing was too shallow, too controlled; it made her posture inflexible, ossified. The cerise silk gown with its painted purple ripples was nicely sexy and very smart, but the orchids on her shoulder made her look like something expensively gift-wrapped. The figure was lush, provocative. If she knew how to walk, those hips could do her a lot of good. There was something oddly appealing about her; maybe it was because she looked Eurasian. But the eyes fastened on people too personally, too intently; she was climbing on them. The reason for this was soon apparent. When the music ended, Miss Hawaii took her chaperone's arm before she somewhat gingerly tackled the stairs, and Sue thought: nearsighted.

Miss Hawaii was approaching. Olga Loomis materialized at Sue's elbow and whispered, "Mepala Yates. Her chaperone is Mrs. Randall."

A few moments later, the pleasantries accomplished, the envoys from Hawaii secure in their welcome and delivered to Mrs. Lockwood for further amenities, Sue looked inquiringly at Bert Blye. He had been standing close by, listening.

"A sweet girl," he said sympathetically, "but I say no."

Sue nodded. "No it is. But a chance, a fair chance, for the Miss Personality award. She makes the effort."

"Yes, a sweet girl," Blye repeated ruefully. "Let me know if you think you see a winner," and he wandered off toward the buffet table.

Olga Loomis sighed and remarked, "I'm disappointed. I was sure he'd say something about giving her a lei."

"He doesn't remember that far back," said Sue. She looked past Olga absently. "Do me a favor, dear," she said softly. "Try Lou Cates at the Hilton. Maybe he knows where Roger is. And use the phone downstairs," she added.

She turned and saw Miss California, and realized with deep regret that she was looking at a girl who could win this year's Pageant but who wasn't going to. This girl had it. Her presence had drama. She held you. She was slender, lissome, with fine bones, her features delicate as a cameo, her eyes languid and self-possessed, catlike. Ash-blond hair fell to her shoulders, a straight and shining waterfall. Her gown was Grecian, of pale-blue chiffon. A silver-mink stole hung carelessly from her arm, almost trailing on the fioor. Her head was tilted up a little, taking the applause with barely a smile but with the quiet delight, the bliss, of a child holding her face up to the rain. The girls who had preceded her had drawn cordial responses, but hers had the thing, the electric pop. Even the orchestra seemed to have a little extra juice going for them, and when they finished their second chorus the drummer tattooed a fine cadenza on his bass drum and cymbals.

7 · MISS CALIFORNIA

THE only reason the room seemed to be standing still, Stacy thought, was because it was spinning so fast. She was elated by the realization and by what it meant. It was two hours since she had turned on, so it was no longer the grass doing it for her. Now she was high on her own, making it by herself. It was like sail planing. You needed something to get you up, but once there, if the air currents were right, you could fly on and on.

Easing her way through the blur of names and faces, Stacy drifted toward the lavish buffet. She picked up an ornate plate and some silver sheathed in a napkin, vowing to diet despite her sense of euphoria. Moving counterclockwise around the huge table, she resisted the rich lobster Thermidor and the butter-drenched escargots. But finally she succumbed to the *paté de fois gras*.

She was scouting the room for a place to settle when she felt a tug at her elbow. "Hi Stacy. Park at our table. There's room for you between Nebraska and Connecticut."

It was Ginny Kerr, the former Miss California and the current Princess America.

"Girls, this is Stacy DeGray, California's latest model," she said as Stacy deposited herself between them. Then, observing Stacy's spartan platter, Ginny laughed. "That's the best thing about going into retirement; I don't have to count calories anymore." She pointed to her heaped dish. "I'm on seconds."

Stacy nibbled slowly at her meager portion, enjoying the small talk and laughter and camaraderie. Suddenly she looked up to see Mama and a slender, gray-haired man approaching.

"That's Lionel Barnes, the Lieutenant Governor," whispered Ginny. "He's coming over to our table."

"Darling," Mama said to Stacy, "the Governor would like to meet you." (He demurred at the promotion, but Mama wouldn't have it.)

"Well, well," said Mr. Barnes, beaming at Stacy. "Mrs. DeGray, you were not exaggerating. Your lovely daughter exceeds her notices. No wonder last year's judges awarded Miss California the crown. She *is* the fairest in the land." And he bowed from the waist.

The silence that followed was lethal. Finally Ginny Kerr, unable to control her cool, turned and looked steadily into the eyes of Mr. Barnes.

"Flatterer," she said, her voice edged with sarcasm. "I'll bet you say that to all the girls. I know. That's what you told *me*—last year."

Stacy made a hasty attempt to calm the troubled waters. "Right state, wrong girl," she said. She gestured toward Ginny. "She's still the champ. But I thank you anyway for the compliment."

The Lieutenant Governor's jaw sagged, like a surgeon who has just learned that he has amputated the wrong leg. His face flushed, he muttered a lame, almost inaudible apology to Ginny Kerr, then made a pitiful retreat.

It had been a delicious moment for Stacy, who thought he had made an honest mistake. Not until later, when Mama had whispered to her, "I got the idea of setting him up for that little scene when I saw you sitting next to Ginny," had Stacy felt chagrined and ill-used.

It figured. Mama was an old pro in the art of upstaging. How she had maneuvered the Lieutenant Governor into serving as the instrument of her little plot, Stacy could not divine. And it was too bad that Ginny Kerr, whom she admired, had to be the victim of Mama's latest coup. At any rate, Stacy was still high and determined that nothing should spoil this triumphant opening night. She flew onward, upward—Superstacy!

And Mama was out of her hair for the moment. She had riveted herself to Dr. Lydecker, who was such an affable little elf, and they seemed to be having a fine time. Stacy had spied them leaving the party area more than once, undoubtedly heading for the bar. Now as they came toward where she was sitting, alone for a rare moment, Stacy guessed they were heading for a refill, but it turned out that she was only partly right.

Stacy could read their lips—and Mama damn well knew she could—but that didn't cramp her style.

"You go on ahead, Doctor," Mama was saying, in her best Clara Bow, "and wait for me breathlessly."

"You won't be long?" he asked anxiously.

"A minute," she purred. "I can't keep away. I just

adore men like you, all skin and bones and delicate meat—oh, how I'd like to fricassee you."

Greater love hath no mother than this, thought Stacy, that she lay down her ass for her daughter.

Dr. Lydecker seemed reluctant to part, even for the minute, but reluctantly he left and Mama came on alone, swinging into high gear, the lights dancing from her silver brocade and jeweled wrists. Stacy could see that something was up; Mama was positively glowing with excitement.

"Yes, Mother?"

"Get yourself together, darling," said Mama commandingly. "You're coming with me."

"Where to?"

Mama's ferocious smile spread itself, enveloping her face. "You're going to be interviewed by Glenda Dowling," she said.

"What?" said Stacy. "When did all this happen?"

Mama shook her head. "Don't you know your mother yet? Don't you know your mother never rests?" Her eyes were brimming with maternal devotion. "I've arranged everything," she said. "She's waiting for you." Stacy got up and Mama inspected her. "Stand back a little," she directed. Her eyes darted everywhere. "Turn. Slowly. Don't be conspicuous. We don't want any of the officials to notice you."

Obediently, Stacy turned. At the far end of the tier, removed from the rest of the party, she saw Sue Rossiter just as her secretary was joining her. They were perhaps thirty feet away, but Stacy had no trouble deciphering Olga Loomis's guarded whisper: "I've got Lou Cates on the phone. Do you want to talk to him?" Sue answered, but Stacy couldn't read her lips because she was facing just a bit too far around. Then they both turned and went downstairs.

Mrs. DeGray took her daughter's arm and began leading the way.

"Just think, there are fourteen other girls here—what wouldn't any of them give for a chance like this? We must make the most of this opportunity. I expect you to be at your brightest. Just remember, darling, what you must impress on Glenda Dowling is that you're something quite special. You're not like the others, you're different."

Mrs. DeGray rattled on, but Stacy no longer heard her. She had tuned out when Mama had uttered a phrase that brought her back to the most desolate years of her life. *"You're not like the others, you're different."*

When she was eleven years old, Stacy had lost her hearing. Meningitis, the doctors said. For three years she had lived in a world of silence, where words were movements made by lips. Why had this happened to her? the child had wondered, unable to comprehend, too young to resolve the question. The only answer they'd given her had been *you're not like the others, you're different.*

And everything had been different—her school, her special teachers, even her few friends, afflicted as she was, who communicated with their fingers. And the others who, remembering that she had once been able to hear, made slow and elaborate contortions with their lips when they spoke to her.

She had learned to live within herself, a solitary child who walked the silent beach, where the ocean rolled in with no sound, where birds fluttered overhead with no sound, where the wind blew through the swaying white-blossomed yucca on nearby cliffs with no sound—a life with no sound of laughter or music and no sound of a little girl crying her heart out, no sound at all. *You're not like the others, you're different.*

Then one day they had taken her on a long journey, to a faraway place where a doctor had performed an operation on her, something new they called a fenestration. Weeks later, when she flew home again, she could hear the giant roar of the motors, and life had opened again. And happy as she had been herself, she was grateful for what it had meant to Mama, because Stacy by then was old enough to understand that she was Mama's whole life, her hope for the future. "You're all I have in the world. In ten years of marriage, you're all I ever got from your father." And Mama meant to protect her investment and make it pay her back.

The years since then had been years of training, learning, hoping, working—and all of it leading, she now realized, to the enshrined place called Surf City, in whose powerful and magical currents she would be swept to ascendancy, even as she was now being carried to where Glenda Dowling was waiting for her.

"Well, here she is, Miss Dowling," Mama proudly announced.

The three judges looked up across the table from their semicircular couch. They hadn't noticed the DeGrays approaching. Nor, from their expressions, had they expected it.

"Yes," said Glenda Dowling blankly, "she certainly is,

isn't she?" Her speech was slurred and an alcoholic vapor cloud wafted around her head.

Mama smiled ingratiatingly. "I was thinking about our little chat and it occurred to me, why not let Stacy tell you about it in her own words?" There was still no glimmer of understanding in Glenda Dowling's lusterless eyes, but she went on again: "You know, that item for your column about how Stacy spent last summer in a New Mexico adobe, working for VISTA?"

"Oh!" said Glenda Dowling loudly, flustered but happy. "Yes, yes, *of course*. Sit down, won't you? Eames, dear thing, move over a bit so Stacy can sit right here between us, and you, my dear Mrs. ah—Eames, will you get us another chair?"

"Oh, no, thank you," said Mama. "I have something to see to," she added archly, "something else you might care to include mentioning in the column—sort of, shall we say, a command performance? But I'll be right back!" And clutching her green feather boa, off she flounced.

A waiter had appeared with a chair, making unnecessary the maneuvering it would have required to get Stacy in on the other side of the table. Stacy sat down, looking after her mother in mounting confusion.

"Let's all have a drink!" Dowling cried lustily. "What do you drink, child?"

Lois Smith put in quickly, "I'm sure Miss Dowling doesn't mean that, Stacy. Wouldn't it be violating a Pageant regulation?"

"The *hell* with it," said Dowling. "We won't tell a soul."

"I don't drink, thank you," Stacy murmured.

"As a matter of fact," Lois went on, addressing Dowling, "didn't you say something about another regulation concerning contestants and judges? I don't think Stacy ought to be here with us."

"Balls!" said Glenda Dowling. "I'm not talking to her as a judge. I'm a newspaper reporter. You all seem to forget that, and you shouldn't, especially anyone who's a friend of Sue Rossiter." She seemed suddenly morose, remembering a previous wound, looking at Lois through half-closed eyes. "You mustn't think I don't like Sue. I'm really very, *extremely*, found of her—we all are, everybody in journalism. Her marriage has been on the rocks for years, but we columnists make it a point not to mention it. She's not divorced, she's not even separated. She just ignores her marriage and so does everybody else. Everybody. And that's because she's *very* high class and lives *very* discreetly, and doesn't give anybody a problem. That's the main thing, not giving anybody a problem, know what I mean?" And she nodded wisely.

Glenda Dowling's abrupt appraisal of Sue Rossiter cast a pall over the table. Bentley, who had been turning from Glenda to Lois and back again, now stared myopically at the tablecloth, clearing his throat.

Lois Smith let the embarrassed silence lay a moment, and then inquired in an even voice: "What do you mean, a problem?"

"Well," said Glenda, in a more conciliatory fashion, "suppose—hypothetically—suppose you're flagrant and you call attention to yourself, it becomes very difficult for journalists to ignore . . . and if it starts looking like someone's going to put it in print, then someone might just as well be first. And if they like you, you're really giving them a problem. That's clear, isn't it?"

"Yes," said Lois. "You've made it perfectly clear."

"Well then, good," said Glenda. "Now let's have that drink and listen to Miss . . . Miss—where did you say you're from?"

"California," said Stacy with infinite relief as she saw Sue Rossiter quickly approaching.

When Sue Rossiter had left the party and gone downstairs to the phone booths with Olga, she had circuitously avoided passing anywhere near the table with the three judges. She feared contact which might easily—the way she felt—ignite the volatile possibilities of the situation. The booths were in the foyer, and a captain stood guard over one of them. As she drew close, Hank Jordan, the orchestra leader, tried to intercept her, but she waved him off with a smile. "See what he wants," she said to Olga, closeting herself in the booth and picking up the phone.

"Hello, Lou?"

"Miss Rossiter?"

"Yes. Lou, do you know where Mr. Megan is?"

"No, Miss Rossiter."

"Did he say anything about coming here?"

"No, he didn't say anything either way."

"Did you give him my message this morning at the Armory?"

"Yes."

"Do you expect to see him later tonight?"

"I can't say."

"If you do, will you tell him to phone me, no matter when?"

"Yes, of course."

She hesitated, then asked, "Lou, is there any trouble?"

He matched her hesitation. "I can't say, Miss Rossiter."

She hung up and left the booth. Olga and Hank Jordan were waiting for her a few feet away. As they came toward her, she saw that Olga was disturbed.

"Sue," she said quietly, "Hank wants to ask you something."

"What is it?"

Jordan said, "Well, I thought I ought to clear it with you, Miss Rossiter. Not that it's all that important, is it? Because we do have entertainment here on other nights."

"What are you talking about?" said Sue in quick alarm.

"One of the chaperones here wants the girl she's with to do a vocal with the band, and—"

She cut him off sharply. "Who was it?"

"She didn't tell me her name, but the girl is Stacy DeGray. She just wants me to introduce her and let her sing one number."

"It's impossible," said Sue flatly.

"I'm sorry. I couldn't see the harm—"

"We have rules against the girls performing in public."

"I'm sorry," he said again. "I had no idea. You know, I'm new here."

"It's not your fault, Hank. Thank you for checking with us."

He dug a hand into his pants pocket, then brought it out and extended it toward Olga. There was a folded twenty-dollar bill in his open palm. "Would you mind returning this to the lady?" he said to Olga. "I might have trouble finding her."

Sue reached out and took the twenty. "I'll do it," she said very quietly. "Thank you again." Jordan nodded politely and walked away. Sue could feel herself shaking. She had closed the money in so tight a fist, her nails were digging into the flesh of her palm.

"It's all right, Sue," said Olga. "Nothing has actually happened." She touched Sue's arm, then held it. "Let's go back," she said. "Max is probably ready to start taking the group pictures. It'll all be over soon."

Sue turned and looked toward the bar entrance. The bar was off the foyer, a room to itself. "See if Dr. Lydecker is in there with Mrs. DeGray," she said. She sounded perfectly calm. "I think I saw them heading there. Tell Mrs. DeGray I'd like to have a word with her." But Olga held back, and Sue shook her head, admonishing her. "You needn't worry, Olga," she said with a faint smile that was half grimace. "Worrying is my province, and I do it beautifully. Go."

"Going," said Olga, but as she took a step she turned slightly and threw a line back over her shoulder. "When was the last time Sue Rossiter stood in Macy's window looking unhappy?" she asked, and continued walking with an unhurried pace to the bar entrance and went inside.

The tight smile on Sue Rossiter's face suddenly blossomed. It was a shammed smile, but consummate, like an artistically wrought wax flower, the required window dressing. Because, always in her public life, there were eyes on her. They were bold eyes, filled with curiosity and longing and envy, staring at her with the Look that celebrities learn to live with. She was being observed on all sides. From the phone booths, the checkroom, by the patrons walking through, by the stewards. A confrontation with Mrs. DeGray before all these eyes might be extremely dangerous. It could easily flare up into an ugly scene.

And then, Sue thought, why was she so upset by her? Hadn't she met Mrs. DeGray's counterpart by the dozens, even the hundreds—the pushy, dreadful, unabashed schemers, oblivious to everything but their drive and ambition? Why was this particular woman capable of bugging her so much? Sue probed deeper into herself for the truth. Wasn't it really because she felt guilt gnawing at her when she was reminded of Stacy?

Olga came out of the bar with Dr. Lydecker, walking toward her. She knew instantly, from Lydecker's troubled, intense gaze, that something else had gone wrong. As they reached her, the little doctor seemed anxious to speak, but Sue asked, "Where is Mrs. DeGray? Isn't she with you?"

Lydecker held his hands out. "She is and she isn't," he shrugged. "I'm waiting for her. She came in about two minutes ago, told me she'd be right back, and went out again."

"But I begged you, Franz, as a favor to me, to keep an eye on her, to stick close to her, to promise her anything just as long as you could prevent her from being an unguided missile."

"Sue, I couldn't have got unstuck if I'd tried. I did what you suggested. I sold her the idea that I could give her daughter tips on winning points from the judges. After she heard that, I couldn't have pried her loose with forceps. She actually made a couple of passes at me. That confounded woman has just about ruined my evening. I wouldn't have done it for anybody but you, and I tried, but I don't know . . . these last ten minutes she started moving too fast for me. She's busy with something."

"God, is she busy," said Sue. "All right, she's got you hung up here. If she gets back before I find her, will you please bring her to me?"

Dr. Lydecker nodded vigorously, and Sue, with Olga trailing half a step behind, returned down the length of the foyer and back into the main room. The moment she walked in she looked toward Glenda Dowling's table, more than half expecting to find Mrs. DeGray there. Instead, with shock and a stab of sickness in her stomach, she saw Stacy sitting with the judges.

Olga had spotted her too. "I'll get her out of there," she quickly volunteered.

"No, Olga," said Sue. "You try and find her mother." And she started for the table, circling the outside of the arena, giving herself that extra split minute to check her state of mind, to prepare for the long minute ahead. Her smile hadn't faded, but she knew it was made of ice, and in the last few steps she infused it with warmth and friendship, the full treatment, the famous smile.

"Good evening, Glenda, Lois, Eames," she said, standing next to Stacy, nodding to each in turn. "I'm sorry I haven't had a chance to come by sooner, but I know you forgive me, we're so—" and interrupting herself, as though the thought were occurring in passing—"Stacy, dear, you should be up there with the others. We're about to take some pictures. Don't you want to be in them?"

"Are you kidding?" said Stacy, getting up immediately.

"Just a minute," said Glenda Dowling, looking piqued. "We're just starting to talk."

"There's a whole week ahead of us for talk," said Sue, trying to laugh it off, "but the pictures are here and now. Run along, dear."

"Thank you," said Stacy. "It would've killed me if I didn't have a souvenir of this evening." She nodded hastily to the judges. "And thank you. A pleasure and a privilege." And she was gone.

Dowling's sour expression softened a bit as she looked after Stacy's retreating form. "Now there, there—" and she hiccuped loudly before she finished— "there goes a *girl.* I'm going to give her a column—well, maybe not a *whole* column, but enough to help, anyway."

"I'm sure you mean well, Glenda," said Sue smoothly, "but don't you realize you're actually jeopardizing that girl's position with this sort of attention?"

Glenda looked up at Sue through narrowing eyes, hostility glinting in them like knives. "Forget it, will you?" she said, her tone changing abruptly.

"I'm sorry, Glenda, but I thought I explained matters this afternoon about the Pageant rules concerning socializing among judges and contestants."

"Now what the hell do you want from me?" said Dowling. "Get off my back, will you *kindly*? Did I invite this girl? Do you know how much I had to do with it? Her mother cornered me in the ladies' room—in the *ladies'* room, goddam it—and she said something about me interviewing her daughter sometime and I said yes just to get rid of her. How the hell should I know she'd bring her here now?"

It's too loud, thought Sue; we're attracting attention; I'm not handling this right. "I'm sorry," she said. "I didn't know the circumstances. Nevertheless, it seems to me—"

"I don't give two farts and a whistle what it seems like to you! And let me tell you something, Miss Rossiter. I'm getting pretty sick of this pageant and the goddam thing hasn't even *started* yet! And if you think you're going to give me a bad time—"

"There's no need—"

"I don't care to discuss it!" Dowling snapped. "And I'm getting the hell out of here this minute." She struggled erect, pushing the table away, then holding on to the edge of it to steady herself. "Eames, will you kindly escort Lois and me home?"

"If you don't mind," said Lois, "I'll stay."

"Ha!" cried Glenda. "All evening you've been in such a goddam hurry to leave, but now you'll stay, hah? Now that you're rid of me, is that it? I might've known. In fact, I did know!" And she began to laugh her cackling sound until she hiccuped again.

Bentley had risen, pale, trapped, dying of embarrassment. He took Dowling's arm in one hand and her mink cape in the other. "Good night," he said to Lois and Sue, unable to meet their eyes, and he began helping Glenda walk, a tug nudging and steering a freighter.

"Sit down a moment, Sue," said Lois softly.

"I can't now. Will you wait for me? It won't take long."

Lois nodded. "I'll wait."

As Sue made her way back to the upper tier, she was trying not to think, not to allow herself the horrible moment of agony realizing what a mess she had made of her minute with Glenda Dowling. The anger in her was a dull ache, and she knew she had to avoid, at all costs, a showdown with Mrs. DeGray. She no longer trusted her poise, her cool diplomacy. She felt helpless. Everything was slipping out of her hands.

And then she was back among them, among the girls and their chaperones as they primped excitedly, chattering, reassuring one another how beautiful they looked, meanwhile jostling for position as Max Gerber arranged them around the longest table. With relief, she spotted Olga, leaving Mrs. DeGray and Dr. Lydecker at one of the rear tables, coming toward her.

"Where did you find her?" Sue asked when Olga approached.

"I found her trying to talk Max into taking a picture of Stacy sitting with the three judges when they were together. She offered him the same twenty, and when he turned her down, she made it fifty. But not Max," said Olga, sighing. "Not our Max."

For the first time since she had taken the twenty from Hank Jordan, Sue remembered she still had it clutched in the fist of her left hand. Painfully, she released her grip. "You give it to her," she said dully. "And please, please keep her away from me."

"Don't I know," said Olga, nodding.

As Olga left her, Sue looked to Max Gerber. He was pointing a forefinger at her, making a pistol with his hand. "Ready on the firing line," he called out, directing her to the center of the waiting group.

Mechanically, she took her place and mechanically she followed all instructions. The picture-taking began and soon seemed endless. Max kept rearranging them, giving all the girls a chance to be photographed standing beside Sue (partly because it was always necessary to be fair to all, and partly because Max would be discreetly selling them prints as he met them again later during the week). Weariness was slowly engulfing her as the ceremony went on, but her perfected smile kept flashing in synchronization with the strobe lights. She was counting the minutes now, and with each blinding flash she knew she was closer to the end of the evening.

Then she was moving around, shaking hands, taking care of the innumerable good-nights. There were only two bad moments to face, and she cut through them swiftly, painlessly. The first was with Stacy, the second with Mrs. DeGray. "Good night," Stacy said in a whisper, "and thank you for rescuing me before." Sue nodded and squeezed her hand. But Mrs. DeGray had tried to take her aside, and Sue, not looking at her, had said something about another time and moved away, betraying nothing.

They were leaving now, thought Stacy, and her spirits had been good to her; they had given her the evening she had asked, and she was thankful. But there was a crush up ahead near the door, what with all the exiting and leave-taking and calling for cabs, and Mama was hanging back. Because of this, instead of being in the foyer, Stacy and her mother were still inside the main room, at the top of the short flight of stairs that led out. Beside her, Mama was chattering away with Dr. Lydecker as they inched forward. Stacy turned and looked back.

Across the room, at the table where the three judges had sat, Stacy saw Sue Rossiter sitting with Mrs. Smith. She was startled by the worn, exhausted look on Sue Rossiter's face, and it piqued her curiosity. She decided to eavesdrop. There was just light enough at their table for Stacy to be able to read their lips.

"But you don't know," Sue was saying. "That incredible woman had arranged to have her daughter get up with the band and sing. It would have been a disaster for the Pageant if we hadn't found out in time. I'm still shaking."

"The girl's looking at us," said Lois.

"Don't look back," said Sue. "Don't give her any sign that might encourage her mother to bring her here."

"She's a lovely girl," said Lois. "It would be a pity if her mother ruined her chance to win."

Sue shook her head. "It doesn't matter, really. She has no chance. She never did. Maybe that's part of what's been bothering me all evening. I couldn't help feeling sorry for her."

"Stacy, dear," Mrs. DeGray called, "aren't you coming?"

But Stacy didn't budge.

"I don't understand," Lois was saying. "Why do you say she has no chance?"

"Because last year's Princess also came from California."

"But what has that got to do with her?"

"It's one of our unwritten laws. No state has ever had two consecutive Pageant winners."

"But isn't it just a coincidence that it's never happened?"

"No, it will never happen. It would hurt the Pageant, so it can't be allowed to happen. The Pageant must be very careful to distribute its honors on a national basis. All this will be explained to you at the briefing for the judges. The current Princess comes from California, so Stacy lost her chance to become Princess the day she became Miss California."

"That's too bad, isn't it?"
"Yes," said Sue Rossiter. "But that's the way it is."
They went on talking, but Stacy closed her eyes. She had gone numb. Faintly she heard her mother's voice. Then it was louder, insistent, beside her. She opened her eyes.
"What's the matter, Stacy? Don't you feel well?"
But she couldn't talk. She seized her mother's arm and held on tightly as they walked through the foyer to the door. Everything was swimming around her. She felt faint, lost, utterly bewildered. Only some minutes later, in the merciful privacy of the cab that was taking them back to their hotel, was she able to release a sound. She buried her head against Mama's shoulder. Great sobs wracked her body, and her tears soaked into Mama's brocade.
"Stacy, baby, what is it?" Mama kept saying, taking her daughter in her arms.
"Oh, Mother, I want to die."
And Stacy continued to cry, unable to stop even when they reached their hotel.

8 · MISS ALASKA

THE wide double window of Bedroom B, Suite 2506, overlooked the plaza separating hotel and boardwalk. As seen from this height, lights from the traffic below flowed, writhed, melted, regrouped. Ten P.M., and Surf City's night life was beginning to swing.

Or if one chose to look upward, there was the great, ungainly blimp cruising aimlessly across a dark sky, an absurd airborne whale. Searchlights from the hotel roof, and from other roofs adjacent, tracked it like a military target as it swam among the stars. A pennant streamer trailing behind it read: 13TH ANNUAL PRINCESS AMERICA PAGEANT.

Motionless at the window, Mildred Waxman stood with her forehead pressed against the cool glass. The shimmer below had the distorted quality of light refracted from Mendenhall Glacier when full sun struck it. A sharp pang of homesickness clawed her.

Beyond the open door to her closet, where the friendly bellhop who had escorted her up from the lobby a few minutes ago had deposited them, her three matched pieces of new luggage (courtesy of the Juneau Chamber of Commerce) awaited attention. There were the inevitable flowers: Alaska's own blue forget-me-nots, with a handwritten note from the Governor. A color TV set (courtesy-loaned by a local Surf City dealer) filled one corner, all seven channels awaiting her pleasure.

Against one wall stood the small spinet piano an Alaskan rooter had ordered for her so that she might practice her specialty in the talent competition—a medley of the stirring Gold Rush tunes identified with her state's early history.

All the comforts of home. And then some.

Home, for Mildred, was the modest bungalow Eli Waxman provided for his wife and only daughter. It commanded a heart-stopping view of those snow-capped peaks which justified Juneau's claim to being most scenic of all America's capitals. But otherwise there was nothing much luxurious about it. By contrast, Suite 2506 was royal.

A girl should be happy to be housed in such elegance, even for a single week. A girl should be excited, on tiptoe with anticipation, bursting with pride. A girl should feel like what the newspapers back home had dubbed her—"the Juno from Juneau."

Instead, Mildred Waxman suffered from a crushing sense of inferiority. What was she doing here in the national finals, she asked herself, when she should be living in that oblivion inhabited by the forgotten also-rans?

A soft silk scarf—yellow, pale green, white in a paisley pattern—circled her throat. She picked at it restlessly.

It had all happened too fast. If she hadn't been caught so far off base, she wouldn't have let it happen at all. When Sidney had told her about submitting her picture in the Miss Alaska preliminaries, she had laughed it off as a flattering joke.

They had been working together in the Alaska Historical Library, collaborating on a team research project for the sophomore course in Eskimo Origins. Sidney had possibly fallen a little in love with her.

A nice boy, Sidney. When he'd asked for her picture, she saw no reason to hurt his feelings by refusing to give it to him. But that was all there had been to it. The term was ending. Papa was somehow squeezing out a round-trip air fare to let her accept the invitation from Uncle Irving and Aunt Bella to visit them in Israel. And with all that to think about, a girl just didn't have many thoughts left over for a too gentle, too studious boy like Sidney.

Israel!

For as far back as she could remember, Mildred had thought of it as a genuine land of milk and honey. Often (loyal American though she was) she had wondered why Papa had not chosen to migrate there with his younger brother. It might so easily have happened, back in those days before she was born when his family had pulled up its roots in Poland. But Papa had seen brighter promise in a vast, rapidly developing territory that seemed destined to become a new American state. So he had come to Alaska, a fleck of foam on the great wave of immigration from Eastern Europe

And that was how it had been for Eli Waxman and, hence, for Eli's daughter. Then, on the eve of her nineteenth birthday, Mildred's dream of a visit to Israel was about to come true. Papa and Mama, who indulged her whenever their small but flourishing sporting-goods store allowed, had scrimped together the wherewithal. The trip was to be her birthday present.

The dream never had envisioned the shocking reality. That there was a constant state of near war in Israel she had known. That that war would leave its mark on her she had never imagined. She supposed she was lucky, really, but it was hard to feel lucky.

July, and Mildred was back home in Juneau, with new and terrifying memories. It was a miracle she hadn't been killed, everyone said, and that was all that really mattered. Mama had tried to fuss over her with chicken soup and a new blouse she had stitched with her sewing machine. Papa had canceled plans for his own fishing vacation near Ketchikan and Tongass Narrows.

There had been no time to think of Sidney. Nor any reason to.

So when the first newspaper reporter telephoned her to verify his story, that she had been invited to enter the preliminaries, she reacted as though someone had just told her thick veins of gold ore had been discovered in the Waxman back yard. It was so wildly improbable, the impossible dream, so out of the blue.

"Aloha!" a voice sounded behind her, cutting off her thoughts. It was a light mellifluous voice. She turned from the window. Leaning against the jamb of the door between Bedroom B and the joint parlor which separated it from Bedroom A, she saw an extraordinarily pretty girl.

She was ripe-figured, graceful even in her negligent pose. Her hair was so black that its highlights seemed blue. She wore it parted in the middle and drawn back from a dramatic widow's peak. Her skin had a gardenia-petal tinge which somehow suggested a strain of Asian or Polynesian blood. She was dressed in a flowing gown of cerise silk which was patterned in op-art fashion with melting demi-shapes in purple. Orchids were pinned to its shoulder.

"Aloha!" she said again. "I hope I didn't startle you." The brown eyes she fixed upon Mildred were smiling and friendly, if perhaps a trifle too intense in their regard. "You're Alaska, aren't you? I'm Hawaii. Mepala Yates, really. Mepala's Polynesian for Mable. We're suite mates. The door was open, so I couldn't resist coming in and introducing myself."

Mildred's fingers relaxed their hold on her scarf. "Hello.

I just got in and was about to unpack. My plane was late. I'm Mildred Waxman."

Mepala edged a few feet further into the bedroom. Mildred envied the way she moved—lithely, bonelessly, like a mermaid. Without being asked, she unlimbered herself on the large bed, her chin supported by her right elbow so as not to disarrange her hair.

"Mepala," Mildred said, "has it occurred to you what a coincidence it is that we're sharing the same suite—Alaska and Hawaii, the two most recent states?"

Mepala shifted her head to her left elbow. "It's design, not coincidence. I hear Norm Prescott, the Pageant's public-relations chief, arranged it that way. He figures it's an angle that will get us a news story."

"They think of everything, don't they?"

"I'm glad I met you tonight, Millie. I was feeling in the dumps. They aren't going to let King Kamehameha stay in my room. They're kicking him out in the morning."

Mildred blinked rapidly. "A . . . a *king* is in your room?"

"My mynah bird. I just couldn't endure leaving him back in the Islands for the whole long week I'll be here. So I brought him along. But there's some idiotic Pageant rule about our having no pets in our rooms. I tried to explain King Kam isn't a bird. He's a person."

"They wouldn't agree with you?"

"Nope. When the Pageant security guard in the lobby tried to take him away from me, King Kam gave him a piece of his mind. And what a mind!" Mepala giggled softly before elaborating. "King Kam was brought up by a sailor. On shore leave, the poor guy couldn't pay his bill at his favorite whorehouse on Kuakini Street—that's in Honolulu's red-light district. The madam took Kam as collateral and held him for six months, but the sailor never redeemed him. Our gardener bought him as a gift for me, never dreaming of the vocabulary King had picked up in the joint. Just about the most refined sentence in his repertoire is 'Screw you, blue balls!' My, that poor guard. When he told me I'd have to get rid of King in the morning, Kam looked at him as if he had also got the message. Then he really cut loose."

Mildred hesitated, but curiosity won out. "What did he say?"

" 'Up yours, mother-fucker!' And a lot worse. 'Blow . . .' " Mepala broke into laughter as she started to recount the episode, found herself unable to continue.

Despite her anxieties, Mildred found that she, too, was

laughing. It was difficult not to feel tranquilized by the offhand, casual manner of this brash, beautiful girl. Not only was Miss Hawaii easy to listen to; she was easy to talk to as well. The story of why Mildred Waxman was here in Surf City in place of the girl who should have been, and of two other girls as well, had been nagging her like a migraine headache. Even though she had met Mepala only minutes ago, she was tempted to confide in her.

"I think I know how King Ka-whatdoyoucallit feels. I've been ready to let loose with a few choice phrases of my own lately. Having to come here. Having to pretend."

"*Having* to come here?" Mepala's eyes, with their faintly Oriental tilt, went wide. "Didn't you want to come? Didn't you fight tooth and nail? *I* did."

"But you won your state competition. I didn't win mine."

"You must have won. You're Miss Alaska. You're here."

"Only because a press plane nosed over at takeoff, leaving Anchorage. They'd flown the four of us up there last week to pose for a publicity layout on the Anchorage Fur Rendezvous—our Mardi Gras of the North. Alma Gregory, she'd placed first and really *is* Miss Alaska. Ethel White Deer, she came in second. Regina Layton, who was third. And fourth place—me. Low girl on the totem pole. I shouldn't have been in the competition at all. Look at me. I'm no beauty like the rest of you. My nose is too long. My eyes are too close together. And . . . and . . ." Mildred halted, fought the hand which of its own volition sought to pluck at the colorful silk scarf.

"Your nose," said Mepala firmly, "is not too long. Your eyes are very pretty, especially when you smile. They remind me of Doris Day's. And your figure's actually sensational. So that's enough of that nonsense. Now, for heaven's sake, tell me. This air crash."

"Well, the Fur Rendezvous isn't until next February. But leaflets pitching it to the tourist trade have to get distributed way in advance. They wanted us—the four finalists—in a shot standing before a big stuffed Kodiak bear reared up on its hind legs."

"With me, so far, it's been posing with surfboards and flower leis," Mepala murmured. "I regret that I only have a hundred and twenty pounds of flesh to give to the Hawaiian Tourist Bureau. So then?"

"We were on the return lap to Juneau when it happened. Someone said later there was slick on the runway. Anyhow, our pilot lost control trying to get us airborne.

Alma got two broken legs in the crack-up. Ethel's back will be in a cast for the next four months. Regina's arm is in a sling. So there was nobody left to come to Surf City but me. It's almost as though I had made wax dolls of the other three girls and stuck pins into them."

"You weren't hurt at all?"

"Only shaken up. That's one thing about me. I have a charmed life." *Or I'm a cat, with nine of them.* Not even with Mepala could she dare discuss that other miraculous eyelash escape when sirens were caterwauling and bombs were ripping the universe apart. "Actually," Mildred went on, "I figured I'd be eliminated right off in the prelims. Only I wasn't. I still don't see why."

"Some day when you've five minutes to spare," said Mepala with deep sincerity, "take a look at yourself in a mirror. A real look. You might be surprised how much the girl looking back at you has going for her."

Mepala yawned. "Forgive my manners," she said, "but my reflexes are still synchronized to Honolulu time." She got up to leave, opened the door which led to their adjoining parlor, looked inside, then stopped short. "Hey, Alaska," she called back. "Want to see King Kam? He's still awake in his cage. This may be your last chance to meet him."

"Introduce me to your vulgar friend."

King Kam was about the size of a parrot, with plumage that was a shimmering, iridescent black. His feet and the snoodlike wattles on either side of his head were yellow, while his beak was half orange and half yellow. His eyes were round and sparkled with roguishness. As soon as he spied Mepala, he began flapping his white-flecked wings and opening his beak.

"Hungry as a whore! Hungry as a whore!" exclaimed Kam. The words were startlingly distinct.

Mepala laughed. "I told you he's intelligent. That's his way of telling me he wants some goodies." She dipped into a plastic container on a table, scooped up some raisins and grapes, then dropped them into the cage. "Okay, Kam," she said. "Have yourself an orgy. But tomorrow, when they take you away from me, it's back to boiled rice."

At the mention of boiled rice, the mynah bird abandoned his delicacies, began fluttering about wildly in his cage.

"Tastes like crap. Tastes like crap."

Mildred's eyes almost popped. "Mepala," she said in wonder, "either I'm dreaming, or you're a ventriloquist."

Mepala's lips formed a mock pout. "The next thing

you'll say is that he's a recording. But King Kam comes from a special breed found only in the Malay jungle. He can *think*. Walk back and forth in front of his cage and I'll prove it."

As Mildred paraded in front of the bird, Mepala bent down toward the cage and spoke clearly. "Mildred is my friend, King. Do you think she's pretty?"

King Kam hopped onto his perch, cocked his head. He uttered a shrill whistle, then: "Pretty. I like her ass. I like her tits."

"Your King is a dirty old lecher," blurted Mildred, her eyes twinkling. "He should be quarantined for life. Now . . . good night." She paused at the door. "Thanks for the laughs, Hawaii. I sure needed them."

Alone in her room, Mildred went about the business of washing and setting her short, dark hair. She was sitting under the drier (installed in every bedroom for the convenience of Pageant participants) when a tiny winking light on the base of the telephone suddenly attracted her eye. Mildred turned off the drier, simultaneously sliding out from her chair. The hum of the appliance faded, and she could hear the ringing which had previously been drowned out.

An intuition that rarely failed warned her that it would be bad news. Who would be calling so late? Papa? Mama? Was something wrong back home? Her hand trembling slightly, she raised the receiver.

An unfamiliar voice said, "Miss Mildred Waxman? This is Lost and Found, Northwest Airlines. Are you missing a piece of luggage—a plastic flight bag?"

Her glance flew across the room to the semi-opened closet door. The luggage the bellboy had stacked so neatly stood in her line of vision. Three matched pieces. No supplementary flight bag. There was a chance it had been tucked somewhere in the rear of the closet, but her subconscious told her not to bet on it.

"I—I don't know. Will you please hold the phone while I check?"

In three strides she was at the closet. She pulled the door full open, activating an overhead bulb. Under its shaft of light she swiftly inspected the floor and the tiers of shelves to either side. The bag was missing, all right. Then her premonition had been correct. It was bad news.

Well, it served her right for cheating. With all the wardrobe changes the week would demand, she had been afraid that her luggage would be overweight. So she had smuggled the flight bag aboard the plane under her topper. Once in her place, she had slipped it under her seat when she was certain no one was watching.

She bit her lips. No need to panic yet. She must find out how the bag had been traced to her. If no one had examined its contents, she could still claim it. Otherwise she would have to disown it completely.

Mildred picked up the phone. "Hello," she spoke into the mouthpiece. "I do have my flight bag. But I think I may have left Seattle with a second one. I changed planes there so fast I can't remember."

It was scarcely plausible. But it would have to do. She paused. "What makes you think the bag you found belongs to me?"

From the other end came Miss Lost and Found's impersonal reply. "The bag has no claim check attached, so we opened it. That's standard procedure. It contains a traveling clock, a small camera, vitamin pills . . ."

"But such things might belong to anyone." They didn't, though. The bag was hers. "Is there any special reason you'd connect it—?"

"There's also a complete collection of cosmetics. Lotions, eyebrow pencils. Creams. All the makeup equipment a Princess America contestant might be carrying. So we thought—"

Mildred closed her eyes. Goodbye, camera, which had been Papa's special farewell gift before she left home. "No, the bag isn't mine," she said indifferently. "But I appreciate your thinking of me."

Numbly, Mildred restored the phone to its cradle. The crisis she had been dreading had arrived. Early tomorrow morning her official chaperone would be calling for her. Could she trust her with her secret and enlist her help? Or would she be duty-bound to report her?

She picked up the Surf City telephone directory on the walnut end table, turned to the classified section. Thumbing hastily to *Drug Stores*, she was referred to *Pharmacists*, and here found the listing she had sought. Terrace Chemists. She had noticed its blinking *All Night Service* sign as the limousine from the airport passed it on the way to the hotel. And it was a safe two miles distant, beyond the boardwalk.

Dialing the number, she got a busy signal. Trying again, after an interminable minute, she established contact with her second anonymous voice of the evening. It was a blessing to know that, in so far as the husky voice at the other end was concerned, she too was anonymous.

"This is . . . Mrs. Martha Jones. I wonder if you could

make up a package for me? A few things I need for a sudden trip. I'll come—I'll send over for them in about twenty minutes if you could have them wrapped and ready."

"Sure can, Mrs. Jones. What's the order?"

Mildred began to call off a variety of items. The night man took them down routinely, repeating each one for confirmation. She gave a gasp of relief when he hung up. Even if he had been suspicious when she had specified that one incriminating item, she was positive he would never associate it with a Princess America contestant. It had been as simple as ordering a Chinese take-out dinner.

I'll come over for them, she started to say. But that, of course, was impossible. There was no chance she could slip past the Pageant security guard posted in the lobby. She would have to find someone to send in her place—someone who would not suspect the real purpose of the errand. In all of Surf City, who?

Why not the bellhop? What had he said his name was? Dave, she thought. Dave Lebow. He would be her carrier pigeon. She pressed the room-service buzzer above the light switch, then sat down on the chair by the spinet.

A few moments later, opening the door in response to his knock, she was pleasantly surprised that he was taller and much more mature-looking than had been her first impression. He could easily be in his late twenties. His broad shoulders in his trim red jacket almost filled the width of the doorway. There was a cleft in his squarish chin that could have been a scar. His eyes, deep in their sockets, were smiling and direct and had the sheen of polished chestnuts.

"Hi Alaska," he said cheerily. "Can I be of any service? During Pageant Week my mission in life is to make you and Miss Hawaii happy."

Mildred returned the smile, then said, "Can you do me a favor? I need someone to run an errand for me. To Terrace Chemists. It's a drugstore up the boardwalk."

"You're ill?" He seemed openly solicitous. "The house doctor—"

"No, it's nothing like that. These are mostly personal items. I left them behind in a flight bag when I changed planes on the Coast."

"We've a pretty complete drugstore in the arcade downstairs."

"I know that," she rushed on glibly, "but one of the items is a sleeping thing. My doctor in Juneau wired the prescription on ahead. He knew I'd be tense and jittery with all the excitement." She shrugged ruefully. "I'm sorry, but that's the pharmacy he wired it to. I've just phoned them. They'll have my package ready to be picked up soon. So if there's somebody you can send for them . . ."

"Sure," Dave said. "I'll go myself. My relief comes on a few minutes from now and I'll be off duty." His smile expanded into a downright grin. He was regarding her with open admiration, yet in a nice way. A warming way. "It would be a *mitzvah* to run a little errand for Miss Alaska."

His use of the Hebrew word *mitzvah* puzzled her. As she dug in her purse for a bill to give him, she couldn't help thinking that his last name, Lebow, sounded more French than Semitic.

She found a twenty-dollar note, handed it to him. "This should cover it," she said.

He gave her a soft salute and departed. To busy herself until he shuttled back, Mildred reached for comb and brush and began teasing her hair. When this chore was over, she moved to the room's Louis Something desk and composed a postcard message to Papa and Mama on one of the chromolithographic likenesses of the hotel provided to each room gratis, along with its Gideon Bible and folders reporting special services available.

Suddenly she heard a key rattling in her door. There was the sound of drunken male laughter. "Oops! Key don't fit."

Then came a giggle and a woman's voice. "Lover boy, you've got the wrong room. We're in 2508. Give me the key."

The key rattled again, a door opened, then slammed. Presently, through the paper-thin wall partition, the coat-of-arms of today's new hotels, Mildred could hear the pillow talk.

"Baby, how much extra to stay the whole night with me?"

"Twenty-five dollars—but you've got to buy me breakfast in bed, too!"

"Deal! Didn't Charlie tell you I was the last of the big spenders? . . . Baby, if you want somethin' to eat, I can let you have it now."

Mildred had vaguely known that Surf City was an open town for commercial passion during businessmen's conventions and other stag affairs. But for a first-rate hotel like this one to let the world's oldest profession thrive during the sacred Pageant Week . . .

A gentle knock on the door after she had written a dozen more cards heralded Dave's return. She let him in, and he set the package down on the end table. The tall young man, no longer in uniform, was wearing slacks and a white turtle-neck sweater. He held out some bills and a handful of silver.

"I paid the druggist seventeen dollars and ten cents, so here's your change." He put it on the table, next to the package.

"You forgot to charge me for your taxi fare. How much did it come to? Both ways, including the tip."

He waved his hands airily. "Not a sou. One of the fellows in my union drove me. Besides, I don't take tips when I'm off duty."

She shook her head. "But you deserve some reward for your noble deed, boy scout. Now please pick up the money and buy yourself a shiny new merit badge."

"No, thanks." His face lit up with an engaging smile. "You don't have to give me anything, really. But if you'd like to swap favors—would you autograph this?"

From the back pocket of his slacks he produced a green strip of pasteboard. He handed it to her and Mildred examined it curiously. The card listed all the states in alphabetical order, and opposite each state was a blank, square box.

"Is this some sort of ballot?"

"Local sweepstakes. The Surf City merchants—markets, gas stations, restaurants, just about everybody—give 'em out like trading stamps during Pageant Week. If anyone can guess the exact finishing order of the five top winners, he wins the grand prize—one of every stock listed on the Big Board." He pointed to the second line. "See here? I've checked Alaska for first place. So I'd certainly like your Jane Hancock on the back of my card."

She looked at him incredulously, almost dropping the ticket.

"Me? But . . . why on earth me?"

"A lot of reasons. I like your style. And you're Jewish, aren't you?"

"I'm as Jewish as Mother Shapiro's gefilte fish."

"Me too. Meet Dave Lebow, formerly Lebowitz. I had it changed legally when I entered medical school."

"You're a med student?"

"Cornell University. I start my senior year in two weeks. The hotel bit in summers, plus tips, covers my room and board. Then, with a scholarship—"

"I rather thought you were miscast as a . . . bellhop."

She scrawled her name on the back of the card, using the pen with which she had written the postcard. "Dave—do you think a Jewish girl could possibly win? Could she really make it as Princess America?"

"Listen," he said. "No one is supposed to mention the Miss America contest around Surf City. They're our biggest rival. It's a dirty word here. But not so many years back Bess Myerson won *that* crown. Look what a big wheel she's been in their pageant ever since."

"So Bess is Jewish? I never really knew. But with a name like Waxman, there isn't much room for doubt, is there?"

"What's in a name? If that bothers you, a Waxman by any other name would smell as sweet. Do as I did. Change it to Wakeman. Or, better still, Wellman."

"I'm not *ashamed* of my name. Or of being Jewish. But there are those prejudices. Extra hurdles. And I—I look Jewish. My nose."

"What's wrong with your nose?"

"It's . . . it's . . . oh, it's so—"

"You ought to have seen the original model of mine. Like a French horn before the panhandler took a whack at it."

"The . . . panhandler?"

"Rhinoplastic surgeon I know. Teaches at my college. Even though he gave me his special economy price for bobbing my schnoz, I'm still in hock for the bill. But I think it was worth it. I'm bucking for a Park Avenue practice. Everything deluxe. No room for comedy."

"That's *my* trouble," she mourned. "Comedy! Oh, my nose isn't a Cyrano, I guess. But it's so long that—"

"Only one silly little Millie-meter longer," he punned. "So forget it." He turned and reached for the door. "Thanks for the souvenir. Sweet dreams, Alaska."

Mildred was sorry to see him go. He had radiated virility, like a smoldering young lion. For just a fleeting moment there she had wanted him to put his arms around her so that his warmth might make her feel safe. He believed in her.

She picked up the package from the end table and took it with her into the bathroom. It opened easily; in fact, as she undid its string, the strands under her fingers seemed not to hold quite so firmly as they should. Had Dave . . . ? But of course not. From the wrapping she extracted the beauty aids and cleansing articles she had ordered, stowed them in a neat array on a cabinet shelf.

All but one white jar.

Mildred studied the three-syllable brand name on the label, and then picked up a single-edged razor blade and began scraping off the print. When the last trace of identification had been removed, she carefully gathered the minute shreds and flushed them down the toilet.

Then, standing tense before the lighted mirror above her dressing table, Mildred unknotted the scarf that covered her throat. A neck graceful as a swan's, with skin of flawless texture, was revealed. But now must come the moment of truth.

She turned on the hot-water tap in the washbasin, let it run over a small face cloth until it was soaked. Then, wringing out the cloth, Mildred brought it up to her throat. For a brief second she held it suspended in mid-air, like a surgeon about to make an incision. With a swift, horizontal, slashlike stroke she rubbed it hard across her throat. Again and again she repeated the motion. Then she tossed the cloth into the hamper. And under the glare from the strong light framing the mirror, her secret stood exposed.

The scar, although long, was only an inch and a half wide. What made it so hideous was the discoloration. Countless black granules polka-dotted the natural white skin, making her neck look like a photographer's negative plate of a star cluster in the Milky Way. Looking into the mirror, Mildred examined her disfigurement with sick recognition and saw herself, because of it, as coinage debased.

She would wear this always; this brand like a mark of Cain—her souvenir from Israel. The specialists at Anchorage, and later at Los Angeles, had told her the same thing. Nothing to be done. Too deep for plastic surgery. Perhaps, if she underwent a series of operations, some improvement. But there would always remain telltale patches. And the expense was prohibitive. A cost Papa could never meet.

The exploding bomb, driving metallic slivers in under her skin, had branded her forever.

She was crying softly, tears without a sound, as she snapped off the bathroom light and undressed in the dark and made her way to bed.

Twenty-five flights below, in the hotel's subterranean arcade that was a miniature shopping center, Dave Lebow, nee Lebowitz, sat at the snack counter of the open-all-night drugstore. He had just finished his usual off-duty coffee and bagel. Four columns of quarters, three of dimes, were neatly stacked in front of him.

"Give me sixteen green ones for this silver, Doc," he said to the white-smocked man behind the counter. "There's an extra four bits here for my check."

Doc Sherman raked in the coins without troubling to count them. He rang up the cash register, poured the coins in the proper compartments, and counted out sixteen singles.

"I'm in the wrong business, kid," he lamented as he handed Dave the bills. "I knock myself out eight hours a night, six days a week, filling prescriptions and tending the counter, and I'll bet my take home pay, after taxes, is less than yours."

"Sure," retorted Dave. "With all the Rockefellers in this hotel I'm getting so rich on dime tips I can buy a bank—a piggy bank. Did I ever tell you how many people stiff me?"

"I was only putting you on. Can't you take a joke? But don't tell me that blond Viennese divorcee with the four ex-husbands doesn't tip you more than a dime when you deliver her daily Martinis—always around matinee time?"

Dave spun around on his stool, stood erect on the floor. Then, after making sure no one was in hearing range, he said, "I have news for you, Doc. First, she's a suicide blonde—dyed by her own hand. In broad daylight, she looks old enough to be on Medicare."

Without counting the bills, he tucked them into his wallet, reciprocating Doc Sherman's prior trustful gesture. As he slipped the wallet into the back pocket of his slacks, his hand encountered the cardboard ballot Mildred Waxman had autographed for him.

The ticket reminded him of something. He walked over to the cosmetic alcove of the store, his eyes scanning the shelves until he spied what he sought. A small, white jar with a three-syllable name on the label—exactly identical to the jar he had earlier delivered to Miss Alaska.

He felt a small stirring of conscience at having peeked into the package while waiting for the intersection lights to change on his trip back from Terrace Chemists. He never should have loosened the string. Yet his motive had been genuine concern for the girl. She had seemed so on edge, so wound up, asking him to run her errand. As if something in the order was a lot more important to her than she was letting on.

And she was such a prize little package herself, that Millie. If she was in trouble of some kind, it was possible he could help her, with his medical-school training and his contacts. That yarn about sleeping pills hadn't checked out when he had inspected the parcel's contents. Everything in it seemed kosher. Except that mysterious jar with the unfamiliar brand name. The price, marked in crayon on its lid, was $9.25. Damned expensive stuff.

Dave walked back to the counter, found Doc Sherman pouring a cup of tea for himself.

"Say, Doc, tell me something."

"Sure. If it isn't something you're too young to know, kid."

"This cosmetic you keep stocked called Hide-a-Mark. What's it for?"

"It's a special, patented salve that covers all kinds of skin marks. Blemishes, smallpox pits, albino patches, moles, rashes, scars."

"I understand it costs more than nine bucks a jar. What makes it better than the stuff the Hollywood stars use for makeup?"

Doc Sherman dunked his tea bag in his cup, swished it around.

"Hollywood makeup can get you by on the screen. But it can't fool the human eye. If it's got a powder base, you can spot the grains. If it's got a cream base, it glistens. But Hide-a-Mark? It'll make a leper's skin as smooth as a baby's ass, and no one would ever know the difference. Of course, you have to apply it every day, particularly after a shower. Or after you shave."

"After you shave? Do men use it?"

"You bet. GIs swear by it. They use it to cover battle scars, skin-graft scars." Doc Sherman leaned over confidentially. "I'll tell you something I've never told anyone but my wife. Remember John Foster Dulles? Ike's Secretary of State? He used to be one of my customers when I had a store in Washington. He'd buy Hide-a-Mark by the case. Used it to conceal a large, ugly, port-wine birthmark on the left side of his face. Can you imagine all the times he was on camera, and nobody ever realized the truth?"

The druggist raised the sodden tea bag. "Why are you so interested in Hide-a-Mark, Dave?"

But young almost-Park-Avenue-doctor David Lebow was already walking away.

BOOK TWO *Monday*

9 · MISS UTAH

LORI's hand groped out, aching for the warm encounter of male flesh. But the bed was empty, as she had known it would be. There was no one to stoke the fire smoldering within her. Everytime it died out, she died a little, too.

She squinted at the luminous dial of her watch and yawned. It was 5 A.M. There was still time for a blissful forty winks before her tiny bedside alarm was set to ring. If only she could turn off the damned ocean outside. Twice every minute the savage breakers hurled themselves against the jetties, raping the night stillness without reprieve.

Friends back home had told her the salt air would make her drowsy. But all night long Lori had found sleep elusive. Her full breasts rose as she breathed in deeply, hoping it would act as a soporific. She would need all her energies for the strenuous day ahead.

Suddenly she cut off her breath as a cloying fragrance engulfed her. She had forgotten that the room was flanked wall to wall with flowers. In true Pageant tradition, well-wishers had sent her wreaths and bouquets heavily garlanded with sego lilies, the official state flower of Utah.

Christ, she thought, the place smells like a funeral chapel. She got out of bed, headed for the open terrace. A flight of sea gulls enjoyed her nudity as she leaned on the iron balustrade, her Diana-like figure shrouded by the moonlight.

Lori looked out on the expanse of sea before her. In the distance ahead she could see the amber and red lights of crawling cruise ships. There were men out there. Virile, rangy, uniformed roosters who did their best to service the sex-starved females prowling the decks in packs. Right now she would give her right arm to change places with one of those predatory passengers. The way she felt, she could take on an entire crew.

Lori was reminded briefly of the handsome naval lieutenant and his two ensigns from the U.S.S. *Wasp* who had met her yesterday at the airport. They had bestowed their top honor upon her—a certificate proclaiming her "The girl we'd most like to pick up in a capsule." She had bussed each one lightly on the cheek. They walked off ten feet tall, awed that they had been kissed by the gorgeous Miss Utah. They didn't dream that she would have readily opened up the hatch for any or all of them.

Enough wishful thinking, she decided. If she didn't get at least an hour's sleep, she'd get up feeling like a victim of Chinese torture. As she crossed the room back to her bed, again the heavy scent of the flowers assailed her. She could kick herself for having forgotten to smuggle a pack of Kools in her luggage. The mentholated cigarette would be perfect to smoke in self-defense against those damned lilies.

Her hands under the covers, Lori unlimbered into her favorite position. Then, as she always did when the fire within her kept her awake, she resorted to the one secret sedative that rarely failed her.

Other girls counted sheep; she counted boys with whom she had made love. "Lori's lambs," she called them. She began with Andy Greene, relived the time she begged him to take her in the dewy grass of a lover's lane, on the night of her fifteenth birthday. Every word, every kiss, every love play was still recorded in the diary of her mind.

A precious tingling radiated from below her hips as she re-enjoyed her gambols with the lambs who had followed Andy. They frolicked about gaily in the corral of her memories. Finally, after they had grazed freely on the lush pastureland there, her internal flame became rekindled. She uttered a sharp cry of relief and sank into an instant sleep.

Lori never thought of herself as sinful. "The first boy you do it with, you *love*," she had once confided in Gerry Cooper, her closest friend. "The second boy, it's because you *like* him a lot. Then, whenever you're with someone you like, you just do it because you like *it*."

When Gerry had agreed with her playgirl philosophy, Lori had felt considerably less wicked. She had never guessed that frumpy Gerry, undesired and undeflowered, was simply giving her lip service, greedy for amorous escapades beyond her own grasp.

It had been a different story, however, the time her older sister, Marge, had been driving home from a dance at the Deepdale Country Club. Marge and her date had been about to pull in at a motel diner for a cup of coffee. Suddenly they had both gasped as the neon sign cast a lavender tint on the faces of a giggling couple. It was Lori and a gawky, self-conscious youth entering a bungalow.

Four hours later, when Lori had come tiptoeing into her room, Marge was waiting for her, pacing the floor like a Bengal tigress.

"You cheap little tramp," she raged. "I was never so embarrassed in my life when we saw you going into that motel. Bob was so shocked he almost lost control of the wheel."

Lori kicked off her mules, unzipped her skirt for the second time that night. "Don't tell me he was mad because we had beaten you kids to the last vacant cabin. You should have gone ten miles up Route Four to that new Howard Johnson place. Bob could have used his credit card."

"You're sick, Lori, sick. You'd go to bed with a boa constrictor. Bob told me all the boys call you 'Drop-a-nickel-in-the-slot Lori.' You need help."

Lori peeled off her sheer stockings. "Oh, don't give me that big-sister jazz. If you're trying to tell me I'm a nympho, come off it. Sure, I sleep around—because I like sex. It's like popcorn. The more you eat, the more you want. But I'm choosy. I won't sleep with nails, snails or puppydog tails. Believe it or not, but I have to be attracted to the guy."

"Like that clod I saw you with at the motel?"

"You don't even know Ben. There's something very nice about him."

"Yes, and I'll bet it's right between his legs." Suddenly Marge knelt down beside Lori, grabbed her harshly by the shoulders.

"Look, Sis, I've got almost three hundred dollars saved from my salary. I want you to take it and see Dr. Quimby. He's a good psychiatrist. Promise me, Lori." She wiped away a mist of tears and held out her hand. Shake?"

"You've got a deal," said Lori. "Now let me hit the sack. I've been up all night."

Lori had kept her word and made an appointment with Dr. Quimby. From the very first visit she had been amused how the tall, stooped psychiatrist avoided staring at her breasts. Four sessions later, when there had been a lull in their dialogue, Quimby had forgotten himself and permitted his scholarly eyes to research her fabulous equipment. The brief exploration had shaken him.

Through half-shuttered eyes Lori had watched his glance begin to travel horizontally down her body as she lay on the couch. She had stretched slightly, just enough so that the hem of her skirt lifted one inch.

It was master timing. When Dr. Quimby's eyes had arrived at her knees he could plainly glimpse the bare flesh of the inner thigh which began where the sheath of nylon hosiery left off.

He had hastily turned away and stared intensely at his note pad. Then, clearing his throat, he had broken the silence. "Lori," he had said, making his voice sound as professional as possible, "perhaps we can make some progress if you tell me about your dreams. What did you dream about since your last visit?"

"Oh, I dream a lot, Doctor. But I almost never remember what they're about after I wake up."

"You said 'almost never,' Lori. Are there any dreams you *do* remember?"

Right then and there she had decided to shock the doctor. She had browsed through Marge's books on Freud and abnormal psychology. Dr. Quimby was probably familiar with all the case histories recorded there, so she would invent her own extravagant dream.

"Yes, there's one dream I can't forget. It's almost like a nightmare. It keeps repeating itself over and over."

"What is it?"

"I'm ashamed to tell you. It's too embarrassing."

"You must tell me, child," he said gently. "I'm your doctor. You must have complete trust in me."

"I'm just afraid that if I tell you this dream you'll lose all respect for me."

"That is impossible, Lori. I give you my word that everything you tell me will be in absolute confidence."

"I keep dreaming that I'm at a dance. All the girls are dressed in lovely gowns. But I'm completely nude."

"A very common dream, Lori. Almost everyone has—"

"I know, Doctor," she had interrupted. "But my dream is different. Listen. I'm standing there as naked as Eve without her fig-leaf. Suddenly the boys begin throwing things at me."

"What things?"

"Brassieres. All colors. All sizes."

"Then what happens?"

"I pick up one of the bras and try to cover myself with it, but it's too small. Then I pick up a larger one, but that won't cover them up, either."

Dr. Quimby's hand was rigid now, utterly unable to write.

"And then you wake up?"

"I wish I did. But the dream gets worse. The dance floor begins to look like the Maiden-Form factory. I keep trying on all the bras, even the very largest ones, but not one fits. Then suddenly the boys stop laughing at me and begin applauding."

"Strange. Do you have an idea why they are applauding you?"

"Yes. When I look down at my chest I see that my breasts have completely shrunk. They've shriveled up and become little purple grapes.

The thought of those marvelous melons scaled down to the size of marbles had appalled Dr. Quimby. He had quickly burst out with an explanation.

"Lori, your dream is simply a manifestation of a guilt complex you have regarding the size of your breasts. Subconsciously you consider them offensive to the sight of men. Hence you persist in punishing yourself by experiencing this recurrent dream."

Lori had placed her hands under her bosom, as if to reassure him that the deflation was definitely a figment of her imagination.

"Tell me the truth, Doctor. Are they abnormal?"

She had seen that his face was all tenderness and that his glasses were almost moist.

"Poor child, you must stop torturing yourself. I assure you your breasts are perfect. If Reubens were alive, he would be proud to paint them."

Exercising iron control, Quimby had quickly changed the subject. Her wantonness, that was the burning problem. He leafed through his notes, found a quote he had underlined.

"Lori, two weeks ago you told me you could only enjoy intercourse with someone you like. I assume the attraction must be physical, mental, or both. Just where do you draw the line?"

"I have one rule, Doctor. I always ask myself, 'Lori, if you had an affair with this boy, and he knocked you up, would you want to bear his child?' If the answer is 'Yes,' we do what comes naturally."

Dr. Quimby had stared down at her recumbent form on the leather couch. Mesmerized by her beauty, he heard himself saying, as if from some great distance, "Lori, dear, would you mind having my child?"

She had fluttered her long lashes, extended her arms, and brushed his crewcut with her palm.

"With you, Doctor, I could stand for a whole litter."

Ten minutes later they were both letting nature take its course.

Lori's alarm, set to go off at 7:15, was pre-empted by the sound of chimes. The melodious notes awakened her. She opened large violet eyes and traced the tones to the communications outlet on the wall over the thermostat. From the perforated disk drifted a familiar voice. It sounded amazingly alert and pleasant for this ungodly hour.

"Rise and shine, girls. This is Sue Rossiter at Pageant headquarters. It is now seven A.M. At exactly eight each of you will be met in your respective lobbies by your official hostess. She will escort you to your private car and you will be driven to the Armory. The weatherman promises seventy-eight degrees today, so you will wear swimsuit, ribbon badge, and take along a lightweight wrap, just in case. Have a good day and . . . See you later!" she ended merrily, giving the sign-off she always used on her afternoon TV show.

There was a faint hum, then a click, and the Pageant's electronic unit that linked all twenty-five hotels and motels together in closed-circuit intimacy went dead.

Lori sat up in bed, rolled her head to look outside. The day was clear and fine. Her nap, though brief, had left her refreshed.

There was a knock on the door. It must be the maid with the breakfast she had ordered last night.

"Just a sec," Lori called out. She jumped from the bed, intercepting a rectangle of golden sunlight as she darted toward the closet. Slipping into a powder-blue housecoat, Lori was about to open the door, then paused. She grimaced as she eyed last night's dress crumpled on a chair, black frothy underwear thrown on top of the dress, brassiere, girdle, and stockings dangling from the night table.

Hastily she bundled the objects together, stuffed them out of sight in the bottom drawer. Then, confident no maid was going to gossip that Miss Utah was a slob, she turned the knob.

An attractive young Puerto Rican woman, trimly clad in a green uniform, pushed a food cart inside. "Good morning, Miss Utah," she said brightly. "I'm Josephina, your maid." She nodded in the direction of the terrace. "Would you like to eat in here or oceanside?"

"I'll eat in here if you don't mind. I got up late and I'll have to rush."

"Well, I mentioned it because Miss Colorado, next door to you is eating on the terrace and I thought you might like each other's company. She's nice, too, like you."

She was sweet, this pretty maid, so anxious to please. Lori warmed to her at once.

Lori sipped the cold orange juice. She noted with satisfaction that the circumference of the dish underneath was inlaid with a design of golden crowns. The motif of the Pageant extended even to the gold-plated utensils on her tray. The end of each knife, fork and spoon was decorated with the same symbolic pattern. She couldn't help thinking what marvelous souvenirs they'd be to take home.

As if divining her thoughts, Josephina spoke. "Pretty, aren't they? Win or lose, each contestant receives a free setting for six, compliments of Briand's Department Store."

Josephina pointed to a folded newspaper on the table. "And there's another surprise for you. Your picture on the front page of the *Press*."

Lori reached for it, curious. It was a picture of her kissing that handsome lieutenant. The caption read: MISS UTAH SINKS NAVY.

Breakfast in her bed from gold-plated service, newspaper headlines, a private car waiting for her downstairs. The glamour of the Pageant was making her giddy. She could hardly eat the English muffin she had already buttered.

Lori gulped down the last of her coffee. "I'm going to get dressed now," she said. "Thanks for everything."

As she stood up, Jospehina lingered a moment. Lori could sense she wanted to say something. She arched her eyebrows. "What is it?"

"I was just wondering, Miss Utah. Would you like me to get rid of the flowers?"

"Josephina, you're an angel and a mind reader. If I ever become a real princess, will you promise to be my lady-in-waiting?"

"That's just what Miss Colorado said. Her room is piled deep with columbines. That's why she's eating on the terrace."

After she had closed the door, Lori congratulated herself. A maid with ESP. How lucky can you get?

After she had washed, she shrugged off her housecoat, opened her suitcase, and flipped through the assortment of silk and nylon swimsuits inside. She selected the stunning yellow metallic suit Marge had brought her from Paris. She slipped into it effortlessly and found a pair of sandals that matched. Her watch indicated seven thirty-five as she sat on a bench before the mirrored dressing table in her bathroom and swiftly applied her makeup.

There remained just one last touch, her ribbon identification badge. Lori fastened it to the center of her suit, directly under her chin. It was an artful job. When she was finished, her breasts remained uncamouflaged by the huge white badge and its twelve inches of blue ribbon.

It was still too early to make her entrance in the lobby. Lori sat down. Behind her, from the beachfront terrace, floated the sound of voices and laughter. She poked her head outside. It was Josephina and a tall blond girl in a black satin bathing suit on the adjacent terrace. Lori noticed that she had a cute little can.

"Colorado, this is Utah," said Josephina.

"I know," said the blonde. "With badges like ours, who needs introductions? Anyway, I'm Barbara Chrysler. And I know you're Lori Macklin, from your picture in the paper."

"I came out here because I heard laughing. Did I miss a good joke?"

"You sure did," said Josephina. She held up two pairs of men's trousers and a couple of jackets. "I came back here to take the dishes away and found these suits on the bed. I said I'd have to report her to the judges. One man in the room, okay. But two is too much."

"I don't know what the gag is," said Lori, "but I'll take the extra man, sight unseen." They didn't realize she was half serious. Those were the first pants she'd seen in ten hours.

"Isn't Josephina priceless?"

"I love her, too," said Lori, "but isn't it time to fill me in?"

"Oh, the suits. They're for my act. I do impersonations of Bert Parks and Johnny Carson. I had them laid out on the bed because I'll need them for rehearsals and they have to be pressed."

"Say, you must be pretty good. I'm stuck with Ophelia's monologue from Hamlet. But yours sounds surefire. The public eats up impersonations."

"Thanks. But I've got other worries."

"You can tell me," said Lori. "I also do impersonations. At this moment I'm a priest."

Barbara laughed. A gentle breeze blew the girlish wisps of her hair behind her lobes as she waited for Josephina to leave. When she heard the door close, she lowered her head.

"I heard that we have to undergo a physical exam today or tomorrow. This physical . . . do they examine us thoroughly? You know what I mean."

"Jesus Christ. You're afraid they'll give you a vaginal and find out you're not a virgin? Well, if they're looking for cherries, let them try the fruit stand at the supermarket."

Barbara's face reddened. "Don't misunderstand me, Lori. I'm still a virgin, but I get sick every time I think of a doctor, even a woman doctor, getting so personal with me."

She hesitated, fingered the ribbon of her badge. "It's a horrible phobia with me. In my first year at college there was one central bathroom in my dorm. I could never take a shower without any of the other girls looking at me. I used to wait until they were all asleep, about eleven. Then I'd shower by myself, even if the water was cold by that time."

"Well, don't press the panic button," said Lori. "The examination is just routine. I'm told they're mainly interested in screening everyone for a heart condition. They'd never give the crown to a girl with heart trouble. For one thing, the excitement could kill her. And she'd never be able to stand the pace touring the country as Princess America."

Lori had heard, too, that the girls would be examined for plastic-inflated breasts. She chose not to mention this item to Barbara lest it upset her still more.

"Now, stop blushing and looking like you dropped a garter," Lori went on. "I was only kidding when I made that crack about cherries. I just didn't want you to feel like a leper if you were an ex-Virginian." Lori glanced at her watch. "Jesus. It's three minutes to countdown. Into the arena we go. Good luck, Colorado."

Barbara watched her dart back into her room. She could be very close to this vivacious girl with her wisecrack humor. As she headed for "the arena," she remembered a line she had read in *Spartacus*: "Gladiator, make no friends."

The corridor to the lobby was a strip of plush, carpeted bowling alley. Quickening her steps, Lori wondered about the chaperone awaiting her. All the chaperones were matrons carefully selected from Surf City's top social strata. It would be just her luck to draw a bitch who was mad at the world because her husband was keeping a mistress.

"Good morning, dear. You look even better than your pictures."

Lori halted. She saw a youngish-looking woman with shingled hair, a patrician face, and a graceful figure.

"I'm Mrs. Birkenbuel, your official Pageant hostess. Actually, I'm your warden and midwife. I think we'll make a good team."

Lori admired the way she was dressed. All class. Her tailored suit was of beige cotton twill. On her left hand was a modest wedding band and a ring with a blue stone. Her perfume was faint and sweet.

"We'd better go now," said Mrs. Birkenbuel. She slipped her arm under Lori's, guided her through a crevice in the wall of people that crowded the lobby. At the coffee shop she tapped on the plate-glass window. A policeman sitting at the counter looked up, shook his head.

"Officer Dorn picked me up at my house this morning. We got here early, so I told him he could have a cup of coffee while we waited for you to come down."

A gold-braided doorman cleared a path for them and they stepped outside. He signaled the parking-lot attendant and a low-slung convertible with a mile of white body between its bumpers rolled into view. All four fenders sported large MISS UTAH pennants fluttering at full mast from their custom-made antennae.

Steve Dorn came up to join them. "How do you like it?" he said as he opened the car's rear door.

"It looks like a battleship," said Lori. "Don't I get to christen it with a bottle of champagne?"

"Lori, this is Officer Steve Dorn. He'll be your driver-escort during the Pageant," said Mrs. Birkenbuel.

Dorn was one of those men who looked taller than his true height, which was five feet eleven inches. Lori looked into his face and knew instantly that she had hit the jackpot.

"Welcome to Surf City, Miss Utah," he said, smiling.

Dorn helped them into the car, slammed the door. He sank into his seat and was just about to pull away when Mrs. Birkenbuel frowned.

"Oh, dear. I forgot to phone my husband's secretary about something. Could you wait a few minutes while I call her?"

Dorn turned off the ignition as she climbed out. "Take your time," he said. "The meter's not running."

Ankles flashing briskly, Mrs. Birkenbuel retraced her way to the lobby. In the back seat, Lori tried to extend her long legs, felt cramped. From his mirror Dorn could see her wrinkle her nose. He sighed as he guessed the trouble. He had never seen a convertible job yet that could handle a driver and a passenger comfortably, unless one of them was a midget.

Well, it was his comfort or hers, and her stems rated priority. It was still better than pounding his beat in the Sixth Precinct, where two of his buddies had been mugged last month. He pressed the power switch at his left. There was a hum, and his bucket seat slid forward. Lori unbent her legs, grateful for the extra inches.

Before she could thank him, Colorado's car shot past. She had been assigned a clean-cut Negro officer for a driver and a mousey-looking hostess. Barbara turned around, waved at Lori.

Dorn watched the car trail off. "The girls sure get prettier every year," he said.

"I don't know if I like that crack," Lori said with mock petulance. "Aren't you supposed to root just for me?"

What the hell does she want me to do, Dorn thought, take a loyalty oath? Then, remembering he was about fifteen years her senior, he softened. "I'll be rooting for you all the way," he said.

"Thanks." She paused. "Do you think I'll be the next Princess?"

"I hope so. If they pick you, I win the cop's pool. A check for two thousand iron soldiers."

Lori calculated rapidly. "I'm flattered. Risking forty dollars of your hard-earned money on a fifty-to-one shot like me?"

Dorn's hand played with the blinker rod of the steering wheel.

"I don't want to hurt your morale, Utah, but I hate to sail under false colors. The money for the pool is always donated by the Chamber of Commerce."

She liked his candor. Under his police cap his dark hair was on the wiry side, a trifle crinkly.

"Have you ever won?"

"Nope. I'm a born loser. I've driven girls in the last six Pageants. Not one even placed in the semifinals." He turned around, smiled. "I hope my bad luck doesn't rub off on you. You can always ask them to assign you another driver, you know."

"And give you up? Don't be ridic. I'd rather lose than switch."

Her boldness bothered him. He looked toward the motel entrance. Where the hell was the Birkenbuel broad? Some chaperone!

Lori's chatter persisted. "What will you do with the pool money if you win?"

"I'd get a new engine for my boat. She's up on rollers at the old Police Garage. I work on her there, nights and weekends."

"And once you've got your motor throbbing?"

The little bitch seemed to want to mean a lot more than the actual words. Jesus! "I'd head straight for the Keys. They say the fishing is great in October."

"Well, the least you could do is take me with you. I'd deserve some sort of finder's fee, wouldn't you say?"

Steve Dorn refused to believe his ears. "And what would I do with my wife while we sailed the ocean deep?"

Lori looked at her scarlet nails, then regarded the nape of his neck. She knew he was studying her reflection in his mirror.

"Oh, you could always have her on the side. I'd allow you visitation rights."

My God, thought Dorn. Roger Megan had been right. At the briefing he had warned them there was always a chance some kid with a Lolita complex might try and give them the business. Megan had also reminded them about the rap waiting for any cop who encouraged such business. Well, he'd better play it cool and ignore the whole bit. This dame was probably harmless, all bark and no bang. Let someone reach for her crotch and she'd chop his hand off. Anyway, here came Mrs. Birkenbuel at last.

"The line was busy, wouldn't you guess?" she explained, hopping into the car. Dorn started up, stepped on the accelerator.

"We were just getting acquainted," said Lori. "Officer Dorn was telling me he likes boats."

The car gathered momentum, approached a crosswalk. The officer on duty raised his arm to the opposing traffic, motioned Dorn through. Lori smiled at the cop, blew him a kiss. They passed a slow-moving bus full of girls on their way to a parochial school. The elderly driver grinned, beeped his horn by way of salute. His passengers spied Lori, and a line of blue-kerchiefed necks craned out the window. Hands flagging wildly, they yelled, "Hooray for Utah."

"Well, at least you've got the Catholic schoolgirl vote," observed Mrs. Birkenbuel.

Great, thought Lori. That and a quarter will buy me a chocolate-covered frozen banana on the boardwalk.

"Wave back to them, dear. Never underestimate the power of the kids. In Fifty-eight, Miss Ohio signed autographs for some boy scouts. They got their entire troop *and* their parents to attend the preliminaries. When she walked onstage, they stampeded the hall. The judges must have been impressed, because they picked her for the semifinals."

"But admission to the prelims is always free," argued Lori. "Don't tell me those kids paid three dollars each to cheer for her at the finals?"

"They sure did. Miss Ohio had invited them to come back with their Brownie cameras and take pictures while she rehearsed her act. Well, one good deed deserves another. The kids showed up at the finals. Some of them had actually hocked their cameras to raise the admission price. When Miss Ohio was introduced, the kids put on the greatest demonstration ever seen here since the rally for Adlai. Anyway, coincidence or not, Ohio won the crown."

The street signs slid past them in neat, alphabetical order, like pages in an atlas. Alabama, Arizona, California, Colorado . . .

"Our efficient city planners," said Mrs. Birkenbuel. "Nobody ever gets lost in Surf City because all the streets running east to west are named alphabetically after states. The north-south ones are named after trees."

"I was never great in geography," said Lori, "but I think somebody short-changed our forty-ninth state. I didn't catch Alaska Avenue."

Mrs. Birkenbuel nodded as the car leaped from Georgia to Idaho. "Sharp girl. Then you've probably noticed that we just skipped Hawaii, too. Serves them both right for entering the Union so late, my husband always says. But they've been added on after Wyoming Avenue—sort of like postscripts."

Two soldiers in an open jeep overtook them, then slowed down to take a longer look at Lori. She responded to their friendly wolf-calls with an outrageous wink.

Ahead toward the left, on Michigan Avenue, loomed the white, arched roof of the Armory. Lori's heartbeat quickened as she saw the huge Pageant banner floating aloft. She waited for Dorn to slow down, but, to her surprise, the car sped on.

Mrs. Birkenbuel patted her bare arm. "You'd like to win this thing, wouldn't you, dear? Just be patient a minute."

Lori stared at her, mystified. They glided on in silence until they reached Utah Avenue.

Dorn swung the car left. "We are now bowing to the Pageant's oldest tradition," he commented. "It's considered good luck for a contestant to ride along her state avenue before she enters the Armory."

"I could use the luck," said Lori. "But doesn't it cancel out if every girl obeys the same tradition?"

Dorn circled the car back to Michigan while Mrs. Birkenbuel reflected on Lori's logic. Her brow furrowed as she reviewed past Pageants, like a wine expert trying to recall the vintage years. She snapped her fingers.

"Of course. Miss Florida, in Sixty-one. She wouldn't let her driver do the honors. Said it was a lot of superstitious nonsense. Got her a lot of publicity, but two days later she broke out with the hives."

Dorn maneuvered the car into a parking space in front of the Armory, directly behind Miss Texas. Lori could see Sue Rossiter on the steps welcoming the girls as they came in, wearing her usual smashing grin.

As Lori got out of the car, Dorn called after her. "Knock 'em dead, Utah."

She gave him the full voltage of her smile. "Thanks a lot," she said.

She knew what she had wanted to tell him, but didn't dare. Steve, darling, if you knew what you were missing, you'd cut your throat.

10 · ROGER MEGAN

JUST before seven on Monday morning, Roger Megan came out of a nightmare as though he had been shot from a cannon.

It had started with Santa Claus . . .

His white beard flowing, Santa was riding perched on the hood of a huge boardwalk rolling chair packed full of canvas sacks. The vehicle flew inches above the snowlike foam along the ocean's edge, drawn by six matched pairs of high-stepping Pageant beauties wearing topless swimsuits. In close pursuit was a pack of yammering wolves. Santa Claus looked back, and suddenly his red cap, his hair and his saintly beard flew off, revealing him to be John Fleming.

With a practiced kick Fleming dumped one of the sacks overboard. It hit the beach hard and ripped open, and Roger Megan crawled out. Bewildered, he looked about him. Santa John and his caravan were disappearing. "But I had a contract!" Megan cried out hoarsely. He got up to run, but with his first step he sank deep into the sand. Within a second he was in past his knees and still going down.

Now the wolves had reached him. They stood in a threatening ring around him, shaggy and silent, watching the sand swallow him up. When only his head was left above surface, the wolves turned away and slowly departed. But not all of them. One wolf remained; he looked remarkably like Felix, a melancholy expression in his eyes. The last Megan heard was the crash of waves coming up like applause at the old Garden on one of his big nights. Then, with a thunderous crack, his eyeballs exploded and the world came to an end.

Megan was instantly, achingly awake. He lay still in his bed, listening to his heart pound, a single thought centered in his mind—the unscheduled visit to John Fleming that he was to make this morning. He had planned it with Felix late the night before; it had been Megan's last wakeful thought.

Gradually his panic subsided. He remembered the strange evolution of the long yesterday, with its poisonous accumulation of fear. He was not surprised it had spilled over into a nightmare. They're getting to me, the bastards, he thought; they're really getting to me, aren't they?

It was D-Day, Operation Pageant, and the assault on the Surf City beaches was under way. The hotel had burst into life at dawn, humming with commotion, with voices and footsteps in the corridors, with radio music and TV morning newscasts osmosing through the walls and floors, with doors slamming. One of them, going off nearby like a land mine, had roused him.

What a switch, he thought—starting the day with a bang instead of ending with one. It was really very funny, hilarious, in a disgusting sort of way. Here he had gone to bed the night before, both solitary and sober, circumstances that were out and out abnormal for him. And the payoff? A sickening nightmare. Ah, the hell with it, he thought; so much for the ascetic life.

With a sigh he gave himself a little feel to cheer himself up, and having re-established contact with hard reality, he rolled out of bed and began moving into his day.

An hour later, after breakfast in the hotel's El Mirasol coffee shop, he began walking north along the boardwalk at a relaxed pace, keeping to the seaside rail. The sky was clean, a pale blue washed with sunlight. Strollers and chairs were out in numbers. From somewhere a vagrant whiff of caramel popcorn floated by with the unsmogged breeze. Well, breathe it in, he thought. The way things are going, this might just turn out to be your last year with the Pageant. One day you're drinking champagne, the next week you're picking grapes.

This was his territory, Meganville, the town from which so many good things came. This was the ocean in which he could drown himself if something went wrong in his territory and the good things stopped coming.

Because the truth was not—as he had trumpeted to Felix—that he was the Pageant's continuity. The Pageant was Megan's continuity. With it he was the famous Megan of the Pageant, invested with glamour and status. Without it he was just another theatrical jack-of-all trades.

Yesterday morning at the Armory, arguing with Felix over Fleming's invitation to Megan's wife, he had swaggered and blustered. He had just come off his bang-up performance for the police chauffeurs, hot with success. But from that exhilarating pinnacle, things had proceeded to go to hell. From then on he had begun encountering annoying little surprises, where nothing happened quite the way it should have, starting with his call to Beverly Hills to tell his wife he wanted her to kill Fleming's invitation.

It had turned out there was nothing for him to say. Claire had already graciously informed Fleming she was unable to accept. "I told him it was impossible because school starts tomorrow, and I can't leave the kids and I can't have them missing the first week of a new semester."

"But school doesn't start until next week," Megan had said, confused.

"Yes, dear, but Mr. Fleming doesn't know that. And he doesn't know that you much prefer being there alone—well, maybe not *exactly* alone, but without your family around."

"I see," Megan said, bristling. "So you're on that again. Can't let a chance go by, can you? Why don't you put a metal band around my leg to see where I migrate?"

"Oh, don't feel so guilty. All I meant was, you have to protect your image and I understand."

It had ended there. And though it had rankled him to be so thoroughly understood, he had put it aside and gone about his business.

Then came the next surprise.

There had been a scheduled meeting to wrap up the loose ends for the Thursday-night Boardwalk Parade in the main conference room of the Armory. Spirits restored, Megan had come waltzing in, thinking he'd spend just enough time to renew friendships with the parade staff, get off a clever line or two and then cut out. But scarcely a soul was there, a few girls busy with paperwork.

They told him the meeting had been postponed until further notice. Why? Nobody knew. An air of uncertainty hung over the enormous room. A secretary volunteered having heard something about a CBS executive asking for a delay. But that made no sense because the network people weren't involved with the parade.

And yet, precisely because it made no sense, the tiny fishhooks of insecurity began tearing at his gut. It was always weird the way one found out things in this business. Later on, when you put together the bits and pieces, the ignored clues vainly signaling an alert, you could see that only a cretin wouldn't at least have suspected something was up. Felix would have sniffed it at once, but Felix wasn't there. He had thoughtfully removed himself when Roger phoned his wife, walking out on him before he finished dialing, not waiting to hear how it had ended.

The charts of the parade route were hung along a wall. Megan looked them over, his interest a bit heightened by now. Nothing seemed changed. All the customary positions were marked off—floats, contestants, bands, judges, the press, chaperones—everything in proper order.

Mildly puzzled, he had shrugged it off. There was to be a CBS-TV production meeting at two, to iron out the mechanics for the Saturday-night coast-to-coast telecast, so if anything was going on, he'd either know by then or find out.

He had just finished lunch at the Wellington Manor and was standing out front, pleasantly awash in Bloody Marys, when Ernie Grayson came by. Grayson was a veteran PR man from CBS-TV, a perennial at the Pageant. They knew each other well enough to shake hands and swap well-here-we-are-again-nice-to-see-yous, then Grayson asked, "Any news yet? Have they decided on anything?"

Megan hesitated the fraction of a moment it took him to decide not to pretend. "Has who decided what?"

"I mean about the parade."

"What about the parade?" Megan asked, going straight ahead.

Grayson seemed suddenly reluctant to go on. "Well, as I understand it," he said cautiously, "they're supposed to be considering whether we televise the parade nationally Thursday night."

"First I've heard of it," said Megan. "Twelve years I've been with the Pageant and the parade has never got more than local coverage."

Grayson nodded. "Yeah, well, that's it," he said awkwardly, turning to go. "Nothing to do but sweat it out, I guess." He waved and disappeared abruptly into the revolving door.

Sweat it out? Megan had let the ominous phrase roll around in his head. Why should Grayson happen to use that expression? What could it possibly mean in relation to the parade being televised? All at once, it seemed, the Bloody Marys had hit him.

After that, Megan had difficulty restraining himself from showing up for the production meeting punctually at two. But he had held to standard procedure and arrived decently, half an hour late. All to no avail. The meeting had not started, nor, as Megan noted immediately, did the prospect seem near—none of the top echelon of the show was there yet. It seemed a curious coincidence.

But there was another. For, as Megan realized, it was the second time that day he had walked into this room, confident of a familiar scene awaiting him, and found something amiss, an unexpected and unexplained development. Some thirty people from every department of the Pageant show were dispersed about the room, chatting in groups, buried in newspapers, doing their nails. The scripts waited undistributed in neat stacks on a long table, behind which stood three empty chairs.

But no executive producer, no producer, no director.

And no information. No one knew why the delay or how long it might last. Megan, appearing unconcerned, did a patient stint of socializing, then got into a hearts game with the camera crew, as though he welcomed this respite among the minor help. But his enthusiasm had waned with the afternoon. Relaxation became repose. More than half the allotted time for the meeting was gone; the ticking sound of cards being slapped down had become a clock. How much longer would he wait?

Then, at three-fifteen, Megan had been called to the phone. It was Felix.

"Roger, there won't be any production meeting today. They're canceling it any minute. I'll explain when I see you. Can we meet at your hotel?"

As Megan had listened to these words, his uncertainty vanished. He no longer had the slightest doubt that there was trouble and that he was in some way involved.

This was their first crisis since Megan had signed Blassingame, Mangon and Wolfe. Until now, though Felix had been unfailingly conscientious, the business relationship had been more or less routine. But if Megan had wondered how Felix might perform in a critical situation, what he had seen so far was impressive.

After phoning Megan at the Armory, Felix had come to Megan's suite with all the answers available at the time. Standing at the window, pulling on a cigar almost half his size, he had begun, "And now for the news of the day," after which, calmly, succinctly, he provided it.

To begin with, said Felix, the rumors had been right, as usual. NBC had pre-empted three hours of its Saturday-night schedule and was going to throw a film against the Pageant show. They would announce it Tuesday and follow with a four-day barrage of publicity. The film was sure to be a big one; they had several blockbusters in the vault, any one of which could be lethal ammunition for a rating blitz.

As soon as CBS had confirmed the foray, only the day before, VP Jim Cornelius had come to Surf City and closeted himself in the Wellington Manor with the show's producers and director. They had come up with a new idea for the show, a change in concept, with extra values that would strengthen its appeal. They would be meeting with Fleming at five to pitch it to him.

"What's this about a change in concept?" asked Megan. "And the extra values; what does that mean?"

"What they always mean by extra values," said Felix dryly. "Names, what else? The basic commodity of the business. A string of names—à la the Oscar ceremonies—coming out to make awards."

"Like which names, for instance?"

"Real eighteen-karat headliners. Rock Hudson, Streisand, Dick Van Dyke, Gleason maybe, Julie Andrews, Dean Martin. Like that."

"And where does that leave me?"

"Oh, you'd still MC the whole show, only you'd be bringing on these others."

Megan let the thought sink in. "Only I'll be bringing on these others," he repeated, nodding as he spoke. "Beautiful," he said bitterly. "It's just great for me. I'll be announcing the important people all night, like a butler in Buckingham Palace."

Felix drew on his cigar and frowned at the rug.

"Who's going to pay for all this?" asked Megan.

"Probably split it somewhere near the middle."

"Fleming going for such a bundle?" Megan shook his head.

"Why not? He spends a dollar. He's generous with you, isn't he?"

"I don't get anything I don't rate."

"True. But you get it without a fight."

"What about the Thursday-night parade? Where does that fit in?"

"Well, if Fleming buys the idea and they go ahead with it, they'll televise the parade live—a half hour special, but it'll really be a disguised promo. Then they'll want to make some changes, stick in some clips of stars they can get on short notice, whether they use them Saturday night or not."

Presently Megan said, "What do you think of the idea? Not for me. We know what it is for me. But what do you think of it for the Pageant?"

"I don't know yet. Offhand it seems attractive, but I have to think about it from Fleming's point of view."

"When do you think you'll know?" said Megan. "After Fleming says okay, I love it—you think you'll know then?"

"What do you want?" Felix said quietly.

"I want to know what you intend to do about it."

"About what?"

"The way I'm being cut down, discounted."

Felix examined his cigar, then said gravely, "Okay, you've convinced me. I'm going to kick Fleming out, tear up the contract with CBS, run the Pageant myself on my own network, and you can be the star."

After a moment, Megan relaxed. "Good," he said. "I like that. You know what really gripes me?" he went on. "Not being told. Couldn't they send word to me there wouldn't be any meetings? Did I have to find out third hand, getting the runaround?"

"That was rotten," said Felix. "But probably unintentional. Confusion, that's all."

So they had chewed it back and forth a little longer without getting anywhere. Nothing to do but wait and—as Ernie Grayson had earlier stated—sweat it out.

"Meanwhile," said Felix, "I'll nose around and call you as soon as there's any word. Do you know where you'll be the next couple of hours?"

Megan nodded. "Here in the hotel, in Lou Cates's room."

"That's nice. From when on?"

"Five o'clock," said Megan, feeling it somehow desirable to add, by way of explanation, "I set it up yesterday."

"In that case, I'd hate to interrupt. I'll leave word, if there is any, and you can call down at your convenience. Anyway, we'll be meeting later at Sue Rossiter's party, right? The place is La Grenouille, right? Enjoy yourself."

And Felix had trotted off, while Megan unobtrusively climbed two flights of stairs to Cates's room, which he occasionally borrowed for a furtive matinee. There he had sought diversion in the arms of a lady whose husband was the Pageant's official jeweler and an account of Megan's for several years.

But this being the sort of day it was, here too Megan's expectations had been blighted. His interval in the depths of passion was only mildly engrossing, and he surfaced regularly every half hour to phone downstairs for messages. All this procedure had got him was word that Miss

Rossiter had called twice and a short livid speech from the lady in bed with him, to the effect that he was an unbelievably insulting son of a bitch and she was leaving.

Back in his own suite, chagrined, chastened, he had inquired again, and this time there was a message from Felix. It said that he would not be at La Grenouille but would leave further word as to when they could get together later. That was all Megan had needed to decide he wasn't going to the party either. Not on Sue Rossiter's terms, as a bystander keeping to the background. It was almost as though she had anticipated and was acting in concert with the CBS effort to downgrade him to a minor role. She could take her party and shove it.

Instead he had made the rounds of various bistros, the habitual gathering places of the in crowd, where one might accidentally run into some of the CBS contingent and glean a nugget or two of raw info. But he did more running than gleaning. He had soon established it was general knowledge that a shake-up in the show was being contemplated, but beyond that no one had any details.

Megan knew more than any of them, and it had given him a perverse satisfaction to indicate as much, with hints and allusions that would be understood only later, when Megan's fall from grace had become apparent. Then they would remember how Megan the Knowledgeable had known the night before and had remained Megan the Unperturbed.

But after several hours of carefully seeding this impression, he could scarcely control his anxiety. Alcohol could have helped, but he wanted to be sober for Felix and had limited himself to one drink at each stop. Finally he had gone back to his hotel to wait for the call so impossibly long in coming.

It had been past midnight when the call arrived, then, shortly afterward, Felix. Even at his best, Felix usually looked as though he'd been dead three days; now a week seemed more likely. The hours since he had last seen Megan had obviously tired him, but he was alert, and his small shining eyes, a bit bloodshot, seemed nevertheless to have regained some of their optimism.

He wasted neither words nor energy. "There's no decision yet. Fleming wants to sleep on it and give them an answer at ten A.M. tomorrow."

Megan groaned. "Now we're hung until tomorrow."

"It could be worse. It could be all over."

"Felix, what do you really think? Level with me."

"Always. What else?" Felix nodded slowly. "Well, to me

the significant thing is that Fleming is taking so long to make up his mind. From my understanding of the man, he's always been against any tampering with the Pageant, right? Obviously, however, the CBS argument has impressed him at least enough to discuss a change in formula and possibly to go along with them. If that happens, we're dead. On the other hand, Fleming really doesn't like the idea of—as he calls it—the Broadway–Hollywood axis taking over and giving the Pageant their aura."

"Are you guessing or you know?"

"I'm quoting the man, so I must know, right? He feels that while it's perfectly okay for show business to call up its big names for a show-business function like the Oscar awards, this is a beauty pageant and the draw should be the Pageant itself."

"Exactly how I see it," said Megan.

Felix smiled wanly. "Yes," he said. "Anyway, he's divided. He's willing to listen to CBS and make a move, but he hesitates to make this one. I think that gives us enough room to try something ourselves, maybe drive a wedge in there. If we can suggest an alternative that Fleming likes better, he could reject the CBS approach without appearing stubborn or standing pat."

"Uh-huh," said Megan sardonically. "All we have to do is dream up a first-rate idea overnight that will keep the whole country from tuning in on *Ben Hur*—or will it be *Gone with the Wind?*"

"I have an idea. Not the greatest, maybe, but it may appeal to Fleming—and it's hard to knock. We'll talk it over. If you like it, tomorrow morning—say, nine A.M., an hour before Cornelius gets there—you'll go in and offer the idea to Fleming for what it's worth, as they say."

"As my own idea? Something I thought up alone?"

"Sure. You can't get hurt even if he doesn't buy it. And if he does, wouldn't you rather have it that way?"

Then Felix had spelled out his proposal. Megan immediately recognized its worth. It had heart, nostalgia, sentiment. It aggrandized the Pageant. It could be put into operation speedily, with a minimum of sweat. And the costs would be negligible. Damned if that canny little Felix didn't show a remarkable grasp of the Pageant scale of values, and the Fleming thinkway. The more they discussed it, the more Megan had felt they might have a winner.

Finally Felix had been ready to leave.

"All in all, Roger, I think we're in fair shape. Even if the breaks go against us. We have to remember that CBS isn't actually attacking you, though it tends to work out that way. No matter what happens, the main thing is for you to do your usual fine job, stay out of trouble and out of gossip. You've had a bad day. Now I suggest a good night's rest and some wholesome sleep—though of course you may have other plans."

"I always have plans," said Megan.

"Day and night? Every day and every night?"

"No, but I'm booked pretty solid."

Felix looked amused, but he shook his head. "It would have been a plus to have your wife here, with or without the kids, but you put a stop to that. Okay, water under the bridge. But why don't you take the advice you gave those cops this morning? Why not lay off the booze and the broads?"

Megan had almost interrupted to explain about his call to the Coast, but instead he smiled and said with a sigh, "Ah, what's the use? Felix, you'll never know."

"What won't I know—about broads?" Felix grunted. "You know, Roger, when I was a kid about seventeen, eighteen, I used to visit a cousin of mine about twice my age, a big-shot lawyer, big spender, big cocksman. He liked me. He wanted me to take up law, and he encouraged me to come around so he could lecture me, steer me. Whenever I'd come by, the first thing he'd say to me was 'Did you get laid yet today?' Once I was there on a Saturday, about eleven o'clock in the morning, and he asked me if I'd been laid yet. Not that it made any difference—the answer was always the same, because I was still a virgin—but when I'd confess and say no, he'd give me a long sad look and say, 'Felix, a day without getting laid is a day wasted.' So I know all about that philosophy. My cousin was just like you."

"You mean a perpetual hot nut?"

"Worse. A pussy-junky."

"*A pussy-junky?*" Megan had burst out laughing. "That's wonderful. A pussy-junky."

"Sure. It's a habit, that's all. Like smoking and drinking."

"But it's a lot better than either of them. Nobody ever died from it."

"It's a habit, a messy, time-wasting, professionally dangerous habit. Why don't you try to kick it? Why should you be a slave to such a habit?"

"Felix, baby," Megan started to say, but he was laughing so hard he couldn't finish. He got out of his chair and walked over to Felix and slapped him on the shoulder.

"Felix, baby," he said, "I agree with you, but you don't understand—it's the best habit I've got!"

But at the door as they shook hands, Megan had said, "Felix, I don't want you to worry. Just one nightcap and I'm off to bed—relatively unloaded but definitely unlaid."

"I know. The supreme sacrifice. But it's for your benefit. Do yourself the favor."

"Tell, me, Felix—you think tomorrow night this time I'll still be a star?"

"Absolutely," said Felix. "It's your occupation. You don't know how to do anything else."

And so Megan's bleak Sunday had quietly drawn to a close on a calmer note, his foreboding diminished, his anxiety under control. Or so he had thought, until his subconscious had clobbered him with a nightmare.

For some minutes now he had been standing at the boardwalk rail, opposite the Hotel Mayfair where Pageant HQ was located, gazing absently at the golden surface of the sea. In a moment or two he would be going up to Fleming. He was ready. Perhaps he had reason, all things considered, to be grateful for the nightmare. It had graphically summed up the stakes. But he had shaken it off. All must be confidence now, all must be awareness. And no mistakes. There was no room for mistakes.

Suddenly he realized that he was staring with gruesome fascination at a single spot on the beach some twenty feet away—the place where, in his nightmare, he had been engulfed and buried in the sand. He felt his hair standing on end. How grotesque that he should know exactly where it was—right here in front of Pageant headquarters.

He turned and walked quickly to the colonnaded entrance to the Mayfair.

Striding through the lobby, Megan made his way to the Pageant's private elevator. At the tenth-floor penthouse he emerged to a luxurious reception room adorned with the flags of the fifty states. Perhaps a dozen people waited, Pageant identification badges prominently displayed, with the harried look of travelers marooned in a terminal, while interoffice traffic flowed around them. Waving to a receptionist, Megan detoured around her table and pushed through a quilted red leather door to the executive-wing library. It seemed unoccupied, but as he crossed the room he heard a guarded whisper from a corner.

Turning toward the sound without breaking step, he

was startled to see an arm sticking out from behind a high-backed Queen Anne chair—a brown-skinned, feminine arm in a cuffed gray sleeve, a wide gold bracelet at the wrist, and a brown, long-fingered hand holding a white telephone.

Continuing on through a door marked Private, Megan entered the inner office, a drawing room filled with light pouring in through north and south walls that were sheets of glass. Across the room, a chic brunette secretary sat at a kidney desk beside the ornately carved door to John Fleming's office.

On a sofa in the center of the room, three men were engaged in a subdued conversation. They were Negroes, two of them middle-aged. The third was conspicuously younger, with a drooping crescent Mexican-style mustache, wearing amber sunglasses and a green corduroy bush jacket. As Megan looked again at the other two, he recognized one of the men. The often photographed features, the imposing forehead and poetic white thatch of hair, were unmistakable. They belonged to Thomas Worthington Walsh, black patriarch and director of the National Freedom League.

"Why, good *morning,* Mr. Megan," the secretary greeted him brightly.

"Good morning to you, Rita my duck. What are chances?"

"You're not expected?"

"No."

She grimaced. "Roger, he's swamped." She lowered her voice. "You have no idea who's in there with him—everybody and his brother; I've lost count—and any minute they'll be starting a very important meeting with these other gentlemen." Her eyes indicated the trio on the sofa. "Then at ten there's another important meeting, with the CBS people. If there's any time open between them, maybe you can squeeze in. Otherwise, the soonest would probably be around eleven or so."

Though he had almost guessed what she would say, Megan listened with despair. Not a thing, not a goddam thing was breaking right. And now what? Resign himself to a delay, knowing it might easily be fatal?

"Eleven sounds a bit late, dear," he said. "Just tell JF I'm here and I'd like to see him—and that I said it's important."

"Will do," she said with an amiable shrug, and, turning, she let herself into Fleming's office so expeditiously that scarcely a sound, a low indistinct babble of voices, came out between the opening and closing of the door.

Megan took off his topcoat and put it on a chair, then moved a few feet to survey himself in an oval mirror on the wall. He looked immaculate and impressive in his Pageant blazer, a dark blue flannel with the Pageant crest embroidered in gold. John Fleming had conferred it on him two years ago, on the occasion of Megan's eleventh anniversary with the organization, in a ceremony that stopped just short of a kiss on the cheeks and a sword on the shoulder. He had been mindful to wear it this morning, a presumably unself-conscious testimonial to his years of loyal service to the cause.

Reflected in the mirror, Megan saw the door from the library swing open. A girl came in, dark and very pretty and elegant—the one whose braceleted arm he had seen—carrying a briefcase. She joined the three men, taking a chair opposite them, her back to Megan, and said something that made the others smile.

Megan saw her only the few seconds it took her to enter and sit down, but everything about her had registered—the lithe body working under her gray tailored suit, the bronze face glowing with yellow light from a chrysanthemum on her shoulder, the long black hair lustrous as raw silk, pulled back and wound around her head like a turban.

Transfixed, Megan kept staring at the group in the mirror. A shudder ran through him. Then from an inside pocket of his blazer he took out a pen and a card case. He slipped out a card engraved with his name. Holding it in the palm of his left hand he wrote, under *ROGER MEGAN: has the honor to inquire whether you would like to sit on his face, and hopes you will call him at the Hilton at 5.*

As he finished writing, Fleming's secretary approached from the office. "Gentlemen," she addressed the seated group, "will you come in, please?" Turning to Megan, who had not budged from the mirror, she added with a wink, "Mr. Fleming would like you to join him, too."

Megan said, "Oh?" He looked vaguely pleased, momentarily confused, and this enabled him to hold back and let the three men precede him as they filed past the secretary through the open door. At the last moment, hesitating again, he muttered. "I'll get my coat out of the way," and with this meaningless remark took the coat to the club chair that stood back to back with the one the girl was in. She had not turned, she had not noticed him. As he put the coat down, Megan managed to drop the card in his hand over the girl's shoulder and into her lap.

And now, turning quickly, he noted with relief that his incredible action had gone unobserved, and hurried into Fleming's office.

11 · JOHN FLEMING

"GENTLEMEN," said John Fleming, "this Meeting was called for Nine o'clock, and it is now Nine o'clock." (JF had a gift for endowing words with capital letters, in thought as well as speech, to connote Larger Meanings.)

"Rita, will you invite the Delegation to come in, please? And Mr. Megan, too." He did not say, as everyone in the room knew, that proceedings were not going to wait because the Mayor was late. His Honor's absence was always fortunate, and more often wished for than realized. Besides, nobody needed him. In Surf City the mayors came and went, but the Hotels and the Pageant Endured. The Power in Surf City was here in this room.

And this was as it should be for an occasion that might well prove a milestone (or millstone, depending on one's bile in these matters) in Black and White Relations. The Historical Overtones were not lost on John Fleming; but neither did they matter. JF had no interest in causes of any kind, political, civic, community or charitable. To him a cause was Somebody Else's Promotion, with nothing in it for JF.

JF was a big, portly man, ponderous as an upright bear. His features were large and pulpy, his eyes an innocent milky blue, with skin as smooth and pink as a baby's. This, combined with his tonsured pate and benign expression, gave him the saintly demeanor of a monk, which he customarily played for all it was worth.

Behind him lay a career that had taken him from pull-in pitchman and nickle-grabber concessionaire to His Serene Highness, Suzerain of Surf City (John the Solvent), but the way had been long and arduous. Many times in his life he had been around scenes where big money was being made, but he could never get a slice. Then one auspicious day (he had by then made it to elite flackery, public-relations consultant; legit) a Surf City hotelman had come to Fleming about running a series of weekend beauty contests for his hotel.

It was the Opportunity of a Lifetime, and Fleming promptly embraced it. He acquitted himself handsomely, with finesse and enterprise, qualities he demonstrated again the next year when he returned on his own, with his own master plan for a national beauty contest, and ballyhooed the Pageant into existence.

The Pageant belonged to JF. It matched its competitors in presenting itself as chartered, civic and nonprofit, but in milking the organization it outdid them all. Securely ensconced behind leases, contracts and licenses, behind invisible salaries and expense accounts, special funds and gifts, JF had created the Pageant's financial structure along lines inspired by the Roman catacombs.

More than one intrepid investigator had been hopelessly confused in its serpentine windings. And from here secret passages led to other subterranean holdings in real estate (his vocation of record, the Fleming & Chesleigh Realty Corp.), pieces of the town's best hotels and choice landed areas.

He had not doubted that sooner or later he would have to deal with some sort of Black America promotion. Very well, it had turned out to be the NFL. The time had come, and John Fleming understood his role—Assigned by Destiny to Make History—but only, as he saw it, if he absolutely had to.

Reaction to the NFL's volley of telegrams had been immediate. This morning a distinguished segment of the local establishment had gathered staunch around Fleming for the Confrontation. The setting was impressive—tapestried walls, alabaster vases, ormolu clocks and Aubusson rugs. Dominating the room was a long oval conference table of inlaid rosewood, with place cards in silver ashtrays before each of the chairs around it. At the center of the table, Fleming stood and looked about him, checking Protocol.

To his right sat Lindstrom from the Chamber of Commerce; Starkey of the Hotelman's Association; Burdine, editor and publisher of the Surf City *Press;* Newhouse from the Pageant's law firm. To his left were three top men from the Pageant's Board of Governors—Ewing, a stockbroker; Chesleigh, JF's realty partner; Littlefield, president of the Surf City Bank & Trust. Seated somewhat apart from the others were two sponsor representatives, Ulrich from Chrysler and Joiner from Ocean Swimsuits. At the far end opposite them sat Police Chief Ed Yoldring and Lieutenant Wesley Douglas, a Negro officer in charge of community-police relations.

Directly across from Fleming were three chairs for the visitors. That left two more, one for Norm Prescott, the other, just added, for Roger Megan, who had come wandering by this morning, probably sleepwalking, and decided to ingratiate himself with a social call, which was probably what he meant by saying it was important. No matter, Megan was welcome. It gave flavor to the gallery.

The room was quite still. The three delegates came in. Fleming nodded and gestured them to their chairs. Thomas Worthington Walsh sat in the middle. On his right was Oscar Attelson, whom JF knew slightly, a lawyer and new selectman and head of the local branch of the NFL.

Attelson was by far the darkest of the trio, a polished ebony, with bushy hair parted as though cleaved by an ax and heavy parched lips edged in purple. He was thin and very stoop-shouldered, and when he looked around, his large glistening eyes seemed to be peering over invisible spectacles.

The younger man was Earl Burrage, and Chief Yoldring had filled JF in on him. ("Bad medicine. Black-power militant, so-called leader of a so-called group named SPUR." "SPUR?" Fleming had asked. "What it means," said Yoldring, "is the Society for the Prevention of Urban Renewal.") Finally Megan came in, looking jaunty, but immediately sobered by the silence and the spectacle. With a glance, Fleming directed him to the chair beside Prescott.

JF picked up a telegram that lay on the table before him. He read it out loud. " 'We are notifying all personnel and sponsors connected with the Thirteenth Annual Princess America Pageant that unless the Pageant meets our demands for racial integration, we will picket the contest, march in protest, demonstrate, and take whatever other action may be necessary. We will also urge all civil rights and progressive organizations to boycott sponsors' products.' " He put the telegram down and regarded the men across the table.

"Gentlemen," he said in a matter-of-fact and friendly voice, "are you accusing the Pageant of racial bias?"

"Mr. Fleming," said Walsh, "the Pageant winner should really be called Princess Lily White America," and he smiled.

"Your telegram mentions demands. Specifically what?"

"We have three. First, there must be at least one Negro contestant in the current Pageant. Second, formal announcement of the end of the color line, to be implemented by franchising Negro organizations to hold preliminary contests. Third, immediate addition of two Negroes to the Pageant's panel of judges."

"Tell me, Mr. Walsh," said Fleming, "for my own edification, and possibly for some others here, assuming that you're right in your accusation, what is the point of fighting to get into the Pageant?"

"The point is, we don't want to be excluded."

"But this is only a pageant," said Fleming, for once dropping a capital letter, "and really such a small affair compared to many of the problems that face colored people. It's like fighting, say, to play on a golf course instead of for a decent home to live in."

"We think they're both worth fighting for. We have housing campaigns going on at present in eleven cities. The Pageant is another problem—a psychological problem, if you will. We want to change the way Negroes think about themselves, to remove that feeling of being unacceptable, prohibited. The Pageant is an affront to us, an area of total exclusion, therefore we must attack it. Now, you say this is like fighting to play on a golf course. We have fought for that and for baseball and tennis. We have fought on a score of fronts, and we will continue to fight—for full participation in American life, nothing less."

"Well, of course, I see your point," said Fleming, "but perhaps not in this instance. Isn't it possible that in this instance you're actually embarked on a course that may very likely be self-defeating in the end?"

"I don't know what you mean."

"Well, in baseball or golf or tennis, after you're admitted to the competition, you have a real chance of winning."

"And in the Pageant?" asked Walsh. Fleming shrugged, and Walsh studied him a moment before he went on. "Do you think there aren't Negro girls who are attractive and talented enough to do well in the Pageant?"

"Mr. Walsh," said Fleming quietly, "you don't seem to recognize that what is attractive by Negro standards may not necessarily be attractive by white standards."

Walsh smiled. "Mr. Fleming, you don't seem to recognize that all it takes to be a Negro is one identifiable Negro ancestor, one great-great grandparent. I personally find African beauty types as becoming as any, but there are Negro girls with Caucasian features and blue eyes—

black, brown, chocolate, coffee, tan, high yellow—who could win anywhere, in an honest and open contest."

"Negro girls have never been excluded from the Pageant. It's simply that they have never won in our preliminary competitions."

"How many have entered these competitions?"

"Frankly, not many. But the choice is their own."

"Perhaps. But I'll bet things will be different when there are contests run by some Negro organizations, with some Negro judges. I'll bet a good many more will choose to enter."

Again Fleming paused. He had not anticipated the meeting becoming a two-man dialogue. Obviously the others were not taking it for granted. They were waiting for JF to show his vaunted skill at the art that had raised him to eminence and prosperity, the manipulation of people to his own ends. He had exhausted the fruitful possibilities of his opening gambit, Fleming decided, and turned to a new one.

"Mr. Walsh, let's examine your demands one at a time, from a practical aspect. You want at least one Negro contestant in the current Pageant. This is impossible. The Pageant has a charter, it has rules, it has procedure, and it is bound by all of them. We have been a year choosing fifty contestants through a series of eliminations, and we're five days away from choosing Princess America. Beyond these fifty contestants, no others are eligible. I could conceivably understand a demand based on next year's Pageant. But this one? Absolutely impossible."

"Not really. There are always ways and means."

"Perhaps you know more about the Pageant than we do?"

"I wouldn't go that far, but I do know that a new girl can be brought in at almost any time and not violate the rules of the Pageant. Suppose one of the present state finalists were to be taken ill, wouldn't her runner-up take her place?"

"Yes," said Fleming slowly. He couldn't imagine what Walsh was driving at. "But no one has been taken ill. Even if that did happen, every contestant already has a runner-up. In fact, with the exception of Miss Alaska, there are four girls behind every girl here—and all previously chosen."

Walsh seemed not to have heard Fleming. "And there are other contingencies," he resumed his thought, "such as the disqualification of a contestant for one reason or another. Isn't that right?"

"I don't think you understood me, Mr. Walsh."

"In what way, Mr. Fleming?"

"I'm trying to explain that only a duly chosen runner-up can replace a contestant. What good would it do you if a contestant was disqualified?"

"If it was the right contestant," said Walsh, "it might do us a lot of good. You see, Mr. Fleming, there *is* a Negro girl who is first runner-up to one of the contestants."

A murmur of surprise swept through the room.

"There is?" said Fleming.

Walsh nodded solemnly.

"Who is it? From which state?"

"That's our secret," said Walsh, smiling faintly, "until and unless you agree to put her into the contest."

"But I've explained we can't do that."

"Of course you can. Disqualify the present winner from her state."

"Disqualify the winner?" Fleming was unable to conceal his astonishment. "For what?"

"That's up to you. You know how to manage things. Find a reason and disqualify her. Then bring in her alternate, the first runner-up. The next day, announce the fact that the New Miss Someone is Negro, and make public the new set-up the Pageant intends to follow—the franchising of Negro sponsoring organizations and the installation of Negro judges."

So now it was out. JF looked around, his eyes traveling from one grim or stolid or expressionless face to another. It hardly seemed possible to Fleming that Thomas Walsh was seriously putting forward such a demand on behalf of the NFL.

"Suppose," said Fleming, "we did just what you propose, Mr. Walsh. Wouldn't it be obvious—having a girl disqualified and her alternate turning out to be Negro—that the whole affair was a frame-up just to accommodate you?"

"Not if it were done right. Only the people in this room know about it, and aside from our delegation you control every one of them."

"That isn't so, Mr. Walsh. But even if it were, how could we prevent you from telling the story later on? It would give the disqualified girl a million-dollar lawsuit."

"You would have to take our word on that."

"I value your word a great deal," said Fleming, "but not quite a million dollars' worth."

Earl Burrage said to Fleming in a soft, satisfied tone, "Then you refuse?"

Fleming said, "I see you've decided to join the conversation, Mr. Burrage."

"I'm not very good at conversation, Jack," said Burrage, spitting out the words. "I came here to listen. You see, Jack, all these years we niggers been going to white folks with a large list of demands in one hand and a prepared cop-out in the other. Now we come with a small list, but we'll either get it all or there'll be no Pageant. Remember that, Jack. I'm a bad nigger. All I want to hear is, do you refuse?"

"We haven't accepted or rejected anything yet. We're still talking. We have until Thursday to decide, don't we? Then let's continue and make everything clear. Let's take demand number two. As you know, every state already has franchised organizations to run the preliminary contests. If we add new ones in these states, it means a duplication of contests. This can only overburden the Pageant and lead to confusion and chaos."

Walsh shook his head. "Not necessarily. Franchises aren't forever. They all have expiration dates, and they all have clauses that enable you to lift them."

"In other words, the same thing—you want us to disqualify some of our franchised organizations?"

"We're not telling you what to do or how to do it, Mr. Fleming. Let's not bog down in a discussion of organizational problems. But there's no question in our minds that if you sincerely decided to open the doors to Negroes, you could solve all the difficulties attendant to it. The same ingenuity that now keeps them out could be employed to allow them in."

"But let's look ahead and see what else might happen, and I'm referring now to your third demand, the appointment of Negro judges. Assuming that everything is being done to your satisfaction, suppose no Negro girls win, or get into the finals. Do you want Negroes to judge white girls?"

"Why not? As things are, you claim Negro girls are eligible, and there is no color line. But they're being judged by whites, are they not, at least theoretically? What's the difference?"

A feeling of frustration had gradually begun to have a numbing effect on Fleming. Burrage seemed to understand it, staring at him with malicious pleasure.

"Mr. Walsh," said Fleming, "suppose we fail to see eye to eye on all of these demands, what do you propose to do about it? Or are you leaving that to our imaginations?"

"You mean," said Walsh, smiling again, "keeping you in

the dark, so to speak?" And he turned and nodded to Oscar Attelson.

Attelson said, "We're pretty sure you already know what we're planning, Mr. Fleming. The police spy system in this town seems to be working fine." He added, with a glance toward Douglas, "That's not directed at you, Lieutenant. Actually, however, we have nothing very unusual in mind—the same old stuff, with maybe a new twist. First, you can expect a picket line around the Armory, including maybe a hundred or so very pretty Negro girls in swimsuits by day and evening gowns at night, and they'll be carrying some rather interesting signs and slogans. Second, we plan to demonstrate twice a day by marching the length of the boardwalk. Third, we'll picket the airport and the railroad and bus terminals so that visitors to Surf City will know what the situation here is all about.

"Fourth and finally, every working Negro in Surf City, no matter what his job, whether he services the hotels or the Pageant or transportation or garbage collection, every single one will go on strike one day this week. That's the only thing we won't tell you now, or warn you about later—which day it will be."

"Does that sum it all up then?" asked Fleming.

"I believe so," said Attelson.

Suddenly Burrage spoke up. "Now just one doggone minute," he said. "I want to say just one thing more about what we're liable to do. I notice you got the police department here, but to my way of thinking, you should have had the fire department too, because that mile and a half of boardwalk is all made of wood, and it burns. And we so burned up with the way things are, we don't mind if everything else gets burned up."

Fleming said, "Does Mr. Burrage speak for you, Mr. Walsh?"

"I speak for myself!" said Burrage angrily. "Me and maybe a couple of hundred other no-good niggers who are willing to fight you honkies the only way you dig!"

"Gentlemen," JF said, laying open his moist palms as though baring his heart, "you may rest assured that we are going to give your proposals the most earnest and sympathetic consideration and do everything in our power to Go Along with you. Obviously, you have presented us with serious problems—problems which we regard not as business problems, not as social problems, but as Human Problems which can and must be resolved with humanity and understanding. Nor are we unaware of our responsibilities to the Entire Nation in these days of great Change and Progress. If I may add a personal statement, I would like to say that I have a Philosophy of Life that guides me in times of stress and crisis, and it is a very simple one."

JF's floating palms levitated again and came to rest in an attitude of benediction. "Many years ago I read a book in which a very old and very wise man, a High Lama, revealed his One Fundamental Rule for Life: 'Be kind.' That, gentlemen, is the philosophy by which I live—Be Kind."

There was a hush as JF finished. Then Earl Burrage's voice knifed through. "Shee-itt, man, you kill me!" he blurted. "What did that high lama get high on?"

In that grotesque moment, everything about John Fleming sagged, his arches, his paunch, his jowls, but not his dignity; he wore it like a toga. He glowered at Burrage, his mind straining for some inspired remark that would put this black-assed sonofabitch in his place, and, none coming, he took refuge in majestic silence. Then Walsh and Attelson rose from their chairs. Almost lugubrious in their studied detachment, with a nod to Fleming, they walked out of the room leaving the door open behind them. Burrage, still suffering gleeful spasms, pulled himself erect and followed.

But as Burrage neared the door, he came to an abrupt stop before the chair where Roger Megan was sitting. Unlike the others, Megan seemed quite relaxed, a smile flickering on his lips.

"Hey, baby, look who's here!" Burrage cried disdainfully. "Megan the mouth! How come you the only laugher? You must think I'm funny, huh?"

Megan surveyed him with cold amusement. Then he got up. "I think you're a riot," he said blandly.

Burrage clapped his hands together softly and wrung them in mock dismay. "Shame on you, a white man talking like that," he reproached Megan, chuckling derisively. "Don't you know riot is a dirty word?"

"On the contrary," said Megan, "there's a good deal to be said for riots. How else can you protest social injustice and come home with a free case of booze and a color TV?"

Burrage's face twitched, his sneer turning splenetic. His jaw muscles danced.

"You're a straight thinker, mouth," he snarled.

"Just telling it like it is, asshole," said Megan, not unkindly, and calmly turned and walked away.

Marvelously, it was over, though Burrage hesitated,

holding back as if trying to think of a rejoinder. Then, with one last baleful look around, he stalked from the room.

As the heavy door swung shut on Burrage, someone let out a laugh, not loud but bursting forth happily, laughing for all of them. Another applauded, and appreciative comments rippled around the room for Roger Megan. All at once, the air-conditioning seemed to be working again.

JF's dewlap shivered with joy. How masterfully Roger had handled Burrage. And the best of it was, it had made JF feel suddenly purged of his recent humiliation—redeemed—for, dressed in his trim royal-blue Pageant blazer, Roger had seemed somehow officially invested and his response to Burrage the word of a Pageant deputy.

"Shall we proceed?" Fleming resumed.

He waited for quiet. The gloom that had earlier settled like fallout had dissipated a little. In this more buoyant atmosphere he hoped now to speed his colleagues the hell out, with a minimum of palaver. He had no time or patience or need to hear from them. He knew where each one stood. And he knew that in the end everything would devolve upon him, a quorum of one.

"Gentlemen, I'm sure there is much to discuss, but unfortunately today's heavy schedule allows me no time for your comments or questions."

He sank gently into his chair. Prescott brought his humidor. Fleming gazed at the cigars, finally took one, then very slowly put it back and chose another. He smoked, contemplating the ash forming on his cigar. Presently he began to speak, addressing no one in particular, with a curiously restrained but unyielding voice.

"I am prepared to concede the franchises. In practice it will all come to nothing. Their people haven't the money to support the effort, or the competence to run it, and if we give them a paper victory they'll play into our hands. And, franchises or not, basic control of the Pageant will remain intact and undiminished, so we need fear no unfortunate or undesirable consequences. Furthermore, since this agreement does not become operative before next year, the installation of Negro judges can probably also be deferred until then. So that, distasteful as these concessions are, their compensatory feature is that they both postpone change. That gives us another chance—and not a bad chance at all—because the way things are going, by next year the separatists may be dominant enough to *fight* integration in the Pageant. We can reasonably hope the mood will be such that Negroes will refuse to enter contests with whites. Our course therefore is to give as little as possible now and stall for time. However," JF went on, "as to their first demand—that we add a Negro contestant to this year's Pageant, somehow appointed or substituted or arranged—if they hold to it, we have no choice but to oppose them. I will not destroy the Pageant to make peace. That is where we stand, my friends."

He lapsed into silence again, distant and insular, and his visitors understood that the audience was over. Their expressions reflecting concern or satisfaction, they got to their feet and began to file out.

In a low voice Fleming called out, "Roger?"

Immediately Megan returned to the table and sat.

"You were very good with Burrage, Roger."

"Thank you, JF."

"What did you want to see me about?"

"It's an idea I think you may like. I know this hardly seems like the time to bring up new projects, but executing it wouldn't be very difficult, and if you do like the idea, we really ought to get started at once."

"Fine," said JF, managing to sound pleased. "Let's hear."

"It's a simple notion. What with all the talk about what NBC may throw opposite us to hurt our ratings, I thought maybe we could make this year's Pageant a very special one, something that would be . . ."

So Megan did know about the CBS proposals. He was here to protect his territorial rights. But something he was saying had nevertheless engaged Fleming's attention.

"Excuse me, Roger," he interrupted. 'Would you mind repeating that last part about a reunion?"

Megan had been pressing, pitching hard. He seemed relieved to have his rhythm broken, and he eased into a more relaxed sell, half sitting on the edge of the conference table with folded arms.

"I was saying," Megan resumed, "let's have a grand reunion of all our twelve past Princesses. A big beautiful production number where they won't have to do anything much, or say more than a few words. They come in from all over America. Those who are married bring their husbands. If they have kids, the kids are there. Everybody wants to know what happens to a Princess America when her year in the limelight is over. We'll show them, and what we have to show is a wonderful testimonial to the standards of the Pageant. The girls who've won the title are still an outstanding group—mothers who've married well, career women, continuing students—in public health, in fashion, teaching, entertainment, publishing. We invite them all, with their families, to come and spend a long weekend with us. A homecoming. The Pageant family reunited. At our expense. We fly them here, wine them and dine them, give them all gifts for all the husbands and children."

He stopped speaking, but only momentarily, feeling constrained to add uncertaintly, "It probably sounds like a lot to undertake on short notice, but if you'll give it a moment's thought . . ." and let it trail off as JF shook his head at him.

"It requires no thought whatever," Fleming pronounced in a subdued, emotional voice. "The thinking has already been done, and splendid, creative thinking it is. Roger, it's brilliant. I congratulate you."

Roger's face lit up slowly, like a chandelier on a rheostat, finally radiant. "Thank you, JF," he murmured, gracefully inclining his head. "I'm glad you like it."

"God, it's beautiful," said Prescott fervently. "It's *got* it. It's a winner."

Fleming rose and with gravity and affection took Megan's right hand and enveloped it with both his own. He looked into Megan's dark, snapping, alert eyes, searching what he hoped were their depths. Twice this morning this tall, handsome, charming, complicated, high-flying, paradoxical fading star had come to his rescue. JF felt the unfamiliar stir of gratitude in his breast and fought back. *Not my rescue. His. One mustn't confuse the motive with the result.* "It couldn't have come at a better time, Roger," he said benignly. "Did you hear what CBS wants to do?"

He let go of Roger's hand, his innocently amused gaze clinically fixed, with difficulty containing his surprise as he heard Roger say, "Yes, it got to me, I suppose unconsciously that was what started me thinking about coming up with something else—because I couldn't agree less with them. They had a basic misunderstanding of the essence of the Pageant."

"Ah?" croaked Fleming. "In what way?"

"We are not show business," said Roger. "We both deal in fairy tales, but ours is infinitely superior, because ours is *real*. All we need do is show the real—not garnish it with stagey glamour. That only obscures the drama. The Pageant is real, and the Pageant is the drama."

"Bravo, Roger," JF breathed. "I've never heard it better expressed."

Smiling modestly, Megan said, "The truth is, I've

learned from you, JF. In fact, you're actually responsible for my getting the idea in the first place. My wife called me yesterday and told me about your kind invitation to spend the week here. Unfortunately, as she told you, this is the children's first week of school, but it was your generous impulse that got me thinking about family reunions and how much they mean to all of us. And there it was—the Pageant family reunited."

"Roger," said JF, "we move on this pronto. You'll phone—no, we'll have both you and Sue on the phone—you do the inviting. I'll have Prescott see to the rest, newspapers, TV promos, radio. Everything."

"I can't tell you how pleased I am," Roger said. But it showed.

As Megan went out, JF's secretary came in. "Mr. Cornelius and the others are here, Mr. Fleming. And there was a message from the Mayor's office. They said he couldn't attend the League meeting because he had a tooth pulled this morning. An emergency."

Fleming said, "I'm sorry to hear it, Rita. Ask Norm Prescott to step in, before Cornelius."

Alone with Norm Prescott, he would take a few moments to gather and hone his thoughts. The Wabash Cannonball was running late, but with a full head of steam and very definitely on the right track for the next stop. *Gentlemen, we must not obscure the Drama. The Pageant is the Drama, because the Pageant is Real!*

Fleming sighed ponderously. "Norman," he said, frowning, "Roger bothers me. I don't know what to make of him. After all these years. Maybe he's a sex maniac, but he's beguiling and attractive, and I can't help liking him. He's got a mind, and he's using it. It seems to me he should be rewarded. A bonus? A five-year contract? Or perhaps make him a VP in some special capacity and draw on his services in an executive post? If I knew I could trust him not to do anything harmful to himself or to us, if I knew definitely whether all this gossip—"

He broke off, nodding sharply with sudden resolution. "Norman, I want him followed. Surveillance day and night and a full report to me every forty-eight hours. I want to know every move he makes while he's here in Surf City. It's time I knew. Let's see what he does with his week."

"Yes, sir. He'll be tailed every minute. I'll have it arranged by noon."

JF took a last pull on the remains of his cigar and tamped it out in a silver ashtray, then buzzed for Rita.

12 · MISS CALIFORNIA

"BUT, Stacy darling, are you sure that Sue Rossiter said you couldn't possibly win?" asked Mrs. DeGray. "I still can't believe they wouldn't let a girl win fair and square." She hesitated a second. "Are you sure you didn't misunderstand her?"

Their driver had stopped at a light. Stacy waited until the car came alive again before she whispered an answer.

"Oh, Mother, how many times do I have to tell you? *I heard her with my own eyes.* I'm practically ex-communicated."

The hearse-length car made a sharp right turn and two blocks ahead they could see the huge monolithic limestone structure that was the Armory.

Police Sergeant Al Herndon, official chauffeur for the DeGrays, having completed the required ceremonial tour of California Avenue for Stacy, shook his head and edged to the curb.

"There are at least a dozen cars stacked up ahead of us," he reported sourly. "New York, Kansas, New Mexico, Illinois. Practically every member of the electoral college except Washington, D.C. I suggest you get out here and walk. Last year I drove Miss Pennsylvania, and we were tied up for twenty minutes. Besides, your chaperone, Mrs. Latham, has been waiting for you inside for at least half an hour."

Stacy nodded. The cop hopped out, opened the door. "Good luck, California." He grinned. "Sock it to 'em, girl!"

The two blocks separating the DeGrays from the Armory was an obstacle course studded with gawkers, amateur photographers and souvenir hucksters. Stacy took in the scene with unblinking eyes. Her face was smoothly made up. Every vestige of the long night's tears had been erased under Mama's supervision. But inside she felt as doomed as a sacrificial virgin. She had risen early this morning and, with shaking fingers, had rolled one of her special cylinders. She had puffed at it desperately in the john before breakfast, praying the floaty effect would get through faster on her empty stomach. But for once the grass had betrayed her. She might just as well have inhaled smog. Worse still, her supply of the stuff was exhausted. All that remained were the lousy leftovers, useless seeds and stems. Making a connection in Surf City would be difficult.

More usually the Armory was a year-round theater for sporting events, political conventions, industrial exhibitions and National Guard drills. The drab interior had all the architectural distinction of an immense airplane hangar. Its walls were cold and featureless. The vaulted roof was supported by a complex spiderweb of exposed steel girders. Its floor, seven acres of paved tarmac, had the warmth of San Quentin's courtyard.

But today an atmosphere of fiesta had invaded it. Flags and official seals of all the fifty states were spaced in varicolored rows along the girders and against the bare walls. Bunting draped the apron of the big stage dominating one end of the hall. Flowers decked each of the rows of tables set for luncheon.

On prominent display alongside the platform reserved for the television crew stood a dozen showcase cabinets, reverently cordoned off like consecrated shrines. Each cabinet had velvet-covered shelves featuring Princess America novelties licensed by the last twelve winners. The fingerprint smudges blurring their windows almost seemed blasphemous.

Through the glass door of the first booth could be seen the modest swimsuit endorsed more than a decade ago by Jane Ellis, Princess No. One. Obsolete now, the suit had earned her $16,000 in royalties.

"Girls, get a load of that third cabinet," Stacy heard a voice from above her say. She turned to look up into the face of a beautiful Amazon with apricot-colored hair set in a gelatinous beehive. Her badge identified her as Miss Wisconsin, and she was tall enough to go out with basketball players. "All the junk in there was endorsed by Sue Rossiter," Miss Wisconsin went on. "Winning the crown that year must have made her a mint."

Wisconsin's observation was accurate indeed. The cabinet was a miniature Marshall Field's. Its shelves were wall-to-walled with Princess America costume jewelry, cosmetics, sports wear, beach wear, gloves, lingerie, boots, a surfboard, tennis racquet, raincoat, luggage, games, coloring books, place mats, shoes, a scrapbook album and cans of health food. There was even a Princess America doll; you wound it up, and it smiled.

But such fat pickings would never be available for herself, Stacy thought bleakly. She filed past the remaining cabinets unseeing, a wedge of depression sunk deep in her brain. The items symbolized the scattered debris of her demolished dream.

Stacy pressed ahead, Mama at her elbow, looking in vain for her chaperone. The place was as busy as New York's international airport; all that was missing were the signs in four languages. Ahead, behind a roped-off section of tables, she spied Glenda Dowling, Eames Bentley and Lois Smith. The faces of the two women and three men sitting with them were ciphers; she assumed they composed the balance of the judges' panel. This was the august jury of eight that would select the thirteenth Princess America.

A petite woman emerged from the crowd and darted toward Stacy. She peered at Stacy's badge. "So *you're* California! Excuse me for not spotting you sooner, but some idiot told me you were a redhead. The only redheads in the house are Miss Massachusetts and Miss Michigan."

Despite her dry and grainy voice, her chaperone was a pleasant woman. Alongside Mama, she was as a bantam to a buzzard. Stacy shook her extended hand; it was cold, filled with tiny bones. After she had introduced herself as Mrs. Cora Latham, she patted Stacy on the arm and smiled warmly.

"You know, dear, I'm glad you're not a redhead. No redhead has ever won the crown. Not that they have a rule against redheads . . ."

Rules? Don't talk to me about the rules, Stacy wanted to scream.

"We're assigned to table eight," Mrs. Latham was saying, indicating a destination far left and forward. "I'll lead the way."

Stacy followed her zigzag route through a series of congested aisles while Mama held fast to her arm, a sucker fish glued to its host. As they passed other chaperones steering their charges to their places, most of them smiled and nodded to Mrs. Latham. Obviously they were old comrades at arms, seasoned veterans of previous Pageant campaigns.

They checked in alongside a table for eight, in the fourth row back from the bunting-iced stage apron. To Stacy's left stood Miss Georgia, a candy-box blonde, her chaperone vigilant beside her like a sentry on duty. Alaska and Hawaii and their official duennas were already seated.

Oblivious to the logistics problem presented by the seating arrangements, Mama plunked herself down in one of the empty chairs. If Mrs. Latham regarded her as a crass interloper, her next words carried no tinge of censure.

"We'd love to have you join us at this table, Mrs. DeGray," she said with iron charm, "but the rules forbid anyone except Pageant personnel from sitting with the contestants. I'm sure you'll enjoy eating at table thirty-two, which has been reserved for you and other guests."

Stacy watched her mother trundle off, disconsolate; she was probably furious that her squatter's rights had not been honored.

All the girls were shamelessly twisting and turning, poise shed to the winds, searching the room for celebrities, sizing up their competitors. Three aisles away, in the front row, Stacy sighted the radiant Ginny Kerr, decorating her table like a living centerpiece. How she hated that face now!

Suddenly there was a roll of the drums, and the band struck up the opening bars of "Sweet Sue."

Out from the wings, chic in peach-toned harem pants which hid her marvelous legs, stepped Sue Rossiter. The traveling mike in her hand seemed as natural as the torch held by the Statue of Liberty.

"Welcome to the Pageant," she began. "All fabulous fifty of you—from Miss Alabama to Miss Wyoming." She smiled directly at her audience, giving them a shot of the Rossiter charisma. "You kids really *are* fabulous, you know. Our statistical department informs me that exactly seventy thousand eight hundred and nine girls entered the Princess America preliminaries this year. You fifty are the cream of that crop. So whenever you feel the pressure great, remind yourself that you outclassed more than seventy thousand contestants to be here. I'm here to give you some useful tips plus a rundown of the most important rules. For openers, I want to show you scenes from color-film tapes of the last two Pageants which feature our finalists in action. I think you can learn from them. So if you'll watch as well as listen . . ."

She snapped her fingers, and the banked lights dimmed, swathing the vast room in semi-eclipse. Behind her, on the stage, twin sections of a huge curtain slid back, baring an enormous white screen.

From a projectionist's booth in the rear a bright beam

zeroed in upon the screen. The film revealed a beautiful girl standing on the great stage of the Armory. She was exhibiting the classic, certified Pageant smile as she walked regally down a runway that bisected the spectators' rows of seats.

"Miss Wyoming, two years ago," Sue's amplified voice commented. "Notice the gown she's wearing. A lovely one. But it almost cost her the crown. When she arrived here it had a dozen tiny buttons fastening the back. She had forgotten that on the night of the finals all the contestants have to change almost instantly from swimsuits to gowns and also put on elbow-length white gloves. Fortunately, Wyoming's chaperone checked it in time, and a Pageant seamstress was called in to substitute a zipper. If any of you brought dresses with a similar problem, report it to your chaperone at once."

The film cut to a slim, redheaded girl clad in a provocative Kelly-green bathing suit.

"Miss Ohio won the swimsuit competition last year. In this event, it's important to remember several points. No bikinis, girls. No padded suits. No falsies. The judges must be given a fair chance to rate you as you really are.

"And while on the subject of gadgets—wiglets, artificial braids and falls are not allowed. No bleached, dyed or tinted hair, either. One girl had to be disqualified last year because she competed wearing false eyelashes. All this may seem unreasonable to some of you. But it's an integral part of the Pageant. Our Princess must be a real girl, not a mechanical contrivance. A girl as wholesome as Snow White. And above all, a lady always.

"Because of these standards, we have formulated other strict taboos. No see-through skirts or blouses. No chewing gum. No drinking of alcoholic beverages. Nor may you smoke during Pageant Week, not even in the privacy of your own hotel room. A maid, a bellhop or a repair man might spot you.

"Your deportment, also, must meet the highest ladylike standards. No off-color talk, please. That includes even juicy quotes from current best sellers and from 'For Adults Only' movies, if you know what I mean. One of our contestants several Pageants back made it all the way to the top ten, but we had to rule her out when she missed a cue during rehearsal, lost her temper, and dropped a four-letter word."

From across the table Stacy caught a muffled giggle. Lifting her eyes over the floral centerpiece, she observed Hawaii leaning toward Alaska, whispering words in decibels too low for audibility. But for Stacy there was no sound barrier.

"I can thank my stars they took King Kam away this morning," Hawaii was saying. "If I had him here for just one minute, I'd be taking the next jet back to Honolulu and Hawaii would be kicked out of the Union.

Gibberish. Or so it seemed to Stacy. Her eyes panned to the table reserved for the press. A reporter was making notes in the confining glow of a pencil flashlight. The illumination was barely sufficient for her to decode his lips as he spoke to a fellow scribe: ". . . little blonde from Georgia. What an eyeful! But they tell me she's got a smashing ninety-seven I.Q. She's so stupid she can only play Scrabble with three letters. She'd need a brain transplant to win . . ."

Stacy flicked a sympathetic look to her left. Georgia appeared unaware of anything going on about her. The images on the screen seemed, judging from her vapid face, absolutely meaningless.

Onstage, Sue Rossiter was saying, "This brings us to another important value. Your stage poise, especially when you're parading on the hundred-and-ten-foot catwalk. Watch closely, now. Here's our eleventh Princess America about to 'walk the plank,' as we call it—and walking it like a queen, despite the fact that her heels are as long and spiky as Lady Macbeth's dagger."

The girl on screen seemed to glide down the catwalk, her luminous smile bestowed impartially upon admirers to the left and to the right. There was no doubt that she had been created by nature for this spell-binding moment.

Sue's practical voice broke the trance. "We will now replay this scene in slow motion. Notice that she walks toes first, just as our posture coach taught her. This way her bottom can't wiggle too provocatively. Notice, too, the way she turns her head from side to side, ignoring no one, charming everyone. Don't be fooled; that captivating head shift is as difficult to master as a complicated Irish reel. Our coach worked with her on it as he did with each of the other contestants. He'll be doing the same with you girls as your appointments come up."

The taped reel was whirling toward its climax. This was the ceremony on stage in which, a year ago, Virginia Louise Kerr had been crowned the twelfth Princess America by her outgoing predecessor, Miss Delaware.

Stacy stared at the sparkling tiara as it was placed atop Ginny's semicurled dark hair, framing her face in piquant loveliness. And unbearable envy suddenly began strangling her. Never had she wanted that crown so much as now.

Now the screen was showing the pair of Princesses embracing each other in a tender close-up, as historic a moment for the fascinated viewers as the meeting of Stanley and Livingstone. Ginny Kerr's face registered modesty and joy, with just a film of mist in her glowing eyes. She personified chastity, faith, hope, wisdom, charity and all the other virtues. An apostle of innocence. The retiring Princess projected honest, congratulatory grace. Then both girls smiled enchantingly, exposing fences of perfect teeth toothpaste mongers had paid a small fortune to advertise during the past two years.

"The smile," Sue said, strolling casually down the apron, mannikin style. "That exclusive Princess America smile. Some of you have already got it down pat, thanks to briefing during your state prelims. But the point can't be made too often. Through the entire week ahead, it's got to be chin up, teeth gleaming, face lit up by a smile. For the public, for the press, and especially for the judges.

"It isn't easy. As official Pageant hostess for the past ten years, I have to practice what I preach, so I know. I'm older than you girls, and it's rough. To tell the truth, I must have my face massaged at the end of the day for muscle fatigue. Just from keeping up that smile. But it has to be kept up. It must never falter. Nervous you may be. Homesick, Scared. Even, sometimes, bored to tears. But you've got to stretch that face and *smile*!

"Next item," Sue continued, "your talent bits. We have a strict time limit on these. You'll have two minutes and thirty seconds, not a moment longer, to show what you can do. Also there will be no Teleprompters. If this comes as bad news for those of you planning to give a long reading or a monologue, see our drama coach immediately. He has a selection of excellent short readings which are easy to memorize.

"Finally," Sue went on, "I hope none of you is counting on using any kind of animal in your routine. Just as pets in your room are taboo, so are animals on stage. Anything that walks, crawls, swims or flies. The Pageant is not a circus."

Sue stepped back to disengage one foot from a loop formed by her mike's dangling wire.

"Well, girls, that takes care of the nitty gritty, except for one special goodie I'm saving for after lunch. Now enjoy yourselves and get acquainted."

The film and the informal lecture were over.

Lights sprang alive, almost blinding by contrast to the dimness they swept away. Overhead, recessed vents hissed their artificial breeze, causing the rows of state banners to flutter vigorously. The band on stage began its musical salute to the fifty contestants starting (alphabetically, of course) with "Stars Fell on Alabama."

Sue Rossiter descended from the stage and began to ricochet from table to table, nodding to a girl here, greeting a chaperone there, and smiling serenely.

As if triggered by the returning lights, a buzz of conversation arose throughout the hall. From the caterer's kitchen in the rear, waiters jogged in, an army bearing trays instead of shields.

Stacy ignored her chicken patty and salad. Food would have choked her. She looked the floor over, resenting the animation and gaiety of her rivals as they bantered with the roving guests.

Years ago, at school dances, Stacy had often used her talent for reading lips to find out what boys thought of her and her friends. It had been a delicious, naughty sport. Today, the stakes were higher. She let her gaze tour the amphitheater to explore the lips of the unsuspecting diners. Like a magpie collecting stray bits of litter, she hopped from face to face. It was like listening in on a party line:

SENATOR HUGO LYONS (bowing low and kissing the hand of Miss Texas): "My dear, I shall continue to hoard the Confederate bonds my father left me. When you become Princess America, the South will rise again."

ROGER MEGAN (to Norm Prescott, observing a wire correspondent surreptitiously heading for an exit): "Ten to one he's hopping across the street to get juiced. They say when he was born the doctor had to slap him twice—once to sober him up."

NORM PRESCOTT (trying to top Megan): "I hear he was arrested last month for being drunk and disorderly. When the cops allowed him to make one phone call, he called the liquor store for more booze."

MISS NEVADA (in an aside to Miss Arizona, while watching Miss New Jersey being photographed by a TV cameraman): "I can't stand that Jersey brat. She looks as if she's posing for her monument."

SUE ROSSITER (pausing at Miss Vermont's table): "Honey, that looks to me like the beginning of a fever blister. If it gets worse, it'll be the kiss of death. You won't be able to smile. I suggest you see Dr. Lydecker right after lunch."

MRS. AMANDA CLARKE (to Virginia Kerr, the reigning Princess America): "Ginny dear, I've looked the field over, and there's not one girl in this year's crop who can hold a candle to you."

FELIX WOLFE (to Norm Prescott, observing Judge Laurel sizing up Miss Utah's figure): "I understand our friend Laurel is quite a Bengal lancer. He once bragged to me he's laid three Oscar winners."

NORM PRESCOTT (waving to an AP correspondent passing by): "We checked him out. He's strictly a name-fucker. A long-form bullshit artist."

MISS ILLINOIS' CHAPERONE (exhibiting a picture in her wallet to the group at her table): "This is Kay Farrell, last year's Miss Maine, whom I chaperoned. Even though she came in second, she earned more than fifty thousand dollars in modeling fees. Besides that, she had a ball all the way."

Small talk, covering most of the seven sins, Stacy concluded after her Peeping Tom excursion. But that tidbit about Kay Farrell offered Stacy a shiny brass ring. There need be no last rites for her. She might be Number Two.

Photographers were now casing the Armory, assessing the fifty candidates for picture possibilities. Aware of their presence, the girls hastened to second-coat their makeup, doubled their former vivacity. A slender man in a mustard-colored sport jacket, tieless, with a camera slung over his shoulders and a large stuffed elephant cuddled under one arm, eased up to Stacy's table and addressed himself to Georgia.

"Hello, sweetie. I'm Sam Trent, *Vue* magazine. How's to give us a pretty picture? One for the GIs to pin up."

Georgia lifted vacant eyes. "Me?"

"Nobody else but you, Georgia peach." As he spoke he shoved the elephant at her, trunk first. "Meet Elmer. Girl with toy. Always makes a cute shot. Now hold Elmer's trunk with both hands and kiss it with those gorgeous lips. Last year we ran a pic of Georgia smooching a donkey, so this will show we're bipartisan."

Georgia caressed the stuffed pet as directed, puckered her lips to kiss the woolen proboscis. Trent leveled his camera, and the shutter's click exploded the flash cube.

"One more shot, doll," said the photographer, keeping his camera level. "Protection, right?"

He got no further. A heavy hand descended in a karate chop and sent the camera crashing to the floor. The photographer twisted around to face a burly six-footer in

Pinkerton uniform. Behind him stood a waxen-faced Sue Rossiter, who had materialized like a ghost at a seance.

"Okay, buster," growled the guard. "Let's see your credentials. Miss Rossiter tells me your magazine is on the Pageant blacklist."

The photographer shrugged. "So I crashed the party. Big deal. Newsmen do it every day of the week. Freedom of the press, you know."

"You're not a newsman," said Sue Rossiter heatedly. "You're a snake who creeps out from under his rock at the drop of a girl's eyelash. *Vue* is a sex publication. Its circulation is strictly for men's smokers and the pervert fringe. Take him down to precinct headquarters, Nick."

"My camera," protested the photographer. He arced down, mongoose-swift, and, before the security guard could prevent his act, pulled out the enclosed film, exposing it to ruinous lights. Then he threw it to the floor, where it lay coiled like a dead adder.

"There's your evidence," he gloated, pointing to the spoiled ribbon of film. "Now lead me to Leavenworth."

"I'd suggest you get yourself a good lawyer," Sue snapped. "The last photographer arrested for trespassing on Pageant grounds was hit with a five-hundred-dollar fine plus a ten-day jail sentence. And you can tell your editor that it's impossible to fix a Surf City judge during Pageant Week."

The Pinkerton man hustled the photographer away and Sue transferred her attention to Georgia's chaperone, a knobby woman who wore a bright yellow dress gored to move gracefully. Her Mediterranean-blue eyes reflected complete mystification as she approached Sue to question her about the incident. Sue motioned her aside, out of earshot of the others at her table.

"Mrs. Traymore," she said, "how long have you been with the Pageant?"

"This is my second year. Last year I chaperoned Miss Kentucky. She finished fourth, if you remember."

"You're familiar with all our official rules?"

"Of course, Miss Rossiter. I've read the manual a dozen times. Why, I even have a copy with me. It's in my purse."

"Good. Would you please take it out?"

Still puzzled, Mrs. Traymore returned to her seat to pick up her pocketbook, a transparent, plastic catch-all. Unclasping the lid, she shuffled through the contents, brushing aside wallet, sunglasses, Kleenex and car keys. At last she fished out a slim blue booklet the size of a vest-pocket diary and offered it to Sue.

Sue rebuffed it with a gesture, said, "I refer you to page eleven, paragraph three. Please read it aloud."

Mrs. Traymore flipped through the pages with nervous fingers until she came to the indicated section.

" 'When dealing with a photographer who requests specific poses of a contestant, it is mandatory that the chaperone prohibit any pictures until she has first checked his press pass to ascertain whether it is stamped with the official Pageant seal. Furthermore, it is the responsibility of the chaperone to see that no photograph is taken which is of questionable taste or can embarrass a contestant or the Pageant.' "

Mrs. Traymore looked confused. "But—but I did check his pass. He showed it to me just before lunch and it looked okay. And he seemed like such a polite young man."

"Mrs. Traymore, I accept your statement that you tried to fulfill your responsibility. But you made a serious error. When you checked the seal on that skunk's pass, you obviously failed to notice that the date was two years old. Your mistake could have embarrassed the Pageant no end and ruined Georgia's chances."

"But I still don't understand why all the fuss," said Mrs. Traymore, still in a state of daze. "It was a perfectly innocent picture he took—Georgia holding a cute toy elephant."

"Cute little elephant, my eye!" Sue said frostily. She thrust the rigid trunk of the stuffed animal at Mrs. Traymore. "Here. Hold the trunk with both your hands, just the way Georgia did. Now kiss the end. Do I have to spell it out?"

Mrs. Traymore's face turned beet red. "You mean . . ."

"Exactly. Just a little retouching and cropping of that eight-inch trunk and that 'polite young man' would have had a dandy item for his dirty magazine."

Almost on the verge of collapse, Georgia's chaperone stared at the toy in disgust.

"Oh, Miss Rossiter . . . I don't know what to say. How could I have been so naïve? Does this mean that from now on I'm *persona non grata?*"

Sue nodded, compassion in her eyes. "I'm sorry, Mrs. Traymore. I've enjoyed our association. But I have no choice. The same rules which apply to our contestants also apply to all Pageant personnel. If we failed to enforce them, we would invite breakdown in discipline."

"I'm fired?"

Sue's lips tightened sadly. Poor Mrs. Traymore. She was getting the ax only because she didn't have a dirty mind. "This is one of the few times I hate my job," Sue said. "I feel like a company fink. Please don't think me unfair or unkind."

"I understand. You won't say anything to the others . . ."

"Don't worry, dear."

Sue watched her dismal departure. Mrs. Traymore was the fifth chaperone she had sacked since joining the Pageant. She made a mental note to remind Norm Prescott to send out a euphemistic release announcing Mrs. Traymore's drop-out and to obtain an immediate replacement from the list of stand-bys.

The band had segued into "Chicago," in honor of Miss Illinois, and Stacy found herself humming the refrain. All at once appetite returned, but the waiters had already cleared the table.

She raised her head, sweeping the arena for Mama and finally located her in the company of two judges whom she had immobilized, shaking them down for their autographs. Foxy female. Not only was Mama ingratiating herself with the judges, but later, tonight, she would use her half-ass skill at handwriting analysis to unravel their personalities, supremely confident she could find an Achilles heel in their characters.

Sue Rossiter had just stopped by Miss Oregon and was handing her a yellow envelope, obviously a telegram. Stacy tuned out the babble around her and bugged Sue's moving lips.

"Judy Kelsey . . . Miss Oregon?" Sue said. "A wire just came for you. Message Center said it was urgent."

Quickly Oregon unsealed the envelope, her on-screen smile dissolving, her complexion paling as she read the message contained.

"What is it, Judy dear?" Sue Rossiter's lips were barely visible, for she had bent over the girl sympathetically and her hair had fallen across her face like a glossy curtain.

Oregon looked up, her eyes wells of grief. "It's my mother, Miss Rossiter. She was bed-ridden with a mild stroke before I left. But she wouldn't hear of my not coming to Surf City. Now Sis says she's in the hospital. In a coma. They can't say how long . . ." Oregon tried to continue, but her voice quavered. "I'll have to take the first plane out . . ."

"I understand," Sue was answering. "But have you thought it out, Judy?"

"Thought what out?"

"You say your mother is in a coma. Would she recognize you at her bedside?"

Oregon looked numb. "N-no. But . . ."

"If she insisted on your coming to Surf City, that must mean she felt your taking part in the Pageant was pretty important. Right?"

"From the first day I entered, Mother talked of nothing else. She drove all over the state with me, cheering me at every prelim. But now . . ."

"What do you imagine she'd want you to do if she could tell you? If you go home now, you're out of the contest. You realize that, don't you?"

"Of course. But if I *don't* go, what kind of selfish, cold-blooded daughter am I? I love my mother."

"May I tell you a true story, dear? You know we rarely plug our competitor, the Miss America Pageant. But back in 1954—are you too young to remember?—a girl named Lee Ann Meriwether suffered the loss of her father. He died only one week before the finals in Atlantic City. While waiting backstage to be introduced to the nation as Miss America, and unaware that she was on camera, Lee raised her eyes heavenward and said—for him alone—'Dad, you know I know how happy you are for me.' When television viewers next saw her, she was walking down the runway like a real champ and smiling through her tears."

"He must have been proud." Oregon was dabbing her eyes with a table napkin. "If . . . he knew."

"I think he did know, dear. And I think your mother will know. What do you think she'd tell you to do if she could advise you?"

"I guess—I guess she'd tell me to stick. To try my darnedest. Mother never quit a fight in her life."

"Then promise me you'll think about that a while before you make any decision?"

Oregon gave Sue a grateful look and nodded.

Sue gripped Judy's arm gently but firmly, as though she could somehow transfuse some of her own strength to the troubled girl. Then, noting that she was fumbling in her purse for her rosary beads, Sue turned to Mrs. Hortense Hayes, the girl's chaperone.

"Hortense," she said, "why don't you take Judy to St. Christopher's Church this evening in time for the Monday novena."

A woman for all seasons, that Sue Rossiter, observed

Stacy. Florence Nightingale. Angel's advocate. Good Samaritan. Censor. Counselor.

The orchestra broke for a ten-minute snack, then reappeared. A tattoo of the drums, and Sue Rossiter had captured the stage again. She faced the audience and waited for the tumult to die.

"Wasn't such an ordeal, was it, these first few hours of the Longest Week?" she began. "I'll bet I know exactly how each of you feels behind those charming smiles. Palms sweating, hearts pounding, goose pimples all over. My own year, if you'll forgive a bit of ancient history, I was so nervous I spilled a Coke in a judge's lap. But the earth kept spinning and I still won the crown. So, if you've got a case of contest jitters—relax.

"Now for a surprise. You are all about to become sorority sisters. By sorority sisters, I mean only this. The entire fifty of you have been divided into three teams as numerically equal as possible—seventeen, seventeen and sixteen. You've been split into Pi Group, Alpha Group and Psi Group. For Princess America Pageant, as you've already caught on."

Sue sashayed gracefully to stage right, the spotlight clinging to her.

"One reason for this is that each group will be engaging in one or another of our various preliminary formalities at identical times. For example, while Pi Group is being interviewed by the judges, Alpha will be getting instructions for the Torchlight Parade. And Psi girls will be busy on the stage, rehearsing their talent acts. As the week goes on, each group, by rotation, will have experienced the same activities."

Sue backtracked to the center of the stage as she talked, then began strolling down the apron, contriving to give each table equal time.

"And now for that goodie I promised you before lunch. It has to do with your chances for being one of the lucky ten girls to land in the semifinals." She stopped at Stacy's table, directed herself to Miss Alaska.

"Millie, what would you say are the odds for a girl making it into the semifinals? Have you ever figured them out?"

Mildred Waxman, slightly flustered by the unexpected limelight, bent over to speak into Sue's lowered mike.

"I sure have," she said, "A girl would have to beat forty other contestants to be among the top ten."

"Exactly. And that sounds like pretty tough odds, doesn't it? But actually—and this is a factor the general public doesn't know—the odds are much more favorable."

Miss Missouri, unable to restrain herself, broke the silence that followed. "I'm from Missouri, Miss Rossiter, so won't you please clarify that last statement?"

There was a soft current of laughter, joined in by Sue herself, and she continued: "I'll explain, Missouri, and I don't think you have to be a math major to understand the point. Beginning Wednesday night, there will be three preliminaries. At each of these, the judges will award points to the girls in each group. After the last prelim, on Friday night, our chief auditor will tabulate the votes. The three girls who have scored the highest in Pi and Alpha groups, plus the top four girls from Psi, will be declared winners. The combined ten winners from all three groups will comprise the list of semifinalists."

Sue paused, giving her audience a few minutes to digest her arithmetic.

"In other words," she went on, "to place in the semifinals you have to beat only fourteen girls if you're in either of the first two groups. And only twelve if you're one of the fortunate sixteen in Psi. That's a lot easier than having to beat *forty* other contestants. Your chaperones will now tell you which group you're in."

Stacy saw Miss Florida's chaperone smile and say, "Good news, Robin. You're in Psi. The only real competition in your group is Miss New Jersey, so I think you'll be a shoo-in."

Stacy herself was in Alpha.

"That about wraps it up," Sue said. "Now, if anyone has a question, I'll be glad to answer it. Just stand up and wait for one of the floor ushers to come over with a traveling mike."

The first question came from Miss Louisiana, a flaxen-haired girl whose voice, surprisingly, was completely devoid of any Southern tinge.

"Miss Rossiter," she said, "I had originally planned to do a two-and-a-half-minute monologue because I was under the impression a Teleprompter would be handy. If I come up now with a recitation that's real short, won't the judges think I'm a dumb bunny with a poor memory?"

"Nonsense, my dear," answered Sue. "Shakespeare said brevity is the soul of wit. But if it will make you feel better, let me remind you that in nineteen sixty-three the girl who won the crown gave a simple ninety-second speech. It was Lincoln's Gettysburg Address."

"Thank you,' said Louisiana and sat down. She leaned

toward her chaperone. "Can you imagine *me* reciting Lincoln?" she whispered. "Pappy would disinherit me!"

Michigan had the floor now. "Miss Rossiter, as you probably know from my fact sheet, my talent specialty will be a native sword dance. It would be much more dramatic if I could do it with a flaming sword. Would it be possible for me to have a source of fire onstage—at least three fire kettles?"

"Last year we accommodated one girl who required an ice rink for her figure-skating act and another who needed a trapeze. So I imagine getting you the fire props you need should be no problem," Sue replied. "Just have your chaperone call Olga Loomis, my secretary. Olga will fix it with Surf City's fire commissioner and you'll be all set."

Sue Rossiter glanced at her watch. "Well, kids, I guess that about wraps it up. Now if there are no more questions . . ."

"Just a moment, please. *I* have a question. A *very* important question."

Stacy couldn't believe her ears. The magnified voice crashing across the vast hall was her mother's. Mama had seized the traveling mike from a passing usher. Looking up, Stacy could see that she clenched the instrument in her hand as though it were a live grenade.

Mama paused until Sue Rossiter gave her a faint nod of recognition, then she said, "Miss Rossiter, I have heard rumors of an unwritten Pageant rule that prohibits the same state from winning the crown two years in a row. Does this tradition mean that my daughter, Stacy DeGray, can't possibly win this year because she's the current Miss California and California won last year?"

Good God, thought Stacy. Sue Rossiter reacted as though she had been turned to stone by the head of the Medusa. Roger Megan, imperturbable, miraculously appeared at Sue Rossiter's side and deftly relieved her of her mike.

"I've been with the Pageant ever since its first year," he said, "so I think I can answer your question better than Sue," Megan said. His voice was sincere, confidential. "Frankly, Mrs. DeGray, the hypothetical situation you describe has never come up in any of the past twelve contests. I can only point out that Luise Rainer won a Hollywood Oscar two years in a row, in nineteen thirty-six and ninteen thirty-seven. Spencer Tracy also copped two consecutive Oscars, in thirty-seven and thirty-eight."

Then, smiling wide-screen so that the orthodontic triumph that were his teeth gained full exposure, Megan went on, preserving his studiously careless style.

"I'm certain that if the Academy of Arts and Sciences can award the same person Oscars back to back, the Pageant can act similarly in the case of two states."

Megan bowed slightly, trying not to look like a pilot who has just narrowly avoided a collision, and returned the mike to Sue Rossiter. Her composure regained, Sue was back in business, cool and assured.

"Immediately after you leave here, girls, Alpha Group will go to Max Gerber's studio to pose for official photographs," she announced. "Pi group will report to our stage-deportment coach for instruction in posture. And Psi Group will head for the dispensary for their routine physical check-ups. Your chaperones will escort you to your appointments."

The lights blinked on and off, signifying the end of the session. Chairs scraped as the girls stood up, joined their chaperones. Stacy got up and began pulling down the edges of her swimsuit, when she felt a strong grip on her arm. Mama.

"Stacy, quick. Look over to the stage. Megan's just walked over to Rossiter. Get a fix on them."

Stacy turned and looked at Megan's lips. A whispered replay echoed from her own lips an instant later.

"Well, Sue doll, did I brainwash the old bag or not? And how do you like the way I remembered those Academy Award dates?"

Stacy shifted her gaze to Sue Rossiter.

"Roger, you may have put over the greatest snow job since the blizzard of eighty-eight—but something tells me that DeGray bitch is going to give us trouble—big trouble."

"So, Mother, that's the way it really is," said Stacy. "But maybe I can end up winning second place. That's not so bad." She turned to go. Mrs. Latham was waiting, and she was worried that their conversation was being overheard.

But Mrs. DeGray held onto her daughter's arm with a bear-trap tenacity.

"*My* Stacy isn't going to settle for Number Two. You're going to listen to your mother. I'm not going to let them shunt you off like an empty freight car on a siding."

"Mother, there's nothing at all you can—"

"We're not going to swallow their 'Yes, Virginia, there is a Santa Claus' crap. I'm going to blast this wide open. I'm going to let the whole world know that the Pageant plays with loaded dice!"

13 · DR. FRANZ LYDECKER

IT was a pleasant office, one that reflected the man rather than the profession. There were, naturally, gilt-lettered diplomas and certificates, laminated and gold-edged, to attest that Franz Lydecker was, indeed, a doctor of medicine, a fellow of the College of Surgeons and a member in good standing of the American Medical Association, to say nothing of honorary status in both the fire and police departments of Surf City.

But there was more because there was more to Franz Lydecker. Much more.

From the brightness of the green-tinted fruitwood paneled walls to the chipped, memento-clogged walnut desk that commanded the airy room, it was first an office of character and only secondly that of a man of medicine.

It was a room devoid of the smell of antiseptic, one that seemed to deny the existence of human ills. And the warmth of the office, its humanism, permeated the entire complex of rooms that was the suite of Surf City's honorary Surgeon General, somehow breathing life into the white porcelain and stainless steel of the examining rooms, and stripping the awe and mystery from the array of diagnostic paraphernalia without which no doctor's office would be complete.

Those who entered the office were always struck by the anomaly. This was not a place of sickness and death; it was a place of health and life. And they rarely, if ever, saw Lydecker's pedigrees hanging on the cheerful walls. They saw instead an incredible collection of beautiful women who gazed fondly from a score of intimately inscribed photographs. They were women of parted, rich lips, whiter-than-white teeth, flawless complexions and enviable cleavage whose faces were known to a generation of movie fans.

'Franz," said one inscription, "you have the coldest hands. All my love, Mona." And another from an Oscar winner: "To the man who rearranged 20 pounds and lifted me from the chorus to stardom. Ever grateful, Tracy." And more, clever words, sincere words, but always words of endearment. Lydecker was loved if not for himself at least for his talents by a group of females that would satiate a sultan and utterly destroy a lesser man.

The subject of this outpouring of devotion now sat behind the walnut desk, a small, baldish man in his mid-fifties, slight to the point of frailness, his slender surgeon's fingers toying with a six-inch replica of an Oscar, a paperweight that was part of the Hollywood memorabilia engulfing the desk. Marilyn Monroe had giggled when she first met Lydecker. "I bet you weigh less than that whatsathing—the stethoscope," she had said.

Between a bronzed bootie Lydecker had received from a star he had coaxed through a pregnancy and a framed letter from Zsa Zsa Gabor written in Hungarian, there was a small ticket from a penny-weight scale. Marilyn had sent it to Lydecker to prove she had held to his diet.

But Dr. Lydecker saw none of this as he rubbed his long fingers over the small statue. Hollywood was behind him. The future was uncertain. There was only now, and now was the Princess America Pageant. In his semiretirement, the Pageant was Lydecker's main endeavor. And now, even that was coming to an end. He thought about that with sadness. Lately, he was thinking about everything with sadness. The curse of age, he thought. Tomorrow comes, but it brings no surprises.

Lydecker put the paperweight down and checked his watch. If John Fleming was right—and he usually was—Dr. Bernstein would arrive at the precise moment of his appointment, which would be within thirty seconds. Lydecker was not surprised when the door opened exactly on time.

"Dr. Lydecker?"

"Yes. Yes, Dr. Bernstein. Come in, please." There was a trace of an accent—German, if you listened closely.

Lydecker rose and motioned the younger man to a comfortable leather chair. "Please sit down and tell me about yourself. We have a half hour before we begin to examine the merchandise." Lydecker's pale-blue eyes watched for a reaction to his flippancy. There was none. He decided the man had no sense of humor.

A frustrated accountant, thought Lydecker. He probably writes his prescriptions with a fine-point pen in very neat, legible letters.

Actually, Dr. Scott Bernstein did look like an accountant, and he did write neat prescriptions. At forty-six, his hair was thin, his middle thick and his brown eyes seemed sharp behind his rimless glasses. He was married, had a son in the Army and no bad habits. Fleming had checked him out with his customary thoroughness. Bernstein was also a good doctor, but that had been secondary.

"My professional background," Bernstein began, but he was interrupted by Lydecker.

"I'm sure it's excellent," he said, sitting again, his fingers linked below his chin. "Perhaps I should fill you in first. We will begin this afternoon. It should take about two days."

"I see," said Bernstein, attentive.

"The examinations are routine but complete," Lydecker explained. "Routine except the ladies are the flowers of our land. Our job is to remove the thorns."

"I don't think I quite understand, sir."

"For God's sake, don't call me sir," Lydecker snapped, surprised at his own reaction. The curse of age, he thought again. Relax. "Look, Dr. Bernstein. Let's relax. We are not here to solve the ills of the world. I don't say it is all fun and games, but it is only a contest. An important contest, granted. But still a contest."

"I'm sorry . . ."

"Please," said Lydecker, waving aside the proffered apology. "I realize the Old Man—Mr. Fleming—has given you to believe this is all very serious. It is. But I am not a man who stands on formality. I run, so to speak, a loose ship. Now, why don't I call you—Scott, is it?—and you call me Franz and we will get along."

"Yes. Of course." Bernstein was flustered. Fleming had led him to believe that to crack a smile would be criminal, and now this little man—what had the *Life* magazine article called him, Doctor of Hollywood?—was reversing the field. It was confusing.

"Why did you take the job?" Lydecker asked, leaning back in his chair, stretching his shoulders to ease the slight tightness, the vague pressure he felt in his sternum region. "The money? The publicity?"

"Actually," said Bernstein, "I took it to meet you, to work with you for a few days. Cosmetic surgery has become the better part of my practice. Your reputation in this field is most impressive."

"Thank you," Lydecker said, flattered. "But *was* would be a better word. For all intents and purposes, I retired four years ago. When my wife and I left Beverly Hills, I became just another semiretired general practitioner. This seemed an ideal location. We winter in Southern California. These offices are primarily for the Pageant. I see a few patients—the Mayor, Frank Collins, who runs the bank, a few."

"Still, you almost wrote the book," Bernstein said. "I hope we can discuss some techniques between examinations."

"Naturally, Scott. It would be my pleasure." Lydecker laughed. "Some of my best work is right here on the walls. Behind you there, the top photograph. Would you believe she was ever absolutely—and I mean absolutely—flat-chested?"

Bernstein rose and studied the photograph. The cleavage was phenomenal. "I would have been a bust without you," it read. Bernstein laughed for the first time. "I never would have guessed," he said, moving to another photograph. "What does she mean by cold hands?" he asked over his shoulder.

"A vaginal condition," Lydecker said.

Bernstein turned. "You had your hand in that?"

"I'm afraid so."

"May I shake your hand, Franz? I'd like to be able to tell the boys at the club that I shook the hand that . . ."

Lydecker laughed and got up to shake Bernstein's hand. The man had a sense of humor after all, he thought. "The Old Man is formidable, isn't he?" Lydecker said, walking to the window and looking out over Surf City, his home now, his own little city.

"Mr. Fleming?"

Lydecker nodded, absently watching the traffic moving two floors below. "Formidable is the word. I couldn't swear to it, but I believe he even had my telephone tapped."

Lydecker smiled to himself and nodded again. He remembered well his first meeting with Fleming, back in that first year, back when beauty contests were anything but legitimate, back when they were still carnival promotions to titillate the suckers. But Fleming had a dream about the American Girl, a national elimination series that would result in the selection of *the* American Girl.

Lydecker had thought the Old Man was crazy. But he had listened, and the more Fleming had talked, the more he had warmed to the idea.

Fleming had said, "But we can't have some goddamned Bolshevik or a scarlet woman winning the contest! Christ, we'd be dead. That's why I need you, Franz. I can get people to check them out politically, but I need someone who knows the female form inside and out to make sure some harlot or rebuilt wallflower doesn't slip through."

And Lydecker had agreed. It was a refreshing idea, a truly natural beauty. He had adjusted so many noses, inflated so many breasts, smoothed out so many wrinkles, pulled up so many sagging necks that the thought of a woman in perfect shape without the aid of surgery or crash diets had intrigued him.

"You can't blame the Old Man for being careful," Lydecker said, leaving the window and walking back to his cluttered desk. "Our first year was a nightmare. Almost half the contestants in the state preliminaries were professional hookers. Others had had abortions. We had a helluva time finding twenty out of forty-eight that were pure and simple enough for the finals."

"I see what you mean," said Bernstein. He pulled out a pipe and lit it.

"I wonder if you do," Lydecker said, seated again, his hands locked. "Spotting the out-and-out call girls was relatively simple; we have an efficient vice squad. But there were the addicts, the weirdies and the syphilitics. Some days this office was a regular clap shack."

"Fascinating," said Bernstein, drawing on his pipe.

"I remember one girl—from some Southern state, I think—who had scars from cigarette burns from her navel right up to her breasts. She claimed it was the only way she could reach orgasm. We even discovered an hermaphrodite and two lesbians in that first crop."

"Fascinating," repeated Bernstein. "I'm surprised the Pageant survived."

"It was touch and go for the first couple of years," Lydecker said. "It was Sue Rossiter who pulled us through. She was beautiful, brainy and talented. After that we got a better class of females. The Princess America Pageant was finally legitimate. We still get some strange ones, but now it's primarily cosmetic surgery or silicone-inflated breasts or some undetected disease. The job has actually become more difficult through the years. But we can't have a Princess America who is a diabetic or on the verge of TB or is slightly deaf. Can you imagine a winner who has to wear a hearing aid?"

"Mr. Fleming said something about a marking system," Bernstein said. "He told me you'd explain it more fully."

"Yes," said Lydecker, rising. "Come into the examining rooms. We have a few moments before our roses arrive, thorns and all."

Bernstein tapped out his pipe in a stand ashtray and

followed the older man into the brightness of the main examining room, off which were several cubicles behind drawn curtains. Still, it was not hospital cold. There was a pot of coffee bubbling on an electric hotplate in one corner, and a stocky woman in a starched white nurse's uniform was half sitting on one of the paper-covered brown leather examining couches. She was casually smoking a cigarette and drinking a cup of coffee.

"This creature is our nurse, Mrs. Bruning—Maggie to her friends," Lydecker said, smiling. "She is absolutely worthless. She is here simply to reassure the girls. Maggie, meet Dr. Scott Bernstein, my successor in this pot of flesh."

"Welcome to Squeezer's Palace," Maggie said, waving an arm. "Franz has been telling me for years that he is looking for telltale lumps or something, but it's a cover. He's actually a dirty old man."

Lydecker laughed and broke a packet of Sanka coffee into a cup of hot water. "Maggie doesn't understand medical detachment," he said. "Have some coffee, Scott, and try to ignore her." Bernstein nodded hello to Mrs. Bruning and poured himself a cup of coffee.

"Maggie, get me the list of contestants and the Mad Mail file," Lydecker said. "I want to explain the devious ways of pageantry to Scott before the girls arrive."

Mrs. Bruning went to a steel file cabinet near one of the windows and returned with two Manila folders, one thin, the other fat with paper.

"Here we have a list of all fifty contestants," Lydecker explained, opening the thin folder. Bernstein looked on with interest, waiting for his coffee to cool. "You will notice there is a box next to each name. If we discover anything that is seriously wrong with the contestant, a black mark is placed in the appropriate box. There is another such list in the hands of the Pageant's private investigators. A black mark next to a girl's name on either list means she is automatically disqualified."

"But what if the judges should pick one of the girls who has been blackballed?" Bernstein questioned.

"Our mechanics for such a situation are simple," Lydecker cut in.

"The two lists go to the chief auditor who tallies the judges' score cards. If one of the contestants who has been black-marked should be the winner, the auditor simply goes on to the next girl in the scoring and the next, if necessary, until an acceptable winner emerges."

Bernstein frowned. "I see that Mr. Fleming runs things with the thoroughness of the Gestapo."

Lydecker put the folder down and picked up the thicker one. "This," he said to Bernstein, "is the Mad Mail. It is our idiot fringe. We have letters from almost every state concerning the contestants. Most are utterly ridiculous, but some require checking."

He thumbed through the mass of letters. "Here is a reasonable letter that says Miss Idaho has had an abortion. We will check that out the best we can. And here is another that names a doctor who is supposed to have given silicone injections to Miss Nevada to enlarge her breasts. And here . . ."

"From whom do these come, these allegations?" Bernstein interrupted.

"From sore losers in the state contests," Lydecker answered. "From jilted lovers, from boy friends who don't want their girls to become too big for them, from cranks, from old biddies and from relatives of finalists who think they can cut down some of the opposition. And from one old lady here in Surf City who writes anonymous letters to us every year concerning ten or fifteen of the girls."

"Who reads them all?"

"The Old Man has a screening committee," Lydecker explained. "Those containing medical charges are passed along to me. For next year's Pageant they'll go to you. Some of the letters are so obviously wild I weed them out immediately. We are usually left with twenty or so that require further medical checking. Ninety-nine percent of the time it's a wild-goose chase. Still, even if it leads us to only one girl who would have otherwise escaped detection, the system is worthwhile. In nineteen sixty-seven for instance, we checked out drug charges against Miss South Carolina and found that she had been treated two years before for an overdose of heroin."

"She was blackballed, I take it," said Bernstein.

"She was. Our winner must reign for a year. If anything like that were to be exposed during her term, the entire Pageant would be demolished." Lydecker closed the folder. "Maggie, see if our lambs have arrived yet. If they have, bring in the first two."

In the adjacent hallway, Stacy DeGray stood at the head of the line watching as Mrs. Rawlins, a senior chaperone, stamped up and down chirping encouragement, wondering as she waited if there was a way of detecting marijuana. She had heard there wasn't, but she couldn't be sure. A telltale sign in the blood? The eyes? *Oh, please . . .*

Maggie opened the office door and told Mrs. Rawlins to

send in the first two. Stacy stiffened, feeling her skin crawl under the swimsuit she and the other contestants still wore. But she moved in through the office on command, she and Marie Somebody who was Miss North Dakota. She recognized Dr. Lydecker but not the other man.

"Just follow Mrs. Bruning," Lydecker said, indicating the nurse. "She will take your histories and give you instructions."

Stacy followed Mrs. Bruning into one of the cubicles. She was handed a white knee-length linen gown.

"Take off your suit and put this on," said Mrs. Bruning, drawing the curtain. Stacy did as she was told, biting her lower lip, wondering, worrying, toying with an insane impulse to run from the office, never to return. But Mrs. Bruning was back, ducking under the curtain, a folder containing medical chart forms in her hand.

"Now," said Mrs. Bruning, "did you have any childhood diseases—measles, chicken pox?" She droned on and Stacy answered the questions mechanically. No, never, she lied. No operations. *Drugs?* No, of course not. Only aspirin or an antibiotic now and then. *Did I say that too quickly? Was it too pat?* The questions continued. *No, it's all right.*

Stacy walked through the rest as though in a dream. X-ray of the chest. Blood from a pin prick on the end of her finger. More blood from her arm, enough to fill a small vial. "We're giving you everything but a saliva test, my dear." Stacy laughed—a flat, humorless laugh.

Then Lydecker was in the cubicle with the other one.

"I'm Dr. Lydecker and this is Dr. Bernstein."

Involuntarily, Stacy pulled her gown tighter to ber body.

"Now, if you will lie on the table," said Lydecker, "we can proceed. You will not have to remove your gown."

Stacy climbed onto the examining table and lay on her back, smoothing the gown over her knees. The two men began to probe and squeeze and feel. Stacy felt like a side of prime beef being tested for fat content and tenderness. Then she was up again to read the eye chart, to follow the tuning fork with each ear, to breathe deeply as the younger man slipped the ice cube end of a stethoscope under her gown and listened intently at the other end.

"Fine," said Bernstein. "That will be all, young lady. You can dress now and send in the next girl on your way out."

Bernstein stepped from the cubicle with Lydecker just as Miss North Dakota was leaving. She smiled brightly at both men and went out through the office.

"Charming girls," said Bernstein.

Lydecker regarded him indulgently, almost patronizingly. "When you have been at this as long as I have, they all begin to look the same. There is a certain boredom in perfection. I think I would rejoice if a truly plain Jane somehow got into the finals."

"If the other forty-eight are anything like these two, I doubt if that will ever happen," Bernstein said, unzippering his tobacco pouch to refill his pipe.

"Oh, it won't happen," Lydecker exclaimed. "But we all have our little dreams. By the way, did you notice anything about our Miss California?"

"Her blood pressure was slightly elevated."

"No, I don't mean the workup on her," Lydecker said. "I mean her attitude. She looked edgy. She seemed to be deathly afraid we would find something."

"I suppose they are all somewhat nervous," Bernstein responded. "I've rarely seen anyone quite at ease during an examination. And here these girls have a lot at stake. I'm sure they suspect they can be disqualified for physical reasons."

"True," Lydecker said, rubbing his chin. "But there are nuances you begin to recognize that don't seem to fit the pattern. Still, she checked out okay. Perhaps I'm just getting old and suspicious." He watched Stacy leave.

Mrs. Bruning led in two more contestants and disappeared into the examining cubicle with one. When she emerged, Lydecker motioned to Bernstein and the two men went in together. Lydecker made the introductions and started the examination while Bernstein looked on. Lydecker was about to probe the girl's breasts when she sat bolt upright and covered her chest with one arm.

Lydecker, surprised by the sudden movement, jumped back a step. "Miss, I can assure you this is routine, it is . . ."

"No, Doctor, it's not that," said the raven-haired beauty who was Miss Wisconsin. "It's just that . . . well . . . I don't have a nipple."

"Is that all?" said Lydecker, vastly relieved. "Well, inverted nipples are not so strange, you know. Many women—"

"No, I don't mean that, Doctor. What I mean is that . . . what I mean is that I only have one . . . just one . . . I mean, the other one is not there at all."

"I don't think I quite understand," said Lydecker, puzzled. Bernstein followed the conversation with fascination.

"I don't know how to explain this," said Miss Wisconsin, embarrassed.

"How . . . ?"

"Reckless necking, I guess you could call it," the girl blurted out. "It was bitten off by a boy." Her head shifted from doctor to doctor in search of an understanding eye. Lydecker fought to keep his face straight. Bernstein didn't know quite what to do. "It was in a car," Miss Wisconsin rushed on, "We were making out and this other car came along and we didn't have the lights on or anything and he banged right into us. Ernie—he's my fiancé—got thrown forward and he just bit it off." She paused. "Does this disqualify me?"

Lydecker smiled reassuringly. "I'm glad you told me, but I wouldn't worry. We require no nudity. Your secret will remain your own. Now lie back and relax while we finish the examination."

"Oh, thank you, Doctor." There were tears in the girl's eyes.

When the two doctors emerged, Bernstein picked up the check list and said, "I suppose that is our first black mark?"

"On the contrary," Lydecker said. "It was such a refreshing confession that I hope the girl does well. A missing nipple is the least of her worries. Besides, she has another one. No, Scott. As long as she doesn't have to show her nipples to the audience, she needn't be disqualified."

"I see I have a few things to learn."

"If you have anything to learn, Scott, it is to be prepared for the unexpected. Three—no, four—years ago I was examining one contestant and discovered, to my great surprise, that she had the name 'Jerry' tattooed on both breasts just below the areolas. She said her fiancé insisted and that she loved him enough to have it done. She begged me to give her a vaginal to prove she was still a virgin. I was tempted to give her a black mark for stupidity, but that is not what we are here for. Had the tattoos been above the aereolas where they might have been seen, I would have flunked her. But they weren't. As I recall, she scored the highest in the talent competition for a trampoline act."

Bernstein laughed uproariously.

Lydecker decided he liked his new replacement.

For the next three hours an enchanting parade of striking young women marched in and out of the cubicles. In that time, five black marks were placed on the tally sheet. Bernstein checked on a Mad Mail letter accusing one girl of having a rebuilt nose. The charge was confirmed when Lydecker examined her and observed the scar tissue inside her nostrils. Miss Idaho displayed a midline pfannstick incision on her stomach, which she claimed had been caused by the removal of an ovarian cyst. Out of the Mad Mail folder came the letter that alleged the girl had had a Caesarean operation, with the name of the attending physician. After a discreet long-distance phone call, placed by Maggie, the Mad Mail had claimed its second victim.

A heart murmur cut down Miss Illinois ("We can't take the chance of Princess America dropping dead on us") and the spongy masses Lydecker's experienced hands felt in the breasts of Miss Kansas could only be the result of silicone injections to enlarge them.

"American women have a breast fetish," Lydecker told Bernstein during a brief respite. "Everything from silicone shots to padded bras and even Scotch tape strategically placed are employed. But Princess America has never been top-heavy, probably never will."

The fifth black mark went next to the name of Miss Arkansas, whose blood pressure read 140 systolic and 70 diastolic and led to a confession that she used amphetamines.

Two of the contestants were singled out for further checking, one who displayed Babinsky's sign, the absence of a reflex action when a needle was scratched along her abdomen, one of the neurological symptoms of the multiple-sclerosis syndrome, the other as a possible diabetic when Lydecker's ophthalmoscope discovered yellowish granules in the fundus of her eyes.

Miss New Jersey, a gorgeous smile glued to her face, sailed through her examination with flying colors. "Will I live, Doctor?" she asked in mock seriousness after he had squeezed her ample breasts. And Bernstein said he should live so long.

In the hallway, Mrs. Rawlins was still treading about, funneling the girls in and out of the office, passing them along to the other chaperones when the examinations were finished. She was down to her last charge for the afternoon—Miss Alaska.

"Cheer up, Millie," Mrs. Rawlins encouraged. "You look as though you are about to be swallowed up alive by some monster." She patted the girl's cheek and waved her into the office.

Mildred Waxman felt naked without her scarf, naked and exposed. She had spent half an hour before her mirror this morning, carefully applying layers of Hide-a-

Mark. Now she would give her right arm for a mirror. Was it still perfectly blended with the natural skin tones? Was it smooth? Would it stand up to searching fingers if they should feel for glands in her throat?

Mildred walked through the outer office without seeing, without feeling. She wondered for the hundredth time why she had let it go this far, why she hadn't told them long before she came to Surf City, where they were all beautiful and perfect beyond belief.

Mildred followed the nurse into the cubicle and accepted the linen gown. She removed her bathing suit and slipped into the loosely fitting gown which came to her collarbone and would go no higher. She answered the questions in a monotone, low and disinterested. Several times Mrs. Bruning had to repeat the questions and strain to hear the answers.

Then she was gone and the curtain moved aside. "I'm Dr. Lydecker," the small man said. "And this is Dr. Bernstein."

"I'm Mildred Waxman."

"Ah, yes. Miss Alaska," Lydecker greeted her warmly.

Bernstein was pleasantly surprised. Here was, of all things, a Jewish girl—from Alaska, of all places. And a finalist. Could she win? She was beautiful, of course. But obviously Jewish. He wondered if there wasn't a list somewhere that had a little black mark next to Miss Alaska's name because she wasn't of the right ethnic stock. From what he had learned so far, there probably was such a list. No, he was being too touchy, too Jewish. He smiled at Mildred.

Mildred returned the smile, a tentative, quick smile, her right hand resting at her throat without touching it, a natural feminine pose which she now thought unnatural and suspicious.

The examination proceeded. Mildred sleep-walked through it, lying down, standing up, breathing deeply, listening, reading the eye chart, being probed and tested. At one point she quietly died as the small man with the kind eyes reached for her throat. But his hand went directly under her chin, the fingers pressing, feeling, but never touching the marred area below. She opened her eyes and began to breathe again.

The little man instructed the other doctor to go out and check some X-ray plates. Then he turned to her and said she could dress, it was over.

Lydecker watched the girl and got the feeling again that something was not quite right. She looked panic-stricken. Why? Had he missed something? Waxman. She was Jewish. Did all Jews carry this haunted, hunted look?

Lydecker had left Germany before World War II, and before Hitler's "Final Solution." Personally, he knew himself innocent of the blood of the murdered Jews. But he could never quite repress a guilty sympathy for anyone Jewish. He was, after all, a German.

No, thought Lydecker. It's my imagination again, Bernstein is perfectly at ease. So are the others, the stars who changed their names, the studio executives, the summer people here in Surf City.

"Doctor?" Mildred was sitting on the edge of the examining table, her hand still resting at the base of her throat.

"Yes?"

"Doctor, I must talk to you—talk to someone." She had to get it done, to get it out, purge herself. He had a kind face—the eyes, like her father's. She felt the hot tears run over her cheeks. "Doctor, I've got to tell you something, but I can't . . ."

Lydecker moved forward, gently taking the girl's arms. "Come now, my dear. Pull yourself together."

Mildred began to sob uncontrollably, her shoulders slumped, her hands raised to half cover her face, the tears now running down between her fingers.

"There, there, Miss Waxman," he said softly. "Tell me what your trouble is. Easy now. Tell me about it. He patted her shoulders, then tucked a finger under her chin and lifted her face, wet, frightened, pleading eyes that averted his.

"I don't belong here," Mildred sobbed. "I'm a fake."

"You are a very beautiful *fraulein,*" Lydecker said softly, unconsciously lapsing into his native tongue. "I don't see . . ."

"Here!" shouted Mildred hysterically, throwing back her head and clawing at her throat. Her nails dug into the covering salve, scraping away patches of it, baring streaks of the black-speckled scar. "Here, Doctor! See for yourself!"

Lydecker stared sympathetically at Mildred's blemished throat. He took her hand and tenderly pulled it away from her neck. He felt her go limp. The sobbing stopped abruptly. She was quiet.

"How long have you had this?"

Mildred looked Lydecker full in the eyes. "Does it matter?" Her voice was composed now. The moment of hysteria had passed and she was emotionally spent. Now, for the first time since it all began, she felt at ease, relaxed.

Lydecker's voice was soothing. "How did it happen?"

"I was in Israel on a visit. There was a bombing . . ."

Lydecker tried to shake the fullness in his chest. He moved Mildred's chin aside and examined the mottled skin. "This cosmetic," he said, his voice still calm, reassuring. "Is it Hide-a-Mark?"

"Yes, Doctor."

Lydecker straightened. "Sit here. I think I have some in my office. Don't move. I'll be right back." He patted her shoulders and left her alone.

Lydecker walked over to a glass cabinet and inspected the shelves, heedless of the growing pressure in his chest, ignoring the distress radiating to his left shoulder.

He found the jar and returned to the cubicle. Bernstein was already there, looking at him questioningly, indicating the exposed portions of Mildred's scar.

"Scott, get me a mirror, please," Lydecker ordered, uncapping the jar. Bernstein, a quizzical expression on his face, did as he was told. Lydecker handed the opened jar to Mildred. "Take this and repair your neck." He turned as Bernstein re-entered with a hand mirror. "Take the mirror. We will wait outside."

Lydecker motioned to Bernstein and the younger doctor followed him out, leaving Mildred alone. She began to cry again, softly, but she moved with practiced ease, holding the mirror in her left hand, applying the Hide-a-Mark with her right.

Outside, Bernstein packed his pipe again and said to Lydecker, "How did you find that? I would never have known."

"Nor would I," Lydecker answered absently. "She told me, showed me. I would never have spotted it." He paused and took a deep breath, fighting the mounting pressure in his chest.

"Are you all right, Franz?" Bernstein's voice was grave.

"It will pass," Lydecker said, extracting a vial of amyl nitrite from his pocket, breaking it and bringing it up to his nose. He breathed deeply and then threw the crushed vial into a wastebasket. "There," he said. "I'm quite all right now."

Mildred came out of the cubicle presently, wearing her swimsuit. Her neck showed no hint of a blemish. Her eyes were dry, her face bright. She handed the jar to Lydecker and opened her mouth to speak.

Lydecker cut her short. "That will be all, Miss

Waxman. I want you to forget everything that happened in there. Do not discuss it with anyone—not even with your chaperone."

"But, Doctor . . ."

"Please, Miss Waxman, do as I say." Lydecker smiled at her. "And good luck to you."

Mildred stood silently for a moment, then turned and walked out through the office and into the birdlike clutches of Mrs. Rawlins. And for the first time in Surf City, Mildred felt as though she belonged.

Bernstein watched her leave, then turned to Lydecker, waiting for him to pick up the check list and make the sixth black mark of the afternoon. Lydecker stood still for some time, his eyes focused somewhere in the middle distance, looking at nothing, apparently deep in thought. When he finally did move, it was not for the check list but for another cup of Sanka.

"Have a cup of coffee, Scott," he said over his shoulder. "That's it for today. Tomorrow we get more lambs. We can talk now if you'd like."

"Yes, that would be fine," answered Bernstein, not moving. "But shouldn't we put a mark next to the Waxman kid's name? I mean . . ."

"I know what you mean," Lydecker said, stirring his coffee with an oral thermometer and, from long habit, checking its temperature. "But Miss Waxman is not to get a black mark."

Bernstein was perplexed. "But, Franz, that thing on her neck. If she were to win and something like that was discovered, wouldn't it hurt the Pageant? The girls are supposed to be flawless."

Lydecker sipped his coffee. "Scott, I love this Pageant. I've heard Megan sing 'Good Luck, Sweet Princess' twelve years running. But for once I'm going to put the girl before the Pageant. Anyway, her chances of winning are as slim as my making twenty consecutive passes at a Vegas crap table. But however slim her chances, I want her to have them."

Lydecker saw the surprise in Bernstein's face and continued: "Scott, let's just say an old man is paying a debt. Next year you will do it your way. But for now I will make the decisions. Have your coffee and we will talk."

In her chair, Maggie smiled. She would miss Lydecker. She would miss him very much.

Bernstein carried himself robotlike to the hotplate and poured himself a cup of coffee. He was confused but resigned. He liked the girl himself. But Lydecker. It was strange. Perhaps a Jewish girl could win. He decided he had a lot to learn.

And behind Bernstein, Lydecker drank his Sanka and smiled to himself.

14 · MISS UTAH

STRICTLY CONFIDENTIAL.

The words were stamped diagonally in red across the face of the envelope. Curious, Lori Macklin separated it from the rest of her late mail. A stack of it had been delivered to her motel door while she and Colorado had been having dinner with some Surf City aldermen and their wives.

The envelope itself was of thick, expensive stock. The engraved return address in the upper left-hand corner was impressive: *American Institute for Psycho-Physical Behavior, United Nations Plaza, New York City, New York.*

The letters she had already skimmed were mainly good-luck messages, most of them bearing Utah postmarks. Friends from her home town, Bountiful. College kids in Provo. Total strangers in Devils Slide and Hurricane and Oasis. Everybody in the state wanted Miss Utah to know they were backing her. *We'll be rooting for you, Lori, all this week . . .*

There were gifts as well. One was a link bracelet dripping gold-plated disks embossed with the dates and places of all the preliminary contests she had won in her triumphant march to Surf City. It had been sent by the members of her college sorority, Tau Beta Tau, and she wore it proudly now. It jangled as she tapped the envelope.

Strictly confidential? Intrigued, she slipped her nail file under the sealed flap. She drew out a blue four-page printed form and a covering letter. The two names on the letterhead rang a bell of recognition. Dr. Elmer McQueen, Chairman. Prof. Frank Mulholland, Director of Research. Of course! The pair was compiling that upcoming and much publicized Mulholland–McQueen Report. It was going to be a superintimate, clinical report on Sex in America, the hottest thing since Kinsey. The team had been working on it for six years. Lori felt a new tingle of interest.

Dear Miss Macklin:
We are writing to you and to each of the other state representatives in the Princess America Pageant in the hope that you will cooperate with us on an important sociological project. Your replies to the accompanying queries will be of special value to the Mulholland–McQueen report. This study is intended as a definitive assessment of the sexual mores of young America in this generation. As such . . .

There was more, explaining the need for candor and honesty. If you were a scientist, you could lift up anybody's bed sheets and peek under them for an eyeful. For this, they would call you dedicated, brilliant, and award you a foundation grant. Crap! Her glance slipped down to the final brief paragraph:

You may rest assured that your replies will be held in utmost confidence. You are not required to sign this questionnaire; nor will even our statisticians be aware of your identity. Therefore, complete frankness is possible. It is the Institute's earnest hope . . .

A small grin began to form at the corners of Lori's lips. Then they pursed mischievously. She spread the folder flat on her lap and bent above it. Each query had a blank space under it for the subject's answer. She browsed through the paragraphs rapidly, checking the range of questions. No birds-and-bees quiz, this. Presently she rose, crossed to the small desk and picked up a ballpoint pen.

Well now, gentlemen. This is going to be a gas! Don't fail to quote me when you make your lecture tours.

It took almost half an hour, but when she had finished she reread her answers with pure satisfaction. This entry ought to blow a fuse in their computers at the pious institute on United Nations Plaza!

Still deep in appreciation of her deviltry, Lori stuffed the folder into the permit-stamped, self-addressed envelope sent by the institute. Running her tongue across the flap, she tasted a faint spearmint flavor but no adhesive. The flap came loose, lazily lifting almost as soon as she tried to press it fast. She made a face, tossed the envelope into a tray on the bureau. Later, when Josephina came by to do her night chores, she'd ask her to Scotch-tape it and deposit it in the lobby mailbox.

She was debating whether first to shower or study her lines when the bedside phone tinkled softly. She picked it up slowly, with the slim, wild hope that the caller might be Steve Dorn.

"Lori? Guess who?"

"Marge Macklin! Of all people! Sis, where are you?"

"Right here in Surf City, honey. At the Regency Hotel up on the boardwalk. I'm on the same floor as Miss Alaska and Miss Hawaii."

"But how did you get here? How long are you—"

"My jet from Rio hit Kennedy at noon. I hitched a local prop flight directly here. I racked up double flight hours last month, so there's time coming to me. Told them I was taking it and they'd have to find themselves some other stewardess until Sunday. I'm sticking here till the Pageant's over."

"Then you'll be around to let me cry on your shoulders when I lose?"

"I'll be here to yell 'Bravo' when you win, silly. How are they treating you?"

"Okay, I guess. Nothing much has happened, really. It's only Monday. We had a briefing from Sue Rossiter at lunch."

There was a pause at the other end. Then: "Lori, you've been . . . behaving since last time I was home?"

"No choice. We have to be saints. And just when I need men like Dr. Barnard needs hearts. Marge, you wouldn't believe this Pageant."

"Lori! Be careful. What if they have your line tapped?"

"Who cares? They keep us all but locked up. Talk about security. Our hotels and motels are like barbed-wire compounds. Bastilles. They practically watch over every pubic hair on all of us."

"Just thank your stars they do. The way you used to carry on . . ."

"Don't lecture. When am I going to see you? Can you drop in tonight?"

Marge hesitated. "I have a dinner date with an old crewmate I ran into. As soon as I shake him I'll hop right over."

"Great. But take your time. I can run through my Ophelia monologue until you get here. I'm in room one eighteen."

Lori broke the connection, still startled by her sister's surprise appearance. It was heartening to know that

Marge, so often thousands of air miles away, was tonight within walking distance.

Yet, as invariably happened when she allowed herself to think seriously about the wide gap between Marge's rigid moral standards and her own hedonistic code, Lori felt plagued by qualms of self-reproach. Two attractive sisters. Same affectionate parents. Same decent environment. Then why was Marge so disgustingly square while she had the soul of a Jezebel? That expensive new psychiatrist Marge was sending her to might be able to explain this paradox. Let him earn his forty bucks per session.

Night had deepened outside while Lori had dashed off her answers on the blue sheets. A slice of moon was playing hide-and-seek with some clouds, and the stars peeped coyly in and out of the scud. Lori stood up and expanded her chest in front of the closet mirror, unbuttoning her robe as she did so. "Mirror, mirror, on the wall. Who's got the fairest tits of them all?"

The tantalizing thoughts Messrs. Mulholland and McQueen stirred had inflamed her desire. Steve Dorn came to mind. If only he were here in this room with her now, right now, this minute. But even if he wanted her, he was a moat away. Noble Princess America regulations saw to that.

No, she was cooped up in here alone and quickly catching fire as she remembered him. Those flat hips which even bulky police gear could not distort. Those eyes with suppressed hell in them that spoke the universal language of Overscrew.

A light rap on the door stopped her musings.

"Come in if you're good-looking," she flung out, not bothering to button her robe. "The door's not locked."

Lori glanced over her shoulder and saw that it was Barbara Chrysler. Spotting the unsealed white rectangle in her hand, Lori nodded with a knowing smile.

"Hi, Colorado. My envelope, too. There must be a glue-factory strike somewhere." She pointed to the tray on the bureau. "Leave yours there with mine. I'll ask Josephina to put stickum on them when she comes around."

Barbara Chrysler dropped her envelope on the tray, slouched down on the edge of the bed.

"Utah—do you really believe they'll keep our replies confidential? I disguised my handwriting, but I'd die of shame if they could trace my answers back to me."

"Don't be a goose. Even if the institute could possibly discover your identity—and I'm sure there's no way they can—they'd want to keep it secret. If it leaked out that they blabbed, they'd have to close down in a month."

The harried look in Colorado's eyes eased. Lori studied her with renewed interest.

"Mind if I ask you a personal question? You can plead the Fifth, if you like."

"Shoot."

"You told me you were a virgin. So how could you have incriminated yourself? You didn't confess to being a les, did you?"

Colorado's cheeks turned rich scarlet. "Remember the question 'Did anyone ever try to corrupt you?' I told them that one summer at camp two of the girls in my bunk used to masturbate each other with their fingers. One night they persuaded me to go out on the field with them and lie down in a circle so we could each fondle the girl next to us. I never joined them again, but I hate to admit that—I liked it."

Lori threw her head back, unable to repress laughter. "So now you can write a book about splendor in the grass and title it 'Chrysler's Corruption.' If it sells half as well as that Portnoy book, you'll make a fortune. Or better still, call it 'The Odd Triple.' "

Apparently seized by second thoughts, Colorado's agitation returned. She reached for her envelope. "This whole deal worries me," she said. "I think I'll tear up my questionnaire. Who needs it? What can I possibly gain by sending it in?"

"Oh, be a sport, Colorado. You don't want to set sexual research back a hundred years. Compared to my answers, yours probably will read like the Dead Sea Scrolls." Lori regarded Barbara soberly. "Unless—unless there's something else you wrote you don't want to tell me."

The girl seemed startled by Lori's shrewd guess. When she spoke, her voice was almost a lament.

"There was one other question. 'If you have any erotic fantasies, describe one of them in detail.' I don't dare tell you how I answered it."

So, Lori reflected to herself, still waters run deep—and dirty. She wondered what sort of unmentionable monkey this modest, prudish girl carried on her back.

Lorid cast a sidelong glance at Colorado's troubled profile. "How are things going?"

"Bluesville. My chaperone told me Miss Kansas in Psi Group is also doing impersonations for her talent routine. One of her imitations will make both of mine look sick."

"So what? You won't be competing against her in the

prelims. You're in Alpha. That's one of the reasons they split us into three teams. It's Pageant policy to avoid placing girls with similar acts in the same sorority. They also see to it that no one group is overloaded with blondes or brunettes."

"It's not the prelims I'm worried about, it's the finals. She's doing a take-off on Tiny Tim, Nehru jacket and all. How can she miss?"

Lori's mind seemed off on a journey, then she snapped her fingers. "At lunch didn't I hear you tell one of the girls that you learned to do a French Apache dance specialty when you were an exchange drama student at the Sorbonne?"

Barbara nodded, puzzlement on her face.

"So," Lori continued, "get yourself a man's cap tomorrow. With the turtle-neck sweater and suit from your Johnny Carson number you'll have yourself a campy Apache costume."

Barbara's eyes brightened with hope. "What a great idea. I'm afraid I'll find myself rusty with some of the steps, but I'll have four days to practice."

Lori responded dryly, mock malice in her tone. "Never mind the thanks. Just make sure you don't come in ahead of me or I'll cut your Fallopian tubes."

They were both laughing heartily when the phone tinkled again. A few moments later Marge Mackliin was at the door, her rosy sunburn complexion contrasting favorably against the cobalt blue of her natty uniform. After an exchange of a hug and a kiss, Lori stepped two paces back and whistled.

"You've still got that nifty airline figure. How do you do it, Sis? Coffee, tea, milk—or Metrecal?"

Marge smiled, at the same time removing her shoulder-strap pouch and tossing it on the bed. "It's simple. I wear green glasses whenever I eat. They make every food that's fattening look like spinach."

Barbara waited until they were introduced, then headed for the open terrace which led to her own room.

"I know you two have an awful lot to catch up on, so I'll turn in now," she said. "Besides, my group is scheduled to have its official photographs taken tomorrow. If I don't get some solid sleep, my eyes will have bags under their bags. They tell me I've got a real case of the Pageant jitters." Her hand on the French door, Barbara turned toward Lori. "Your sister's really gorgeous, Utah. What's Sue Rossiter got that she hasn't?"

"Come back here," Marge Macklin hailed out. "A compliment like that deserves a reward. She dug into her pouch on the bed, came up with a vial half filled with pink pills. "Take these. Guaranteed not to hook you. Pleasant dreams and a fresh start tomorrow."

"You're sure they're harmless?"

"I've used them for years, honey, whenever I can't adjust to the difference in time zones after long flights. And these won't give you a hangover."

Hesitant but grateful, Colorado accepted the capsules and left.

"Lovely girl," Marge remarked. "Not as pretty as you, but much more attractive than Miss Alaska, whom I've seen at my hotel." She dipped into the pocket of her stewardess jacket, withdrew a cigarette case and a silver lighter. "Will it bother you if I smoke? I know the rules say you can't indulge."

"Don't let me stop you," Lori said. She reached for her plastic cap. "I'm going to take a quick shower. In the meanwhile, make yourself comfy. There's fruit and candy all over the place from my scads of admirers. And you can watch TV if you like."

Lori disappeared into the bathroom, leaving the door partially open. Marge lit a cigarette, then turned on the television, skipping from channel to channel. A rerun starring Cary Grant in a dated Hitchcock production caught her fancy, even though she had seen it twice before. She settled back in a chair, crossed her slim legs, and started to inhale.

After a few puffs, sighting no ashtray within reach, she got up and prowled the room until she finally located one on the bureau. It had been buried behind a huge fruit basket wrapped in flame-colored cellophane. She was flicking the ash when the letters on the tray beside it attracted her eye. Enticed by the address typed on the surface, she picked up the topmost envelope and found, to her surprise, that it was unsealed. She had heard of the institute. All they were interested in was sex, sex, sex. Why was her sister on their mailing list?

The open envelope invited inspection. The thrumming sound of water in the bathroom assured her that Lori was still under the shower. Without hesitation, Marge extracted the enclosed blue folder. Her eyes raced over the contents, perplexed. It was a sex questionnaire, as she had half suspected, but the answers were not in Lori's handwriting. This envelope had probably been left here by that nice Colorado kid, she surmised.

The sound of pelting water continued. It was safe to

pry. She removed the folder from the second envelope, scanned the first page. Like the other one, it consisted of a series of printed questions. The answers below each, in a loose, careless scrawl, she instantly recognized as Lori's handwriting. Her heart pumping wildly, she began to read the opening paragraphs.

Q: Do you find that boys respect you more than other girls because you are beautiful?
A: *Natch. They always take me to the more expensive motels.*
Q: Being pretty, do you ever go out on a blind date?
A: *I'd go out with a deaf or dumb date . . . as long as the guy had a long one.*
Q: Do you believe in sex before marriage?
A: *I believe in sex before the next question.*
Q: Are you a virgin?
A: *Darlings, you've heard of social drinkers? Well, I'm a social fornicator.*
Q: According to our surveys, the normal married woman will experience sexual relations with her husband approximately 4,800 times during her marriage. Does this figure gratify you or repulse you?
A: *It terrifies. 4,800 times is just a year's average for me.*

Suddenly the water was cut off and Marge could hear the shower door being slid back. "I'll be out in a sec," Lori called out over Cary Grant's British accent.

It would be too risky to continue reading the entire questionnaire, Marge decided. She turned the folder. The final blank space, almost a third of a page, was not prefaced by a formal question. It merely asked: Comments? On it Lori had written:

Can't you boys do something scientific to make future Princess America contests fairer for us girls? This Pageant awards points for just about everything —except what really counts. Talent? Swimsuits? How do we look in evening gowns? Balls!

Now, you fellows know it's how a girl looks out of her clothes that really matters. It's how she can sock it to you on the mattress. Well, isn't it?

Yet are points given for Best Bedmanship? Does being able to take on a whole basketball team in fifty clocked minutes (as I did once) get you anywhere in this race? And how about awarding points for Original

Positions? I know sixty-nine. After all, dear sexologists, isn't position everything in life?

A minute later, when Lori came into the room, Marge seemed absorbed in the movie. Her cigarette, almost burned down to its cork tip, was balanced precariously on the rim of the ashtray, which she had parked on the arm of her chair. The two envelopes were next to the fruit basket, exactly where they had been before.

A trail of scented powder followed Lori as she went for the door. Marge eyed her quizzically as she pushed in the lock on the knob, connected the loose chain to the bolt on the wall.

Lori turned around. "Now I'm as safe as a gold brick in Fort Knox," she said. "So be a dear and give me a cigarette. And no sermon, please. I rate something for good behavior."

The little hypocrite, Marge thought. She handed her the silver case, watched in silence as Lori took a cigarette, lit it, and inhaled greedily.

"Mmmm, that was good," Lori said, releasing the column of smoke. "Now I'm beginning to feel like a winner."

"Lori, do you think you have a chance to win first place?"

"I don't know, Marge. The competish this year is terrific. The smart money has it that California, New Jersey and Florida are the best bets. Honest, the girls are such knockouts I'd be lucky to cop the prize in the crackerjack box." She hesitated, smiled. "I think the only way I can win is if I did an el foldo for each of the male judges."

Marge's body went stiff. She crushed her cigarette in the ashtray with extra vigor. "Lori, you know I don't like to hear you talk like that."

"Don't flap, Marge. The truth is I've reformed completely and become a sweet little Mary Poppins. Dr. Odrich did such a great brainwashing job on me I've stored my pussy in the deep freeze. The only time I shake my ass is when I do my isometric exercises. When I finish college I'll join the Mormon Tabernacle Choir and sing hymns until my Prince Charming comes along. Is that what you'd like to hear?"

"Yes. I only hope I hear it before Mom and Dad find out about you. That reminds me." She opened her purse, drew out two one-hundred-dollar bills from a long snakeskin wallet. When Marge placed them on the bureau, Lori saw that they were new and crisp.

"That's for Dr. Odrich. Just in case I don't see you for a while. They're switching me to the Houston–Chicago run next week."

"Thanks, Marge." She sighed. "I don't know if I'll ever be able to pay you back."

"Don't worry. I'll put a lien on your contest winnings."

"Fat chance. Even if by some miracle I placed first or second, they tie up all the loot for one year. And the money for the scholarships they award each loser goes directly to the school. No college, no cash. They do that to discourage dropouts."

"How goes it with Dr. Odrich? Making any progress?"

"Well, for one thing he has me sitting in a chair. Says a couch is bad for my posture. And he keeps insisting I'm a nympho. So I suggested that he commit me to the Harvard dormitory. As soon as the chambermaids started looking good to me, I'd know I was cured."

Marge clenched her fists, concentrated on keeping her voice level. Her face was a tight mask of self-control.

"What did he say to that?"

"He said isolating me with a group of men would be like putting Count Dracula in charge of a blood bank."

"I agree with him," burst out Marge, no longer able to conceal her emotions. "Your mind is like a filthy French postcard. When will you realize that you can't wisecrack your way through life?"

"Look, Marge, you're my sister and I love you. You're a great looker, you've got boy friends, and I'm sure you've had a dozen proposals. But you're pushing twenty-eight and still unmarried. Why? I'll tell you. Because you're frigid. Sex makes you freeze. You think it's dirty and ugly. If you ever get married, I pity your husband. He'll discover your clit is an icicle. And the only way you'll be able to hold him is to fake having an orgasm. You're the one who should see a psychiatrist."

Marge's lower lip was quivering. "What you say about me may be true," she flared. "But what's to become of you if you go on the way you are?"

"I'd rather end up as a prostitute than be an old maid. Besides, I'm *not* a nympho. I can draw the line on sex anytime I want to."

Marge laughed scornfully.

"You sound like the guy about to jump off the Empire State Building who says he can stop falling when he reaches the thirtieth floor."

Ignoring the analogy, Lori walked over to the fruit basket, began tearing at the orange cellophane. She bent over the basket studiously, finally selected a small pyramid of grapes.

"Oh, Lori, Lori, what am I going to do with you?" pleaded Marge.

"Why don't you write a letter to Dear Abby and ask her?"

"I don't have to send her a letter. Yours told me enough. Taking on a basketball team in fifty clocked minutes. Why don't you add a P.S. and tell them your body is community property?"

Lori whirled around, dumbfounded.

"You read my personal mail! I'll never forgive you for that as long as I live." The cluster of grapes fell from her hand and she brought it against her sister's cheek in a sweeping stroke, slapping her so hard the impact stung her palm. "Now get the hell out of here," she shrilled, her brain smoking with rage. "I never want to see you again."

Marge stood frozen, shaken by the fury of Lori's attack. She was helpless to think, unable to explain. The feeble words of apology she tried to spill out became knotted in her vocal cords.

Her cheek still smarting from Lori's blow, she walked numbly toward the door. She had just disengaged the chain from the bolt when there was the rattle of a key in the lock, then a sharp knock.

"Miss Utah. Is anything wrong?"

Lori was at the door in almost a single bound. "Christ!" she whispered. "It's the maid. We'll have to put on an act of some kind, or there may be talk. She's a goddamned mind reader."

Marge nodded eagerly, anxious to be a co-conspirator, hopeful this was a signal from Lori that blood was thicker than water.

"Come in, Josephina," Lori sang out brightly. "There's nobody here but us chickens."

Josephina let herself in, using the house key. Her eyes glowed with admiration as she surveyed the two girls.

"Very pretty chickens," she said. "And you look alike enough to have come from the same rooster."

Marge watched Josephina cross over to the bed to pull down the covers. "Lori told me you could read minds, but I didn't believe her," she said. "I'm her older sister, Marge."

Josephina raised her head a few inches, her hands meanwhile propping the pillows against the headboard. "I wasn't due to make up this room yet. But I heard loud voices . . ."

"I was helping Lori rehearse a scene from Shakespeare," Marge volunteered. "For her talent skit. I guess we ran away with ourselves."

Josephina stood up. "I was all the way down the hall, so of course I couldn't hear any of the words. But it must be an exciting scene, with so much yelling. What play is it from?"

"The Taming of the Shrew," Lori answered quickly, her eyes fixed steadily at Marge. "It's about a nasty bitch who finally gets what she deserves."

"Which of you two played the part of the shrew?" asked Josephina, guileless.

"Me," offered Lori. "Marge is too sweet to play such a lousy character."

Marge gave her sister a grateful look, sensing that her remark was meant to be taken as an olive branch. She decided to leave now. To remain alone with her after Josephina left would be asking for it. She went over to Lori to kiss her goodbye, was met with a warm embrace that surprised her. It was as if the explosive confrontation between the two had never occurred.

"Good night, Sis," said Lori when they broke apart. "You're an angel to have come over to wish me good luck."

And you're a devil, Marge wanted to say, but thought better of it.

Josephina occupied herself about the room after Marge had left, discreetly disposing of the cigarette stubs without comment. When she came across the two envelopes on the tray, her uncanny extrasensory perception instantly became activated. "You want me to seal these for you and mail them?" she asked.

Lori nodded absently. All at once she felt tired, drained by the timetable demands of the past fourteen hours. She wriggled out of her robe and, completely nude, slid in between the pastel sheets of her bed. Thoughtfully Josephina turned off the lights, then left the room, gently closing the self-locking door behind her.

But sleep would not come. Lori told herself she was a fool not to have asked Marge for some of the pills she had given Colorado.

She found herself envying Colorado; the kid's only hangup in life was an erotic fantasy she had confided anonymously to her questionnaire. Lori had chosen to answer that same question with an outrageous fib intended to shock the institute. But now, as she fought a losing battle with the demons bent on robbing her of sleep, her mind spun out an erotic fantasy she wished she'd thought of earlier:

Colorado had told her she always slept with the terrace door open. Chances were she'd take another sleeping pill before the contest was over. Beginning tomorrow, each night Lori would tiptoe down the terrace and pause at Barbara's door. If she heard heavy breathing she would slip into her room and "borrow" the Apache costume from her closet. Back in her own quarters, she would put on the pants, turtleneck sweater and jacket. Her hair, pushed up into a bun, would be hidden under the cap. Sunglasses and sandals would complete the man's disguise. Then she'd hop over the low balcony railing and walk across the sand until she reached steps leading to the boardwalk. Four blocks down, at Maple Street, she'd turn left until she came to the old police garage at Delaware Avenue. There she'd find Steve alone, busy with his boat. As soon as he saw her he would grin with delight. There would be a gentle reprimand. Then he would pull her into his arms and destroy her with sex . . .

Again and again Lori reviewed the fantasy in her mind, always savoring the ecstatic ending. And the longer she dwelled on it, the more she convinced herself that it would be simple to convert the fantasy into a reality.

She sank her head deep into the soft pillow and smiled to herself in the darkness. Of course it would work! Colorado was certain to take at least one more sleeping pill to ward off the Pageant jitters. And by innocently questioning Steve when he drove her around tomorrow she would easily determine what nights he would be working at the garage.

But there was one small detail she must remember to take care of to make the entire plan fail-safe. Her breasts. Under the turtle-neck sweater they would appear more prominent than ever. She'd be spotted as a girl the moment anyone passed her.

Well, she knew how to take care of *that* detail.

She shut her eyes and tried once again to fall asleep. The night was still long. She slid one hand under the sheet and began to count "Lori's lambs."

15 · ROGER MEGAN

BRIMMING with excitement, walking on air, Roger Megan was at his suite promptly at five to await a call from the girl he had asked to sit on his face. Nor did he doubt that she would phone. All day he had tried not to think about it, to save it for last, the olive in the martini.

But he had not succeeded. Life around the darling Pageant contestants was apt to be stimulating indeed, and instead of distracting him as always, they had only fired his expectancy to the kindling point. Now, luxuriously fatigued, stripped to underwear and a silk robe, frosty glass in hand, he reclined in an armchair and gave over freely to anticipation of the evening and its promise of sexual pleasures.

But the minutes and martinis kept mounting. The call had not materialized. And little by little Roger felt his heart shrinking and his liver enlarging.

Lou Cates, hovering nearby wary as a cat (his employer bore few trials with less grace than waiting to hear from ladies who were either late or not going to be heard from at all), rattled the ice in a chrome pitcher. Slowly, Roger's gaze found him, fixed him with a death ray.

"Yes, faithful retainer, what is it?"

"Fresh batch maybe?"

Roger pondered and said judiciously, "No, we go the rest of the way on tequila." He remembered her shapely legs, the spirited way she walked. Legs like a race horse, with an ass to match. "Did you want to remind me what time it is?"

"Five forty-nine. Will you be waiting much longer?"

"I don't know. How's that grab you?"

"Very firmly, sire." Cates poured tequila into a snifter and handed it to Roger. "May I make so bold as to ask if there is something especially special about this one?"

Megan held the glass up to eye level, squinting through the clear amber liquid, and smiled mournfully, like a brave invalid. "Lou," he said, "I think I can safely say this is something even you wouldn't believe." He sipped, then downed the rest.

"That," said Cates, "I can believe," and, filling the glass again, he stood the bottle on the floor beside Roger's chair and went into the bedroom.

There were two phones in Megan's suite. In the twenty minutes following his arrival they had rung five times, twice overlapping. Prescott had called with reassuring news that Princess 1961 had been reached in Jamaica and was set. Gus the masseur wanted to know why his appointment had been canceled. ("But that's just when you need it the most, Mr. Megan, when you don't feel up to it.") Sue Rossiter, ostensibly inviting him to join a group at her place for a drink before dinner, waiting for him to drop a word about later that night. *Newsweek,* confirming Wednesday's interview and fishing for possibly trenchant quotes concerning the reputed NFL impasse. Jay Mallett, the Pageant's show director, inquiring about Megan's availability to look at a draft of the reunion spot. ("Roger, I hate to bust into your evening, but JF *suggested* we get your reaction before he sees it.")

And from then on, strangely, not another ring.

Roger drank and stared morosely at the phone at arm's length on a taboret. It had been cut off by vandals at the switchboard. It had died; we all have to go sometime. It had been diverted to another room, where an optometrist from South Dakota was quietly accepting Roger's calls and preparing to start a new life.

Suddenly it rang. Roger leaped, caught himself, and then with great calm reached for the phone; but his hand, he noticed, was trembling.

"Hello."

"Roger?"

Megan's eyes closed and he heaved a terrible sigh. "Hi, Felix. What's up?"

"You tell me. I'm in New York. Something at the office, and I'll have to stay over, so I won't be seeing you later at the Merri-Cola reception."

"That's logical."

"But you're going, of course?"

"Of course."

"Good, I'm glad to hear it. Anything with the League?"

"Just rumors. Two or three an hour." Megan paused. "So what else is new, Felix?"

"Oh, yes. I ran into David Merrick at Sardi's. He's

thinking of offering you the lead in a musical based on the Miss Galaxy beauty contest. He's got a wow of a title. 'Around the World with Eighty Girls.' "

"What's the plot?"

"When the play opens, you've already banged seventy-seven of the contestants. Then, in the next three acts, you have to screw Miss Italy, Miss Israel and Miss America. I told him if you take the part, you'll have to recap your pecker."

"Very funny."

"Roger, you don't sound like you sounded at lunch. Is something wrong? Something I don't know about?"

"Trouble in paradise? God forbid. And also JF, who watches over us. Life at this glamorous seaside haven continues graciously and all is well except that some sonofabitch optometrist from South Dakota is getting my calls."

"What? How is that possible? How do you know?"

"Deduction."

"Oh, I see. Well, don't worry, it can't last. Anybody else getting your calls should be fucked dead by morning."

"You should live so," said Megan sadly.

"You're turning Jewish?"

"As a matter of fact, I'm feeling somewhat Jewish at the moment, but I was considering turning Negro."

"Well, good luck, *zei gesundt,* and I'll see you tomorrow."

"It's a thrill and a privilege talking to you," said Roger. With one hand he replaced the phone, with the other he picked up his glass and drained it. Then he tilted his head back, opened his jaws wide and roared softly, a wounded lion.

Cates was at the bed laying out a white dinner jacket when Roger walked into the room. "All done?" he asked.

"Uh-huh." Roger lit a cigarette and leaned back against the dresser, propped on his elbows. "Lou, stop what you're doing a minute. And look at me. I want to see your face when I lay this on you." Obligingly, Cates turned. He clasped his hands, attentive, impassive. "The idea," Roger resumed, "was to let you meet her later without warning. A great big beautiful surprise. But . . ." He shrugged and said, "Guess who's not coming for dinner."

"The dinner," said Cates.

"Fink," said Roger, shaking his head. "You ruined my line. I'll get you for this."

"Promises, promises."

Roger contemplated him calmly for a moment, getting back his timing. Then he said, "Hazel Sanders."

Cates blinked. His eyebrows went up slowly and stayed up. "Hazel Sanders!" he echoed.

Megan hugged himself. "Well, say something?"

"Fantastic," said Cates. "Never in a million years. Where on earth did you run into her?"

"In Fleming's outer office."

"This can't be a put-on? What would be the point?'

"Exactly, schmuck," Roger said fondly. "It's legit. She was there with Walsh and the others from the League. What the connection is beats me, but apparently there is one."

"Didn't you ask her?"

"We never talked. She didn't even realize I was there. I was looking in a mirror with my back to her when I saw her come in. I thought I'd gone bananas. I couldn't believe it. Then the others went in to Fleming, and I dropped a note into her lap and followed them. Just my card with a few words, asking her to call me here at five." What those few words had been, Roger found himself reluctant to say. "I thought she would, but I really can't blame her."

Presently, after a compassionate interval, Cates asked, "Has she changed? You had no trouble recognizing her?"

"Instantly." Roger sighed and took a long pull on his cigarette. "One look. The sweet face, the big black eyes, the walk, the legs. I felt sick."

But as he spoke, it struck him as odd that the possibility of error had never once crossed his mind. He had, after all, seen her only briefly in a small oval mirror, a gimcrack antique with its distorting surface darkened by flecks of sooty gold leaf. What if he had been wrong? What if he had given his card—with his licorish handwritten message—to someone he didn't know? A mistake like that could hold its own with Napoleon's decision to winter in Moscow.

"In fact," said Roger, grimacing unhappily, "I don't feel too great right now."

"Tequila does it every time," said Cates.

"Tequila my ass. I've been thinking about her, waiting all day. What do I do next? How do I find her?"

"Offhand, it doesn't sound difficult. Are you showering?"

"No," said Roger after a moment, "I'm moving in just the right amount of fog. A shower would kill it."

Nevertheless, for insurance, he had another drink, and, on the theory that too much insurance is better than too little, still another. So that by the time he went in to wash and shave again, he was carrying close to the maximum his portfolio could afford.

What baffled him was the hurt he felt. And this was really absurd, for as Robbie Burns says of such matters (Roger had reached the point of declaiming aloud to the mirror, his captive audience), *The best laid schemes o' mice an' men gang aft a-gley*. And more specifically, the best schemed lays. Under the circumstances—for, as Megan had often stated: "A star without pussy is no star"—hurt was inevitable, as well as impersonal, and nothing more was involved. Except perhaps a wee Scotch, which—gorgeous coincidence!—was Black Label, thus enabling him to toast the bard and the broad simultaneously. Gallant, if not actually princely, in defeat, sir.

Emerging then to the bedroom with a high-minded purpose, as he was passing the phone it went off. He whirled, seized it before the first ring had ended, a thing alive, a bird caught taking wing. He brought the mouthpiece close to his lips. "Is it you?" he whispered, and hearing the melodious voice that responded with laughter, he shivered and closed his eyes and smiled.

"I think so. How are you, Roger?"

"Hazel, Hazel, Hazel," he said softly. "How wonderful to hear you again. I almost lost hope. How have you been? No, don't answer. Don't say anything. We'll talk when we meet. Where are you now?"

"I can't see you, Roger."

His eyes opened. "What? Why not?"

"Oh, lots of reasons." Polite, placid. "I'm sorry."

"Hazel, you can't mean it?"

"I'm very busy, Roger. I have things to do."

"Hazel, no matter what . . ." he began, and broke off with a groan. "I can't talk to you like this. I must look at you. I must be with you. Tell me where you are."

"Roger, listen to me—"

"No, not until you meet me. Please, Hazel, don't do this. Just for a little while, just to see you again. Hazel, I must see you, damn it!"

"Hey there," she murmured, "Get yo'se'f together. Tell you what. I'm at League headquarters, but I'm leaving for home and I'll be in until seven-thirty or so. If you'd like to come by for about half an hour, well, fine."

"Did you say home? Are you living here?"

"Temporarily. I've been here since May. I sublet a flat."

After a pause that he knew was too long, much too long, he asked, "Is it safe?"
"Yes," she said, "it's safe. You'll see."
"What's the address?"
"Seventeen Tarpon Road. It's on the far west side, three blocks south of the old causeway. There's a print shop downstairs, the Hammond Press. I'm above it."
"Thank you, love," he said quietly. "See you soon." Slowly, abstractedly—his mind was racing and in several directions—he put the receiver down and turned to find Cates in the doorway to the sitting room, observing him with a lemony smile. "Dr. Watson, I have an errand for you," Roger said thoughtfully. "Go down and rent a car. Something inconspicuous. I'll walk to Ocean Drive and turn south. You can pick me up somewhere along the line. Follow?"
"Like a leopard," said Cates. "Do you still want the white jacket?"
Roger nodded. "And my navy rain coat over it. I'll be going on from there to the reception. Ring me when you're all set. And before you go, tell me what that curious look on your curious face means."
"I was thinking how long it's been since I heard you pitch like that."
"Like what?"
"Like a lover."
Megan's grin developed slowly. "Which is it you underestimate in me—the artist or the beast?"
"Well," said Cates, "the artist, occasionally, maybe. But never the beast."
And taking his hat he left.

In Roger Megan's private chronology, years were identified by their Pageant numeration and remembered by the advent of successive crises and women in a life that lacked for neither. Accordingly, the year of the eighth Pageant was the year of disaster in Florida, when he was turning forty, frightened by the first tremors of a career cracking under him. It was also when and where he had found Hazel Sanders.
Though he had known her only briefly, less than three weeks, her presence pervaded memories light-years away now, but as the mind flies instantly restored, vivid and immediate. Swamp lilies on black water as she surfaced among them. The wind ceaselessly soughing through groves of yellow pine, the air charged with their aroma and an attar distilled by her body as she lay in his arms. A blue

heron lazily rising against the immense sky with a mudfish flopping in its bill. He had called it a crane, and Hazel had taught him that cranes stretched their necks out in flight, while herons kept theirs curved back against the breast.

Five years ago, following the close of the eighth Pageant, Roger had gone to Hampton Springs, a small backwater Gulf town in the unspoiled northwest Florida panhandle country, remote from most of the blessings of tourism. There, in the still lingering dog days of subtropical summer, he had joined a large company on location making a pilot-plus-two for a TV series. Animals were very big that year in television, and astute producers were hitching their wagons to bears, dogs and dolphins.

Roger's producer, an ungifted faggot noted for his connections and brocade vests, had chosen the cracker backwoods because it was the scene of Marjorie Kinnan Rawling's great success, *The Yearling,* about a boy and his pet fawn, with one of whom he apparently identified. The company had set up camp near the confluence of the Gulf and the Fenholloway River. In this locale of overpowering beauty the wilderness abounded with prodigal varieties of animal life, with fish and reptiles and waterfowl, most of which were penciled in as co-stars for future chapters.

Roger was cast as the somewhat felonious hero, in bush jacket and visored cap, with a pipe in his teeth, a glint in his eye, and a boat for charter. His best friend was a noble game warden, struggling against marauding poachers, and his romance a shady lady gone to virtue who ran a picturesquely ramshackle hotel in an oystering village. The betting in the industry was that this dreary pastiche ("Roger, it's *Key Largo, Rain* and *Green Mansions* rolled into one!"), widely hailed for creative trail-blazing, couldn't miss. But it not only missed, it effectively ended Roger's burgeoning efforts in TV dramas. It also gave the quietus to whatever hope he had for features and, in the words of one critic, cast a pall over seasons to come.

Roger knew it early. Because he saw the venture was doomed, the work was hard and unrewarding and the heat oppressive. Booze in reasonable quantities was a help, but it could not replace kooze, and kooze—as Roger discovered with disbelief, despondency, and, finally, quiet horror—was unavailable. There were women around, actresses, script girls, secretaries, half of them worth a tussle, but in their tight community of trailers the clandestineness essential for a star was impossible. Soon the good ones were paired off with the crew, provoking neither notice nor gabble, and the others never came close enough to get grabbed.

Denied *droit du seigneur,* and in fact any *droits* at all, he was ready to bestow a little *noblesse oblige* on the associate producer, a diet-wasted divorcee, whereupon he learned to his chagrin that he would have to wait his turn, and this, he forlornly decided, was really too infra dig.

The shooting schedule was erratic, and though Roger was frequently idled, he was on call often enough to preclude even a brief foray in Tampa, not far down the coast, let alone the other glittering Floridian resort towns studding the peninsula. (*"You know, Lou, some nights, when the wind is right and it gets very quiet, I can hear them sucking in Palm Beach."*)

As the wretched days passed, Roger took to spending his sporadic leisure hours sailing a small cabin cruiser. One steamy afternoon, following the coast north along Apalachee Bay to investigate the promise of a town named Panacea, he caught sight of a canvas-topped pale-blue jeep running south on the sandy road winding with the shoreline. There was a girl in it, wearing a wide-brimmed yellow hat. He waved. She waved back, speeding on. Immediately he came about, pursuing her dust cloud, but the jeep never slackened and presently she was gone. Gone, and with her all that might have been; goodbye.

He resumed his way north, but the not quite encounter had put worms in his day, and after a while he turned for home. On the way back, he spied the blue jeep again. It was parked at the foot of a dilapidated pier that led out to the ruins of a shingle-and-tar paper shack on stilts, the roof alive with water birds. Through binoculars he saw the girl sitting near the shack, propped against an askew piling, reading a book. She wore the same floppy yellow hat and a yellow bikini, and ogling her, what at first he hoped would turn out to be splendidly suntanned skin was soon revealed as Negro.

It seemed pointless to go on. Not because she was Negro. It was not in Roger's nature to be deterred in his universal appreciation of womanhood by superficialities, but this was Florida, the old Florida of the deep South and rednecks and turpentine darkies who knew their place. But in yellow bikinis?

On he came. His ravaged condition would not permit otherwise. He had to have a look. The boat glided across the calm shoaly water to the pier, and she and the motionless birds on the roof watched with interest as he tied up a few feet away.

She was fairly dark, a dusky velvet cocoa that glistened bronze in sunlight. She was young and blooming, full thighs, full breasts, hips curved smooth with baby fat, and a round belly with a deep navel. Shaded under her maize scallop-brimmed hat was an open charming face, as much Asian as African, high cheekbones leading to brightly black eyes, a small upturned nose, and a wide good-natured mouth, her lips painted cherry.

His heart had leaped at the sight of her, and he felt sick to think of the terrible chasms between them, but when he heard her voice—the softly slurred musical surface—he knew he must have her.

"Well, burn my clothes!" she exclaimed mildly, sitting up as recognition burst upon her. "You look just like Roger Megan. . . . Is it? . . . I mean, are you?"

"Yes," Roger had answered, smiling, gratified down to his toenails, "it is, and I am. What's yours?"

Hazel was then twenty-one. She came from near Tallahassee, where her father taught high-school math. She had gone to Clark U. in Atlanta for two years, majoring in sociology and journalism, then transferred to Dillard in New Orleans, where she would return later in the month for her senior year. She had spent the summer vacation driving a mobile library truck for the Leon County Interdenominational Federation and helping a voter registration campaign. Now she was staying with a cousin two miles up the road, stretching her bones and taking things easy before going back to school.

This and more Roger drew from her in half an hour with easy efficiency, as though filling out a fact sheet for a Pageant contestant. SPECIAL TRAINING: *Piano and Clarinet.* FAVORITE HOBBY: *Writing and Nature Study.* FAVORITE SPORT: *Swimming, Hiking, Bowling.* AMBITION: *To receive a Master's degree in Sociology and to write professionally.* OTHER FACTS: *Has no special boy friend. Likes to go out, but is unacquainted in this area and welcomes the rest.*

After that, having located her in time and space, he homed in to study the lovely animal, talking amiably, wittily, familiarly, guided and corrected by a shading of her voice, a flicker of expression, delighting and disarming her. Truly, as Megan was unduly fond of saying, his best performances were invariably offstage.

Twice again they had met at the pier that week, without appointment, communicating with a sensitive obliquity by which he let her know that his free intervals were unpredictable, and she mentioned that she was usually there every day. But when, the first time, he found her before noon, and the second near six o'clock as day was fading, he realized what long hours she was devoting to vigil, and he saw that he had it made. She came aboard the boat, and that evening, anchored in a cove at one of the neighboring keys, catbirds, fireflies and all, he took her in his arms and it began.

After that, early every day Cates drove the ten miles to the trysting place, to tell her if and when Roger could come. They had been together perhaps seven or eight times in the brief span they knew each other before she left for New Orleans. Their last meeting was the only one they planned ahead, and the only time they spent a night together. They sailed to their verdant deserted key, came ashore with blankets, and talked and drank and made love and slept under the stars.

In the morning, before the mist had burned away, he brought her back to the pier. The limpid water undulated gently, heavy as enamel, heavy as his heart. Hand in hand they walked the weathered boards to her car. She got in. The jeep was drenched with dew, and she ran the windshield wipers while the engine warmed and sent clouds of gray smoke rolling out over the bay. He poked his head in through the open side curtain and kissed her.

Hazel, we're going to stay in touch, aren't we?

Yes, if you want to . . .

Waving to each other, their romance ended as it had begun, and whatever they had been to each other was over.

After Roger left Florida, soon afterward, he wrote to her, a rambling emotional letter, and though she answered promptly, he had already plunged back into the turmoil and tribulations of the show-biz rat race, and months passed before he wrote again. It had seemed likely he was coming to New Orleans for a TV special on the Mardi Gras, but the project fell through and that was the last she heard from him.

Yet for a long while the memory of her would recur mysteriously, incandescently, to leave him with a burden of melancholy. It was always a sense of regret that his retrospection and rumination could not assess or put to rest. Because there was nothing to regret. She had come to him, a glorious piece of ass, his apartheid Aphrodite, to solace and cheer him, and she returned to those empyrean regions, inaccessible to him, from which she had come.

Tarpon Road lay in an isolated cantle on the wrong side of the turnpike and the causeways, at the outskirts of the Negro sector of town. Beyond it began a boggy wasteland of sedge and cattails, of decaying marsh and sandy barrens. It was an area the gala souvenir maps of Surf City omitted as irrelevant, and even with directions Megan had to search out his destination.

The block he wanted seemed to have been zoned for automotive blight. On one side was a lot with junked cars and a scorified brick skeleton that had been a garage. Across the street was a boarded-up gas station, and a hundred feet farther down another that still functioned but was closed, night lights on. Between them, separated from both by wire-fenced lots luxuriant with towering seeds and wild flowers, was a green frame building. A store occupied the ground floor, shielded by padlocked ironwork, on one window *The Hammond Press* and under it the numeral seventeen. The upper story was half-timbered, with three curtained windows, the middle one framing an air-conditioner.

Cates nursed the car to a stop. No one was about. Only a hum of traffic from the turnpike disturbed the enveloping stillness. It was a quarter to seven.

"You will remember to give her my regards?" said Cates.

"What?" said Roger, then: "Your regards, yes, of course." His mind was in utter disarray. Gathering his coat around him, he nodded to Cates, "Later," and was out of the car and walking before it had pulled away.

A slate path deep in crab grass led to the side entrance of the house and a gravel driveway where a dusty maroon Mustang stood parked.

He pressed a bell in the doorjamb. The latch clacked. He pushed in, climbed a thinly carpeted dark flight to a landing and another door, knocked lightly.

"It's open," Hazel's voice called.

She was standing in the center of a spacious room, her cool smile faintly quizzical, lips parted as though about to speak. Her hair, longer than he remembered it, tumbled uncombed, unreeled black floss, to her shoulders. A kaftan of striped green and gold lamé dropped from her throat in sweeping folds to a shaggy rose rug at her feet. Her hands hung at her sides, a silver hairbrush in her right, a cigarette in her left, smoke curling upward in a lazy whorl. She returned his gaze expectantly, patiently.

"A little older," he said at length, slowly nodding, "and

even more lovely, maybe because of it. You look wonderful, Hazel."

"You, too," she said, "Just like on television." Her smile had changed during his protracted scrutiny, grown softer and indulgent. "Especially in that jacket," she added.

Move, Megan thought. No talk. Physical contact. Take her hand and kiss it and see what develops.

But his first step set her in motion, sidling gracefully toward a white door on her left, almost not so much shying away as responding to a lead in an improvised, if ancient, minuet. "Will you excuse me, Roger?" she was saying. "I just stepped out of a tub. Take off your coat and make yourself a drink. I'll be dressed in no time."

The white door opened, revealing to Megan's angled view a segment of a bedroom—part of a screened window, part of a low bed with a cerise quilted headboard—and she vanished within.

He stared at the closed door. *Well, Megan, that wasn't too good, was it?* He could see her at this moment, slipping out of her robe, naked before a long mirror, brushing her hair, bouncing those beautiful brown tits of hers. He would walk in on her (the more you plan, the worse it'll go) and throw her on the bed and bury his head in her cunt and put an end to this bullshit.

Slowly he removed his coat and laid it on a Victorian rattan chair. On a sideboard were assorted bottles and glasses and an ice bucket. Scotch, Holland gin, vodka from Poland, Goldwasser, Hungarian wine, Ouzo, Portuguese brandy. This one he definitely needed; an act of mercy. He poured vodka and sipped it. The right decision. Kindness from Poland.

On one wall was a collection of photographs featuring Hazel against a variety of foreign backgrounds. Hazel on an ornate stone balcony overlooking an Italian bay. With two tall young blacks in African dress before a marble fountain. With a group of men and women, black and white, at a sidewalk café. Feeding pigeons in a plaza. With one of the blacks from the fountain, standing with bicycles at the edge of a cliff. And with the same black again, both in parkas, carrying skis, against a vast white slope.

Nice looking stud, Megan thought. What was the expression Hazel had used that first day they met, when he had been questioning her about boy friends? *"You mean do I have a main enthusiasm? The answer is none. None to speak of."* Her directness had pleased him. The evening she had come aboard his boat, and he had kissed her and known he was going to make her, he had asked her, "Are you a virgin?" "No," she had said, and added gravely, "Does that spoil it for you?" And before he could think of what to say, she had gone on, smilingly, "Tell you what though, Roger—you'll be my first white man."

Hazel came out of the bedroom. "How you doing?" she asked. She had gathered her hair in a Psyche knot and put on a high-bodiced orange and black minidress, and she was barefoot.

He motioned toward the pictures. "You've been traveling?"

"Yes, three years abroad, mostly studying and working, but I did get to move around quite a bit."

"International spy?"

"Sort of." She took some wine and turned to him. "I worked for the War Resisters League. Wonderful years really. I was very happy in Europe. I didn't want to leave."

"Why did you?"

"Well, I met Tom Walsh in London last year, and he said, 'Hazel, I want you to come back home and work for a black league.' He made me feel I had to. I knew it anyway." She smiled. "And it's interesting work. And it's important work."

"What do you do? What sort of work?"

"Every sort. The whole spectrum of League activity. My title is executive assistant for communications media, but it doesn't mean a thing. I go wherever Walsh thinks I can be useful. Like Surf City. I was assigned here when we started getting ready to take on the Pageant."

Roger nodded. "You've taken it on, all right."

"Yes, haven't we? . . . Why don't you sit?"

"I'd rather stand." They were some fifteen feet apart; he had not moved from the wall with the photographs, and she was still at the sideboard. He wanted another drink, but he could not get at the vodka without seeming to approach her, and he would not risk being misunderstood and pressing her again to evasive action. Not until the climate changed. Vamp till ready, he thought. "You know," he said, "it's hard to believe that I'm seeing you again. You can't imagine how astonished I was when I realized it was you in Fleming's office. I didn't know what to do."

"Well," she said with a little laugh, "it didn't take you too long to think of something. And you have no idea how astonished *I* was. Of course, I knew you were here and I thought it barely possible we might run into each other. But hardly like that."

"Suppose we hadn't? Wouldn't you have called me anyway? Before the week was over?"

"I doubt it. Probably not. What for?"

"What for? To meet. To talk. Like this. To see each other again." But she just kept smiling at him, and he said, "But you did call."

"Yes, I was afraid next time you might embarrass me publicly instead of privately."

"You mean what I wrote on my card?" She nodded. Acid welled in his throat, an instant's searing. "You didn't think it was funny?"

"No. Actually I thought it was vulgar."

"I didn't think of it that way."

"I know you didn't."

"I thought of it as intimate."

"It was that too. I had to burn it. Just as I had to burn the two letters you sent me, and I didn't want to." She paused, and when he remained silent she said, "Have I hurt you?"

"A little, but I see I've hurt you, and I'm sorry. I was writing the way we used to talk—the way I used to talk. You were never offended."

"It was a novelty then. And things were different then."

"Then," said Roger, and he sighed, and having acknowledged the then—and that it was indeed different from the now, and he damned well knew it—he walked slowly to the sideboard and stood close to her, inhaling her perfume as he poured more vodka. "Here's to then," he said, turning to her with his drink raised.

Their eyes met. "Why not?" she said and clinked glasses.

Before this she had not touched her wine. Now she drank all of it. Roger refilled her glass and backed away a step or two. Her eyes were luminous.

"You've remained single?" he asked.

"Yes."

"How come?"

"Maybe nobody asked me."

"Why are you teasing me?"

"Is that what I'm doing? Hmmmm. Well, I really don't know what the answer is. I've been asked, yes. It's nice to be asked. And it must be nice to say yes, but I guess I just never wanted to say it."

"Have you been in love?"

"Oh, Roger, don't be so serious. You used to make me laugh. That's why I liked you so much."

"I did?"

"Don't you remember how much I'd laugh when I was with you?"

"And that's why you liked me?"

"I liked you because you always made the effort . . . so I knew you were involved with me . . . because it's hard to put on an act like that."

How strange this girl was, how full of surprises. There were three different thoughts in what she had said, one coiled inside another. He started to speak, to say what?—then shook his head and retreated for cover to his drink.

"Don' strain yo' tonsils," she said with a gentle smile, and as she spoke the telephone rang in the bedroom and she excused herself and ran on her toes to answer it.

Megan stood there, breathing in the still scented air, remembering suddenly (was it the sight of her pink soles as she ran?) an afternoon they had wandered one of the keys in the bay, a hummock of palmetto and cat-briar tangles and swamp, held together by twining roots of red mangroves. They had been at the island's edge, sitting against the swollen trunk of a tupelo, watching a chicken turtle munch hibiscus flowers. Hazel had been bathing her feet, bruised and scratched from trudging about shoeless, and they were invisible in the water turned as coppery as her skin by tannic acid from the mangrove roots.

"What is this with you and shoes?" he had said. "You even drive barefoot. Child of nature or what?" She had smiled and said, "Child of hang-up, more likely. I was seven years old before I had a pair of shoes that really fit me. A Negro shoe store had opened in Madison. It was a long trip, fifty-five miles, but they let me try the shoes on before my mother paid for them."

"Didn't they let you try them on in the other stores?"

She had looked at him and said, almost laughing, "Cullud folks putting their feet into shoes that white folks might buy?"

He could hear her talking quietly, shortly, then the click of the phone, then moving around the room. When she came out she was wearing black patent pumps and carrying a russet suede coat that she laid on the studio couch. She seemed preoccupied, her gaze absently searching the room.

"Bad news?" he asked.

"Not yet," she said. "Walsh and Fleming are meeting again, but it's a waste of time."

A dozen replies flitted through his mind, but in the end he said nothing. Because silence was better than all of them, silence protected him. He watched her as she found on a table the cigarettes she had evidently been looking for, lighting one before he could offer, maintaining the distance between them.

"How did you get here?" she asked.

"Cates dropped me off. I almost forgot—he sends you his best regards."

"He's still with you? That sweet man. Will you tell him hello for me?"

"Yes. Hello and goodbye."

"Roger," she said and shook her head at him, then: "How are you going back? Is he coming for you?"

"I'll call him at the hotel when you think it's time for me to leave."

She frowned. "You can't. Not from this phone."

"Why not?"

"The police have a bug on it. Are you surprised?"

"Yes. No. What difference? It's no good, right?"

"Right. You should have had Cates come back for you in half an hour. I told you that was all the time I had."

"I know, but I thought maybe you might change your mind."

"Impossible. I was due back at eight. But that's been postponed, and now I have to go to Westbridge—and I don't suppose I can let you off somewhere. A diner? But you couldn't wait there, could you?"

"No, it's all so complicated, isn't it?"

She picked up her coat and put it on. "There's only one way to do this. I'll take you to Westbridge. You can call Cates from there when I'm ready to leave, and we'll arrange to meet some place where you can change cars. Unless," she hesitated, "it'll make you too late for where you were going."

Roger slowly finished his drink and set his glass down with the cold gloom of someone placing a chessman one move from resignation. "It doesn't matter," he said. He was already five years too late, he thought, for where he had been going.

Twilight was falling, soft as soot, and a dusky red sun was half gone. They were driving through marshland, traversed only by spider-legged pylons carrying power lines. A wind was rising, bringing from somewhere the clatter of a passing train.

Roger cursed himself for having forgotten to take along his tinted glasses. So he sat beside Hazel, crouched in a bucket seat that let him sink down with his head low. Roger was grateful for its depth, especially when a state trooper's car passed them. She drove well, fast but without flash. All the same, he could sense her nervousness.

Why was she going to Westbridge? They turned in a hairpin curve, came to a side-angled fork and turned sharply again.

"You seem to know all the back roads," he said.

"Boondocks are my natural habitat."

"It's nice of you to do this for me."

"What else could I do?" It was not ungracious, merely the truth. "I have as much to lose as you do. Among other things we happen to be on opposite sides of a crucial local issue."

"No," he said. "We're on the same side. I'm not against anything the League asked for."

"Earl Burrage told me what you said to him."

"That was different. I just didn't like his style. His kind makes things impossible. Do you agree with him?"

She took a moment to answer. "I don't. The League is integrationist, and I'm working for them. Even though sometimes I'm not sure I still believe in that objective." She paused, then went on quietly, "Maybe it depends on what happens in Surf City. Tom Walsh is a great man. He is bedrock. He's foreseen a lot, but can he still see ahead with the same clarity? I would like to think so, and I'm trying to help, but everything we've been doing here, attempting here, is on the line now."

Roger sighed. "But how can you win? Fleming is over a barrel. Even if he wanted to, there isn't time to do what the League wants. Walsh may be a great man, but why did he wait until the day before the Pageant opened to make his demands?"

"Oh, get under the stove," she said, "What day before the Pageant? We've been after Fleming for a year. Letter after letter. The man never answered one of them."

"Huh?" said Roger, turning to look at her. Her lips were pressed in a thin caustic smile. "That's news to me," he said.

"It's news to most people. The only place it isn't news is in the newspapers."

"But nothing? No results at all?"

"Ye-e-e-s," she drawled, "we got results. Harassment, intimidation, phones tapped, police spies, false arrests. Like the print shop, where I live. We were turning out a weekly broadside for the League and we had a wild parade of officials slapping us with violations—fire laws, building codes, ordinances, you name it—and summonses and fines and injunctions. Finally last month they shut the place down for good. Claimed they were printing pornography—do they ever think of anything else? So we had to print in Elton and smuggle it in like drugs. But that's just kid stuff. They're really going to start moving on us now that they see we weren't just beating our chops."

"Well," he said, "I still think the old buzzard would welcome a reasonable way out."

"What does reasonable mean? Like the offer he made this afternoon?"

"What was the offer?"

"Franchises and judges and contestants next year, and two or three Negro girls as guests of the Pageant this year."

"I see. Walsh turned it down, I gather?"

"Walsh isn't next-year minded. The contestant principle can be established this year, and guest status doesn't do it. He wants them to be Entries at Large."

"No chance. Fleming can't go that far."

"Why not?"

"That would violate a principle of the Pageant. Every contestant represents a specific place, a state. On what basis could they choose Entries at Large? Where would they come from? And who would make the choice?"

"Simple. Let the League invite half a dozen black contest winners from various parts of the country."

"Half a dozen seems like a lot."

"Oh, I'm just talking. Walsh would be satisfied with less. In fact, I heard him remark that if he had to settle for only one, he'd be quite happy with the girl who took first in Washington, D.C., this past June. So he's not really holding out for very much. Our principle against yours. Against the Pageant's," she amended.

"Still . . ." Roger began, and broke off. Suddenly they had emerged from a scraggly wooded area to a macadam highway with a fair sprinkling of traffic in its four lanes.

"Better get lower," said Hazel. "There's a light up ahead. I should've warned you."

Roger crouched down painfully, half on the floorboard. The car swung into the far right lane, diminishing speed, then picking up again.

"The green's with us," she said. "Just a few minutes more. Are you very uncomfortable?"

"Only inside my head," he replied. He was very near to

her legs now, her marvelous legs, near enough to send a hand sliding up past her knees.

The car veered right to a rougher, telfordized surface and slowed abruptly. Azure light momentarily flooded the dark interior where he huddled in a fetal position. Startled, he twisted around to peer over the window and saw receding a lighted blue neon sign at the roadside: *Judah Cypress Funeral Chapel.* Before them loomed a large white frame house with a colonnaded veranda. They rolled past it to cut into a driveway, eased into a courtyard and came to a stop deep in shadow under low-hanging trees.

"Stay put," she said quietly. "They have a watchman."

She got out of the car and walked toward the house. The sharp report of a screen door closing, then a man's voice. Barely audible sounds of a dialogue. The screen door resounded *splat!* again and Hazel returned. She leaned into the car and whispered, "There's a building straight ahead. Give me half a minute to open the door and follow me. Come out this side."

She was gone again. Megan counted to thirty, then slid out over the driver's seat, keeping low. There was a long flat-roofed building across the yard under a huge elm. Stooping, he ran for it. Hazel was just inside the door. As he lurched past the threshold she closed the door behind him and turned the lock. Then she snapped on an overhead light.

They were in an office, a cramped tidy room furnished in metal and black vinyl, with two narrow windows in the front wall and two narrow doors in the wall directly opposite, hung with prints of Biblical scenes in which all the characters were either brown or black.

"Where are we?" he asked.

Hazel had checked the blinds and replaced the harsh ceiling fixture with two shaded desk lamps. She took off her coat, grinning at him. "This is a mortuary. Make yourself at home."

"Hilarious. May I ask what this is all about?"

"The owner is a friend. He lets us use the place."

"For what?"

"For confidential League business. We're past the county line here, and Fleming's fuzz can't get at us—at least that's our theory and so far it's worked. Would you like a whisk broom for your coat? No? Do relax. You look so tense."

He slumped in a chrome-legged armchair and lit a cigarette, eyes following her across the room to a small safe embedded in the floor. "This is where we keep the bodies," she said. Squatting on her heels, she carefully manipulated the dial.

He gazed at her forlornly, at the majestic buttocks straining her miniskirt. She opened the safe, removed a ledger and took it to a desk. There, thumbing through the ledger, she began writing on a long yellow pad.

Minutes passed, marked only by an occasional rustle of paper where she worked, her oval face shining softly in reflected light. The room and the silence pressed in on him.

"What are you doing?" he asked.

She smiled, not looking up. "Really want to know?"

"Unless you don't trust me. Opposite sides."

"It doesn't matter anymore. Not at this stage." She turned a page in the ledger and told him, "These are the names, addresses and phone numbers of our strike stewards. Where we can contact them on short notice."

"And you expect to be using them?"

"I think we've realized it's just a question of when."

Roger sighed. "I hate to hear it. It'll ruin my week."

She smiled again. "Let's hope so."

What was it he had wanted to ask her about? Something they had discussed in the car. A brilliant idea, hovering just beyond recall. The Great Compromiser, with feet of Henry Clay, and the end of slave trade in the D of C, but what? His lucid intervals were less frequent. For a long time he stared at a print on the wall near him, which showed a black Noah on his ark releasing a dove, and therefore clearly was a mistake, unless it was an albino blackbird. He felt cut off, immersed in loneliness.

Presently she rose. "That's it. You can make your call now. I'll tell you what to say." She took the ledger back to the safe and locked it away and, turning, saw that he had not budged. "What are you waiting for?"

A long ash fell from his cigarette to his coat. "I want to talk to you."

"You keep saying that. Haven't we been talking?"

"I mean about us."

She was going for her coat. "I'm in a hurry, Roger, aren't you?"

He pushed himself up from his chair. "I must know when I'm going to see you again."

She stopped and slowly swung around to face him, her head cocked, her glance sidewise, as though flirting behind a fan, smiling at some unexpected gallantry. "Why, anytime," she said. "Whenever you like. Where do you want to meet me? In a cave somewhere? Or at my place in Dinge Alley?"

He stared at her and said quietly, "What kind of a thing is that to say?"

"Is it too much to say? Too true to say? Too unspeakable to say?" She surveyed him with cool interest. "You see, Roger, we've never really talked, except once, the night we spent together, the last time I saw you. Except for that night, you made it a practice never to refer to the most important thing we shared—our difference in color. I say shared, but it was separate and unequal. No, don't interrupt. Hear me out."

"Can't I defend myself?"

"Don't. There's nothing to defend. I understood. At least, I thought I did at the time. It was your way of telling me that it didn't even rate a mention, that it didn't matter. But of course the difference was there, and the basic condition it imposed on us—of always having to hide—was something we both accepted. It really was no problem. I could always tell myself that there were very sound reasons for our hiding that had nothing to do with color—you were married, you were in the public eye. And so I went along.

"But that last night, when we both got drunk, I heard from you. You called me hot chocolate. And Aphrodite and aphrodisiac, only you spelled it out, *a-f-r-o*. Once you started blubbering and said I made you feel like Gauguin. And then you told me a curious thing. Black is the star, you kept saying. 'Never forget it, Hazel, black is the star.' When I asked what you meant, you explained that it was one of the primary laws of your world—that whenever a white and a black get married, and one of them is in show business, the black is always the star. And I thought and I thought, and I couldn't think of an exception. Sammy Davis is the star. Lena is the star. Pearl is the star. Leslie is the star. And then I realized that it wasn't just show business, it was true in everything, in all of our world. Whenever a white and a black get married, the black must have special qualifications—status, money, accomplishment, talent—to make up for being black. Well, of course, I knew I didn't have them, and you were the star. But I was astounded. I'd thought we were just having a summer romance, and it was all right with me. I was so surprised you'd think of me in connection with marriage. I had loved it when you called me hot chocolate, but you changed everything. You had acted as if color meant nothing, that it was irrelevant, and then the first time you brought it up, it was to tell me that it was an insuperable barrier between us."

Her voice died away tonelessly. Megan stood dumbstruck, his insides churning. Listening to her, he felt like a sleepwalker come awake in a strange place, still sunk in dreams. Though that night five years gone had remained an indelible memory, it had been abandoned in some recess of his brain and sealed off by drink.

Bewildered, guilty, he asked, "But can't both be true?"

"What if they are?" Her eyes were fever bright, though she had spoken with scarcely a betrayal of emotion, as if repeating by rote thoughts long ago shaped and resolved. "To hell with it. It's not for me. I could have an affair with you and be discreet because you're married and a celebrity—but I refuse to hide because I'm black . . . with no special qualifications . . . and no saving attributes or virtues."

Silence enveloped them. Presently Megan went to the desk Hazel had used and took the telephone. Then he paused, and, turning his head to her, he said, "I can't think too straight right now, but please listen, and maybe I'll get across. I don't care what I said. I didn't lie to you, did I? I don't give a damn about this black and white shit, and I never did. I have a very troubled life, and I've got my hands full just making it from one week to the next. If you don't want to meet me on the sneak once in a while, okay, don't. That's the only way it can be with us. But if you do want to, and you could do it for one reason but not for another, well then, goddam it, why can't you pick the reason that helps you? The real difference between us is we want different things. You want to feel sorry for yourself, and I want your ass."

With a bitter and disdainful smile, she said, "My hero."

He lifted the receiver and went rigid. There were explosive sounds outside, a sudden violent commotion, a man's voice shouting, the hard swift slap of running feet on pavement, receding, and the voice again, farther off. Megan and Hazel stared at each other, entranced in fright, waiting. Suspended in mid-air in his hand, the phone hummed like a distant alarm. The footsteps returned. On the front door now, a heavy, rapid knocking, and the man's voice: "Miss Sanders, it's me, Frank!"

Frantically she gestured toward the wall with the two doors. "Just a minute," she called out.

Megan unclenched his hand and put the phone down. Which door? The near one meant circling a glasstopped table. The other was in almost a straight line; he chose it, flew across the room, his senses galvanized alert. The doorknob turned in his palm and the door gave inward. He opened it enough to slide through into the darkness beyond, and quietly closed it.

Listening intently, the sweat running down his face as it pressed against the door, he could hear Hazel and the man conversing but nothing of what they said. He thought of the butt-filled ashtray he had left on a table, and feared it could trap him. *But you don't understand, we're old friends, we've known each other for years, met in Florida, isn't that so, Miss Sanders?*

The room seemed airless, suffocating, charged with a peculiar smell, a musty amalgam of wood shavings and wet umbrellas. He found his lighter, flicked it on. The feeble gas flame lit a yellow sphere around him. He was in the mortuary's warehouse. The room was filled with coffins and their accessories, some on wooden platforms, some on tiers of broad shelves, boxes with silver handles, stacked rectangular piles of thin foam-rubber pads, bolts of quilted satin, pink and white and lavender. With utmost caution he moved among them, scanning the walls. There must be windows and, if not windows, other doors, else how were these coffins brought in and out?

All at once, light spilled weakly around him from behind; he whirled to find Hazel standing in the doorway he had left. She leaned against the jamb, her outlined form surrounded by an aureole, beckoning him with a forefinger. He walked her shadow, as on a dark path to her.

Her face was drawn. She seemed utterly spent. She told him softly, "There was someone outside in the yard. He was trying to look in through one of the windows. The watchman chased him, but he got away."

Roger said, "Maybe it was just a house prowl, a burglar."

"No. A burglar would avoid a lighted place."

"What do you think?"

She shook her head. "I can't think. Maybe somebody knew I was coming here. Maybe I was followed." She paused. "Or maybe you're the one being followed."

"Impossible," he said with emphasis. "Why would anyone want to spy on me?"

Reflexly he reached out to touch her, to comfort her, taking her hand. It was their first physical contact in all the time they had been together. A voluptuous current sparked across the tactile synapse, and they shivered in the power of their commitment. It transcended all thought and reason, all denial, all defenses.

He kissed her hand and put her palm to his face and pulled her to him. She yielded to his arms, to his caress of her cheeks, her temples. He took her nape and tilted her head back and they kissed tenderly, barely brushing lips, tasting each other, their tongues gently explorative. How acutely he remembered her fragrance. Their mouths were locked, sucking breath from each other. His hands traced her spine and embraced the twin moons of her hind, pressing her to him, her lissome warmth curved to his loins. Eyes closed, he swam in a sea of gold, the gold of the bay water in sunlight the first time he had seen her, the gold in the mirror where he had found her again.

He swept her up in his arms and carried her deeper into the storeroom, to a low platform heaped with coffin pads, and slowly laid her down.

"Not here, not now," she whispered, holding on to his arms.

"Yes, baby."

Unopposed, he raised her dress, peeled away her pale lacy underpants. In the nebular light he drank in the wealth of her body, its planes and dips and hollows, its smooth glades and cambers. With a shudder, he shook off his coat and knelt beside her, in this prayerful posture kissing her belly's flexuous sweep from the navel to the finespun pubic floss, where, descending, his tongue fluttered and she groaned.

And now, rampant, his swollen penis out, he climbed on top of her and her thighs parted under him. God, what a lucky cock, he thought enviously, the only part of his body to be able fully to savor her bounty.

Despite all his efforts to hold on to awareness, he was lost, he ceased to be. His vision blurred to mist, his hearing recorded only the blood pounding in his head as heart and balls pumped away together. Nothing was left of him but a quaking rump attached to a massive iron instrument, a divine rod, whose imperious movements it followed. Somewhere on earth there was one perfect cunt for every cock, and they spent their lives hunting for each other—this one was his. Arching to meet his ferocious plunging, she whimpered and moaned, brimful of him. When finally he shot into her, in as far as he could go, she thrust up her groin and found somehow a last fraction of an inch of him to engorge.

With a gasp, he slowly collapsed on her, head to head, his lips to her face, breathing in hoarse gulps. After a while, when he grew quiet, he heard her say in his ear, "That's what I call being fucked."

"Yes, baby," he whispered.

A minute passed. She stirred under him. He was still in her. Her upper torso was moving, jerking spasmodically. Tears fell on him. She was sobbing, clutching him to her.

"What is it, baby?" he asked in pain. "What's the matter?"

She shook her head and more tears wet his face. "I wish I were white," she said.

It was almost nine-thirty by the time Roger had effected the transfer from Hazel's car to the one where Lou Cates waited, a mile out of Westbridge, on a road lonely enough to be unobserved. The circuitous way back to Surf City would be long, entailing a detour of the marshland short cut. But it was taking longer still, for Roger had told Lou he wanted to drive around aimlessly awhile before they returned.

"You'll miss the Merri-Cola reception, what's left of it."

"I can't go anyway. My clothes are a mess."

"There's still time to get back to the hotel and change."

"But I'm a mess too. Just drive and let me sit here and not think and collect myself."

He had been with Hazel somewhat less than three hours. Seldom in his life had he been through so much in so short a span; seldom had he been so moved. The nightbound countryside, dimly bathed in orange moonlight, had a healing effect on him, and, despite the deafening chirping of insects that rose from the fields on all sides, he was able to find inner silence and peace from the turbulence of his thoughts.

At length, as they were cutting past the edge of a town, he suggested they stop somewhere for a bottle of something, and Cates, nodding, allowed himself a smile of relief and observed, "Ah, back to normal."

The remark was truer than Cates knew. Above and beyond all he felt, in the midst of his ferment and confusion, Roger had grown increasingly and incredibly horny. His cock lay unwashed in his soiled pants, as big and stiff as a drum major's baton.

For all the sufficiency and the luxuriance of his intercourse with Hazel—indeed, *because* of it—he was still unsated. Nothing would satisfy him now but a glut of gash. And so, thinking and drinking as they sped back to Surf City, his mind turned to Sue Rossiter.

It was almost eleven when they reached town. From a street booth he phoned the reception and asked for Sue, but it was over and everyone had left. He tried her hotel, but she was not in. He called the Hilton for messages, but there was nothing. In desperation he went through a list of contingency kooze, but they were all off on other contingencies.

Reduced finally to cruising the watering places where he might score jackal style, he bundled his coat around him and bent an elbow at half a dozen bars, casting his smile with no success. There was something wild about him, a look that warned away even the tramps. Only a woman who wanted to take a beating would have found him attractive now.

By one A.M., roaring drunk, literally roaring at the last place, alone and dreadfully depressed, he took a taxi to his hotel. In the lobby, the bell captain intercepted him and handed him a note sealed in a Hilton envelope.

"Mr Cates asked me to give you this when you came in, sir."

He tore it open and read: *Merry Christmas from Santa Claus.* Baffled, exasperated, indignant, he crushed the note and stuffed it into a pocket. To his roiled brain it summoned up a vague recall of the nightmare with which he had wakened to this extraordinary day, the fearful dream of Santa JF dumping him to a wolfpack. In the elevator on his way up he thought of going to Cates's room to throw him out the window, but he was too wary; it could wait till morning. He staggered down the corridor to his door.

He turned the lock and entered. There was light in his bedroom and music softly floated out. He went to it. Sue Rossiter was sitting up in his bed, wearing his pajama top.

She put down the book she was holding, her eyes filled with welcome, and said in her low sweet voice, "Surprise, darling."

He stared at her, transfixed. "How did you get in?"

"Lou gave me the key."

Slowly, Roger's smile grew until it became a thing of glory.

"Merry Christmas," he said as he began to tear off his clothes.

BOOK THREE *Tuesday*

16 · MISS ALASKA

THEY arrived at the Armory like debutantes flocking to a cotillion.

Entering the vast hall with her forty-nine rivals, Mildred Waxman was still overwhelmed by the incredible amnesty granted her yesterday by Dr. Lydecker.

But how long could her luck hold out? She squeezed her purse to feel the reassuring bulge of the small jar inside. If her phenomenal *mazel* continued, then maybe, just *maybe,* that jar could be her key to the crown. A wild notion, her common sense insisted. She had as much chance of winning as Nasser of becoming a rabbi.

The air-conditioned hall was cool as a cave. Norm Prescott was already on stage.

"Good morning, glamour girls," Prescott's amplified voice blanketed their gossip. "All of you say 'cheese.' "

"CHEESE!" echoed a chorus of Greek goddesses.

"Perfect!" said Prescott. "Such lovely smiles. And especially for so early in the morning. My wife wouldn't smile before eight A.M. even if I tickled her nose with a new mink."

The girls tittered and Prescott lowered his head in a ghost bow. They didn't know it, but he was subbing for Megan, as well as using his lines. Megan had awakened him half an hour ago to confide that he had a first-degree hangover. Norm had dressed hurriedly, picked up Olga Loomis in his Mercedes, and cursed at the constipated traffic delaying their rush to the Armory.

Prescott stalked across the big stage. "As most of you have probably guessed," he spoke into the mike, "this entire morning belongs to our sponsors . . . the firms who put up the money for your scholarships. They've sent a team of top photographers to take group shots of you kids endorsing their products. So, whether you place first or last, your faces will appear in national magazines, newspapers, on billboards and over one hundred TV stations."

There was a buzz of excitement from the girls until Prescott's voice boomed out again. He waved his free hand. "Right up here for the first picture. It's for the American Millinery Association. They're out to recapture the lost youth market. They're betting an ad campaign featuring all you Pageant pretties wearing hats will bring them back in style."

A dolly truck stacked with hat boxes was rolled on stage as he talked. The celebrated Duncan brothers, Chris and Eric, had already set up their camera artillery. As the girls pressed forward to ascend the stage, two prop boys took turns calling out the state inscribed on each box-lid. It was like Army mail call. Whenever a state was named, a girl stepped forward to claim her hatbox.

Olga Loomis sat in the front row. From this command post, she could supervise each routine. A sheet fastened to a clipboard on her lap listed the sequence in which the commercials were to be shot. The stop watch on her wrist was for making certain no sponsor consumed more than fifteen minutes for his takes.

Swiftly the girls put on their hats. Then Chris Duncan deployed his subjects into three lines on the steps of a makeshift bleacher stand. He fired cues at them like darts from a blowgun.

"Nevada, move left just one step. Your feather's blocking Ohio's face ... Head toward me, Alabama, I'm catching you in profile ... Missouri, slip your state ribbon down a few inches; I can't see the first two letters ..."

He kept them in their places for a series of rapid shots. Meanwhile brother Eric took photographs from different angles. When the fifteen minutes had expired, Chris Duncan wagged his hand at the girls, as if brushing away attic cobwebs.

The girls had hardly started to stretch when Olga Loomis took over.

"Next setup, everybody!" she said. "This one's a Merri Cola commercial. As soon as you've taken off the hats and touched up your hair, we'll be ready."

With a sigh of relief, Mildred removed the bonnet model she had worn. Its velvet strap under her chin, almost in the area of her camouflaged scar, had been perilously close. She wondered if some of the Hide-a-Mark ointment had been rubbed off.

Meanwhile, Eric Duncan had been checking the scenery for the next assignment. This time, one row of girls was directed to sit on the stage floor. Those behind them were ordered to lean against a rustic fence.

The prop boys passed among the girls, handing out soft-drink bottles.

"What I want," said Eric Duncan, "is all bottles raised toward my camera. Like you're all saying, 'Here's to Merri Cola!' "

With each bottle lofted, with fifty bright smiles and one hundred eyes shining ecstatic approval of the nation's top soft drink, the shutter snapped several times and the pictures moved on into history.

Sponsor after sponsor had his photographic innings. Colognes. Play clothes. Costume jewelry. Sunglasses. A national air line.

A break in the normal routine came suddenly and unexpectedly. One of the sponsors was a women's wear chain, Silks 'n Satins. In previous pageants the firm had posed the contestants in flowing housecoats, slacks and rain togs. But this year the sponsor wanted to push a new specialty.

As the girls started for their dressing rooms to change into his latest product, Olga Loomis, who had accompanied them to check on arrangements, returned breathlessly and made a beeline for Norm Prescott. She whispered urgently. Prescott in turn wheeled on the chain's representative, a mustached man in a seersucker suit.

"I'm sorry, Mr. Flexner. The black lace nightgowns are out."

"The hell they are!" he said testily. "We're expanding into lingerie this fall. We'll feature—"

"Not with our girls. The Pageant doesn't permit photographs of contestants in underwear. Next year you'll be requesting Lady Godiva shots."

"Look here, Prescott. My company—"

"Save your breath. Our rules on good taste are explicit."

"So is our intention to get our money's worth. Do you think we're paying your ten grand pirate fee to take pictures of girls wearing clothes Rebecca of Sunnybrook Farm wouldn't be caught dead in? Do you want me to go to Fleming himself?"

"You do just that, Mr. Flexner." Prescott peered coolly at his wristwatch. "He'll be in his office for the next hour."

The company rep stormed from the hall. The photographing continued with a series featuring the girls sitting under hair-driers.

"Did you hear that?" whispered Lori Macklin to Mildred during a one-minute break. "Ten big ones for each endorsement? They must have raked in almost one hundred grand during the past few hours. No wonder they call Fleming 'The Merchant of Venus.' "

"Ten thousand?" That's a lot of money for just one photograph," observed Mildred in an awed voice.

"Wise up," Lori said. "Only companies who have contracts with the Pageant are eligible. That's what it costs them for an exclusive shot of fifty certified American beauties glorifying some crummy product. So every time we hear a click, honey, it's really Fleming's cash register. Cash is his favorite four-letter word. If you ask me, we ought to organize a Princess America Protective Union. They're getting us for coolie rates."

An announcement from Olga Loomis ended their conversation. "Last shot, kids," she said. "After that, some of you will be asked to pose for individual commercials. Now, this final one's for Snow-White Toothpaste, to introduce their new toothbrush."

The prop boys began distributing toothbrushes. After the allotted fifteen minutes, the girls broke ranks while Olga once again took the mike. She began to read from a new list.

"Maine, you'll be showing Indiana how to make a Down East Sandwich—recipe courtesy of the Maine Sardine Council. New Mexico, you'll be displaying Navajo silver jewelry. Hawaii, Paradise Pineapples wants you for a luau shot. Louisiana, there's a shrimp picture for Gulf Coast Prawns. Alaska—"

Hearing her name called out, Mildred felt a glow of pleasant surprise. Who could possibly want her for a promo?

"Alaska, you're booked to model fashion shots for Northern Lights Ski Togs . . ."

The Northern Lights set was located along the lefthand aisle. The photographer, Phil Sargent, was waiting for her. He was tall, blue-eyed, and puffed at a meerschaum pipe.

"Miss Waxman? I know you must be tired. So I'll try to make this short and sweet."

Mildred turned her head and explored the set. A backdrop draped against the wall dominated the scene. On it, a sweep of snow and sky, with a curtain of spectacular northern lights overhead, was painted in facsimile. The effect was a remarkable arctic illusion.

Sargent indicated a heap of furs on a table.

"My firm is introducing a new Alaska line," he explained. "It should make big fashion news for next winter's sports crowd. Fairbanks Fox. Nome Nutria. Sitka

Seal." He paused to draw on his pipe. "Have you ever ridden on a dog sled?"

Mildred shook her head. "Only in my dreams, after I read *Call of the Wild.*"

"Well, your dreams are about to come true. Meet your personal driver. Jasper Bear Claw, the best dog-trainer in Alaska."

He gestured at a swarthy man in a fur parka heading toward them. Behind him, leashed to his hand, panted a team of six Alaskan malamutes, their pink tongues lolling. Bringing up the rear, a couple of prop men carried a genuine dog sled.

The sled was quickly set up in front of the backdrop. With a grunt, Jasper Bear Claw slid into the driver's seat and assumed the reins. His canine sextet was strung out single file.

"Miss Waxman, you'll wear the seal piece first, please."

The next hour was a chore Mildred knew she would always remember. Donning fur after fur, she kept posing on the sled behind Bear Claw trying to look like a frost-proof passenger mushing through a wilderness of white. Sargent kept peppering directions.

"Try to look like you'd be shivering if the fur didn't keep you cozy . . . Open your mouth slightly so it'll look as if your breath can be seen in the cold. We'll airbrush in the vapor on the negative . . ."

The lights kept beating at her like bludgeons. She was feeling as enervated as a sunstroke victim when Sargent smiled and said, "Just one last shot, sweetie. Put this on and we'll have you out of here in a wink."

He handed her a two-pelt mink choker. "This is going to be a closeup. It's cheap ranch mink. But on you it'll look like a million. Should help us sell an entire warehouse of the skins."

Obediently, she fastened the tight-fitting fur around her throat. Then the camera clicked, incredibly, for a final time.

Mildred tugged off the neckpiece as Sargent turned aside to confer with Jasper Bear Claw. Then, for no special reason, she looked down casually at the fur in her hands. What she saw made her react as if a lightning bolt had just missed her by a foot. A long, greasy streak stained the sheen of one of the pelts.

Instinctively, Mildred slapped the choker back around her throat. She knew what must be visible there. The past hour's hectic pace had kept her so preoccupied she had failed to realize that the switching from one neck-circling parka hood to another had caused disastrous erosion. And this last, strangling contact with the mink choker had undoubtedly rubbed away enough of the protective cosmetic to expose at least part of her scar.

The photographer still had his back toward her. He had seen nothing. Frantically, Mildred shoved the furs higher under her chin.

If she could only make it to the john . . . If she could have just five private minutes in one of the pay cubicles with the jar nesting inside her handbag . . .

Sargent was finishing with Bear Claw. He was turning to face her. With his cameraman's eye trained for detail, the moment he took back the pelts . . .

The john!

Her heart racing, Mildred braced herself and began to walk away. It would work. It had to work, because if it didn't . . .

"Miss Waxman!"

She could pretend not to hear him. With all those voices gabbling, with hammers beginning to dismantle scenery, it would be perfectly natural if she didn't respond. Just a few more steps would carry her out of his voice range. He wouldn't chase a girl on her way to the . . .

"Miss Waxman! The mink skins!"

Mildred turned back, her face a death mask.

"The neckpiece, Miss Waxman. We want you to keep it. A present from Northern Lights because you've worked like a Trojan for us today."

She thanked him profusely, feeling like a victim who has just escaped the Iron Maiden. He relit his dead pipe, then stared at her in puzzlement.

"You're not going to wear it back to your room? The mercury's in the eighties outside. Let me have it wrapped for you."

Mildred let her eyes stray toward the john. "I was about to meet one of the girls in the powder room," she improvised. "I'd like her to see me wearing it. Then you can wrap it for me."

Sargent nodded, exhaling an aromatic cloud of smoke. "Of course."

Mildred took a step forward, stopped. She opened her purse, inspected the contents, and frowned. She looked up into Sargent's sapphire eyes.

"This is very embarrassing," she said demurely. "But can you lend me a dime?"

17 · MISS FLORIDA

IN the main lobby of the Lido Royale, the *Today* board for Tuesday listed the event in red letters: *12:30-2:00* P.M. . . . *Miss Florida Luncheon . . . Roof Garden.*

For Art Waldo, largely responsible for planning it, the occasion was emphatically red-letter. It was the first of three gala social salvos to be fired off in honor of Robin Gervais. This blast, for an inbred group, was sponsored by the Orlando Jaycees. Thursday there would be another luncheon, national in scope, given by the Florida Tourist Development Association. It would be followed Friday night by a lavish late buffet, courtesy of the Florida fruit exchange.

All was going merrily and Mr. Waldo cautiously congratulated himself. There were thirty-five guests, most of them VIPs from the Sunshine State, political, cultural, commercial. Serenading the group was a trio of strolling guitarists, Cuban refugees, playing endless variations on "Perfidia." And no less than six photographers were cruising the scene. Two were in Waldo's employ, hired in case too few responded to his publicity releases, but he was elated to see that Robin was drawing on her own. The word was out—Miss Florida was clearly a prominent contender.

But now, as he observed another massive toast being hoisted to something Floridian, Waldo had misgivings. Such cordiality, such enthusiasm. Was it possible their foaming beakers of orange juice had been fortified with something more invigorating than Vitamin D? Technically, only nonalcoholic beverages could be served. Whether or not they were being laced was another matter.

But, as he damn well knew, everything mattered. The tiniest infraction of the rules could wreck Robin's chances. This, he decided, was really the province of her new official Pageant chaperone, Mrs. Louisa Willow, who had taken over from Aunt Charlotte the day before. He sought her out.

Mrs. Willow was posing in a group shot, but by some telepathic means which had been instantly established at their first meeting, she turned, looked at Waldo, and nodded. Waldo beamed. He liked her enormously. They had so much in common—excess weight, a gnawing hunger for a winner (neither had, in their years of Pageant service, come closer than the quarter finals), and a convert's faith that Robin would lead them from the wilderness. A moment later she disengaged herself and came to him, a large cheerful woman in a garden frock and matching picture hat.

"My goodness," she said, "are you as hot as you look?"

"Well," said Waldo, "frankly, I don't feel so hot," and he grinned at his pun. He lowered his voice. "Tell me, do you think they're drinking?"

"I'm sure of it. And in this heat. But then, you Florida people are accustomed to it."

"The heat?"

"And the drinking."

"I deny everything."

She returned his smile. "Is that all you wanted?"

"No, I really wanted to ask you to run away with me to Pago Pago."

"Aren't you a dear," she said, squeezing his hand. "Let me think about it."

His eyes followed her fondly as she rejoined the party. How fortunate they had been, having Mrs. Willow assigned to Robin, a wise, unflappable veteran, a woman both soothing and stimulating. Already, it seemed to him, he could detect her influence on Robin. Secretly he had worried, especially these last weeks, whether the arduous summer grind of being Miss Florida had wrung too much out of her. She had often seemed bored, withdrawn from her surroundings.

But this afternoon she was, far more than just figuratively, the life of the party. This relaxed new mood, this easy concentration of thought and energy on the Pageant's demands, was exactly what she needed for the tense days ahead. Which Mrs. Willow was so admirably equipped to insure. In all, thought Waldo, a hell of a stroke of good luck.

Just then a clipped voice behind him said, "A great turnout, Mr. Waldo, a great affair. My compliments."

Waldo had started, less from surprise than recognition that it was General Gervais. He turned, resisting an impulse to do it by the numbers. "Thank you, sir," he said. "Deeply gratified."

The general nodded, looking somewhat pleased for a fleeting moment. He had come in civilian clothes, but even so he looked like a brigadier. His tropical poplins remained unwrinkled, as starched as his posture. He had been keeping to himself, walking about with a proprietary air as though on a tour of inspection. Now, with his hands clasped behind his back, the ever-present cigar locked in his teeth, he seesawed gently on his heels and seemed to be waiting for a report of some kind.

Finally Waldo thought of something to say.

"I've been meaning to ask you, sir, when you expect your pilots back." The general nodded again and said nothing. Obviously this statement required further explanation. Waldo plunged on. "You see, sir, if they're to be here for the weekend, I ought to start hunting reservations. As it is, two rooms may be impossible."

"That's very kind of you, Mr. Waldo," said Gervais. He paused. "But only Major Spofford is coming, so one room will be quite sufficient . . . You look surprised, Mr. Waldo."

"I am," said Waldo, baffled. "Of the two, I thought the captain was the more interested in the Pageant. Fact is, he said something to me about arriving early Thursday morning."

The general's smile spread slowly. It seemed to Waldo he was struggling to say nothing more, but the same force that had made him smile now made him speak. Waving his cigar with a gesture of dismissal, he said in so underplayed a manner that it lay bare his effort to achieve it, "Captain Brioni was unexpectedly transferred. By Thursday he'll be in Okinawa."

"Okinawa?" Waldo echoed tonelessly.

"That's the Army," said Gervais, puffing away. Then he added, "This information is confidential, Mr. Waldo. I expect you to keep it entirely to yourself."

Without waiting for comment, the general turned abruptly and resumed his tour.

And this to Art Waldo, all at once depressed, made sense because an order needed no answer. For one miserable-making moment it had acutely brought back his melancholy memories of the Army, of the dog-shit time in his life when he had nothing to say about who he was or where he was or what he was doing.

Across the roof garden he saw Robin sitting in animated conversation with half a dozen heavy-lidded males.

Beautifully poised, gracious, natural, she had it all, true warmth and true dignity. How could Gervais have such a daughter? Only their years of separation, the decisive years of her upbringing by her aunt, could explain it.

A thrill of fear raced through Waldo as suddenly he heard the sounds of disaster—a shriek from Robin, china shattering, outcries of dismay. A plate of syrupy ice cream had fallen off the table into her lap. She had jumped up, a chocolate smear spread across her pleated white skirt, staring fascinated at the damage. Then looking up at the consternation around her, she burst out laughing. "Nobody leave till I get back!" she cried, and, refusing to allow either her aunt or Mrs. Willow to go with her, she made a deep flourishing curtsy and ran laughing to the elevator.

Everyone applauded.

"What a girl," Waldo said under his breath.

In her room, Robin stripped quickly to her underthings and put her skirt to soak in the bathtub. Then she took out a suitcase, unlocked it, and found a hidden olive-green box the size of a cigarette lighter. It was a miniaturized walkie-talkie, a new marvel of electronics, still classified Army equipment. The week before, Paul had unofficially borrowed a pair of these instruments from a Signal Corps crony for use in Surf City. One he had given Robin; the other was with him, close at hand, in constant readiness for her call.

Gingerly she extended the telescoped antenna to a wand-like eight inches, then jiggled a tiny red lever, once, twice. After a moment a faint buzz answered her signal. She pressed the *Send* node and spoke into a perforated hollow, saying, "Robin calling Batman ... Over," and moved her thumb to the *Receive*.

Paul Brioni's voice came in, softly, clearly. "This is Batman. Where are you, darling?"

"In my room. Where are you?"

"At a motel, where else? I'm sunbathing at the pool and losing my mind. Why haven't I heard from you?"

"Darling, don't be a monster. Didn't I call four times yesterday? This is the first minute I've had alone since I woke up, and I had to ruin a skirt to get it, so let's not waste time. I love you. . . . Over."

"I love you too. What's that about ruining a skirt?"

"I dumped ice cream on it so I could sneak a few minutes to talk to you. How much do you love me?"

"I'll show you next time I see you."

"I can't wait."

"Neither can I. It kills me to think we're only half a

mile apart. Listen, I have a great idea. You stay there and say you're sick, and I'll get a physician's black satchel and come over disguised as Dr. Kildare. What do you think? . . . Over."

"Brilliant. They've intercepted nine phony doctors so far today. I think about you all the time, do you?"

"What else is there to do? I'm hung here—my room to the pool to the restaurant, and that's it. I'm afraid to go out just to take a walk or try another place to eat. It's like I pulled a bank job and this is my hideout."

"But, sweetie, why can't you take the gadget with you? Then if you don't answer, I'll know you're some place where you can't talk at the moment and I'll wait, if I can."

"Yes, dear, but I'm registered at the Plaza in New York, and that's where I'm supposed to be. What if I bumped into your aunt or Mr. Waldo, or what's her name, Mrs. Willow? Not to mention a certain general who told me to stay away until Friday. . . . Over."

"I say phooey on all of them. In spades."

There was a pause, then Paul's voice came in, not quite under control. "Well, anyway you made me laugh, and that's something. You sound good, darling, very, very good."

"You should have heard me this morning. Very, very bad."

"You mean the physical?"

"No, that was fine, actually. This was later, at the talent meeting. Sue Rossiter told us that Missouri and I were doing practically the same act—both of us violin solos and both playing a Grieg etude. She suggested one of us might at least choose a different composer, which of course would mean preparing a whole new piece in three days, and where we'd find time for it God knows, so we both said no. But Mr. Waldo said we'd probably cancel each other out, and Aunt Charlotte suggested why don't I do my gypsy fiddle thing—you know, what I did at the Heart Fund benefit in July, remember? Are you listening, darling? . . . . Over."

"Yes. Gypsy fiddle at the Heart Fund. So?"

"Well, it may not be great fiddle in a classical sense, but it's different and effective, and I could have it in shape in a couple of hours. So I began to think. And then Aunt Charlotte came up with a real groovy idea—why not wear a gypsy costume and do it right? Knock their eyes out, agree?"

"Agree, but where can you get a gypsy costume?"

"That's no problem, dear. There are plenty of costumers in New York, only it gets complicated having them bring out enough stuff to choose from, and time, expense, et cetera. But we worked it out very simply. Mrs. Willow knows a gypsy place on the boardwalk near Oak Street—you know, fortunetellers?—and she went there and it's all set. They're letting me pick a whole outfit from their own things. And that's where I'm going in about half an hour. By the way, what did you do last night?"

"I read the sex manual you gave me for my birthday."

"Then next time we're together I want you to do everything to me in Chapter Five."

"After we try Chapter Four."

"Sweetie, I could talk to you all day, but they're waiting for me. I love you. . . . Over."

"And under, and especially in between. Kiss."

"Kiss."

Some minutes later, cool and crisp in an ivory cotton print, Robin returned to the roof garden. The photographers went into a last flurry of action as she began to make her leisurely rounds of goodbyes, a model of cheer and *politesse*. And so refreshingly modest, as someone commented, observing her blush to a compliment. "Robin," a lady had said to her, "I don't know what it is, but you've got something remarkable in you."

How right she was, Robin was thinking.

The trip to Oak Street entailed five blocks and five hundred broiling but gawking pedestrians enroute. The temperature was at blood heat, the air as shimmery as molten glass. Just short of her destination, the gleaming white convertible made a brief stop to let Robin out and spun away, Mrs. Willow waving her parasol and calling, "Forty-five minutes, dear!" Half hidden under a huge leghorn hat, Robin climbed a ramp to the boardwalk without undue haste, turned a corner, and became anonymous.

The place leaped at her, a red-painted storefront garishly adorned with limp triangular day-glo pennants of the kind usually seen at gas stations. In both its windows were large colorful signs saying MADAME ANDRASHI, AUTHENTIC HUNGARIAN GYPSY COUNSELOR, under which appeared a zodiac, a diagrammed hand, a compartmentalized head, and the words *Palmist, Phrenologist, Astrologer, Tea Served, Air-Conditioned.* She walked in, to be greeted by a sight that was hilariously like a cartoon that needed no caption.

There was Madame Andrashi, the middle-aged authentic air-conditioned Hungarian gypsy, swathed in brilliant silks, bedecked with jewelry, seated at a small green-draped table. A crystal ball at her left, she was studying a racing form. She looked up at Robin and diamonds set in her teeth flashed as she smiled.

"I'm Miss Gervais," said Robin, "from the Pageant."

Madame shook her head. "It's not necessary to say. I have eyes. You are very beautiful. You are going to win." Her speech was soft and slurred and altogether charming.

"How well do you do with horses?" Robin grinned.

"Hah!" cried Madame Andrashi, a tender nerve touched. "If I was good with horses, I would have nothing to do with people," and she shrugged with comic sadness.

"You have some clothes to show me?" Robin asked, looking to a nondescript multicolored bundle on a chair in a corner, her heart sinking.

"Yes, but not those," said Madame, getting up. "Those are for you not to like them, in case the lady came with you—the lady who watches you," she explained more fully, to Robin's further confusion. "Then I say to you, why don't you go in the back, where we have much more clothes to see? Then you go and I stay here with the lady and read her fortune. But—" she smiled grandly, with authentic Hungarian gypsy wisdom and guile—"you are alone, so we don't have to do this. Come with me."

Robin might not have moved had not Madame Andrashi taken her by the hand. Yet she was not afraid as she let herself be led through a succession of curtains, all reaching from cloth-hidden ceilings to carpeted floors, then more curtains, at length through beaded curtains to a warren evidently living quarters. Here were covered studio beds, some Dante chairs, a bentwood rocker, Moroccan hassocks, and a color TV set with a towering antenna entwined with paper flowers. The walls were lined with sandy jute burlap, and the tentlike effect was cool and insulated from the world. On an oval dining table lay a profusion of apparel and accessories.

"You look through these and see what you like," said Madame.

"But what about size?' Robin asked. "How can I tell?"

"The way we dress it is not so important," Madame smiled. "But you can try on. Take your time. I will be outside."

"But can't you help me choose the—"

"No. I will be outside," said Madame. "When you are finished, come out. I will wait for you." And she disappeared through the curtains.

Robin turned her attention to the table heaped with clothes. What she saw delighted her. She sorted them, running her hands through them—lacy camisoles, studded belts, crinolines, embroidered satin slippers, cambric petticoats, bandannas, velvet bodices—clothes from another time, another world. Excitedly she held up a patchwork dirndl, an antique whose riotous elegance captured her at once. How much more, she thought, there was in this little room than she had bargained for.

Never had Robin thought more to the point. From behind, a strong pair of arms slid around her, encircling her waist, pressing her to a body unmistakably a man's and a voice chuckled in her ear, "How's my little gypsy fiddler?"

"Paul!" Robin cried. She almost fainted.

He turned her to him, holding her. "Quiet," he whispered, "everything's under control. I fixed it with Madame Andrashi. Who's out front—Mrs. Willow?"

She stared at him. He was peeling sunburn, wearing slacks and a knit shirt that had been her first present to him. "No," she said, trying to think, "I'm alone. She'll come for me."

"How soon?"

"Forty minutes, maybe."

"How long will it take you to find a costume?"

"I don't know . . . not long . . ."

"Good," he breathed, kissing her lips, her nose, biting her neck, his hands roaming her body. Suddenly he picked her up and carried her to a bed. Their eyes locked as he pulled up her dress and took off her underpants. Silently he got between her raised thighs and started rolling a condom on his penis.

"No," she said urgently, taking him in her hand and removing the rubber skin. "I want you without it."

He shook his head, but he was helpless to resist as she guided him into her. And then, after a few savage thrusts, the bed heaving under them, he groaned and tried to pull out as he felt himself nearing climax. But she clasped her legs and her arms around him, clutching him to her, refusing to let him withdraw, whispering fiercely, "Come in me . . . come in me."

"Oh God," he said, and let himself go, his unprotected seed pulsating into her again and again.

They lay quietly together and she caressed him, and presently he sat up. "Why?" he asked. "Why, darling?'

"Because it doesn't matter," she said softly. "I'm pregnant, my love." She took his hand and squeezed it, responding to the pain and fright in his eyes, the disbelief, the wanting to disbelieve. "I know, darling, I found out for sure two weeks ago. It must have happened the second time. I counted."

For several minutes he sat there, face cupped in his hands, looking at Robin occasionally, then away again to his thoughts. After a while he said gently, "Maybe it's the best thing that could have happened. Now we have no choice."

"Choice about what?" she asked, stroking his lips.

"About you and the Pageant," he said. "Now we have to tell your father the truth. We've been married three months, and you're pregnant and that's it." Quietly she said, "That's impossible, Paul. I can't."

"But how can you go on?" He was reasoning with her. "What about the physical you took this morning? They're going to find out, don't you see?"

"No dear. They didn't test for it. I don't know why, but they didn't. Nobody knows or suspects. There's no reason to say anything. Next week, after the Pageant is over, we'll put our heads together and decide what to do."

"But what can we do except tell him, sooner or later?"

"There are such things as abortions, you know." She nodded at him. "After the Pageant I'll be free again. I can fly to New York for a weekend and get it done."

"Never," he said, and repeated, "Never." And then he stirred and said, "What if you win?"

She kissed his cheek. "The odds are forty-nine to one."

"Robin, you're crazy! We can't take the chance."

Again she kissed him. "You're still in shock, darling. I've had time to think about it. I can't tell Dad I ruined my chance for winning. It would kill him to know I had thrown away everything that means so much to him. Let things work themselves out naturally. The Pageant will come to an end, I'll be a graceful loser, and then we'll work things out one way or another. Who knows—Dad may even promote you to major when he finds out you've given him a grandchild."

Her hand was brushing his thigh, playing with him, touching his rigidity, holding it. "Last chance to fill up before the desert," she said.

He shuddered and opened her up again.

Half an hour later, emerging to blinding sunlight with Mrs. Willow from Madame Andrashi's authentic Hungarian bazaar and rendezvous, Robin carried an armload of Madame's frippery and her own beautiful thoughts.

"I must say," remarked Mrs. Willow, "you seem to have made excellent use of the time."

"Thank you," said Robin, smiling. Her eyes shone. How intuitive everyone was today.

18 · JOHN FLEMING

THE crown sparkled at the center of the massive rosewood table, attracting all eyes. An exquisitely designed tiara, its faceted jewels outlined a pattern dainty as a dew-spangled cobweb. These scaled upward to a low eminence studded with a stone the size of a pea. Then the gems receded into the base, a shining silver band, until they became tiny radiant pellets.

Fleming surveyed the scene with much more satisfaction than he had experienced here at roughly the same hour yesterday, when he had been grappling with the militant Walsh delegation. Today, the chamber was not a battleground. It was a schoolroom.

And he was the teacher.

Fleming canvassed the faces of the eight Pageant judges assembled for briefing. Almost all of them stared at the tiara.

"Ladies and gentlemen," he began, "I've been watching you study the crown which you will award to some fortunate young lady on Saturday night."

He gestured casually toward the light-refracting ornament. "Actually, my friends, that diadem is of little intrinsic value. It contains not a single diamond and is worth less than four hundred dollars. All of the gems are common stones. Spinel, zircon, rutile and titania. The band itself is made of sterling. But we all know, cheap as it is, that crown is ardently desired by every one of our fifty girls. The choice as to which one will wear it throughout this coming year is entirely up to you.

"Over the years this Pageant has been served by many important judges, most of them household names. Statesmen, stars of stage and screen, distinguished men of letters, industrialists, leaders in all the arts, college presidents. We can even boast having been honored with one Nobel Prize winner. I feel justified in saying, however, that no group has ever been of a higher caliber or more widely respected than yourselves."

He let them preen a bit, if so inclined.

Athene Ciardi, that ageless Greek opera tornado, bloomed before him like an overgrown orchid.

Her Tosca, her Butterfly, her Mimi and Lucia, all had sparked near riots of adoration in opera houses from Milan to Manhattan. Although she was probably in her sixties, and the famous jet-black hair she let flow loose when she sang an electrifying Medea was dyed, she still retained the Great Presence.

Julius Laurel, owner of a popular line of beauty products and a Pageant sponsor, sat with one finger to cheek in the pose of the Thinker. In his white turtle neck and black suit of an Edwardian cut, he resembled a minister. The Hollywood writing witch, Glenda Dowling, looked as if she had a chip on her tongue and could hardly wait to spit it out. The glaze in her reddened eyes hinted that she had already been nipping at her Margaritas.

In contrast, Lois Potter Smith seemed cool and neat and natural. She was wearing a crisp linen dress, pale pink, like a reflection of the faint color in her delicate cheeks.

Fleming's glance halted briefly when he came to Sue Rossiter and Roger Megan, seated at the far end of the table opposite him. They were here not as pupils but teaching assistants. Sue smiled back warmly and Megan nodded.

Fleming's eyes started up the other side of the table. Dimitri Guitard, the Crown Prince of Hairdressers, gazed back soulfully, projecting that wounded-doe look his Jet Set clientele found devastating. Adrian Koch scrubbed diligently at a gravy stain on his cheap ascot. His faded salt-and-pepper jacket belied his substantial salary as director of a major museum of modern art. Eames Bentley, the movie producer, was now wearing Ben Franklin half-glasses and was making senseless doodles on his notebook with a gold-plated ballpoint.

And in the chair immediately to Fleming's left sat Lily Williams, a Federal judge.

"First," continued Fleming, "a brief prologue. What concerns us all are the rules, the standards, the evaluations which make our selection of a Princess America truly meaningful. Beauty alone is not a sufficient credential. Our Princess-elect must have many other attributes.

"If Detroit releases a new line of cars with a defect, the flawed models can be recalled for correction. But when the Pageant releases a Princess who turns out to be imperfect, there is no way of recalling her. It is vital, therefore, that we be ultra-cautious in our final choice. We must screen all contestants as carefully as possible."

Adrian Koch interrupted. "Question?"

"Certainly, Mr. Koch."

"You said 'screen.' Does that imply the girls undergo some FBI-type security check?"

"Correct. We have millions of dollars at stake here. Our preliminary contest franchises. The investment in commercials by our sponsors. And most important of all—" Fleming permitted himself a benign, noble smile—"the scholarships of all our fine young women ride on the Pageant's continuing prestige. Should we make even one serious error . . ." A shudder ripped over his fleshy, silk-suited frame.

Watching from the foot of the table, Roger Megan suppressed a sardonic grimace. *You sanctimonious hypocrite! Who are you conning? It's the dough in your own pocket you're worried about. And the power you wield in Surf City. You'd take it up the ass seven nights a week before you'd let all that slip through your fat paws.*

Fleming turned toward a uniformed page who had been standing against the wall. The page stepped forward and removed a green velvet shroud which had been draping an easel behind Fleming.

A blackboard had been positioned on the easel. On it, the letters P-A-G-E-A-N-T had been neatly chalked in a vertical column. Next to each of these capitals other letters had been added, spelling out a series of words:

P oise
A dvertisers
G ood Health
E roticism
A ccusations
N ature
T radition

Fleming stood up, picked up a slim pointer from the table.

"You must excuse me if this prop seems a bit too gimmicky," he said. "But I've been using it for twelve years and it does the job."

The wooden tip stabbed out and landed under "P" for Poise.

"The thirteenth Princess, whoever she may be, will spend much of her year meeting dignitaries from all over the world. Ginny Kerr, for instance, has been received at the White House by the President. She's had an audience with the Pope in Rome. At Buckingham Palace, she was presented to the Queen. At Cape Kennedy, she met the Apollo Eleven moon astronauts. Also, she must face the general public. Franchise holders. Sales groups. Local dealers employed by our sponsors. They will all expect her participation in their promotions and at their conventions. At many of these functions there inevitably will be drinking. Men she meets may make improper suggestions. She must fend these off tactfully.

"As custodians of the Pageant's standards, we ask that when you interview the girls you test them for poise. The Princess you select must be able to think fast in any emergency. Be rattled by no situation she may encounter. And she must be graciously diplomatic at all times, so that she offends no one. . . . Yes, Miss Dowling?"

Glenda Dowling blinked behind a fog of cigarette smoke. Looking at her, thought Fleming, was almost as much fun as snake-watching at the reptile house. "Can we ask the girls questions about sex? Or is that taboo?"

"By all means, ask the contestants anything you wish," Fleming replied smoothly. "Pull no punches. I repeat, your purpose in interrogating them is to learn how these girls handle embarrassing inquiries. Sue, my dear, I see you have your hand raised. Have you anything to add on this point?"

Sue Rossiter shifted position in her chair and leaned forward.

"Yes, JF. I just wanted to mention that the letter 'P' on our blackboard also stands for 'Photogenic.' Every one of our contestants must be officially photographed by Max Gerber. I'm sure all of you are familiar with Mr. Gerber's camera work. Prints of the pictures he takes will be sent to you as soon as they are ready. You will then be asked to vote on them, grading the girls secret points for their photogenic assets."

Lily Williams straightened up as if about to question the constitutionality of a courtroom issue. "Points on picture evidence only? We came to Surf City to pass on the merits of fifty live girls, did we not?"

"Of course you did, Judge," rejoined Sue. "But all of us, I think, have known individuals who were attractive in person, yet photographed miserably. Some kinds of beauty just fail to register for a camera lens. What practical use would there be for a Princess, however lovely, whose good looks didn't come through in news shots and advertising layouts? We simply must choose a Princess whose pictures do her justice. Possibly even more than justice. So please, we beg all of you to exercise the greatest care in scoring Max's pictures."

The nodding of heads around the table indicated unanimous approval of Sue's remarks. Fleming plunged on.

"We come next to the first 'A' on our blackboard—'Advertisers.' The lifeblood of the Pageant is the financial support of these respected business concerns. Without them . . ." Fleming made a sorrowful gesture implying Waterloo.

"Now, ladies and gentlemen, I have a distressing matter to report," he went on. "Miss Oregon has been disqualified, as of this morning, on this particular count."

Dimitri Guitard made a graceful hand movement which both registered protest and displayed the platimum ID bracelet on his wrist. "But that's Judy Girl!"

"Miss Judy Kelsey. Yes, Mr. Guitard."

"A fine young lady, I thought. We were chatting at yesterday's luncheon."

"Our decision has nothing to do with Miss Kelsey personally, I assure you. It's entirely a legal matter. We have a rule that if a contestant is a minor, one of her parents must sign her contract with the Pageant. Otherwise, it's not valid. When our security staff checked Judy's contract, they discovered that she herself had written—I won't say forged—the signature purporting to be her mother's. Therefore, she is out of the running as Princess America."

"But, Mr. Fleming," pursued Dimitri Guitard, "her father's been dead for several years, so he couldn't sign. And her mother had a stroke. She's in a coma, dying in all probability. How could she sign? Judy only—"

"Only did what she felt expedient under the circumstances, I'm sure. But as Judge Williams here can tell you, this does not alter the legality of the case."

"I simply fail to grasp what difference—"

"Suppose Mrs. Kelsey does die, Mr. Guitard. Suppose the guardian the courts appoint for Judy refuses to honor a fraudulent signature. How then can she fulfill her commitments to our sponsors? Where might that leave advertisers who have invested thousands in the Pageant and then could not use the Princess in their promotions?"

"But her mother's dying. Man, can't you bend those ironclad rules a fraction?"

"Unfortunately, a contract is evaluated by law rather than compassion."

"But it's so unfair!"

"Would it be fair to forty-nine other girls to jeopardize their scholarships by permitting a situation which might cause sponsors to withdraw their support? Our major rival, as you doubtless know, is the Miss America Pageant in Atlantic City. A Miss Venus Ramey won with them back in—Sue, was it nineteen forty-five or forty-four?"

"Nineteen forty-four, JF," Sue murmured promptly.

Fleming continued. "Miss Ramey, a minor, was living away from home and signed her mother's name to a contract very similar to ours. The Ramey girl had not expected to win. But she did."

"Next day, conscience prompted her to confess to the officials. What had seemed to her a trifling technicality was actually a matter involving thousands of dollars. All contracts between sponsors and the contest were declared invalid. Financially speaking, everyone involved took a bath that year. We can't risk a similar disaster."

Fleming paused for comments. None came.

"Our next consideration is 'G' for 'Good Health.' If he were not working around the clock to complete physical examinations of all our fifty young ladies, Dr. Lydecker would be with us now to explain how he and his staff screen the girls for health problems.

"The rigors of a year as Princess America would surprise you. Touring the country and the world on a nonstop schedule is a strenuous ordeal. A girl with a weak heart, tuberculosis, or latent multiple sclerosis—any serious physical condition—would be unfit for duty. Such girls also must be secretly disqualified."

"Secretly?" challenged Glenda Dowling. "Are you telling us you can keep a girl's disqualification a secret?"

Fleming nodded gravely. "Absolutely. Even if a contestant is disqualified, she continues to participate in all Pageant activities until Saturday night. The girl herself, and the public, is never the wiser. The points she rolls up are simply negated by our chief auditor in the final tabulation. The actual winner is the still qualified entrant who accumulates the highest score."

"Makes sense to me, and I'm a sponsor," said Julius Laurel, looking up from his preying-mantis pose.

Fleming shot him a thankful smile. "Next, ladies and gentlemen, we have 'E' for 'Eroticism.' A while back, I was asked if questions on sex were taboo. I answered that they definitely are not. We ask them ourselves. But in a circuitous way, which guarantees us honest answers."

From the table he picked up a sheaf of envelopes, to each of which a blue folder was stapled.

"It goes without saying our Princess must possess high personal morals. As a symbol of America's young womanhood, she must not offend society's accepted norms of behavior. Sexual behavior.

"Checking out so intimate a matter is extremely delicate. So we have developed a special technique. You've all heard of the McQueen–Holland Report. For several seasons the Pageant has made a generous contribution to help support their studies of America's sexual mores. In exchange, they query our girls. All questionnaires received from Pageant contestants are delivered to us by special messenger immediately upon receipt. In this way, we glean information some of the girls might hide if they knew we had access to it."

He rifled the envelopes and folders. "Here are a few received this morning."

Lily Williams spoke. "Each of our state winners responds with such data?"

"Not all of them, no. A number of the girls don't cooperate. But each year an average of thirty replies filter in. They've helped us greatly in past contests."

"Helped? How?"

"I can cite many examples, Judge. Two years ago, for instance, we had a contestant from a Western state, wholesome as a Grandma Moses card, who turned out to be addicted to pornographic magazines. She admitted to our anonymous questionnaire that her locker at school was plastered with pin-ups of nude men from salacious magazines and that . . ."

Judge Williams made a staying gesture with one splay-fingered hand, as though silencing a talkative witness on the stand.

"I get the point, Mr. Fleming. Thank you."

"Here, as I said—" and Fleming scowled faintly, irked at her dismissal—"here are a batch of replies from current contestants. One of these is a shocking document. By her own words, the girl is truly amoral."

Glenda Dowling bent forward eagerly. "Can you read us a sample?"

Fleming reddened. It took him some time to select a line he could quote in mixed company.

"Ah, yes! Here she says something about 'taking on an entire basketball team in fifty clocked minutes.' " Fleming lifted his head from the folder. "I prefer not to read aloud her other comments. But I'll pass the folder down the table so each of you can study it."

Fleming handed the folder to Adrian Koch, who began

to scan the contents. His eyes, sleepy at first, kindled sharply as he read.

"I do not understand," Madame Ciardi said. "Anon-ee-mouse, you say. Theese mean nobody knows who ees answer, yes? So what good eet do for Pageant? No way you can tell which girl in fifty ees writing answer."

Fleming regarded her indulgently. "A very discerning question, Madame. But, you see, we have a little extra trick working for us here."

He leaned forward and flicked the switch of a small lamp set to the left of his seat on the table. Then he thrust the envelope in which the folder had been mailed under its lens.

"Each envelope bears a name, written in invisible ink," he said. "It becomes permanently legible under ultraviolet light."

"What a sneaky trick!" Dimitri Guitard's voice was furious.

"Dirty pool," grumbled Koch.

"Not at all, gentlemen. A practical necessity. Now, the name of the girl whose folder we passed around is—" Fleming squinted to study the exposed letters—"is Barbara Chrysler."

"Miss Colorado?" For once the judicial calm of Lily Williams was shaken. "But I talked with her only yesterday, at the Armory. She seemed so . . . innocent."

"That's a mistake we of the Pageant cannot afford to make, Your Honor. Judging any book by its cover. Her questionnaire reveals a nymphomaniac's personality. Her answers would make Sadie Thompson blush with shame."

Her Honor frowned reflectively. "Miss Colorado is to be disqualified, then?"

"Automatically." But Judge Williams' obvious disappointment prompted Fleming to add a softening touch. "It really doesn't make much difference. We'd have been forced to disqualify her anyway. The name, you know. Chrysler. Pontiac is one of our sponsors this year."

"And that—" the Williams scowl had deepened—"is enough to kill the girl's chances?"

"Consider the advertiser, Judge. If she won, how would he feel, seeing a competitor's name splashed across every one of the ads featuring Princess America?"

"Hell!" snorted Koch. "If you're speaking of competitors, how about the Miss America contest? I caught their nineteen sixty-eight pageant. The winner was Judith Ford. Yet Oldsmobile was one of their sponsors."

Fleming ran a finger under a collar which suddenly

hugged too tightly. "We'll let the Miss America people go to their church, shall we, Mr. Koch? And we'll go to ours."

Glenda Dowling had at last succeeded in grabbing the folder out of Guitard's slender fingers and was clucking as she read its pages. She tossed the blue sheets aside and squared her thin lips at Fleming.

"Suppose the majority of the girls turn out like this one? Would you disqualify them, too? Would you cop out with an announcement, 'Pageant canceled on account of carnal knowledge'?"

Fleming drew himself up regally. "We live in a permissive era, Miss Dowling. Yet I assure you the majority of the young women in our contest are as pure as—"

"Moon dust, Mr. Fleming? Only one rotten apple in the Pageant's barrel? You expect me to buy that?"

"It may come as a surprise to you, Miss Dowling, but virginity has not vanished from America. Far from it. These promiscuous hippie types are in a distinct minority."

"Barbara Chrysler being one of those sexpots?"

"We've all examined her replies to the institute's questions. But I can show you a dozen samples quite the opposite." Fleming shuffled the folders in front of him, picked one out. "Any of us would be proud of a daughter who had written these modest, somewhat embarrassed, yet evidently honest reponses."

"And who, may I ask, is this Mary Poppins?"

"Look for yourself." Fleming handed her a second folder, first passing its attached envelope under the ultraviolet beam. Seconds later the name invisibly printed on its surface became exposed.

"Lori Macklin! That's Miss Utah." Glenda Dowling exclaimed. She studied each word on the questionnaire with the curiosity of a kid reading the ingredients from a candy wrapper. When she had finished, her thin tongue moistened her dry lips.

"I can't believe it," she finally erupted. "I'd have bet half my circulation the Macklin girl was the Pageant Pushover."

Eames Bentley pumped on the stub of his cigar, unmindful of the mountainous ash on the verge of an immediate breakaway.

"Come now, Glenda," he said. "Let's not be prejudiced. I, too, read Miss Utah's questionnaire. All my experience, all my instincts, tell me her answers are one hundred percent honest. So let's be fair to the girl until—" Bentley drew again on his cigar and, miraculously, the ash remained frozen—"until Mr. Fleming devises a clever way to trick the girls into taking a lie-detector test."

"Now, let's go on to our second 'A.' " Fleming said, his face red. "It stands for 'Accusations.' Each year, during Pageant Week, we receive a flood of crank letters. There seem to be poison pens at work everywhere. A sad commentary on human nature."

From the table he lifted a pack of envelopes.

"Here we have a sampling of mail delivered since Saturday. One unsigned letter informs us that Miss South Dakota's father is an ex-convict who recently served time for arson. Here's one from 'A Friend,' charging that Miss Minnesota once eloped and had the marriage annulled. And a third, alleging Miss Iowa takes heroin."

Lois Potter shook her head mournfully. "Obviously malicious gossip. Or lies inspired by jealousy. My magazine gets the same type of crackpot mail whenever we profile a famous personality."

"I agree with you, but—"

"You used the word "unsigned," Mr. Fleming," Lily Williams cut in. "Inadmissible evidence, is it not? Surely no unsigned accusation can carry weight against a contestant?"

"Certainly not, Judge. No unsupported charge. However, each of these letters has been Xeroxed and passed along to our security staff. Each charge is discreetly investigated. If false, it does the girl no harm."

Sue Rossiter interrupted. "Last year, Judge, we received a letter telling us that a contestant had once attempted suicide. We checked that, as we always do. When an investigator in her town went to her local library, he discovered that she read only morbid books. Books concerned with death, embalming, self-destruction, and necrophilia. Quite obviously, this girl was disturbed. A risky bet for our Princess America. So we disqualified her."

Fleming took it again, as smoothly as a tennis pro returning an easy serve.

"The point to note here, ladies and gentlemen, is that we must cope with such accusations. Ninety-nine percent, of course, are what Lois Potter calls them. Jealousy. Lies. Spite. There are many, many haters out there. Yet they can't be ignored. At this very moment, for example, Dr. Lydecker is checking an informant's charge that one of our girls had a rhinoplasty. The letter even names the specialist who performed the nose bob.

"And this brings us to 'N' for 'Nature." Our Princess

must be a natural beauty, not a product of cosmetic surgery. No hidden deformities. No artifices of any kind. We trust that in awarding your points you will keep this constantly in mind. *Natural* beauty."

"Now, then, for the final letter of our acrostic," Fleming went on. " 'T' for 'Tradition.' "

He gazed about the table serenely. "You are all familiar, I'm sure, with many of the traditions which have grown up with us as the Pageant has grown. The Boardwalk Parade on Thursday evening. The trio of elimination shows. The suspenseful crowning ceremony on the final evening. These are all generally known. But there are other traditions we observe. Confidential ones. By that I—

"I'm glad you opened that door," broke in Glenda Dowling. "I have a sticky question."

Fleming braced himself. He felt like a fly caught in hot tar. "Certainly, Miss Dowling."

"At the Armory lunch yesterday the mother of Miss California asked whether you have an unwritten rule which prohibits back-to-back winners. Against girls from the same state becoming Princess in two consecutive years. True or false?"

Fleming stepped out onto the high wire gingerly. "So far this has never been a problem. It would be most unfortunate for us should it become one."

"Don't diddle me, Mr. Fleming. True or false? Virginia Kerr is from California. Does that mean this year's Miss California might as well have stayed home? Stacy DeGray has as much going for her, in my opinion, as—"

"Again, dear lady, we cannot dictate your decisions. But advertising sponsors from other areas of the country would be—shall we say—upset if California seemed to have developed a monopoly on Princesses. We throw the standards of the Pageant on your mercy. It has been an unwritten tradition—"

"Are you trying to tell us, Mr. Fleming, that this contest is fixed?"

Skewered on that final word, Fleming stood quivering, unable to bottle his emotions. This Dowling dragon had a syndicated column in which to spill her bile. She was openly high on the DeGray girl and she was perfectly capable of starting a messianic newspaper crusade over her darling Stacy. What, then, would happen to the Pageant? He thought of the Teapot Dome scandal. He recalled the Black Sox baseball fiasco. His blood chilled.

"Well, Mr. Fleming? It's fixed or it isn't fixed. Which?"

Roger Megan came forward in his chair, all boyish charm, to ease his boss off the hook.

"Certainly it's not fixed, Miss Dowling," Megan said. "We go to extreme lengths to insure that there won't be the slightest suspicion of favoritism in our selection."

"A two-sided coin. The obverse of favoritism is prejudice. Why should Stacy be discriminated against? Sponsors, says Mr. Fleming. You call that justice?"

"Miss Dowling, we'd have everything to lose. Suppose it came out that one of our contests had been rigged. Remember what happened a few years back when fixing on the big TV quiz shows was exposed? Top ratings didn't save them. They were wiped off the air."

"As this Pageant could be wiped without a trace."

"Indeed it could. We'd lose the confidence of the public and of the very sponsors Mr. Fleming mentions. A very great deal of sincere and selfless labor, by many dedicated people, would go down the drain. I happen to be a devoted reader of your column, Miss Dowling. I think I know you quite well, from the warmth and intimacy of your writing. I don't believe that you want this to happen."

"I want the principle of the fair shake established here."

"Miss California will get exactly that. You and your fellow judges are absolutely free to award her the highest score you honestly believe she deserves." There were other ways, Megan knew, to spin the Stacy kid out of orbit. Plenty of them. "If she wins, she wins. And I must add, she's a lucky young girl to have someone like you in her corner."

The sincerity in his voice totally disarmed her. Slowly, the fire of battle faded from her eyes.

"Why thank you, Mr. Megan. As long as fairness is observed . . ."

Fleming tried to conceal his elation. Roger had already hit the ball over the fence. Now all he had to do was run the bases.

"We'll be fair, Miss Dowling," Megan said. "Scrupulously. I personally promise you that. And I'm sure we can count on you to be fair, as well. To give the other contestants equal and unbiased consideration, I mean."

"Why shouldn't I?"

"Coming from Hollywood, as you do, it might be easy for you to become—unconsciously—Miss California's champion. There's home-state pride in all of us. I have to admit to plenty of it in myself."

"I certainly hope I'm capable of judgments without prejudice."

Megan smiled.

"We know you are. We know you will not withhold a single point from a single girl if you feel she deserves it. This Pageant selects its judges with the greatest of thought and care. We seek only the cream. And frankly, we have utter confidence in your complete objectivity."

Glenda Dowling settled back with a placated nod which spoke well for objectivity.

Jesus! thought Fleming, *the man's a magician! He's the engine that pulls the Pageant express. That sincere look could melt rock. No wonder he's rolled in half the beds from here to Miami Beach.*

Aloud, he said: "The briefing for the thirteenth Princess America Pageant is hereby concluded. Meeting adjourned."

Leaving the room, Roger Megan caught up with Sue Rossiter. "Sue, love," he whispered out of the side of his mouth, "that was a great Christmas present you gave me last evening. Is Santa Claus coming down my chimney again tonight?"

"Please, Roger. I want to be able to walk to the Pageant."

19 · PRINCESS AMERICA

THE sunken tub was almost the size of a moon crater. Arched backward in warm suds which all but engulfed her, Ginny Kerr wondered how it would be a week from now. When the super-year was over. When she had been phased out as Princess America and replaced by a new beauty champ.

She stretched languorously, lowering her chin into the tide of perfumed bubbles. The fragrant scent was like some pagan incense. Six months ago, a leading cosmetic house had signed her to introduce this product in TV commercials. As a bonus, they had sent her enough cases of the stuff to last through menopause.

A sliver of regret escaped her. Now that she was turning in her crown, the flow of free loot she had known during her fabulous year would shrivel up. The Princess is dead! Long live the Princess! She couldn't help thinking how, almost a year ago last September, she had awakened on Saturday morning, never dreaming that at midnight it would be her foot that would fit into the glass slipper.

Well, the Cinderella extravaganza was over, and she was now a lame-duck heroine. But if this was to be her Last Hurrah, what a way to go. When John Fleming had designed this luxurious bath for the Princess America suite in the St. George Hotel's east wing penthouse, he obviously had kept the Hanging Gardens of Babylon in mind.

Blush-tinted marble had been squandered about by a budget-reckless hand. Lavish expanses of mirror were built into each wall, reflecting her image from four sides. A Persian brazier of pierced brass decorated the tub's foot. From concealed spigots it hosed hot or cold fountains in response to the pressure of her fingers upon gold-plated levers. Statues of six Nubian pages stood sightlessly about the huge room's periphery, each polychromed and dazzlingly polished.

The windows were draped in Thai silk, pink and dove gray, veined with silver strands. The subdued lights were held by carved and gilded male arms which projected from the walls like cloves from a ham. Matching arms extended bath towels as thick and smooth as clouds. Ginny had a strong feeling that she need only clap her hands for the Grand Eunuch to appear.

She would rather have clapped to summon Ian. Who, Lord knows, was no eunuch.

The mere thought and he appeared. She need never even rub a lamp to evoke Ian MacLaren—in her thoughts, at least. The tall, angular body. The somewhat longish face, almost too severe, with its high cheekbones and its eyes deepset under brows which jutted like the prows of ships. They were a clear hazel, those eyes, with a wary solemnity to them most of the time. Until something amused him, when they could blaze alive like shooting sparks.

His hair was good Scots hair, red when the sunlight struck it but otherwise an oxidized brown. He wore tweeds with a casual elegance which implied he did not know they existed. He had small use for men who spent much thought on wardrobes. Yet he was the one male she knew who could wear kilts as if he had been born to wear them. The MacLaren plaid—rich blue overlaid with green and threaded with red and yellow—looked as natural on this man as skin.

He had been educated in London, so there was no marked Scottish burr to his voice. Yet the Highlands were his birthplace, his boy place. He never had forgotten them. Ginny had not known him an hour before he was speaking of old feuds with the Campbells, the Buchanans and the MacGregors as if they were current upheavals in Southeast Asia.

In the twelfth century or thereabouts, a pitched battle had been waged at a place called Strathyre over some insult to a MacLaren. The Buchanans of Leny had been all but annihilated. It all was real, all present tense to him. Ian recounted the event with a gusto some men saved for tallying their bedroom conquests.

He was good in a bedroom, too. Very good indeed.

Remembering just how good, Ginny stirred lazily in the perfumed foam. And suddenly this impending sunset of her reigning year did not seem an occasion to be mourned, after all. With Ian waiting, the world was her runway.

Their meeting really had not been a pick-up. More of a happening.

It was a Sunday morning in March. She had come to New York for the opening of a big industrial show at the Coliseum. Early their second day in town, and with her chaperone's understanding consent, Ginny had left the hotel and hired a horse at one of the stables off Amsterdam Avenue. Almost the worst thing about being Princess America, for Virginia Kerr, was how seldom her crowded schedule allowed her to swing into a saddle.

The chestnut filly she had rented, though spirited, was no real challenge to her. Ginny had often jumped mounts loath to accept a bit, who would tolerate only a hackamore. She had twice been in serious competition for a spot on the United States Equestrian Team in the Olympics. Her mirror at home was framed in blue ribbon rosettes from horse shows in a dozen states.

It was early and the bridle path in Central Park was all but deserted. Loping along, she breathed deep of air which had not yet succumbed to the day's pollution; air with a late-winter chill in it The sun had barely come up over the towers to the east. Shadows of naked trees made filigrees on slopes refusing to show even a promise of green to come.

As she cantered, she was dimly aware of thudding hoofbeats other than her chestnut's. They came from behind and were paced at about the same tempo as her own. Another early-morning rider was out in the park, doing his own thing.

And then . . .

Up ahead, on the bicycle path to her right, a youth on a red bike suddenly lost control of his vehicle when a wheel bumped into a clump of unleafed forsythia. The bike swerved sharply left, directly in front of her horse's path. Ginny braced herself for the inevitable collision but, miraculously, the bike blurred past her. Startled by the narrow escape, she was for a fatal instant inattentive to her filly. And in that split second the panicked chestnut chose to rear and bolt. Expert horsewoman though she was, Ginny felt the rein torn from her grasp.

Alarmed now, she readied for a runaway. It never happened. Instead, a firm hand caught her dangling lines. The rider behind her had spurred up so fast that his reflex astonished her.

"Well!" he said, quite as if he blamed her. "They warned me America is pested with Sunday drivers. I didn't know one also had to worry about Sunday riders."

British. His voice told her that, although his rangy ruggedness suggested Marlboro Country. She felt her cheeks crimson at his gibe.

"And what's wrong with the way I ride?"

"The mount you picked. Too skittish. A good horsewoman should have known that."

"I've handled horses with more spirit than this one since they stopped changing my diapers!"

"Horses did that? Talented blighters they'd have to be."

In spite of herself, she favored the stranger with a faint smile. "Thanks for the foreign aid, but I've got to go now."

The smile he returned seemed able to break the back of winter. "I'd better ride along with you, what? You're still shaking."

She was darned if she'd let him find her an easy Central Park pick-up.

"I'm turning back to the stables. Sorry, Mr. . . ."

"MacLaren," he said calmly, refusing to be snubbed. "Ian MacLaren. What's the matter? Still shook up in spite of those diapers?"

"I happen to have a busy morning ahead of me, that's all."

"I like a girl with pride. Needn't be ashamed of a scare, though."

"I am *not* scared. Will you please stop saying that?"

"The lady doth protest too much." He paused to pat the flank of his horse with gentle strokes. "Look, you're my responsibility, in a way. So I'll turn in my own mount and take you somewhere for some reviving coffee."

"You'll do nothing of the sort, thank you. I am *very* busy."

"There's a little place I like south side of the park. We'll go there, I think. Even at this hour they sport what you Americans call a real hairy crowd. And the brioches are most edible."

She answered as though speaking to a retarded child, slowly and distinctly.

"I'm not going anywhere with you, Mr. MacLaren. Not anywhere at all. I'm turning back my horse and keeping my appointment. Some of us in America work for a living."

"May I ask what work you do?"

"I happen to be Princess America. Just now, I'm helping to publicize one of the exhibits at the Coliseum. So if you'll let me pass—"

"Princess? You're joking with me. Americans aren't permitted titles."

Despite the blow to her ego, Ginny was amused that he had never heard of her. For almost seven months now, in fifty far-flung states, her name had been a household word. From the pages of magazines and newspapers, from television screens, from advertising billboards everywhere, her face beamed daily upon millions. Yet to this foreign character she was as anonymous as the telephone operator one dialed for a weather report. She could hardly wait to write Norm Prescott about her experience; she was certain it would activate his ulcers into an uproar.

"While we're having coffee you can tell me what you really do," he persisted. "And I promise not to report you to the Committee on Un-American Activities."

The smile she flashed was as bright as a landing-strip beacon, and she could feel the cold wind on her teeth. "Lead on, MacDuff!"

Fifteen minutes later, seated at a table with a red-checkered cloth, she was hearing how his ancestors had ambushed the Buchanans at the Battle of Strathyre. Incredibly, she found herself kneading the napkin in her lap and rooting for the Clan MacLaren to triumph.

He worked, he had told her that first day, for an international bank headquartered in London. His business in America was to prospect for fruitful investment opportunities. This meant that he traveled constantly, coast to coast. It was astonishing how many cities he had managed to turn up in thereafter, just as Princess America was cutting the ribbon at a supermarket opening or crowning a local beauty queen. Her schedule, of course, was widely publicized. It was no great trick for him to arrange coincidences. Still, she never knew when or where the lightning would strike.

Ian. . . .

That morning she had met him, for the first time since her limelight year began, she had lied to her chaperone. Her excuse for returning late had been as brittle as spun glass. Inherently a decent, moral girl, Ginny did not take her responsibilities as Princess America lightly. She had been entrusted with an image. She had fully intended to honor that trust.

But the human heart, as she was to discover, can be quite beyond honor.

The day after that canter in the park, Amanda Clarke had awakened with a slight temperature—the herald, as it turned out, of a mild attack of the Hong Kong flu. Unquestioningly confident of Ginny's integrity, Amanda had readily yielded to her urgings that she remain in bed for the day.

A photographic appointment—Princess America was endorsing a new line of air luggage—led off the morning's agenda. When Ginny went down alone in the hotel elevator on her way to keep the date, Ian was in the lobby.

"What on earth are you doing here, MacLaren?"

"What else but waiting? To satisfy myself that you *do* exist. It's simple logic you can't really be one of the *daoine sidhg.*"

"The—the what?"

"The Good People. The fairy folk. I remembered you as every bit the bonnie. All night long I had these remarkable lying-awake dreams about you. Ach, and it's got to stop. It's bad for a man's business judgments, losing his sleep."

"Spoken like a true Scotsman!" Damn it, did her voice have to quiver?

"When your mind's on a lass," he said sternly, "it can't consider more important matters. Prime chances go down the drain. So a MacLaren does something about it." Then he had tucked her arm through his and propelled her out to a taxi.

She half suspected he would take her down to City Hall. Instead, he had accompanied her to the studio where he had sat impatiently in the reception room while she posed under the hot lights, faking the radiant expectation of a bride. When she was free at last, but only to move on to her duties at the Coliseum show, he trailed along. And with every moment they were together, it became more desperately necessary to assure herself that this wild electricity he generated within her wouldn't blow out her fuses.

He had proposed to her, as she knew he would, late that afternoon, in the rear booth of a Longchamps restaurant near her hotel.

"We don't waste time in my part of the world," he had told her, quite unromantically. "So I'm asking you to marry me. I'll make a better husband than any chap you'll ever meet this side of the Atlantic."

She had touched his hand, and a hot pulse inside her she had never known before began hammering. "Ian, dear, I can't marry you—or anyone else—until next October. The small print in my Princess America contract forbids me to get married until my reigning year is over. We'll just have to wait."

Since her first date, at fourteen, Ginny had firmly been convinced that sex was the most important factor in her life; that she would be a stupid fool to lose her virginity before her wedding night; and that a premarital affair would be the worst disaster that could happen to her. Now, for the first time in her life, she began to have serious doubts as to these convictions. If Ian had asked her now—as she had to admit to herself—he could have had her.

The trouble was, he didn't ask. She and Amanda checked out of their hotel two days later, headed for a State Fair in Iowa.

When he did show up somewhere, there was endless scheming to win them any time alone together. Ginny was genuinely shocked by her natural skill for intrigue which those arrangements brought to the surface. Hating them, she still invented elaborate lies which traded shamelessly on Amanda's unsuspecting trust. Those devious excuses. Those stealthy exits from shared hotel rooms after her chaperone's gentle snores began. The phony "dental appointment" in Albuquerque. The faked visit to an "old classmate" in Tacoma. Was this conniving creature the same person she always had been—until now? If the real Virginia Louise Kerr had been asked to stand up, would she have recognized herself?

And still Ian did not ask for what she ached to give him. If he couldn't have her honorably, he wouldn't take her dishonorably. Damn the code and the honor and the ethics of the MacLaren clan!

By the Memorial Day weekend, when a brief recess in their schedule allowed Ginny to return home to her family and Amanda to wing eastward to her husband and stepdaughter, she had grown almost desperate in her need to crack his enraging restraint.

June was a mere riffle of the calendar away when he checked in at a motor lodge just outside her home town. As so often before, but this time in her parents' familiar living room, a telephone had rung.

"*Creag an Turic!*" the voice said.

"Ian! Darling!"

"It is my intention to take you out to dinner, Miss Kerr. At seven."

He arrived to collect her in a Hertz rental, was charming to her parents for the ten minutes his punctilious manners required and drove her off to the most elegant restaurant in the vicinity. Poor Ian! He could not even have suspected that a spider spinning webs sat beside him.

At dinner, demure but determined, she took control of the conversation and got him talking about his beloved Highlands.

When he paused, she decided it was time to move in for the kill. "Do you really dress there in the traditional Highland style?" she asked. "In kilts and sporran and the rest?"

"On grand occasions we do."

"You must look magnificent."

"Ach, darling, many wear the gear better than I."

"Ian, have you got it with you now? You told me once you always pack it for good luck. I'd trade my whole Princess career to see you in full regimentals—just once."

"Unlikely. I'd look like an oaf if I appeared in public."

"Not in public. At your motel. We could stop there—oh, don't look so shocked, you prig—on our way back. You could model for me. It wouldn't take twenty minutes."

"And would be most improper. For a young lass of good reputation to—"

"A good reputation is supposed to be a girl's best defense against gossip, isn't it? Anyway, who's going to know? This once the Pageant isn't watching us."

It took more argument to overcome his reluctance, but half an hour later the door to his motor-lodge cabin was closing behind them. In the impersonal cedar-paneled room, with its ample bed all but shouting for attention in the center, Ian—visibly embarrassed—paid a brief visit to the closet. Then he strode toward the connecting bath, modestly closing the door. Ginny sank into a Danish modern chair to wait.

"Well, then," he said uneasily when he emerged. "Here it is."

The thing inside her that never would lie still in his presence leaped like a stag from cover. The kilt was a swirl of MacLaren tartan as he strode toward her. The doublet fitted his wide shoulders and slim waist like a coat of paint. Its buttons were made of antler and its ornaments were cairngorm. The sporran swayed as he walked, and she scarcely could tear her gaze from the movement. In his high hose a *sgian dubh* dagger looked ready to stab the nearest enemy.

"My God!" she breathed in genuine awe. "The Monarch of the Glen!"

"A disappointment to you, I'm thinking."

"A revelation. You're gorgeous! Turn around. Let me see how it is in motion."

Obediently, he pivoted in a full circle. "And now that you've seen it—"

"Here comes the oldest question in the world. What *does* a Scotsman wear under his kilts? I've heard it asked a hundred times. I never heard the answer."

He was standing close by her chair. His long face reddened.

"The answer, lass, is nothing."

She could have restrained the hand that groped out for him only by cutting it off at the wrist. And it was not toward his wicked-looking dagger that she reached, but between naked knees and tartan hem. Russet hairs curled silky and thick under her fingertips as they slid under—and up. From above, she heard him gasp.

"So this *is* the answer, Ian dear. You were telling me the truth."

She felt his throb of response to that light touch which had found what it was seeking. He moaned a few words in Gaelic she did not understand and caught her up out of her chair as if she were weightless. He put her down on the bed as if she might break if not gently handled. But despite the gentleness there was purpose now. One hand slipped down behind her back, the other reached for her dress zipper. Then he was stretching out beside her, thrusting his plaid pleats out of their way.

"Ian," she whispered as his muscle grew to fit her body. "Oh, Ian, I've waited so long."

"You'll wait no longer, forbye. I'll hurt you no more than I must, my darling."

There was an interval of precious pain as he took her, swift as a stroke of lightning. After that, as the long and slow and tender movements began, it was fulfillment all the way. All these weeks of restless anticipation, she had not been wrong. Ian MacLaren had been built for the act of love.

She had luxuriated in the suds so long that she felt waterlogged. Rubbed down and glowing, Ginny slid into a green silk housecoat and padded out into the suite's emperor-sized parlor. The room was paneled in pale wood which had been stripped and waxed and polished; and all four walls bore, at mathematically spaced intervals, framed portraits of the former Princess Americas. Each had been painted by a contemporary artist. The eleven former winners graced the room like a corsage of American beauties. In the place of special prominence over an elaborately carved marble fireplace, the latest of the series—the twelfth—had been hung. Her portrait.

This compliment was traditional. Ginny paused for a moment, looking up with real pleasure at the canvas for which she had posed so many tedious hours.

Percy Kilbourne, the famous artist in whose drafty Vermont studio she had sat regally on a thronelike chair until every muscle in her body screamed with weariness, had done an excellent job. The face was delicately molded, the flesh tones of a breathing reality, the tiny crown, like a halo, a glittering ornament to hair alive with the healthy patina of countless brushings. It was really Virginia Louise Kerr who smiled down on her.

Ian said so; and Ian never was the gentlest of critics.

"You know what first struck me about you?" he had observed, on the afternoon she had pulled strings to let him attend a private viewing of the finished portrait. "You walk like somebody God put on earth to descend curving staircases. The chap's caught that. You really *are* a Princess, dash it."

She had been deeply moved. "Thank you, kind sir."

"For what? For admitting you measure up to MacLaren standards?"

The painting still was new enough for Ginny to find fresh things in it every time she studied it. But come next season, there would be another face to enshrine above the marble mantel. Ginny Kerr's portrait would be relegated to its permanent place among the other ex-Princesses circling the walls, merely one more item in a collection which always reminded her of that gallery of past Presidents in the Green Room at the White House.

And who would displace her? Who would be the thirteenth Princess? From her previous day's mingling with many of the candidates, she had grudgingly decided that the obvious front runner was the bumptious, mirror-addicted Miss New Jersey. It wouldn't surprise Ginny a bit if Jersey was at this very minute busy composing her acceptance speech. The bitch in Ginny couldn't help musing that if Jersey won the contest, they could never find a crown large enough to fit her swelled head.

One of the girls at the armory luncheon had told a supposedly true anecdote about Miss New Jersey. It seems she had been caught in a summer storm with a boyfriend, and sudden lightning flashed. The girl had turned calmly to her escort and said, "God just took my picture."

The suite was hot and oddly airless. Ginny had not really

been aware of this while in the tub, assuming bath steam to be responsible. But now, as she crossed the parlor toward a French table by the corridor window, the closeness was oppressive. She loosened her robe a trifle.

The table was so loaded with a pyramid of fan mail that its frail period legs seemed to bow further under the weight. For the next several minutes Ginny was busy slitting open envelopes. Their contents were predictable. Requests for her autograph. Marriage proposals from lonely soldiers, many with snapshots enclosed. Requests for money—bold, pathetic or ingenious. Letters from anxious mothers seeking advice on how to start daughters on the beauty-contest trail.

The heat in the room had become more intolerable. Ginny felt her forehead misting and looked about the room with a slowly dawning realization. The air-conditioner had stopped working. And of course the windows were sealed shut, as they always were in hotels and trains dedicated to the infallibility of mechanisms.

She was just about to reach for the phone to complain downstairs when the PA unit in the wall came to life.

"Hi, girls. This is Sue Rossiter. A power failure has knocked out the air-conditioning systems in most of the hotels along the boardwalk. If your hotel is one of the unlucky ones, please be patient. Emergency crews are already busy trying to correct the trouble. So keep your cool, everyone, and thanks for bearing with us."

Well, at least she wasn't the only one. She decided to dress swiftly so she'd be ready the minute her chaperone arrived. Ready for evening chores, which consisted tonight of dinner with various Surf City VIPs to be given in her honor at some swank restaurant farther up the boardwalk.

Ginny had been ready and waiting several minutes, fanning herself with the hotel's huge menu to keep her makeup from beading, when Amanda Clarke let herself in. She took three steps into the room, stopped dead, and spoke in horror.

"It's an oven! My God, Virginia, they're baking you alive!"

"The air-conditioner has had it," Ginny said.

"But what are they doing about it? This room is *gruesome*!"

"I don't think they're doing anything. After all, I'm practically a Princess Emeritus."

An envelope in Amanda's hand pre-empted her attention. "Telegram for you. They gave it to me at the desk."

Ginny's heartbeat quickened as she used the letter opener. Ian? A moment later, despite the letdown that it was not from him, she was laughing aloud.

"Delighted inform you thirteen hundred seven write-in votes your name California State Legislature primary." She read it through twice, speculating whether it could be a practical joke. But it was signed by the head of Judge Kerr's political party in their home district, a man she knew well.

"Some jokers wrote me in for the Legislature. I guess I should be flattered. But how whacky can you get?"

Amanda cocked one grizzled eyebrow. Short, squarishly sturdy, on the sunny side of fifty, she was a woman who spoke her mind.

"Not whacky at all. Why *not* the Legislature?"

"But I'm not even out of college. No one could seriously—"

"You're a law student, aren't you? Probably you know more law right now than half the fools who make them. If you want a political career, while you're green in the public memory would be the time to start."

"Green is the word. I've never even licked stamps in a campaign."

"Laugh if you like. But one nineteen fifty-five Miss America finalist—don't tell Roger Megan I ever mentioned the name—ran against Lureen Wallace for Governor. Why not you, in this confusing Year of Our Lord?"

Amanda had begun to mop her forehead, feeling wretched from the room's heat. "Child, plug your pretty pink ears. I'm about to use some four-letter words. Even *I* have a boiling point—and I've just reached it."

Ginny laughed in amusement at Amanda's complaint. During these eleven months they had spent together, intimate companions, she had developed a deep and genuine affection for the woman who stood now with indignation puffing out her rose-petal cheeks as if she were a blowfish.

Amanda Clarke had a bride's complexion, a firecracker temper, eyes the color of bluebells, and silver hair which curled naturally into a ringlet mop. Her plump, prettyish face was underlined by a double chin. She dressed for the most part in simple shirtwaist numbers which might have been ordered from a Sears, Roebuck catalogue but which actually came out of one of the costliest ateliers on Fifth Avenue. The branches of her family tree included one *Mayflower* passenger, two Revolutionary War generals, and a great-aunt who had married a Vice President.

"Well?" she huffed. "What are we going to do about this?"

"Smile. That's the Pageant cure-all, isn't it?"

"But you can't spend the night here. You'd suffocate."

"There isn't an empty room in Surf City this week, as you well know. And think what Mr. Fleming would say if I got arrested for sleeping on the boardwalk."

Amanda's sniff disposed of Fleming. "I know the answer. You'll come with me aboard *Buttercup*. We can put you up if you don't mind sharing a cabin with DeDe. She and Otis and I are the only passengers aboard, except the crew. At least one can breathe on the water."

The prospect was alluring as Ginny thought of a sea breeze. "You're sure I wouldn't be—?"

"We'd adore it. You're something of a heroine to DeDe, you know. Anyhow, I have a surprise out there for you. A sort of graduation present."

"You sold me! Let's do it!"

"I'll arrange for the tender to pick us up as early as we can break free from dinner. Eat lightly. We'll have a late supper on the boat. Now, you remember who it is you're shedding your radiance on tonight? The mayor. The city councilmen. Their wives—"

20 · MISS ALASKA

DAVE LEBOW backed out of Suite 2508, towing a service cart with him.

The blonde under the coverlet yawned as she watched him go. The two bills she had tipped him were still palmed in one hand. Remnants of her late lunch littered the cart's flat top. Remnants of a rough night littered her face. Her makeup was as messed as her hair.

Once freshened for a new evening's foray, with her eyes sparkling, she was probably a blue-plate dish. But this early—and for broads like her, even the tag end of afternoon was early—she looked under the weather. The eyes which followed his departure seemed sedated. They took in his trim body in tight pants and red jacket, but only because he was male. Sheer reflex on her part. She wasn't really interested. Bellhops didn't make enough money to interest ladies of the night.

He swung his wagon toward the service elevators and started wheeling it down the corridor. The next suite interested him more: 2506. Miss Alaska's.

There was something extra special about her. At odd moments, memory of her liquid brown eyes and her shy smile kept drifting back. He wondered if she was in her room or involved with some phase of her busy Pageant schedule.

He halted as the door of an elevator ahead slid open. A freckled little teeny-bopper in a plaid miniskirt and green sweater emerged. He paused as her frail juvenile legs headed for Mildred's suite.

The kid tapped lightly on the door. "Miss Alaska," she called out in a thin voice. She waited a few moments, tapped again. No response forthcoming, she tried the knob and pushed. The door must have been unlocked, for it swung three-quarters open. The kid stepped inside.

"Miss Alaska!" she repeated. "Are you here?"

The whole inner side of the door was a sheet mirror.

As Dave drew abreast, an oblique reflection came into view. He braked his cart. The angled glass displayed a surprising tableau.

Mother-naked, Miss Alaska stood transfixed on the threshold of the suite's sun terrace. One hand was clutched over her throat. The other hand moved swiftly to cover a puff of dark pubic fleece.

"W-what are you doing here?" Dave heard her gasp. "You frightened me. I thought you were a prowler."

The kid stood her ground uncertainly, a shaky rock of Gibraltar. "You're Miss Alaska?"

"Get out of here, little girl!" Mildred stared at the young intruder as though she were Rosemary's baby.

"The door was open. And I didn't see any 'Do Not Disturb' sign. So I thought it was okay to—"

"What do you want?"

"I'd love to have your autograph," the thin voice pleaded. "Please!" She extended a white folder she had been carrying under her left arm.

Mildred hesitated, then said, "All right. But wait outside while I slip on my robe. I was taking a sunbath when you broke in."

"I'm sorry, I really am," the kid apologized, retreating into the hall. She pulled the door shut with her and the mirror image vanished.

The youngster turned, almost bumping into Dave. "I'm waiting to get Miss Alaska's autograph," she explained. "I've seen her only once in the lobby, but I just adore her." She sighed dreamily. "Do you think she might write something special? Then if she gets to be Princess I can tell the kids we're real pals. Maybe like 'To Evelyn, My Dearest and Greatest Fan.' My name is Evelyn."

Dave regarded her yearning eyes and smiled. Evelyn might be brash, but she wasn't one of those hotel imps who play push-the-button with the elevators all day.

He was about to reply when Mildred opened the door clad in a terrycloth robe, its collar turned up.

Evelyn dug into the pocket of her skirt. "Here's a pen," she offered eagerly. "Gee, wait till the kids see!" She held up the white folder. "You can write on this."

"Hold it, Alaska!" It was Dave's voice. Urgent. A command. The teeny-bopper spun about, startled. Pen in hand, Mildred looked up at him, startled.

He gave her a friendly nod. "Hi!"

"H-h-hi!" she echoed, flustered. Confusion made her even prettier.

A real doll. The terrycloth robe didn't put blinders on

his memory. What he had just seen in reflection wasn't wiped from his mind's eye.

Hey!

Every so often, on a room-service call, he had bumbled accidentally into the wrong suite and confronted a female occupant in the nude, coming out of the shower or about to get dressed. In the embarrassing few seconds it took him to back out, her reaction had always been the same. One hand would speed to screen the twat. The other would streak to cover the boobs.

But Mildred's first hand had flown straight for her throat!

Something clicked in his head. That package he had picked up for her at the pharmacy. That goo to cover a blemish or birthmark. He had wondered if she really had one, because certainly nothing showed.

But now he knew. It was her neck that was marred.

"You're staring at me." Mildred inched the robe's collar still higher.

"No," Dave lied. "At what you're holding. It's a menu from our Cockatoo Room."

She looked down as if until now she had not been aware of what was in her hand. "Yes?"

"This kid wants you to autograph it?"

Little Evelyn eyed him timidly. "I didn't steal it, Mister. The waiter gave it to my mother for a souvenir."

"But it could get Miss Alaska in trouble," Dave said. "If—"

"My girl friend's got five signatures already," Evelyn interrupted. "Just in the two days we've been in Surf City."

"Then that's five contestants who may lose points."

Mildred frowned faintly. "But . . . why?"

"Got your Pageant rulebook handy, Alaska?"

It lay on the Italianate writing desk inside. She brought it out quickly. He flipped it open and rippled the leaves.

"Here we are. One of the judges gave me a copy two years ago instead of a tip, so I practically know it by heart. Page five, paragraph three. 'Each contestant will promise to conduct herself in such fashion as will not embarrass the Pageant or be penalized by a loss of points as determined by the judges . . .' "

"I still don't understand."

"It's simple. Only proper autograph books are approved. That's on page twelve. No menus. No napkins. No postcards. No programs. No plaster casts. Nothing impromptu. As they see it, it's beneath the Pageant's dignity. Really, I guess, it's a sensible precaution."

"But against what?"

"Use your imagination. Some schlock promoter could easily sneak in almost anything he wanted a beauty queen to endorse. None of you has had much experience being a public figure. You'd likely be rattled and not notice what you were signing, among a lot of assorted papers. I saw it happen last year to Miss New Mexico. Some joker had tricked her into signing a petition for legalizing panty raids."

"I didn't realize . . ."

Dave lifted the menu from Mildred's hands and returned it to the child. "I'm sorry, Evelyn. But we both want Miss Alaska to win. And breaking one of the rules may hurt her."

The scrawny shoulders under the green sweater sagged in defeat. Dispiritedly, Evelyn started to walk toward the elevator.

On impulse, Dave called after her. "Hey, Evelyn!"

Silently, she turned back. Tears seemed about to irrigate her freckled face.

"Here." He proffered the two singles the whore had tipped him. "They sell autograph albums at the drugstore in the lobby arcade. Tell Doc Sherman that Dave sent you, and he'll give you one that's a bargain. Then come back here and I'm sure Miss Alaska will be happy to oblige. Even with 'dearest and greatest fan.' "

The solemn face lit up. Grasping the bills, Evelyn darted for the elevators.

Alone with Dave now, Mildred stared at him curiously. "But you had me sign my name on that lottery card."

"That was different."

"I don't see why."

"It was for luck. To bring me luck. And I'm your friend. I wouldn't flash it around and get you in a jam."

"I know you wouldn't, Dave. You're so . . . nice. Doing that for the kid."

"A nothing, lady. *Ciao!*" He hesitated, reluctant to end the moment yet unable to prolong it, and set the cart in motion.

21 · GENERAL GERVAIS

GENERAL GERVAIS followed the WAC sergeant down the hospital corridor, swinging along in the civilian tropical worsteds his errand required.

"Here we are, Mr. Jones," she said. "Ward H. There's your nephew, last on the left."

As "Mr. Jones"—uncle to "Private Jones," recovering from wounds suffered in Vietnam—all Gervais could do was thank her stiffly.

Gervais walked along a line of wheelchairs arrayed before the ward's multiple windows. In each wheelchair, staring out at the illuminated hospital gardens below, hunched a figure in a maroon bathrobe. Some held books or magazines. Some sat with hands laced listlessly in laps. A few glanced up at him as he went by. In the gray monotony of their days, even the passing of a stranger broke up the hour-after-hour sameness.

Reaching the chair Sergeant Hoskins had indicated, he bent slightly.

"Well, well, well, Peter! And how are they treating you heroes here, anyway?"

The young man in the chair had been peering down at the garden paths. His pale eyes held something of the curiosity of a child studying an ant colony. On walks radiating wheel-spoke style from the Army Convalescent Center itself, diminutive figures were moving: nurses wheeling patients, visitors arriving and departing, rehab cases testing new artificial legs.

The eyes lifted almost reluctantly.

"Hello, Uncle Fred."

"Your Aunt Alice asked me to bring you these home-baked brownies, boy."

"Thanks. I guess she remembers how much I like them."

None of the other occupants in the ward was likely to guess that anything important had been said in this stilted exchange. Actually, the triple repetition of the "well" had been like a business card. It identified its bearer. The "Uncle Fred" had been a coded response, to which the name "Alice" and mention of brownies had added an official seal.

Private Peter Jones—which was not the real name or rank of the wheelchair's tenant—could now trust the stranger he faced.

The paper bag which Gervais had brought with him, containing home-baked brownies, was handed over. Peter drew out a rich square, let his eyes linger for a moment at its studding of chopped walnuts.

He took a bite, savoring it thoughtfully.

"They're all right, boy?" Gervais made it sound genuinely anxious. "Alice spent all afternoon yesterday baking. Nothing too good for Pete, she said."

"They're swell, Uncle Fred. Just swell. Want to try one?"

"Well, they're meant for you. I don't like to—"

"Go on, go on. There's plenty. Must be a dozen in there still."

A brownie changed hands. If it concealed a slip of paper, which Gervais instantly creased into his palm, not even the next casualty down the line could have noticed. A roster, secretly compiled, had been delivered.

It enumerated the enlisted personnel connected with an underground military newspaper called *Dog Tag*. Highly critical of Pentagon policy, *Dog Tag* was printed and circulated from post to post through subterranean channels the brass had long been unable to identify. But huddled day after day in his wheelchair, a young GI could listen in on many whispers, inspire many confidences.

"Aunt Alice will be very glad to hear you liked her present, Peter."

"She's a real Betty Crocker. Hers are the best."

"When I tell her what you said, she'll want to send you another present."

If to Peter Jones another present implied a pay raise or a promotion, no one else in Ward H had reason to suspect.

"Well, I reckon I'd better be making tracks, Pete. They told me downstairs you still aren't up to long visits."

"Yes, sir. And thanks for coming. And thank Aunt Alice."

Gervais had to concentrate on suppressing his normal military stride as he quit the ward. It was hard to alter the habit of a long career. Yet the many dull eyes which watched him go all had been soldier eyes. A martial walk could strip his disguise so that his tropical suit might as well be a dress uniform.

Only when outside in the corridor did he dare relax. Art Waldo, he thought then. Waldo's argument about the public doubting his claim of official business in Surf City, and figuring Robin's skyborne arrival to be an exercise in special privilege. If the public knew what had just taken place in Ward H, there'd be no room for quibbles.

The list now folded into his pocket was invaluable. One by one, quietly, the agitators it named could be rounded up and muzzled. Their dirty efforts to undermine morale could be hamstrung. A good intelligence man, Jones.

But the public, of course, must never know. None of their business. So the potential danger to Robin still stood. He moved along resolutely. A smell of disinfectant hung heavy. The air itself was close and hot. He cursed the power failure that had knocked out the air-conditioning system.

Outside on the top hospital step, he dragged in his first breath of an evening gone to total darkness while he had been indoors. It seemed only a little cooler. A few minutes later he found his rented sedan in the parking lot and coasted down into the city proper.

But once he had restored the car to the agency office, he found himself grudgingly unwilling to return to his motel, the Sea Turtle. For two past evenings, he had watched all the television he could endure. Trying to keep out of public view, just in case somebody recognized him and inferred something damaging to Robin from his presence, was like hunkering down in a foxhole to wait for a battle to begin.

He was alone now and in civilian dress. There wasn't one chance in a million for him to be pegged as General Gervais, influential father. He wanted a breath of cooling air, if in all this sultry sweatbox of a night one could be found stirring.

He walked.

The boardwalk, when he hit it, was operating at full blast. Gaudy arcades faced the sea like pigeons on a balustrade. (*"Win a watch! Win a kewpie!"*) Behind pizza-parlor windows, white-aproned geniuses spun platters of dough in impossible arcs. Booths displayed flashy costume jewelry. Enormous Teddy bears, offered as prizes, stared from the shelves of a ring-toss concession. The pervading scent of caramel popcorn was unappetizing in the stagnant air.

Gervais walked on.

Under his tread, the weathered herringbone of the wooden planks showed wear and splinters. The strollers, black and white, pressed in both directions like contrary tides.

From a dance pavilion, a scratched needle beat out canned rock. At soft-drink stands, fountains of purple and orange liquids geysered under plastic domes. (*"Bingo tonight! No waiting! New game just beginning, friends!"*) Across a low railing, if anyone cared, the dark sea stirred and shimmered.

As Gervais halted to light a fresh cigar, the seedy storefront before him diverted his attention. MADAME ANDRASHI, AUTHENTIC HUNGARIAN GYPSY COUNSELOR, a sign read. Under it was a list of Madame's occult accomplishments.

Gervais hesitated chiefly because the heat of the evening was getting to him and the effort of continued movement had become unwelcome. His cigar lit, he examined the window displays.

In one, a phrenology chart was prominent. The shaved head it featured was subdivided like the prospectus map for a real-estate development. Each plot bore its arcane label: *Sublimity. Ideality. Self-Esteem. Combativeness . . .*

This last rang a bell. A Gervais trait, Combativeness. What you wanted you fought for. No surrender. *Continuity. Benevolence. Parental Love* . . . I ought to have a big bump on my head there, he thought. Nothing I won't do for my daughter.

Robin!

She was back in his thoughts. Robin Gervais. Miss Florida. Thirteenth Princess America.

When Saturday night rolled around, was Robin going to make it?

The window signs again caught his eyes. From Madame Andrashi, they boasted, the future withheld no secrets. Balls! And yet—?

Gervais paused thoughtfully. He always had been titillated by the claims of palmists, seers and astrologers. No True Believer, he habitually checked out his daily horoscope in his morning newspaper. It amused him. And just suppose there *was* anything to all this manure they spread around?

What tipped the scales was the small sign reading *Air-Conditioned*. Mopping a damp forehead, he opened the door.

Madame sat smearing fresh polish on her fingernails.

She looked up quickly as he entered. In their creepy sockets her eyes glowed with avarice. Scented smoke coiled from a dangling censer in one corner. The dim room reeked of it.

She smiled mechanically.

"You have come to inquire of the future." It was a statement, not a query. Her voice was surprisingly pleasant. He had expected a harp whine.

"You're supposed to be able to foresee it. Yes, Madame?"

She motioned him to a camp chair across the draped table from her. Setting aside her manicure paraphernalia, she brought a crystal ball into position. The glass looked dirty. Gervais already was regretting that he had entered her den.

"Your birthdate?" Madame demanded. "The day, the hour, the minute, the place, Gentleman."

"I was born April twenty-fifth. Three-fifteen in the morning. At Ocala, Florida."

"Taurus," she said. "The Bull." She nodded gravely and stared for a moment at the smudged sphere. She looked up with a piercing glance, as if about to reveal dark mysteries. What she said was "Five dollars. You pay in advance."

"When I was a kid, fortune tellers used to like their palms crossed with silver."

"Inflation has hit all the spirits, sir, the same as anybody else."

He put down a bill on the baronet satin cloth between them. "I hope you're worth it."

"I tell only what the crystal reveals. Of course—for another five dollars, I can also read the palm. Here there is no threat of cloudiness, no misinterpretation. In a man's hand lie all the lines which tie his days together, from cradle to grave."

Gervais was surprised at himself for not standing up and walking out. But the old fake had something. In her gypsy silks, she looked like a half-asstrologer. Delighted with his wit, he produced a second bill. This one he set down closer to himself.

"Okay, let's hear the spiel. If you tell me anything real, the extra's yours."

"You do not trust Andrashi? She has read the palms of kings, sir."

"I just like to get a run for my money."

"Then hold out your hand to me."

The touch of her painted claws was cool and light. For a long moment she examined his flattened palm.

"You are a widower, yes?" It came at him in a gusty sigh, perfumed with rye.

He nodded.

"I see here a great tragedy in your past life. It touches upon your wife."

He felt himself go rigid. How in hell could she know? Was this boardwalk boozer in tawdry rags going to tell him how Celeste had died?

Was he going to sit here in a midway rat trap and hear himself accused of driving an innocent woman—a woman he loved—to suicide?

Whatever else might have been on the tip of her tongue, it remained unspoken.

There was a jangle of the doorbell just beyond his shoulder. Madame arose and waddled on stiletto heels to answer it. General Gervais sank back in his chair, shivering. And only moments ago he had been mopping himself from the heat!

It wasn't possible she could see into his past, of course. It was only hokum. A lucky guess. But those eyes of hers . . .

He was staring about him, fixing upon anything but that obscene glass orb on the table. At first, the tiny object on the carpet a few inches from his shoe seemed merely a light refraction. Gervais bent with idle curiosity to search for the gleam's source. Madame, at the door, was mumbling with whoever had rung for her. She seemed to be accepting a package.

The object he had picked up was a minuscule gold figure. A charm. Obviously, part of a woman's bracelet. He saw where the attaching link had been broken. He rolled it slowly between his fingertips. It was a diminutive Christ of the Andes, arms outspread. He recognized it instantly.

He turned the bauble over. There was a date on its underside. He himself had ordered it engraved there. It was meant to remind her of their shared tour of South American republics, that spring when he had served as security expert for the Vice President's good-will expedition. Each of those golden charms she wore—the Taj Mahal, the Eiffel Tower, the dome of St. Peter's, all the rest—had been added to her collection, one by one, by Gervais himself. Each commemorated some journey on which he had taken her. He knew them well.

Robin has been here, here in this crummy hole. And recently. Today.

Madame returned from the door carrying the gray cardboard container for a take-out pizza. She set it on the table top, heedless of the fact that it was seeping grease.

"My voices," she explained, "speak louder on a full belly. You like pizza, yes? I cut you a slice. Enough for both of us."

"Thanks, no," he somehow managed. "But don't let me stop you, Madame."

"It will wait if the gentleman is in a hurry."

"Eat it while it's hot. And while you're eating, *I'll* tell *your* fortune—absolutely free of charge."

"My fortune? Hah!"

"Not the future. I'm no good at that. But I can read the past."

Her smirk became skeptical. She tore into a pizza wedge.

"I see a very beautiful girl. She visited you, Madame. Quite recently."

"The town is this week filled with beautiful girls." Madame shrugged.

"This girl has a rare poise. It comes from travel all over the world. She is warm and gracious. Her eyes are black. Her hair is brown. Her figure is perfect. Her smile—"

Madame's own smile had been diminishing noticeably. The masticating jaws ground to a halt. She said nothing, but kept studying Gervais through narrowing eyes.

"This girl who came here was not alone." That much was a safe guess. Her chaperone, or Charlotte, was supposed to accompany Robin everywhere. But he had a chilling premonition that her companion had been neither of them. "Am I right?"

Madame nodded imperceptibly. He knew she had not intended to. The real technique of her ancient trade was to watch alertly for any slight indications a subject might give. These would tell how close some random, vague shot had hit. She would then build from there, cleverly enticing the subject to reveal what she promptly fed back to him.

And so it was now with General Gervais, muscling in on her racket. As he launched his real gamble, he watched her even more intently than she was watching him.

"She was with a young man. Handsome. Of Italian extraction. Not in uniform, yet carrying himself like an officer."

"They did not come at the same time. She . . ." Madame bit down on it hard, much as she had upon the pizza.

The rest was easy. "He had bribed you to provide them with a meeting place, And while they were here together—you furnished them privacy."

"Christ Jesus!" breathed the gypsy. "You have the evil eye. Nothing is hidden." She leaned toward him, beads clacking faintly. "I think we talk business, you and I."

"Business, Madame Andrashi?"

"I could well use a partner here. The take is not bad, even in the off season. At time like now, with a convention or a pageant, there's a fortune to be made. I cannot guess how you do it. But with a talent like yours, with experience like mine—"

"I'm already employed, thank you. This is only—you might call it a parlor trick. But I can tell you more. This girl who came here is in the Pageant."

"I swore to them I wouldn't tell. But yes."

"Do you—" and for the instant their roles reversed again—"think she can win?"

"She could. She is a Gemini. The stars will be favorable to her on Saturday night. Except . . ."

Gervais drew in the incense-heavy air. "Except what? What are you telling me?"

"You know without me. Tell it to yourself—Gentleman. Already I have said too much." She pushed back her chair. Her lupine eyes dropped hopefully toward that second bill on the table. With a tight, cold smile, Gervais picked it up. Then, on second thought, he tossed it back on the table.

Returned to the bonfire heat of the boardwalk, he swung in the direction of his motel. Two words kept blinking on and off in his brain like the garish neon signs along his route. One was *bastard*. The second read *Brioni*.

Bastard to have used his spell to corrupt Robin, as that tape so painfully proved. Bastard to have lured her into a dangerous rendezvous. Bastard to have rated his own goddam letch above her chance at the title. Bastard doubled and redoubled.

Okinawa was too good for a Paul Brioni. The original Devil's Island would have been more like it.

And as for Charlotte and that blob of lard, Louisa Willow, it was lucky for both of them that they weren't in his Army.

Sentries had been shot for deserting their posts. He'd have remanded them both to the stockade, were he able. He'd have condemned them to solitary. He'd have strung them up by their thumbs.

His teeth clamped down on his panatela.

I'll cut Brioni's transfer orders tomorrow.

Gemini? Horse shit! Nothing in the stars is going to lock up this contest for my girl, nor make certain she wins it. There's only one way to do that. Robin needs her father, not the zodiac.

By God Almighty, there are advantages to being a general! Only top echelon Intelligence personnel have access to SEARCH. But if this new supercomputer our Pentagon has spent millions developing is worth a fart, it's going to get my daughter the crown.

You'll see, Robin!

You'll see, Celeste!

22 · PRINCESS AMERICA

THE *Buttercup*, Virginia Kerr knew from various bits Amanda had told her, was the special pride and joy of her husband, Otis Kenton Clarke. An expensive, three-masted staysail schooner with a spinnaker boom almost the length of a ballroom, she had made something of a tradition of anchoring off Surf City at Pageant time. Last September, while only Miss California, Ginny had watched her coming in through binoculars and had thought she moved like a countess swaying to a Viennese waltz.

Guided by a young crewman in faded dungarees, who found it impossible to unfasten his eyes from Ginny, the tender which had come ashore for them neared the schooner. The ice-white Terylene sails, furled now, seemed like the folded wings of giant angels.

"She's beautiful!" Ginny's murmur was reverent.

"My husband thinks so. But with him beauty isn't altogether a matter of aesthetics. It's the performance built into *Buttercup*'s lines that really gets Otis. It's what he calls her valor."

"She looks as if she could outsail almost anything. He races her in international competition, didn't you tell me?"

"Constantly. That competitive drive sometimes frightens me. 'To strive, to seek, to find, and not to yield'—Tennyson might have been writing about Otis in 'Ulysses.' "

This almost wistful note in Amanda's voice was new to Ginny, but not the picture of Amanda's mate as an amateur seaman. Early in their association she had learned that he spent most of his time cruising his yacht—sailing her to Bermuda or the Bahamas and as far north as Nova Scotia. Otis Clarke was senior partner in one of Wall Street's most prestigious brokerage firms but semiretired now and devoting most of his tremendous vitality to the sea.

A moment later the tender swung alongside and they

were climbing the yacht's ladder. Ginny found herself upon a capacious deck and in the bosom of the Clarke family.

It was not, she long had privately felt, much of a family. How could it be? Otis was off sailing or racing most of the time. Amanda had manacled herself to the Princess America Pageant and for the past seven years had toured as official chaperone to a succession of Princesses. She was reunited with her husband and DeDe only on such almost ritual occasions as Pageant Week, Easter and Christmas. Whatever attraction had impelled these two to marry, it obviously had ebbed with the years to a platonic, undemanding friendship.

DeDe was Otis Clarke's only child, Amanda's stepdaughter. She had been perched on the railing watching the tender's approach, but as Amanda and Ginny set foot on deck she hopped down and came forward with a pert, ragamuffin salute.

"You're California, aren't you? Hi! I'm DeDe, your Welcome Wagon hostess aboard *Buttercup*. And this is my father, Captain Bligh."

It was not precisely a respectful introduction, and Ginny could see that it annoyed Otis Clarke. His one visible eye cast an angry glance in the girl's direction. Its left-hand mate was masked, almost too dramatically, by a patch of claret velvet. The naked eye had the savage glare of a modern corsair. Poor Wall Street!

"We're delighted Amanda has brought you out to us, Virginia," he said. "Far more comfortable here on a night like this, I'm sure, than it possibly can be ashore."

"Encourage him," said DeDe, "and he will presently bore you speechless with a guided tour. Refuse to take it, and you will be trussed up and keel-hauled until you yield."

Having again barbed her father, the girl returned to her roost on the railing. Here she balanced with birdlike gaze fixed brightly on the wicker chair toward which Otis Clarke had ushered Ginny.

DeDe was small, about nineteen, with the wiry build of an athletic boy just past puberty. Her face was thin, marked with a fierceness which she no doubt inherited from her father. Yet it was a face determined, in the current Mod fashion, to appear necrotic. Too heavy and too white a makeup. Blackly circled eyes. Lashes mascaraed to the stiff sharpness of fork tines.

She addressed herself to Ginny. "I'm going to have a martini. Join me?"

"DeDe, you know there's a Pageant rule against drinking." The corsair eye impaled her. "I wish I could make it apply to you."

"Sorry, Pops. I didn't think Ginny was still under house arrest out here."

Ginny had taken advantage of the brief sparring match to study her host more closely. He had returned to his previous position, in a comfortable deck chair. Unobtrusively, Amanda had sat down beside him and was auditing their exchange of thrusts unhappily.

The master of all he surveyed, that was Otis K. Clarke.

His weathered face had begun to collapse into the ruin of age which everything else about him belligerently refused to accept. His hair grew whiter than Amanda's, short and bristly. Inky in contrast to that silver stubble, his eyebrows were really one brow campaigning across his face in a single foray.

"What do you really think of this Pageant business, Virginia?" Leaning toward his wife's guest, he was easily gracious. His sword tip evidently was reserved for DeDe, as was hers for him. "The whole idea of it, I mean?"

"Considering the college scholarships it finances—"

"I didn't have that angle in mind, exactly. Has it ever struck you that we in America are far too much hung up on the cult of beauty? In fact, that's our own home-grown phrase, isn't it—the Beautiful People? In Europe it's very different, as perhaps you discovered while you and Amanda were there."

"Different in what way, Mr. Clarke?"

"Europeans place so much less stress on mere physical perfection. With them it's beauty of the mind, the personality. Over here, what Ninon de Lenclos still could hold her adoring courtiers at the age of ninety?"

"I think you're selling Princess America short, sir," answered Ginny, rallying promptly to the defense—as was perhaps her socially skillful host's subtle intention. "A girl has to show a lot more than a pretty face to survive even the preliminaries."

"Has there ever been an ugly winner?"

"Well—no. I guess we do still like attractive packaging for the solider virtues. But if you'll check out the values other than measurements which rate winning points from each year's judges—the talents, the ambitions, the capabilities—"

The debate Clarke had so adroitly launched still continued spiritedly when a balding, white-jacketed steward appeared with small tables which he set up beside each chair.

Their "late supper" proved to be one of the most exquisite meals Ginny ever had enjoyed. Before it was over, she regretted having eaten anything at all at that earlier boardwalk shore dinner—and wondered fleetingly how Ian was going to like marrying a fat girl.

The chef in the galley, Auguste, might have been a genius lured from a four-star Paris restaurant. He was a *café-au-lait* Haitian, of whom Ginny had caught one brief glimpse when he came on deck to replenish Clarke's Irish-and-soda. Despite the delicacies he created, he was thin as a celery stalk

DeDe was obviously avid for reports on the Pageant, never failing to address Ginny as "California"—which she evidently regarded as being In.

"My daughter," Otis Clarke dryly observed, his good eye flickering toward her, "fancies herself a theatrical career. Wild nonsense, of course. She has no talent whatever."

"You'd know about talent?" DeDe flashed. "You had to have your own poems brought out by a vanity press. No trade publisher would give them listroom."

Ginny blinked. Had she heard correctly? "Poems, Mr. Clarke?"

"Daddy celebrates the mysteries of the ocean deep in odes and lyrics," taunted his daughter. " 'A tall ship and a star to steer her by.' Only not half so good."

"That will do, DeDe," cut in Amanda firmly, noting her husband's displeasure.

"If I can't be honest about his scribbles, tell him to lay off my acting." She turned her feverish eyes back to Ginny. "I've really been quite active in professional theater, California. Did you know that?"

"One half season as a Rockette at Radio City, to keep the record straight," Otis Clarke said. It was a retaliatory stab. "And that was a disaster all the way. Wasn't it, DeDe?"

Amanda stood up as if only the pleasantest badinage had been exchanged.

"We've finished, Freddie. You may clear away. And now, Ginny dear, for that surprise I promised. I'll only be a moment. Keep out of the line of fire while I'm gone. They really adore each other—I hope."

The short, stocky figure was back on deck before father and daughter had relaxed from fighting-cock stance. She brought with her from the forward cabin two lumpy, oversized leather-bound scrapbooks.

"I've been clipping everything I could find in print about you, all year long, and pasting them up," Amanda said. "I meant to give these to you on Sunday. But tonight is even better. Princess America . . . this is your life!"

DeDe asserted herself quickly. "I helped, California. I clipped most of them. I've been following your year closer than any other girl Amanda's ever played watchdog to. You're the most beautiful Princess in the whole dozen, that's what I think."

Ginny opened the top volume. On the front page was a shot of herself riding a float in the Parade of Roses preceding the Rose Bowl Game. New Year's Day. The start of the year which, had she but known it then, was to bring Ian into her world. Gazing at the smiling girl, crowned, ribboned like an ambassador, white-gloved arm lifted gaily to the crowd, she had a surprising reaction. *Maybe I'll remember it this way the rest of my days. Not the year I was Princess, but the year I met Ian MacLaren.*

"We've traveled over two hundred thousand miles together, my dear," Amanda murmured. "It's all there. To remind you, decades from now, how it was."

"Oh, yes!" Ginny forced her attention back to present matters. "Here's our audience with the Pope. We were in Rome for the International Fashion Awards, remember? I was so excited I almost turned Catholic."

Another page, another picture. "Look, here you are waving your hand to the crowd at the Dartmouth Winter Carnival."

Ginny laughed. "The temperature was freezing and all I was wearing was a wool sweater and skirt. I was waving my hand to keep warm. Sue Rossiter taught me that trick."

She continued to turn the pages, each photograph stirring fresh memories. "Here I am at the Automobile Show! Remember how I absolutely craved this groovy sports number they have me posing in here? When would I ever have found free time to drive it, I wonder?"

"After next Saturday. But I'm glad you recovered from the fever. It was absurdly overpriced, even with the discount they offered you."

"I'll bet you've been offered everything, California," DeDe said, a wisp of envy in her voice.

"Perhaps not quite everything." That odd overtone marred Clarke's voice again.

"And the television panel." Ginny struggled not to notice their interplay. It made her uneasy. "I was positive I'd muff every quiz question and make a coast-to-coast dolt of myself. But that cute MC pitched me all the easy ones, bless him."

"They weren't all that easy," said Amanda. "I was proud of you."

DeDe again: "I'm proud of you, too, California. What was it *really* like?"

"It? Oh, you mean this past year? Well—I don't know exactly how to sum it up. It's been an experience. A wonderful, wonderful one. But—"

" 'But,' " echoed Otis Clarke. He was regarding her now with genuine attention. Perhaps he liked a girl who could field curiosity about her personal life. "I take it that means your ecstasy was qualified?"

"There are drawbacks to almost everything, sir, aren't there?"

"To being Princess America? Amanda never would admit it."

"Of course she would. She knows the rough parts as well as I do. Always being on. Always having to wear a tailored suit that won't wrinkle, and a hat and gloves—so that you look like a Princess when the photographers meet your plane. Hopping from one town to the next so fast you can't recall their names. Doing your own hair when you're dying for two hours in a beauty parlor, because one of your franchised sponsors sells a do-it-yourself hair-set kit."

"I'd put up with all that," sighed DeDe, "just to walk out into a spotlight once and know that every girl in the audience wished she was you."

"It isn't that simple," Amanda cut in. "You should have traveled with Ginny for a week if you think it's any picnic. Working with totally different people every day. Clinging to Pageant standards of poise no matter what stumbling blocks they toss in your way. Coping with fog and blizzards that make air flights hours late, or cancel them altogether, when welcoming committees are waiting and advertised events demand your presence."

Now that the door was opened, Amanda warmed to her subject.

"Think of the sponsors who have to be kept happy—at the opening of a bottling plant, when a new TV commercial for nail polish is to be taped, when automobile models are introduced, when a line of fabrics debuts. They all demand Princess America in person. And how about the civic groups featuring her for their charity events? And the hundreds of visits to Army hospitals and colleges and church convocations and children's clinics? And the stadiums where she has to throw out the first baseball? And the Community Chest luncheons? And the poster-posing for national health drives and U.S. Bond promotions?"

DeDe shrugged. "You must have loved it or you wouldn't have stayed with it all these years."

"I happen to believe in the Princess America Pageant," answered her stepmother. Amanda's voice carried the same conviction found in patients who defend their psychiatrists. "It's one of the largest scholarship programs for young women in our country today. If the world ever needed educated citizens, certainly it's now."

"Education?" DeDe said cynically. "Don't you mean you like the hoopla?"

"Last year alone, the program awarded over a half million dollars in scholarships. To almost seven hundred girls. It's wonderful being a part of something like that. One feels useful. Needed."

Which Amanda was not, quite evidently, in this tight family circle. Otis lived on his schooner. DeDe was tended, in their huge apartment hung above the East River, by a competent staff of servants. The girl was too old for parental supervision and seemed none too fond of her father's second wife. Amanda's last four words explained tellingly her fierce compulsion to make the Pageant her life.

In the few beats of silence which followed that statement of faith, the gentle creak of the hull became audible. *Buttercup* dipped haughtily on the long swells headed in toward shore. Aport, Surf City's lights glittered distantly like the strewn output of King Solomon's mines.

"An exhausting schedule," Clarke admitted, reaching again for his whiskey. "I'm amazed you two can plan it all. Or even keep your dates straight."

"All that is done for us," Ginny explained. "By our Pageant business manager, Alan Stone. He handles all our activities. It's his job to schedule all appearances, make flight reservations, and chart routes so there'll be as little backtracking as possible. He even has to figure free time when Mrs. Clarke and I can get back to visit with our families. Not that we ask for too much time off! Every day we work means another fat fee, and you don't earn those on the old porch swing."

DeDe giggled. "In another line of work you might."

"Enough of that." Her father's visible eye turned

toward her coldly. "Tell me, Virginia. From all this mobile sweat shop, you must have a few pet memories."

"Oh, yes! I'll never forget the time in Wyoming when they let me ride a bronc in the Pioneer Days rodeo. They were all betting he'd throw me, but I held on for ninety seconds. And there was the time we made the movie short on water skiing at Cypress Gardens. I'd never skied before. I had to learn how."

"I wish I could have taught you," DeDe said. "I'm sensational at it. Maybe we could take a trip sometime, just you and I, and—"

"Unlikely," Clarke said, and tilted his glass until ice clicked against his dentures. "Virginia will have her own affairs to pick up, after Saturday. She's probably traveled enough for a lifetime. Don't pester her."

"We'll finish looking at the scrapbooks another time." Amanda arose. "I don't want you dragged out for your morning schedule. We're due back ashore at nine o'clock, Ginny. Time for bed."

DeDe's cabin, which she was to share for the night, lay aft of the open deck. As they closed its door, DeDe chuckled.

"Time for bed!" She mimicked Amanda's tone with a startling fidelity. Maybe Otis Clarke was unfair about her lack of talent.

Alongside the wide bunk, flagrantly in view, a silver wine cooler packed with a crushed iceberg thrust up two bottle necks, foil-wrapped and angled like an antenna. DeDe backed toward the cooler with a sly wink.

"Champagne." She grinned. "Don't you adore it, California?"

"Who doesn't? Your mother promised to treat me to some as soon as I'm unfrocked and the new Princess takes over."

"Why wait? We've something to celebrate. You're here at last on *Buttercup*. I know you're not supposed to drink and Amanda is a demon about regulations. But who will know? *I'll* never snitch."

"But the rules—"

"Shove the rules. They don't apply outside the three-mile limit. We're in international waters." DeDe's strong young thumbs were working a cork. Cautiously, she held a folded towel over the neck to muffle the pop. "Oh, not really three miles out. But you can commit one small crime tonight. I've already committed two myself, stealing

Freddie's wine-locker key and then bribing Auguste to smuggle in the cooler and glasses."

While she spoke, she had been pouring into a hollow stemmed goblet. When it was four-fifths full, she extended it to Ginny. Ginny fought one final round with conscience. And conscience lost. After all, it would be jumping the gun only a little. And this far out from shore there wasn't the slightest chance the Pageant's unsullied reputation could be harmed.

"I hope you like this champagne." DeDe's voice was apologetic. "Frankly, I don't know if the year was a good one or a disaster."

"Right now," Ginny answered with a boldness that surprised her, "I'd drink witch hazel. Thanks."

"To California!" DeDe was toasting her warmly. "My idea of the ideal Princess America! For me, all the others are only Xerox copies of you."

"Thanks," Ginny said again, somewhat embarrassed. Despite her year in a blaze of publicity, she always felt flustered by obvious flattery. To change the subject, she added quickly, "Your mother has told me a lot about you. But she never mentioned you wanting a career in the theater. The Rockettes, was it?"

"As darling Daddy was quick to point out, only for half a season."

"You didn't like stage life as much as you'd expected?"

DeDe grimaced. "Oh, the life was okay. But the salary was absurd. Ninety-nine dollars a week, and that was twenty-six bucks lower than they paid a beginning stagehand. We had to rehearse a hundred and twenty hours, no pay at all, for the nine new shows the Music Hall puts on every year. For twenty-one days running, we'd do four shows a day with only a ninety-minute break between. And no days off. Then, during the six-day rest you eventually rated, they'd call you as a replacement if one of the cast got sick. The girls developed a telephone code ring so they wouldn't get tapped when it was the Music Hall calling. And for all that, you know what we were making? We figured it came to about two cents a kick, that's what!"

Sipping as she listened, Ginny was surprised. "I wouldn't think that economics would be a problem. Not for you."

"I had to make Daddy take me seriously, didn't I?" DeDe was reaching to fill both glasses again. "He only admires two things. Important money and records for *Buttercup* to log in a major race."

"What made you quit the Rockettes? Just the money?"

"Well, no. I was getting bunions. And have you ever worked that Music Hall stage? You need a preliminary course in survival. There's solid concrete under the linoleum. You jar your back teeth loose trying to dance on it. And the occupational hazards—wow! Christmas Nativity scenes—when the camels crap right where you're supposed to start the high-kick routine. Easters, they're apt to do a Running Between the Raindrops thing and leave you puddles to mush through."

"Sounds more rugged than my own schedule," Ginny sympathized.

Again, the chilled bottle was busy between them.

"So when the worm finally turned and the kids went out on strike, demanding a raise, I quit. I couldn't buy marching up and down in a picket line. That's not theater, that's labor. Anyhow, by then I'd had—oh, sort of misunderstandings with a couple of the girls. I was fed up. That wasn't serious stage. I want to be a real actress."

"Have you studied for it? There's an awful lot to learn."

"Giving me Amanda's noble higher-education bit?" DeDe made a rude sound. "I have my own method for studying my art."

"What's that?"

"I go to the movies. Ones where the show is continuous, and I have a rough idea as to what the plot is about. The first time they run the feature, I sit with my eyes closed. I hear the dialogue but I don't see the actors. I try to visualize every scene in my mind and plan the business I'd be doing if I had to speak each line. Cross the room here. Light a cigarette here. Stare out of the window after a long speech. And so on. Then, the second time round, I keep my eyes open and watch more than I listen. I check on how right my direction was. Often it turns out the director's ideas are much more dramatic than mine. That's how I learn."

"It sounds like a pretty original method."

Ginny was staring detachedly at her glass. The level of pale topaz liquid in it never seemed to lower, no matter how much she drank. She heard a soft, delighted giggle and realized it was her own.

"The bubbles," she said thickly, "making my nose tickle."

There was a gurgling sound and her glass was full again, as if by witchcraft. DeDe was tilting a new champagne bottle. Ginny had not even heard the second cork pop.

"Ought to get to bed," she said, responding to the automatic curfew sent out by her subconscious. "Tomorrow—'nother day."

"A good idea. Did you bring any gear, California?"

"No gear. Straight from dinner. Always must travel light. For Princess America, baggage limit can't be over forty pounds. You know that? Basic wardrobe for luncheons, lectures, dinners, flagpole sitting. Baggage gets lost, have to be presentable in what we stand up in. At all times."

It had been a feat to get out that "presentable" without a slur. She felt proud of herself, almost expecting a round of applause.

DeDe was pouring again. "Never mind. You can wear half of my jammies. I've only one set aboard, because the laundry went ashore this morning. Which half, California?"

"I don't want to be . . . nuisance. Sleep in my slip."

"I wouldn't hear of it!" Laughing, DeDe yanked open a chest drawer and produced pajamas—green silk with little pink clovers scattered over them like measles. "Which half, beautiful Princess?"

"Tops, if that's okay."

Following DeDe's lead, she began to peel off her sheath and underthings. Somehow she managed to roll her sheer nylons down her calves. DeDe, naked by now, was in front of the dressing-table mirror, cold-creaming that absurd hippie makeup from her narrow face. But in the glass she was studying the curving line of Ginny's flesh with unconcealed admiration.

"You're one gorgeous doll, California. But I guess you know that."

The bright reflected eyes seemed almost febrile. But Ginny was too preoccupied to notice. Getting the right arm into the right sleeve was her main problem right now.

"Nightcap!" announced DeDe, wearing the pajama bottoms. Her negligible breasts were as tanned as her arms and back. Except for their hard, dark nipples, they might have been a boy's. With the paint wiped from her face, she no longer had that mortuary look. But Ginny felt sorry for her. Something inside this girl was wrong. She seemed as sad as a clown.

"No thanks. I don't think—"

"Party pooper! Come on, don't be so square!"

Ginny sank onto the bunk they were to share.

"No more, really. I'll be a mess tomorrow. Can't afford that."

Further conversation was an effort. The champagne had fogged her senses of sight and hearing. But somehow the unwanted stemmed glass was in her hand again and she was sipping.

"Who writes to you most?" DeDe's gaze became bolder.

"Girls or men? I bet a lot of girls wish they knew you."

"Mail—about an even split. Lots of mail, though. Lots."

"How do you answer them? The girls who wish they knew you?"

Norm Prescott had drilled the procedure into her. Answer their questions. With the truth, if that fits policy. With the party line, if you have to cover up. But answer. The Princess is always very cooperative. Everybody's darling, see? "Family helps me." She was trying to think clearly, trying to come up with the required information. It was a query she had coped with often before. People liked to know about Princess America's fan mail. "Most of it gets shipped home. My folks send out the cards. Cards with my picture. Lots of requests for my picture. Business manager answers appeals—money, bookings, endorsements. Special ones, I drop notes. Your mother, too."

"My stepmother. Screw her. The special ones, California? The girls?"

"Good night," Ginny said abruptly. Fatigue and a wave of champagne giddiness combined to engulf her. She fell back on her pillow, limp as a punctured tube, already 85 percent asleep.

The other 15 percent was dimly conscious of hands rolling her over, making room for DeDe to crawl in at her side. The boat rocked. Boat. At sea. All at sea. That was why directions seemed distorted. Why DeDe's voice seemed to come from somewhere near the bunk's foot.

"Good night, sweet Princess!" She felt a kiss on her lips.

There was a veil of time after these words during which she was aware of nothing. Black chiffon, layers of it, seemed to hold her like winding sheets. There was only emptiness beyond that casing. Utter void.

But she could feel the rocking. Tide swell was at the boat like a foot on a cradle's treadle. Back and forth. Back and forth.

Then—suddenly—something else.

She moaned thickly. "Please . . . don't . . ."

But it didn't stop. The pressure spreading her legs apart was gentle though insistent. And something hot and wet and quick was there.

It must be a dog—some little dog—licking, whimpering, wanting to be loved. She pushed vaguely, to discourage the puppy. It kept on licking, whining softly.

But there was no dog aboard the Buttercup.

Suddenly Ginny tried to sit up, the movement a convulsive jerk. Horror and nausea combined to set every nerve in her body on screaming edge. *"Stop that!"*

But the weight which pinioned her legs did not shift. The tempo of what was happening down there only increased. As did the whimpering.

Black chiffon. No light anywhere. The cabin was dark, although she could not recall when its lights had been switched off. Out of the black chiffon, hands were at her thighs, lifting the green pajama jacket higher.

"Let me go! Let . . . me . . . *go!*"

DeDe gasped like a long-distance runner at the tape. "Don't move, California . . . please . . . just a little longer. I'm almost on the moon."

"I'll call for help! I swear I will!" But Ginny was retching as she tried to speak, and the words were lost in the raw spew sound.

"Don't move. I'll give you anything you want. Just let me—"

"No! No!" Ginny kicked with all the force she could muster. But she was held as if by gyves, and DeDe hung on. Like the honey bear who slips his red tongue into the nest of sleeping bees to steal honey. "Don't be shocked . . . I've had one other Princess before . . ." Then a spasm shook her like a Kansas twister, arching her. "Oh, Christ! Oh, Jesus! *Here I come!*"

In the instant she felt that imprisoning weight quiver and relax, Ginny wrenched herself free and was off the bunk and up on her feet. Heedless of her scanty covering, whipped by hysteria and guided only by memory, she lunged toward where the cabin door should be.

The catch was under her trembling fingers almost as she reached for it. She flung the panel wide, hurled herself past the high marine threshold and darted across the dark deck.

Soft night wrapped the *Buttercup* as in a womb. The full moon, which had hung low on the horizon when supper ended, had disappeared behind a cloud. Half the boardwalk neons ashore had dropped away like spangles from an old gown. Overhead, the red riding lights of the schooner swayed as the tall masts tilted. But she saw none of this. She was a fox, with a desperate huntress at her heels. DeDe was chasing after her.

"Virginia!" It was a different kind of begging now. A frightened, almost futile begging. "California! Wait, please wait! Let me explain." But nothing could have stopped her headlong flight.

"Ginny—don't tell them. You don't understand. It's happened before. If Daddy finds out this time . . ."

What the rope in her path was, or why someone had left it coiled, treacherous on the deck, Ginny never knew. But her bare foot caught in it, checking her mad stampede. Simultaneously the boat dipped. The devilish timing pitched her over the low railing, plunging her into the black depths below. The water was like a glacial current and a strong tide was running. Ginny struggled against the sucking greed of it. But the champagne and horror had crippled her reflexes.

Waves were rising all around her. The walls of liquid onyx reared higher, higher. Like locoed black stallions, trampling . . . higher . . .

I'm going to die, Ginny thought, feeling the ravenous icy ink in which she struggled suck her down again. Ian, darling, I'm going to drown.

Past midnight, Surf City's famous beach was all but deserted. The thousands of bathers who frequented it on any normal warm day, let alone the extra hordes this unseasonable September scorcher had brought out, had gone home.

But because the night was still insufferably hot, a few late lingerers dotted the sand—some of them lovers, the rest stretched out on terrycloth towels to get what relief they could. Only a skeleton force of the Surf City Beach Patrol remained on duty, watchful if no longer anticipating emergencies.

Steve Dorn slowed Miss Utah's convertible near the edge of the boardwalk, lit a cigarette, and looked across the water. It stirred and shimmered faintly like black satin on a woman's breast. Utah's breasts came instantly to mind.

That Lori Macklin could spell trouble for a guy. Trouble in spades. The way she'd been tossing it at him all day. A promising smile whenever Mrs. Birkenbuel's attention was diverted. A light brush of hand on hand as he held open the car door for her. A provocative swaying of hips as she walked, as if to show him where the action was. They all telegraphed the message loud and clear. *It's here just waiting for you, Buster . . . Come and get it!*

Well-serviced married man though he was, he was strongly tempted to go and get it. During the day just past he had become more and more convinced that this one wasn't another little cock teaser, as he'd figured at first. This kid would really deliver.

Sitting in the parked car, half listening to reports sputtering over the shortwave radio, Dorn struggled to think down his semierection. Dynamite. Poison. Catastrophe. Just you remember that, Steve, my boy.

For the past few years, during the summer months, Dorn was always transferred to duty with the elite corps that made up the Beach Patrol. He knew this four-mile stretch of sand like his own appendicitis scar. He was well aware of every danger spot where an offset (what laymen referred to, erroneously, as undertow) might form.

Actually that moving water did not operate beneath the surface; nor did it pull a bather under. What happened was that the mushy sand was almost as fluid as the sea itself. Waves got whipped by wind and tides and currents, churning up the bottom below. A hole big enough for elephants to mate in could be gouged out in minutes. Water, forever seeking out its lowest level, would flood into these hollow troughs so fast that its momentum could sweep 150 bathers to sea at once. That was what they meant when they blamed an undertow for some fresh tragedy. The unlucky bastard had got himself caught in a sudden offset.

It was panic that caused the drownings. If a victim kept his cool, he could hold enough air in his lungs to stay afloat until help reached him. But the average swimmer let fear take over. He'd begin to struggle and thrash in the water, sinking, gasping desperately for air and taking salt water into his lungs instead. The saline inhalation, causing spasms of the larynx, would cut off his windpipe as if he'd tied a granny knot in it. After that, the sea had him cold.

Steve chuckled philosophically. Nothing to chill the hots like a self-lecture in oceanography. He was almost his own man once more. He would not think again of Utah's 36-23-35 proportions. Not until he was safely in bed with Nancy, whose pelvic r.p.m. could make him break every holding pattern he had ever devised to delay his orgasm. Home, James! He reached for the car's ignition key.

". . . off the three-master *Buttercup*. S.O.S. S.O.S. Beach Patrol!"

The words leaped at him from the radio speaker on the dashboard. *Buttercup*. The Clarke sailing yacht. She had put in opposite this very spot at twilight yesterday. He had seen her at anchor on his way to the hotel this morning. He knew almost exactly where she lay.

Dorn was out of his bucket seat in a wink, reacting like Pavlov's dog. As he pounded down the soft sand, the cop on duty at Stand Sixteen—nearest of the line spaced two hundred yards apart across the entire length of the beach—already was in motion. They joined forces a few paces short of the seventeen-foot bank skiff which sat on two wooden rollers almost at the edge of the tide. Each stand in the series was equipped with its own skiff. The guard on duty here recognized him.

"Steve! The *Buttercup*'s out there. My can of worms."

"Everybody's can, Ed."

They moved like parts of one well-oiled machine. The doughnut—a ring-shaped buoy affixed to sixty feet of line—was ready in its place aboard. They maneuvered the skiff expertly into floatable water. Oars fell into their locks and dipped in perfect unison without a word being spoken.

A lifeboat rescue is work only for thoroughly experienced personnel. Two men in a boat, no matter how high the seas, could just about double the speed of even a champion swimmer. They could row five hundred feet in a minute and a half. That was half the average drowning time.

They were out into the full swell when the flare of a distress rocket opened a hole in the darkness. It had gone up not too far ahead. It flowered against the sky, a minicomet, briefly illuminating the high waves which seethed below it. Whoever was in that sea must be in bad trouble.

They did not talk. The combers rolling beachward were giving them tough enough odds. They concentrated as a single brain, a single body, on the job at hand.

That poor bastard up ahead, whoever he might be, must have given up hope by now. *Let him be alive,* Steve urged Somebody, although he was not a religious man. *Just let the poor slob be alive.*

They were close by the *Buttercup* now. Even as a black cutout against less solid black, she was big and beautiful.

"Over there, Steve!" Ed had spotted it first.

The bobbing head was barely visible as the sea lifted it. They shifted course without missing an oar dip and bore down on the spot.

"How's your pitching arm?" Ed grated.

"Ready for the strike zone." Steve rose carefully in the rolling skiff, bringing the doughnut up with him. Balanced on spread legs, he bellowed into the night.

"Ahoy! Catch hold of this, Mac! We'll drag you in!"

The line to which the buoy was attached snaked out. Dorn's aim was accurate. He saw the buoyant circle strike surface a scant four feet from that dark head. But the rag doll rising and falling with its matrix wave made no move to grab it.

"Shit!" he muttered. "Too far gone!" Off came the jacket, the uniform pants. The shirt. The shoes. He split water in a long, shallow dive and came up swimming. He was a strong swimmer, raised from boyhood in the surf, and he closed the gap between him and the rag doll in three strokes.

Just as the body began to slide under, Dorn managed one arm around it. No struggle here. No wrestling match. He had dead weight to lug. The skiff heaved beside him as he turned back. Ed's arms reached over its gunwale to relieve him of his sodden burden. Steve hoisted himself, dripping, in its wake.

As they swung alongside the *Buttercup* its ladder was already dropping down to the water. A powerful searchlight coned down at them. A few moments later, the inert form draped over his shoulder, Steve had reached the deck. At once, a tense knot of jabbering figures closed in on him.

"Stand back!" he barked, not even glancing at them.

It was not until he had lowered his cargo on the scrubbed planking that he saw it was a girl. An almost naked girl. She was blue with the onset of cyanosis.

He was down on his knees beside her almost before she touched floor. One practiced move had her head tilted back with her chin pointed upward. Another had tugged her jaw into an unnatural jut, so that the base of her tongue would keep clear of the back of her throat and leave an air passage open.

With an extended finger for a swab, he wiped away whatever might be obstructing her mouth—food matter, brine, blood. Then thumb and forefinger pinched her nostrils tight, to seal otherwise escaping breath within her nose.

Opening his mouth to a wide oval, he fixed it tightly over hers. He blew. He blew again. He kept on blowing, pacing himself. Twelve breaths per minute. In goes the good air, out goes the bad air. The routine was second nature.

When he removed his lips to listen for that gasp which should accompany air exchange, there was none. Moving fast, he rolled her over on her side and struck a series of ungentle blows between her shoulder blades. They were intended to dislodge any extraneous material which might be cutting off air. Again his thrust finger served as a swab. He rolled her back, rechecking head and jaw positions. Was she dead already? He didn't like that blue skin.

Grimly, he bent to his task again.

The kiss was intolerable. It possessed her mouth. It demanded something. On her mouth, this time; but just before it hadn't been on her mouth. Unbearable. Wrong. Perverted.

Ginny stirred weakly. The protest inside her was strong, yet she could not make her body fight. The weight was on top of her—just as it had been in the cabin. So the nightmare of drowning had been false horror. She never had escaped from the bunk at all.

"No . . ." She gagged, sick at the effort. "Please, oh, please . . ."

"She's coming around!" somebody said, a galaxy away.

"Thank God! Oh, thank God! Ginny, darling, it's Amanda!"

"Keep back, lady. We still need air here. She's not out of the woods yet."

This last was a male voice, deep and gruff. This kiss stopped while the voice spoke, but then it began again.

But if it was a man's voice, then it couldn't be DeDe.

It seemed to be terribly important that she open her eyes and check this point. What man? Why was he kissing her? She was on a boat, because she could feel it tilting.

Boat? Oh, yes, *Buttercup*. The cabin was on *Buttercup*. The pride and joy of Otis Kenyon Clarke. Who wore a piratical red velvet patch. Whose daughter was a high-kicking Rockette lesbian.

Slowly, she opened her eyes. The circle of faces seemed to shimmer before her. They all were staring down at her as if she were a bear in a pit. Why was she lying on the deck? Wet, too. Shivering.

Somebody seemed to hear her thinking this, because hands began wrapping her in a blanket. The man took his mouth away and settled back to watch them make a cocoon of her.

Oddly, it was Freddie she recognized first. He was

gaping at her with his thin jaw asag, like a gate on a broken hinge. And there was Amanda, crying, face blotched and streaked with tears; Amanda, who never cried.

And, cloaked in another blanket, stood the sad, sad little clown.

DeDe! The girl was staring down like the rest. But unlike the others, through eyes enormous with horror. They were the most terrified eyes Ginny had ever seen. They were pleading with her wordlessly, desperately.

Don't tell them! those distended eyes implored. *Oh, God, don't tell!*

Shuddering, Ginny turned her face away. At the first hint of movement, the man crouched above her took over. "Easy, girl. Easy."

She stared up directly into his face. His hair was very dark and crinkly. His smile was wide and warm. He was dripping wet and almost as naked as she was.

"Where did you come from? You weren't here for supper."

"Out of the sea," he said. "How're you feeling?"

"Lousy, thank you. Absolutely lousy."

"I'll tell you what you're going to do. You're going to lie down in a nice warm spot for about an hour. You're going to take about two fingers of whiskey neat. And then I'm going to get you to a hospital."

Amanda's indrawn breath was a chalk squeak on slate. "Hospital, Officer? But . . . unless you're sure it's necessary—"

"A precaution, ma'am. There could be a shock reaction. She's better off the rest of tonight where a doctor can watch her."

"Of course then, if it's for Ginny's good. But—"

"You don't have to worry about publicity, Mrs. Clarke. I've recognized her. So would reporters, that's what you're thinking. But nobody wants to hurt the Pageant. I'll get her into the police infirmary by the back way."

"Tomorrow, we—"

"Tomorrow, if she's fit to leave, that'll be that. Nothing on the record. Nothing in the headlines."

"You can't know how grateful we'll all be. Ginny, too. The Pageant's good name means so much to us." It wasn't like Amanda to babble. "I still can't understand how this awful thing happened. Ginny, dearest, can't you tell us?"

"It was . . ." But those great, stricken eyes, just beyond Amanda's solid shoulder, were beseeching her.

"DeDe said you were walking in your sleep. You never did before."

The pitiful little clown was on the scaffold, pleading with the executioner.

Ginny shuddered again. Somehow, she had to stop the questions. "I had a bad dream. I woke up scared. I ran on deck . . . panicky. Tripped on a rope . . . fell over the rail . . ."

Ginny heard a long-held breath expelled. It sounded like a little girl's sob.

The *Buttercup*'s tender, ferrying Ginny and Steve Dorn ashore, was lost to darkness within seconds of quitting the schooner's side. Ed had departed earlier, oaring his skiff back to its beach post.

Except for the crewman in charge of the tender, the Clarke employees had retired to quarters to make the most of what was left of a broken night. Amanda had gulped a double sedative, eyes still red, cheeks still puffy.

DeDe huddled on the forward railing, almost at the bow. She had not looked after the tender as it departed. She had not dared to. Her thin hands still were shaking, and there were tiny red half-moons in their palms where her nails had dug in. The breeze which had been blowing earlier continued, lifting the short red curls from her forehead. The boat rocked gently, like two sweethearts in a hammock. A woman holding her girl lover, purring, crooning . . .

It isn't evil. It isn't bad. It's only . . . different.

The waves were white lace ruffles. Like the Parisienne panties in that can-can number at the Music Hall. A row of shapely legs kicked high, flaunting the frills to tantalize the audience. And not only the audience, either.

I didn't ask to be this way. It's not my fault.

Everyone was asleep. She was the only person left in the world. And she ached not to be. Not to be alone like this, but *with* someone.

I could have shown you things you never dreamed of, California. Why did you have to spoil it? Why did you run?

She straightened slowly, turning at last toward her own cabin. Her bare feet made no sound on the star-washed deck. The cabin door moved at her touch and let her past. She didn't remember the lights being on before. Yet they were burning now. The cabin, every detail of it, stood out crystal clear.

Her father was leaning against the dressing table, staring across the little distance which separated them as she paused in surprise.

"Daddy! I—I thought . . ."

His one exposed eye held on her tense face for rather too long a moment. Then it cut toward the bunk. Two pillows lay there side by side. Only one showed any rumpling of use. The eye moved back, cold as a lizard's skin.

"So you tried it again. Again, after that last time."

"I never—I didn't—I mean, it was all a mistake, I—"

"A mistake that forced Ginny to jump into the ocean to be safe from you?"

"I wasn't even touching her when she went over. Daddy, I swear—"

"Do you happen to remember what it cost me to keep that Music Hall business from smearing my name—and yours—across the tabloids? Do you know that girl will sit cozy for the rest of her days from what I had to pay her to keep mum? Christ, what did I ever do to deserve you?"

A spark of defiance struck. "You wanted a son, didn't you? A boy? Well, maybe that's how I got to be the way I am. Trying to be what you wanted. Trying to be like you."

"Like *me?* Dear, merciful God, I'm no fucking fruit!"

"You've chased women all your life. I've watched it since I was a small girl. Getting some slut under you in bed was more important than pulling off your next business deal. Always, always!"

"At least I gave them something they could rise to." Otis Clarke took a long stride that brought them close. He slapped her so hard that she collapsed across the bunk. "You! You and your big, hungry mouth!"

BOOK FOUR *Wednesday*

23 · MISS FLORIDA

BY Wednesday morning, the oppressive heat had abated. A refreshing easterly wind, idling in from the Atlantic, had blessed the coast. It rippled the flowered cloths on four circular tables ranged around the Olympic-sized pool of the Imperial Hotel.

Colored umbrellas, like scoops of sherbert, shaded each table. Orange, lemon, pink and green. Two Pageant judges sat at each table. Passing before them in prearranged sequence, pairs of contestants were making the rounds.

Robin Gervais, approaching the first table alongside Miss New Jersey, was determined to be friendly with her bouncy rival.

"They're about to start shooting," she remarked. "Now I know how it feels to stand up before a firing squad."

"Really?" Swaggering along beside her, Jersey shrugged her shoulders. "They don't bother me. A pack of squares, except for that cute hairdresser. I'll have them eating out of my hand."

Robin compressed her lips ever so slightly. She was reminded of a gorgeous, petite, but extremely vain girl she had known in high school. When they had run her picture in the senior classbook, a cruel but deserved line under it read "Giant economy-size conceit packaged in a small container."

Darlene Bryant was far more impossible to take.

Under the orange umbrella, Glenda Dowling and Julius Laurel awaited them. Laurel rose gallantly, invited the girls to sit down. Glenda Dowling shook her head, her jowls bobbing.

Tilted back in his wicker chair, Laurel gave both girls an affable smile. "We want you both to relax," he began. "This is not a Spanish Inquisition."

The squeals of two little girls in red bikinis squabbling in the pool for possession of an inflated seahorse overlapped his words.

"Let me briefly explain the reason for this interview," he resumed when their shouts abated. "For the next ten minutes, Miss Dowling and I are going to ask you hypothetical questions. Most of them will be deliberately embarrassing. A few will be conventional."

Laurel paused as a waitress came by with a tray bearing four glasses filled to the brim with Merri-Cola and crushed ice. She deposited them on the table along with some straws without shedding a single drop.

"We—and our colleagues at the next three tables you will visit—will score your answers on the basis of three factors," Laurel continued. "Speed in responding. Tact and diplomacy. Humor. Our intent is to determine if you have the potential to maintain the poise, dignity and graciousness of a Princess America."

Off to Robin's right, a curly-haired, muscle-beach specimen bounced on a diving board, testing its play. Presently, his eyes fixed on Robin and held. She was unaware of him.

She was thinking of Paul.

Something was wrong. At the fortuneteller's parlor yesterday, he had asked her to contact him before breakfast this morning. The sun had barely spilled into her room when she had activated her miniature walkie-talkie.

"Robin calling Batman . . . "

But when she flicked to *Receive*—nothing. Not a hum.

"Come in, Batman . . . " But the silence had continued.

It wasn't at all like Paul. He had been so insistent about wanting to wish her luck before meeting with the judges. What could have come up? Where could he be?

The worry that nagged her did not show at all on her calm face as she met the scrutiny of her inquisitors. She, in turn, was assessing them.

Julius Laurel looked as remote and noble as a marble knight atop a medieval tomb. Glenda Dowling was smiling balefully, revealing fangs like a basilisk's. *She doesn't like me,* Robin sensed. *I wonder why?*

Actually, could she have observed the Dowling mind through a transparent plastic skull, she would have seen gleaming knives inside. A dozen of them. Each sharpened to stab a contestant she considered to be a genuine threat to Stacy DeGray.

Miss Florida and Miss New Jersey were her targets at the moment.

In Fleming's office yesterday, Glenda had been carried away by Rodger Megan's eloquence and had let him practically hypnotize her into promising that her judging would be impartial. But since then, flowers from that delightful Mrs. DeGray had arrived in her hotel room. And with them, a charming note which made it abundantly clear how highly the two DeGrays, *mère et fille*, regarded their sister Californian.

The flowers and the note had set Glenda thinking. And she had redecided that Stacy was going to win.

So the two of them, woman and girl, judge and contestant, sat eyeing each other warily across a circle of tablecloth. Julius Laurel made the kickoff.

"Miss New Jersey," he began, "if you become Princess America, you will probably earn more than two hundred and fifty thousand dollars. Is that why you'd like to win the contest?"

"Well-ll . . . " Darlene was playing her dimples. "Everybody knows Daddy's loaded. He's set up a million-dollar trust fund for me. So I'd donate the money to worthy charities."

Laurel's sculptured face remained unreadable as it veered toward Robin.

"Miss Florida?"

Robin weighed the pros and cons swiftly. If she answered "Yes," she'd seem mercenary. A flat "No" would hardly sound convincing. Jersey's answer, whether truthful or calculated to impress the judges, would be hard to top.

"Mr. Laurel, I don't want to win for myself," she said. "I've won lots of contests. I'd like to win primarily because of my state. Florida's never had a winner."

Clever cop-out, Laurel thought to himself. But could she keep it up?

He consulted the list of questions on his pad, selected another fire-cracker, and addressed Miss New Jersey.

"Tell me, young woman, what do you think of girls who pose in the nude for magazines like *Playboy?*"

Jersey's eyes registered contempt. "They're disgusting. Friends have told me I've a better figure than almost any one of them. Yet I wouldn't expose my body to the public. It's just plain revolting."

"And you, Miss Florida?"

Red light. Stop. This was another loaded question, Robin realized. Agree with Darlene, and I'm a prude. Disagree, and I'm a sexpot.

"I'm afraid I can't answer your question, Mr. Laurel," she said. "You see, I never read magazines like *Playboy.*"

A hint of a grin passed over Laurel's austere lips. Florida was making mincemeat out of her opponent.

"Next question, Miss New Jersey. Purely hypothetical. Suppose you're smooching with a boy friend in his parked car. Suppose he wants you to go the limit. How would you cool him off?"

Jersey's answer was prompt. "Slap his face. I'd let him know I'm a perfect lady."

Robin smiled when she answered. "I'd tell him I never give samples—only references."

This time, Laurel chuckled audibly. This Florida kid knew all the answers. She was cleverer than any of the contestants he had interviewed up to now. She had brains as well as bust.

Once again he referred to his pad. Then: "Miss New Jersey, have you ever worn false eyelashes?"

Darlene squirmed in her chair. She sensed this was a trap. The Pageant rules, she knew, forbid beauty artifices.

"Please excuse me if I sound immodest, Mr. Laurel," she answered coyly. "But I really don't think I need them. Boys always tell me they're wild about my eyes."

"I see. Miss Florida?"

Robin recognized the real pitfall. Laurel Products included, among other luxury cosmetic items, false eyelashes. She considered this fact, wanting her response to outscore Darlene's. That she felt keenly competitive surprised her. Certainly, with a duck in the oven, she had no wish to win the crown—quite the reverse. All she wanted was to make a respectable showing—at least finish among the five semifinalists—for her father's sake. To gentle him up for a later surprise. Yet now . . .

It's Darlene, Robin thought. *Her vanity gives me a swift pain. She has enough brass in her to build an old-fashioned bed. I'd like to steal points from her so nice kids like Hawaii, Colorado and Alaska would have a better chance.*

"Miss Florida?" Laurel nudged.

"I once saw a groovy pair I liked in a boutique. Made by your company. I almost splurged and bought them, but I figured out that each time I lost a lash it would cost me eighty-three cents!"

With an angry little snort, Glenda Dowling took over. She had silently been appraising the two girls. Jersey was a pretty little piece, but phony, conceited and often obnoxious. She really didn't matter. Robin Gervais was a different breed of cat. Lovely. Cool. Unruffled. Modestly charming. All the qualities one looked for in a Princess America. In short, a top contender.

This girl, thought Glenda, is *Stacy DeGray's most dan-*

gerous competition. But she's not going to get by me that easily. She's going to stub her toe at this station stop so badly, even Laurel's stock in her will go down.

Glendy Dowling leveled her eyes at Darlene.

"Miss New Jersey, let's suppose that after several years of marriage you discover your husband can't give you a baby. Suppose he asks you to submit to artificial insemination. Would you go along?"

"Of course not," Darlene answered indignantly. "I'd suggest that we adopt a child."

An obvious answer, Glenda told herself. But the Gervais girl would either have to echo it or respond with one even lamer.

"And you, Miss Florida?" Glenda asked. "Would you accept a test-tube baby if your husband were sterile?"

But I don't have that problem, Robin thought proudly. *I'm one of the lucky ones. I'm married to a man who can fill me full of himself. I'm married to Paul. And his baby is warm and safe in my womb. And it's going to be a perfect baby, because he's its father!*

"Come, Miss Florida," Glenda persisted. "Would you have a baby by artificial insemination?"

Robin answered sweetly and innocent-eyed. "I just don't believe I could conceive of such a situation, Miss Dowling."

Laurel laughed heartily. The girl was like a blob of mercury impossible to pin down. He must remember to quote her answer to the other judges.

With sour resentment, Glenda Dowling watched him checking the highest box on his Florida card. It would counteract the bottom rating she had just given the girl. If Robin did as well with the other judges, she would run away with the interview competition.

The Hollywood columnist bore down harder with her next question.

"Miss New Jersey, suppose the President of the United States asked you to give yourself body and soul to an enemy agent. In order to obtain information vital to national security. What would you say?"

Jersey reflected soberly. This was another trap. If she said "Yes," obviously the judges would regard her as immoral and permissive.

"I'd tell him I'm no Mata Hari," she replied.

Glenda's eyes shifted to Robin. "And you, Miss Florida?"

Robin's candid gaze met hers, and Glenda knew that

the girl must be aware of the undeclared war between them. Would she fall flat on her face answering this one?

"Miss Dowling," Robin replied, "I'm a very patriotic American. So I would do anything my President requested."

A broad smile on his face, again Laurel gave Robin the top rating. Glenda Dowling glowered.

"My final question," the cosmetics king cut in, looking up from his pad. "Miss New Jersey, a lovely girl like you undoubtedly will be married soon. How many children would you want?"

Darlene pondered. She was smart enough to realize that Robin had massacred her in every round. Well, this time she'd outwit Florida with a response that catered to the Pageant image.

"But child-bearing often ruins a woman's figure!" she protested. "No Princess America should let down her public so foolishly, even *after* her big year."

"None for you, then. How many for Florida?"

"Oh, lots!" Robin's face lit up eagerly. "A dozen if we can!"

"No more than twelve?"

"Well, not thirteen, anyway. I'm superstitious."

Glenda saw, with indignant frustration, that Laurel had given Robin a perfect report card.

"And now *my* final question," she rasped. She had dreamed up a real hot potato. She didn't give a damn how Jersey answered it. But it would force Florida to cut her own throat.

"Miss New Jersey, if you personally had the power to select the next Princess America—if it all depended on your honesty—would you choose Miss Florida or yourself?"

Julius Laurel bent forward, intrigued by Dowling's question. It was a real Hobson's choice. If Jersey recommended herself, she'd appear too conceited. If she named Florida, she'd be boosting her opponent.

Darlene wrestled with her emotions unhappily. She felt like Jack Benny in that classic skit in which the holdup man pointed a gun at him and asked: "Your money or your life?"

Finally she answered, "If I have to be honest, I guess I'd pick myself."

Glenda chortled to herself. If Florida chose herself, it would be a draw. If she selected Jersey, Laurel would have to admit she was insincere.

"And now, Miss Florida, your choice?"

Robin answered unhesitatingly.

"Miss Dowling, if such a decision were actually put up to me—my honest answer is that I'd go to you for advice."

Glenda's eyes frosted over like January windows. "Why would you come to me? You think I have some particular iron in the fire?"

"Not at all. You'd be completely fair, of course. All I meant is that you're much more experienced than I am in judging—don't they call it star quality?"

After the girls had been processed by the judges, there was a brief break for john-visiting in the hotel's lower arcade. Robin lingered behind. When she was certain they were all out of sight, she slipped into a phone booth.

She sat down on the supporting arm, opened her summer purse, and took out her precious green box. It was her half of the walkie-talkie she shared with Paul. She raised the antenna, flipped the red lever twice, and held in her breath.

There was no signal.

Where are you, Paul? Why don't you answer, darling? I'm scared . . . scared.

She tried again. Her heart almost burst when a clear buzz answered. She quickly pressed the *Send* button and spoke into the tiny gadget. "Robin calling Batman. . . . Over."

"Robin, sweetheart." It was Paul. His voice was a tense whisper, barely audible. "Your father is transferring me to Okinawa. I'm in his suite right now. He's on the phone, ordering a staff car to take me to the airport. Keep thinking how much I love you. And win the contest! I'll . . ."

Silence.

Confused, bewildered, Robin returned the green box to her purse. Why was her father sending her husband half a world away?

It was the only question of the morning she was unable to answer.

24 · THE PRELIMINARIES

THE three dressing rooms backstage at the Armory were alive with young laughter, expectations and the scent of hair spray. It was a time for crossed fingers.

Here, this evening and the next two, a third of the contestants would parade on the catwalk in evening gowns and another third in bathing suits. They would leave the stage proper to the final third, who would present their talent skits.

At the conclusion of all three preliminary evenings, by this rotation procedure, each girl would have participated in all three categories.

In dressing room C, a powder dust bowl, the sixteen girls in Psi Group sat facing their individual mirrors. Their chaperones were diligently advising them to add or subtract rouge and lipstick.

The majority of the girls, finally cosmeticized to their satisfaction, got up and left, to mingle with other contestants backstage. But four of the group remained in the room, staring at their reflections with secret thoughts.

Hopes. Fears. Fantasies.

Miss Alaska: *I've had crazy luck so far, but it's bound to be overdrawn soon. But what if, by some wild fluke, my streak continues? Just suppose—just suppose I came in first or second. With all that money, I could find a surgeon somewhere who could fix my scar.*

Miss Montana: *Mother and Dad phoned they'd come see me Saturday night. I wonder if they'll come together. They haven't seen each other for five years, ever since the separation. I'd rather they make up than win.*

Miss Hawaii: *With all this* pilikia *they're making about keeping a black girl out of the contest, maybe they'll compromise by letting a Hawaiian take the crown. Fat chance! When the judges stack me up against Florida, California and Jersey, they'll rate me*—pilau!

Miss New Jersey: *Tonight I've got a hand that will win the pot. I'll steal the show. By acclamation!*

Miss Montana gave herself a last look, stood up. "I wish I knew more about how the judges rate us," she said to her chaperone.

"From what I understand, dear, they vote by secret ballot. Two CPAs serve as tellers. Each judge has the option of awarding from one to ten points to each girl in each category. The ballots go to the chief auditor for tabulation after Friday night's preliminary. The three girls who score the highest in Alpha and Pi groups, and the four in your group, all get into the semifinals."

Despite the muffling, thick red curtain which was lowered over the stage, they could hear the mounting hum as the audience began to dribble in. Mildred Waxman stood up and joined the others backstage, partly to ease the tension churning her insides. Mr. Megan had told them there would be two thousand people out there tonight, eight thousand on Saturday night. She had never performed before an audience so large. She wanted to double up.

She was in costume already for her Gold Rush number, the ruffle-petticoated garb of a Yukon dance-hall girl. It was complete to fishnet stockings and satin pumps with rhinestone buckles. And into her short, dark hair she had pinned a gleaming bow topped by a tiny cluster of egrets. Even the cock-feather boa wrapped about her throat, covering the Hide-a-Mark application, was carefully in character.

A peephole punctured the curtain, allowing a monocular view of the audience. Some of the girls lined up to squint through it and study the house, searching for relatives and well-wishers they expected to find there. Presently, noticing the position vacated, Mildred stepped up.

She was surprised to see that the Armory had been completely reconverted since she had attended the orientation lunch. Gone were the rows of tables; gone every earlier decorative detail except one. Up above the balcony level, the fifty state banners still furled overhead. But beneath them a long runway now stabbed out from the center of the stage like an accusing finger.

To either side of the runway, tiers and tiers of collapsible seats flanked out. The result was a roomy auditorium. Down front, directly under the lip of the stage, was the section reserved for the judges, sponsors and their wives and other Pageant VIPs. This early, only four of the seats of judgment were occupied.

There would be nobody out there from Alaska. All this distance, who could come? Not even her folks, back home minding the store. And why would anybody want to make the long trek? Not to root for a fourth-place stand-in!

Despite those hundreds of people out there and all the hubbub of backstage activity around her, Mildred had never felt so alone in all her life. She would even have welcomed gruff Jasper Bear Claw.

And then, like the sudden appearance of a rainbow, she spotted him. Dave. He was sitting in the front row of the right balcony, scanning a program. Was he searching for her name? Her heart thumped in her chest. He had played hooky from his union meeting and come here. For her! Just for a moment, Mildred felt able to lick a dozen times her weight in Alaskan huskies.

Roger Megan arrived backstage creating a stir. He passed among the girls, exhibiting well-tailored shoulders and a breezy smile.

"You're cute as a kitten tonight," he assured Miss New Mexico, who was jittery and clutching her sheet music as if it were a life raft.

"That shade of pink will register out front like a million dollars." This with a paternal pat on Miss Arkansas' shoulder. "You'll look like a rose garden."

And for Mildred herself: "If we could backlight you with the Aurora Borealis, honey, you couldn't look greater."

Privately, Mildred doubted that Megan actually knew one contestant from another. But he sounded so sincere that every girl he spoke to wanted to believe that he had singled her out for special attention.

Sue Rossiter appeared in a gown of white chiffon which seemed to float about her. She was immediately surrounded by a gaggle of girls.

"Miss Rossiter, I simply couldn't cut my monologue to less than three minutes. Will I be disqualified if it runs overtime tonight?"

"The music for my routine, Miss Rossiter. The orchestra conductor lost his copy."

Miss Maine was limping like the loser in a lobster fight. "My shoe, my shoe!" she wailed. "The left heel fell off."

With a competence gained from her years with the Pageant, Sue calmed the fretful girls, providing an eleventh-hour remedy to solve each crisis. She broke out of the huddle to where a bathing-suited Miss Illinois stood nervously fingering a silver crucifix suspended from a thin chain around her neck.

"Sandy, dear, I'm sorry," Sue said gently, "but you can't wear a religious medal out on the runway. It might prejudice the judges."

The girl protested unhappily. "But I always wear it for good luck."

"I want you to have all the luck there is, too, dear. Here, I'll keep it for you until the swimsuit parade is over."

Overhearing the conversation, Roger Megan made a comment to a nearby stagehand. "I watched that Illinois kid rehearse. Her talent skit is so hammy she couldn't win if she stuffed her pussy with four-leaf clovers."

Out front, musical instruments began to limber up. A hush fell over the packed auditorium as the Pageant Overture began. The houselights dimmed. The footlights came up. And Rodger Megan was parting the closed curtains, bursting into view with that familiar, intimate grin. The thin layer of panchromatic makeup he wore on his face looked like a natural, healthy suntan.

Applause surged to meet him like a strong tide running. After a few slight bows, Megan raised his hand. He was King Canute commanding the sea to subside. The Pageant's golden boy.

"Here we are again, friends. For the thirteenth time—golly, can it really be that many?—we're about to start picking *the* Princess from among fifty, nifty eligibles. Right here tonight. Your applause is not supposed to influence the votes of the judges, you know. But it certainly can encourage the girl you may be rooting for to do just a wee bit better than her best. So, when she comes on—let her hear it!"

He crossed the stage with that cocky swagger step they expected of him, grasped the metal stalk of the microphone.

"Each one of our young lovelies is hoping to score a passel of points tonight. Fifty beautiful optimists."

He worked back to center stage before delivering his opening sally.

"You've all heard the definition of an optimist? He's a fellow who figures he can apply to his bank for a home-improvement loan to have his wife murdered."

The stale joke drew only a few giggles from the darkened house. Unperturbed, Megan continued. "So you know I swiped that gag from Bob Hope? Well, I'm a sort of Robin Hood. I steal jokes only from Jack Benny, Alan King, Red Skelton—you know, the rich comedians."

The ad lib won loud guffaws. This was the way he

wanted to play them. Easy, loose, no socko yaks. Most of that pretty flock of amateur turkeys fluttering around backstage were going to bomb. But if they put on too dismal a performance, if people grew restless, he could always juice up the pace and carry the load himself. If necessary, once he shook off the rust of two months' unemployment, he could even make their stomachs hurt.

"I guarantee one thing. And that's the top quality of the fine talents we'll be enjoying here tonight. Because each of our contestants is bright and gifted."

He knew his promises were like pie crusts, made to be broken.

"I know they say brains are what you look for in a girl after you've looked at everything else. But tonight don't sell them short. You're in for a treat. I've been watching our little stars rehearse. I tell you, I was bowled over. They're great in all categories. So why keep you waiting longer? Here they are! The girls who keep America beautiful!"

Alpha Group, competing in evening gowns, appeared first. Each girl was ushered into the limelight by her state's signature tune which accompanied her along the runway. Miss Michigan, confident enough of her seraphic face to be wearing her red hair in a Maggie-and-Jiggs topknot, and dressed in moiré taffeta, gave the judges a beguiling smile. Texas, in a hammered white satin gown, looked like a young bride approaching the altar.

As each girl returned to the stage she halted in front of a blue-chalk guideline on the floor, so that when all seventeen were aligned they formed a chain stretching between the two proscenium arches. The applause which had greeted each individual girl now heightened to pay tribute to the entire radiant line.

One after another, as Megan announced state names like a station master—"Georgia! Delaware! Mississippi! Nevada!"—each girl advanced toward the footlights. She turned to show her left profile; pivoted to display her back; yet again to flash her right profile; then completed the full revolution by facing forward and stepping back into her original place.

The ballots for this phase of the judging had a column of boxes in which to rate specific charms with points from one to ten. Personality. Grooming. Poise. Grace of movement. Coiffeur. Symmetry of figure. Pencils scratched industriously.

As the two tellers gathered the ballots, music escorted the contestants into the wings. Remaining on stage, Megan led the applause. He knew precisely how long to milk it, just when to cut it off.

"And now, folks, the part of our show that most people think of first when you mention Surf City. Our bathing beauties! Mother, may I go out to swim? Yes, my darling daughter. But *only* if you look like a Pageant princess out there on the sand, honey!"

The orchestra began to frolic through "By the Sea." From the wings filed the evening's second squad. The seventeen contestants in Pi Group, to engage in the swimsuit competition.

Flashbulbs in the hands of shutterbugs exploding around them, the girls made their leisurely, cadence-timed trips up and down the runway. Even though the Pageant's standards of propriety ruled out bikinis, the shapely anatomy which was exposed looked good enough to pinch.

Reassembled onstage, the girls began a simple seaside ballet. Its purpose was for the contestants to be judged for grace in motion. Medicine balls were tossed about. Swimmers pretended to emerge from the waves and towel themselves with colorful terrycloths. But the number lacked style. Most of the girls performed as routinely as trained seals. Miss Missouri kept dropping the ball and looking like a sad-eyed Labrador retriever each time she picked it up.

The orchestra reprised with "By the Sea" as the bathing beauties trooped off. Once again, Megan let his invaluable inner scale weigh the applause. Once again, the eight little gods in the front seats made their evaluations. Figures were appraised, flaws discounted, ballots scored and collected.

"Next," Megan announced, "that feast of talent I promised you earlier. The girls in Psi Group. Some of these kids can project every emotion from delight to dementia. Item One on tonight's bill of fare is . . . Miss Iowa. Otherwise known as Maryjean Logan. If you've never heard an angel play the harp, here's your chance. So listen good!"

The curtains spliced apart and a pale but game Miss Iowa moved toward the massive golden instrument revealed in a puddle of spotlight. The band supplied a few bars of "That's Where the Tall Corn Grows" to get her to center stage. The audience gave her a warm welcome, ready and willing to be pleased.

"Ladies and gentlemen . . . " Her voice wavered, but she kept it on the march. "I'd like to share with you two solos from the works of Oliver Messiaen. It's been said of

Messiaen's music that he eavesdropped on nature. In these fantasies I think you can really hear the birds calling. First, *'La Bouscarie.'* Then, *'Reveil des Oiseaux.'* "

Her face taut, Maryjean sat down on the ballroom chair alongside the harp, brought it against her shoulder and began to pluck the strings. There was a round of applause when she cascaded a series of rich notes one after another. The reaction from the audience gave her all the courage she needed. Her lips parted in a wide, secure smile. Then, fingers flying, she proved her complete mastery of the instrument by making it surrender the bird-call effects she had promised.

Roger Megan had not seen the girl rehearse, so he had been dreading that her music would be as lousy as her schoolgirl French. But the kid wasn't bad, not bad at all. She was a credit to some home-town teacher back there in the prairies.

The audience's appreciation was heartier when the young harpist, having worked her way out of a complex crescendo, stood up, made a little-girl curtsy, and exited into the wings.

Megan waited for the applause to taper off. Then he stepped back into the spotlight. The curtains meanwhile whispered shut, and a stage crew began wheeling the harp out of view.

"Next, you lucky people, Miss Hawaii is going to do a Polynesian courtship dance for you. It's really a Samoan number. But she brings it to you as performed in her own native Honolulu. And when you've seen it, you'll be yelling for Some Moah."

There were good-natured groans and a few cat calls. This was just the reaction he had sought. They loved him. They felt at home with him. He gestured toward stage left. "Mepala Yates! Miss Hawaii!"

For her act, Mepala had wrapped her chassis in a tapa-patterned *pareu* and let her blue-black hair flow free. Around her neck hung fresh leis flown in early that morning from the Islands. The orchestra brought her on with "Sweet Leilani," and then, as her hands began to ripple, slid into the gourd rhythm of her special music.

Mepala's body began to undulate in the lazy way of a basket cobra swaying to a fakir's flute. But as the beat quickened, so did her sinuous contortions. Two stroboscope lights had been brought in, one in each of the wings. Their revolving gelatines kaleidoscoped vivid colors over her slim figure as the ritual dance accelerated into higher speed.

Faster and faster raced the barbaric tempo. Mepala's writhing kept pace with it.

The leis began to revolve around her bare shoulders like hula hoops. Her hips were rotating wantonly, insinuating the very act of love. Her softly curved belly was vibrating with the offer she made to an invisible mate for whom she symbolically danced. Bang, bang, bang thrust her pelvis against the whirling rainbow of colored lights.

Out in the dark house, somebody whistled. It was a long, shrill, lusting slice of sound. The coarse salute of the drugstore cowboy. Other covetous wolf calls followed. The courtship ritual had found a responsive audience.

"Roger!" Just out of sight in the wings, Sue Rossiter stood shaking. "What's she *doing* out there? My God, it's coitus to music! In all the years of the Pageant we've never—"

"She's out!" Megan snapped. "*Out!* I'll clue in the auditor to disqualify her."

"But didn't you watch her rehearse? Couldn't you have caught this then?"

"There was nothing like this in the rehearsal. The dizzy little tart did a spun-sugar thing that was mostly old-fashioned shimmy. She only had recorded music then. The live band's gotten to her. It's hotted her up like Spanish fly."

"Stop her now. Stop her before we're raided."

Megan was already pressing a buzzer. At the signal a small bulb blinked in the orchestra pit, and the music stopped. The spinning lights clicked off, leaving only the overhead spot on. The abrupt cessation of sound and visual effects caught Mepala flat-footed, in mid-writhe.

She realized something was wrong but had enough showmanship instinct to sign off in the traditional Polynesian manner—arms extended forward, with both palms facing down, head lowering in a swift bow. Then she scampered for the lowering curtains, ducking between them just in time.

Male spectators were on their feet in every section of the auditorium, clapping boisterously and bellowing for an encore.

"After that she'd be lucky to make anything but Princess Minsky!" Roger muttered.

But the infectious smile was revved up to full horsepower as he strode quickly on stage, arms raised to quell the uproar.

"Well, say, they have a pretty strenuous way of getting engaged out there in the Pacific, don't they, folks? While

Miss Hawaii catches her breath, here's something in a different style. Miss Montana wants you to catch her impression of one of our greatest show-biz stars. Ready, Montana? We give you—Chevalier!"

Mildred watched Montana rise unsteadily to her feet. Poor kid! Any resemblance between this wobbly-kneed zombie and the debonair French octogenarian was invisible. The dapper dinner jacket, the jaunty straw hat, the cane, all added up to zero. They were wiped out by the girl's utter panic.

Megan pointed again toward the wings. "Here we have it, people. The pride of the boulevards. The great Maurice!"

Then, suspecting the girl had stage fright, Megan tried to stall. "You'll have to wait a few moments, folks. Miss Montana's still recovering from her nonstop flight to Surf City. The awful movie she saw on the plane made her deathly ill. No fooling, halfway through the picture the stewardess had to lower the oxygen masks."

The gag made them laugh, but it failed to win a reprieve for the frantic girl. She stared vacantly in the direction of Megan's voice, petrified. She tried to talk, but the muscles of her throat refused to work. With a sharp, painful moan, Montana pitched forward in a dead faint.

Sue Rossiter was in motion almost at once, reaching the girl's side and kneeling down in a pool of snowy chiffon to cradle Montana's head. Standing nearby, Mildred felt pity for her. From behind, a stagehand muttered to a companion.

"Tough break! Weeks of getting ready—all down the crapper."

Dr. Franz Lydecker popped up, a Kildare-on-the-spot.

"Another case of 'Pageant Panic,'" he said sympathetically in his slight German accent. "It happens at least once every year. If they'd only let me give the nervous Nellies a mild tranquilizer before the show . . ."

He directed the nearest hands to carry Montana to a backstage first-aid room, with Sue trailing along. And out in front Megan was keeping the show on the tracks.

"Oh-oh! The old maestro got his cue cards shuffled, friends. Le Grand Chevalier is on tomorrow night. Right now, it's Miss New Mexico's turn."

With the crowd still electrified by Mepala's dance, Miss New Mexico had three strikes against her. There was only a bare patter of applause after she struggled laboriously through a passage from a Disraeli speech, reciting her lines as if picking pearls from an oyster tray.

Meanwhile, wandering backstage, Mildred found Mepala sitting numbly in a chair against the brick rear wall. There were tears on her smooth cheeks.

Uncertain how she might be useful, yet wanting to help, Mildred reached for Mepala's hand and clasped it tightly. Mildred sensed that she wept for the brief moment of triumph which had been snatched from her grasp.

Mepala seemed unaware of anyone beside her. Then, fingers locking around Mildred's, she looked up.

"Thanks, *hoaloha*," she whispered gratefully. "That means 'friend.' "

"They thought your dance was too—"

"It got me uptight. The music. I forgot where I was. I just had to let go."

"You zapped the audience, anyway. Did you hear them cheering?"

"I heard," she said miserably. "They cheered me right out of competition. Well, that's the story of my life. I always get the sticky end of the lollipop."

"Don't let it throw you, Hawaii. I read in an article that Joan Blondell was rejected in the Miss Dallas preliminary of the Miss Universe contest. And I could give you a load of other examples. With your looks and figure you could make it big as a fashion model. That's how Arlene Dahl, Lauren Bacall and Grace Kelly started, and they all became movie stars."

"Thanks for the pep talk." Mepala's voice had a false tinkle. "Just remember to tell your grandchildren to catch me on the late late show."

On the stage, Megan was clowning desperately to make the audience forget Mepala's dance had ever happened. From his mental file of state gags he selected one with which to introduce Stacy DeGray.

"Next, Miss California! Do you know what's a clear day in California? It's when the smog lifts and you can see the fog."

The quip went over better than last year and he decided to dust off his other state jokes for Saturday. "Here's Stacy DeGray, to give us an exhibition of Extrasensory Perception!"

California stepped out in a swirl of pale net. She took the mike confidently. "Ladies and gentlemen, I think E.S.P. is a fascinating science," she said. "I'd like to try an experiment in rapport with you. Mr. Megan, just so everyone can see what's happening, could the overhead lights be turned on for a minute?"

Megan made a signal and lights fanned out over the orchestra.

"Now then!" Stacy addressed the audience. "Will each of you face the person beside you and whisper what you're thinking about? Anything at all, so long as you won't be embarrassed if I reveal it. Once the second person has the thought, will *both* of you concentrate on it? That way, two minds will be projecting each thought in my direction."

While Stacy stood smiling, men and women in the audience pondered and then whispered to their neighbors. The bright lights brought their moving lips clearly into focus for her.

"Ready?" she asked, when lips had ceased to stir. "The lady in the green dress. You were thinking, *My daughter is the spitting image of Miss Virginia.* Right?"

A gasp from the woman in green was all the confirmation needed.

"And you, sir, to the right of the aisle—didn't you think: *Got to get our firm on the list of Pageant sponsors next year . . . ?*"

"How the devil—" the man blurted, then grinned sheepishly.

One after another, for as many as the time limit allowed, Stacy exposed the thoughts "projected" by her startled guinea pigs. She met with no failures. Her experiment in E.S.P. had been a smash, her performance as smooth as Cornish cream. A sly grimace as she swept from the stage left the audience with an implication of we-know-this-is-only-a party-stunt-don't-we? The applause was explosive.

"Well!" commented Megan. "Our little lady's talent *does* make a believer out of a fellow! And now, a switch from parapsychology to nostalgia. Come back with me, friends, to the riproaring days of the Alaska Gold Rush!"

And then Mildred went rigid. Her entrance cue!

Paralysis froze her. To move an inch was impossible.

"Miss Alaska, folks! Here's Mildred Waxman, the Juno from Juneau—bringing us a medley of dance-hall tunes from those good old days when our forty-ninth state was young!"

"You're on," prodded Mepala. "Mildred—that's *you.*"

A vision of Miss Montana in her Chevalier tuxedo danced through her head. Only now Montana's face was her own face.

"Help me, God!" Mildred whispered. "I'm going to do it, too—faint."

Megan scowled uneasily as he glanced toward the wings, fearful of another awkward stage wait. The way this evening was going, only a sudden power blackout could prevent a complete disaster. He had to cover Alaska's delay somehow.

"This girl might have been that famous Lady Known as Lou in your grandfather's day," he winged it. "And *he* might have been the face on the barroom floor."

Mepala's hands pushed firmly from behind. "You're supposed to be *out* there!"

There was a wall rising in front of Mildred. A wall of blinding light. Behind it was a frightening darkness. In that darkness, blurred faces were arrayed in a pattern as formless as raindrops on a window. Faces . . . disembodied faces . . . staring faces.

Hundreds and hundreds of faces . . .

"And here she is, folks!" Megan called out. "Meet Miss Alaska!"

Not a line from any of her well-rehearsed songs stuck in Mildred's memory. Not a bar of the raucous music. Her mind was a complete blank. All she knew was that the strangers out there were waiting to see her flop. She would be walking into a valley of death.

And then she heard it. One pair of hands sounding like thunderclaps.

Dave!

As she turned toward that resounding solo percussion, it began to proliferate in other sections. To the left, to the right, straight ahead, and then as a bloc eruption from one part of the balcony. Applause swelled from a trickle to the roar of a Niagara.

Men were rising to their feet, most of them young. Through the barrier of glare she could make out several figures in a variety of hotel service uniforms—tight pants, brief jackets. In colors of red, purple, blue, green and maroon.

Wonder dawned in her as she realized what was happening. Dave had kidnapped the members of his local union and brought them here with him in a body. *The whole union.* Hundreds of them. God alone knew how he had managed it; maybe union members rallied to a brother's call for help the way donors answered an emergency appeal for blood. Their enthusiasm spread like a flash of fire in a canyon. The general audience was caught up in it and joined the applause.

The constituency in the balcony dragged out inflated balloons from concealment under their chairs. Released in unison, a barrage of the gay spheres, each with ALASKA printed on it in gold letters, floated down all over the hall. From their pockets the legion of bellhops produced still more balloons and began puffing like blowfish to inflate them.

"Jesus!" Megan whispered as the second wave of balloons descended. "It's the biggest blow job in the history of the Pageant!"

The tumult continued. And over the entire din, or at least so she imagined, Mildred could make out the steady clapping of one pair of hands. The hands which had triggered this inspiring demonstration.

She faced the area where she had sighted Dave Lebow earlier. She could not make him out now, because of a stinging mist in her eyes. But she shot a smile in his direction that paled the footlights' dazzle.

On her way to the piano, for an extra bit of business, she gave her rump a spicy bar-girl twist that set its lace ruffles flurrying. Her fingers hit the keyboard without so much as a warm-up flexing. The rowdy rhythm of "A Hot Time in the Old Town" pounded at the audience, as if from a souped-up jukebox. Fishnet-stockinged legs pumped pedals vigorously as the tune about-faced into "Goodbye, Dolly Gray" and turned another corner into "Just Break the News to Mother."

In the judges' box, glances met. Eyebrows lifted in approval. Pencils began to jab at score cards. But up on the stage, Miss Alaska was oblivious to the world.

Assaulting a piano which could just as well have been the nickelodeon in the original Last Chance Saloon, she was gloriously belting out a "Maple Leaf Rag" guaranteed to bring the saints marching in on the double.

Alaska was succeeded by several other girls in Psi Group, most of them bush leaguers. Some sang, one tap-danced, and a blonde with Jean Harlow hair played "La Paloma" on a marimba. They had about as much pizazz as rejects from a Ted Mack show. Megan consoled himself with the thought that there was only one more act on the bill. He was nearing the end of a hard day's night and couldn't wait to wash down its memory with a hooker of Scotch.

"And now, folks, Miss New Jersey for the final act. So here she is—Darlene Bryant! 'Daredevil Darlene,' they call her, because she can tiptoe on a high wire as easily as you and I can amble down the boardwalk."

Out of the wings emerged New Jersey, clad in a satin

black leotard. The diamond-studded headband in her laquered hair sparkled in the spotlight.

Her curtains slid back, bringing into view two elevated platforms supported by fiberglass stepladders twenty feet high. A cable of steel wire stretched between the two platforms for a distance of twenty-five feet. Waving gallantly at the audience, Jersey pirouetted and began to scale the right stepladder. She reached the top rung just as the stagehands below had rigged up the safety net.

She glanced down at the stage. A shadow of annoyance crossed her face.

"Mr. Megan," she called out loudly. "Would you please have them remove the net? I always do my act better without it. It distracts my attention and makes me feel nervous."

Megan looked up at her, shocked. The scheming little skunk. She knew damned well, from rehearsal dry runs, that the net was an absolute must and that he couldn't permit her to perform without it. He mobilized his thoughts swiftly.

"Darlene honey, nobody doubts your skill on your courage. But all the girls in the Pageant are covered by insurance. We signed an agreement to take every safety precaution possible."

But Jersey persisted with her pretense of naïveté.

"I'll be glad to sign a waiver releasing everyone—anything they want. I've done this stunt hundreds of times without a net."

Some of the spectators in the audience began to hiss and boo. Instead of a ringmaster, Megan felt like a neutral umpire getting Bronx cheers from Met fans angry at a close decision.

He hugged the mike nearer to his mouth. "Friends, nothing would thrill me more than to watch our girl do her act like a real circus trouper. But I know you'll understand that I personally can't take the responsibility to allow it." He threw them some bullshit. "Perhaps, if our miss gets into the finals, we can arrange a special exception for her."

Jersey's voice drifted down sweetly from her high perch.

"Thanks, Mr. Megan. I didn't mean to put you on the spot. I simply didn't realize . . . "

The hell she didn't, Megan fumed to himself. The brat had planned the whole bit as a grandstand play to impress the judges and the audience. And it had worked superbly. Craning his neck to watch her step out on the taut wire, the flexible balancing pole swaying in her hands, he wished she would freeze like Montana.

But she proceeded expertly, sure-footed as a cat burglar. Unshaken by the ominous roll of the drums. Undaunted by the glare from the spotlight. Unfazed by the gasps and screams from the audience. Halfway across the cable she paused, pretending to falter precariously, then righted herself triumphantly into a perfect vertical stance.

When she had spanned the entire treacherous gap and arrived safely at the opposite platform, the applause was like a twenty-one-gun salute. They gave her a standing ovation.

Miss New Jersey had stolen the show.

And looking up into the cat-that-swallowed-the-canary glint that lit her eyes, Megan fervently hoped that if she made the finals, they *would* eliminate the net.

So that she might fall on her ass and be picked up with a blotter.

25 · GENERAL GERVAIS

THE room was dark, lit only by the glowing tip of a half-smoked panatela. Deep in thought, General Clinton Gervais crouched on the edge of one of the suite's two single beds.

The silent promises he had made on the boardwalk last night, to a living daughter and to a ghost, still gripped him. *Robin is going to win that crown. SEARCH is going to nail it for her.*

But the thing had to be played smart. And safe.

He remembered something Waldo had passed on to him earlier in the day. He reached out and turned on the reading light by the night table. From its surface she picked up a thin booklet. The copy on its cover stated simply:

THIRTEENTH ANNUAL PRINCESS AMERICA PAGEANT
ROSTER OF OFFICIAL PERSONNEL
1970 Edition

The pamphlet was a handout supplied by Norman Prescott's publicity office. It had been prepared for members of the news media and public-relations flak. To experienced journalists, the printed names offered a Klondike of contracts for offbeat stories and interviews. A brief foreword "suggested" that all stories obtained from these sources be cleared by Prescott's office so that they could be checked for "accuracy" and "embarrassing errors."

Gervais turned the pages slowly, studying them carefully.

What Gervais found of special interest was the column listing the eight judges and their qualifications. They were the tribunal who would determine which girl would become the thirteenth Princess. They were the nerve centers he would have to squeeze in order to execute his plan.

Gervais stared at the list sourly. It lacked the one important factor he required. Although it contained the home address and telephone number of everyone named, it did not furnish their Social Security numbers.

Of course, there was no earthly reason why those digits should have been added next to the names in the Pageant roster any more than the numerals on their license plates. But their absence represented an Achilles' heel in his plan.

These missing numbers were what SEARCH, located in a secret, multimillion-dollar, eighty-two-acre complex, fed upon. Unless SEARCH was programmed with these vital numbers, its mammoth belly full of gears, circuits, and 13,000 miles of electronic wiring would not spew out the classified information he needed.

There was only one way Gervais could obtain these numbers. With resolute decision, he reached for the telephone on the night stand. It was a model on which direct dialing was possible, bypassing the motel switchboard.

His index finger spun a series. The number was unlisted, known to very few. But an emergency night staff operated the Social Security office at late hours.

"Yes?" The voice came clipped, almost hostile, from the other end.

Gervais spoke a code word. "Ferret."

"One moment. Hold."

The delay was anticipated. He knew they would have to check out Ferret against a list of accredited personnel in their code book.

"Okay, Ferret," a voice presently came through. "State name, rank and serial number."

"Gervais, Clinton, Brigadier General, U.S.A. 08937429."

"What can we do for you, General?"

The names of the eight judges were on the tip of his tongue. He had but to reel them off and eight sets of numbers would promptly be relayed back to him. Eight sequences which then could be tossed like bones to the greedy beast that was SEARCH.

Equipped with them, the Orwellian mechanical monster would click out its findings on each judge at fantastic speed. Political background. Marital status. Travel habits. A full medical history. Whether the subject had a police record, or had ever been involved in a dishonorable escapade in high school or college. Army record. Scandals involving a relative, business associate or friend . . .

But first he must have those Social Security numbers.

Gervais was on the verge of requesting them when a wave of apprehension gripped him. If Robin won—*when* Robin won—there would be a blaze of nationwide publicity. Suppose someone at the SS agency grew curious and ran a search-back? Their records would reveal that Clinton Gervais had asked about the eight Pageant judges. He would be vulnerable to suspicion of manipulation.

"General?" The distant voice was impatient.

"False alarm. Sorry," he said with a forced levity. "My aide just brought me the data I needed. It was misfiled. Thanks, anyway."

He hung up, distraught. He had been on the brink of disaster. He was always a careful planner, too cautious to make tactical errors. Fortunately he had aborted his misstep in time. But he was still nowhere in sight of his objective.

He sat for a moment, thinking desperately. If frontal assault was inadvisable, then, as the Army had long ago taught him, one maneuvered a sneak attack from the rear. But the ass end of a computer was difficult to locate. What now, Gervais?

All at once a name leaped at him. Art Waldo.

Gervais sat for a few moments pondering. Then he shot up from the bed's rim with the spring of a young man in fighting trim. He let the panatela die in the ashtray and headed purposefully for the door.

The long motel corridor was deserted. The rooms which lined it had been almost exclusively taken over by Surf City visitors. At this hour, with the first preliminary in full swing, there were few strangers about.

Art Waldo's room was at the end of the passageway, adjoining one which had been reserved for Major Spofford. By now, his co-pilot, Captain Paul Brioni—and the general's mouth quivered as if it had just tasted acid—was already over the Pacific.

He knocked sharply at Waldo's door. A voice said, "Come in."

Waldo was at his portable typewriter, hacking out a Robin puff to be wired back to Florida local papers.

"General!" Waldo said in surprise as he struggled erect, almost tipping over the chair in his elephantine clumsiness.

Gervais nodded curtly. He closed the door behind him. Without invitation, he crossed to the room's most comfortable chair.

"Anything wrong, sir?"

"Waldo, how would you like to be the man behind the winner on Saturday night? We can do it, Art. You and I can do it."

"I'd like to buy that dream, General. But it's the judges who pick the Princess."

"Some of them are going to vote for Robin anyway. That's not a father speaking, that's common sense. You've looked over her competition. Well?"

"Robin's one of the best, sir. Maybe *the* best. But there's always a dark horse—"

"So some votes we don't worry about. But we do need a clear majority. We need enough high scores so there's no doubt she shows her heels to the pack."

"Yes, General, of course," Waldo's jowls flapped. But—"

One reason he had come almost to hate General Gervais was the man's habit of rolling roughshod over anyone else's words. "So what I need from you are eight Social Security numbers."

"Social Security?"

"The numbers of the Pageant judges. There must be some way you can get hold of them."

Waldo stared at his visitor. "I'm not a pickpocket, General. I can't heist their wallets."

"Naturally not. But you will find a way."

He might as well, thought Waldo unhappily, have added, *"And that's an order."* No matter how casually the general might be attired—even dressed in slacks and polo shirt as he was now—Robin's father always seemed to him to be wearing his star and bucking for a second one. You might resent the hell out of that top-brass tone in which he spoke. Still, you had to fight yourself to keep from jumping to obey it.

"I'd have to know more about what you have in mind, sir, before I—"

"Do I have to spell it out? I have full access to the National Security Agency at Fort Meade, Maryland. NSA has just installed a new super-computer. They call it SEARCH—for Secret Evidence, Authentic Records and Confidential Histories. It's programmed with the profiles of millions of people in the country. Everyone who has a Social Security number. *Complete* profiles, Waldo. Everything pertinent."

"I still don't see what Social Security numbers—"

"The records are coded to them. SEARCH has to be activated by a number to come up with a dossier. There must be at least some dark secret in its guts that at least one of the judges would want kept private. And when we discover it, we squeeze . . . "

For one of the few times in his opportunistic life,

Waldo was genuinely shocked. "*Blackmail*, General?" He shook his head violently. "Count me out!"

The craggy face opposite him tightened.

"I don't like your choice of words, man," Gervais snapped.

"I didn't mean to offend you," Waldo retreated. "But what else can you call it?"

"You can call it my personal antiballistic system," Gervais snarled. "Or tactical manipulation, to get your guns into firing range. You can call it fuck-a-rabbit. I don't give a damn what you call it. But don't accuse me of anything illegal."

Why the hell did Gervais always have to speak like a military communique?

"No, sir, of course not," Waldo said. "But—"

"The point is you may become a six-time loser in this beauty business. You don't want that to happen, do you? So you'll get me those numbers."

"I don't know how I can do that, General. Wouldn't it be easier for *you?*"

Gervais came up out of his chair the way a switchblade flicks open. He strode a few steps to Waldo's side, standing straight as if his spine were made of metal. He caught Waldo's arm and gave it a judo twist. The general's eyes, abnormally bright, seemed to bulge. Anger corded the tendons of his throat.

The bastard's a psychotic, Waldo thought in panic. *A real Section Eight psycho. Oh, Jesus. Who was it who said, "Power does not merely corrupt; it invites paranoia?"*

"Listen, Waldo," the general said fiercely. "Robin's going to win this crown, you understand that? Not just because she's my daughter, damn you. Because I owe it to her mother. To make up for killing her."

"K-killing?" Waldo squeaked. "But I always thought—they told me—I mean, didn't Mrs. Gervais die in some terrible accident?"

"I know what they told you. They told you she committed suicide."

"Yes, sir. I didn't want to upset you, but—"

"She slashed her wrists one night and sat in her bathtub until . . . That's in the coroner's report. But I might as well have held the razor."

"You? I—I don't understand."

"I drove her to it. I made her do it. I made her want to die."

It was odd how whenever he remembered Celeste the

first thing that came back to him was an awareness of her perfume.

The scent of her first, and then the ghost. The wide eyes, gray as autumn smoke. The slim, fragile figure hurrying to greet him, arms uplifted, glowing face tilted for his kiss.

"I know what you've been up to, you slut! I know what you've done!"

"Clinton—darling—what are you saying?"

"You think an officer in the Intelligence can be made a fool of behind his back? I can prove what you've been up to while I was away."

"Prove? Clinton, I don't understand."

"You've been screwing—oh, Christ knows who he is. Or who they are. But you've had them in my bed. You've taken them into you. Whore!"

"Never. Darling, never once. I don't know why you think these things, but—"

"I'll tell you why. Even those weekends before we were married, when you'd come up to the Point to hops—even back then, one lover wasn't enough for you. I used to half die inside, watching them dancing with their arms around you. And you laughing up at them as if to say they could—could take you in any dark corner on the parade ground."

"Clinton! I love you!"

"I didn't dare trust you, not even after Robin was born. So when they gave me this assignment to Intelligence and I had to be away so much—I set a little trap."

"Clinton, whatever this is—we can work it out. It's some mistake. But you're shouting. Please keep your voice down, dear. Thank heaven Robin's off visiting Charlotte. But Anna's right here in the kitchen. We don't want the maid to hear these things you're saying. Please!"

"Let her hear! I don't care if the whole world hears! It was so simple, the way I rigged it. The vaginal jelly you use with your diaphragm. Every time I had to run a mission, I marked a tiny notch on the tube. When I came home, I only had to check your medicine cabinet to find out if you'd used any."

"You must know, then, that I didn't. Not ever."

"Three months back, when I came home unexpectedly, I saw you had. The tube was rolled up well past my mark. I should have faced you with it then. But you seemed so happy to have me home. You were so warm and eager under me, that night. I thought I had to be wrong."

"And you were, Clinton. You were very wrong if you thought—"

"So tonight I checked again. The same filthy story. Rolled up past where it should be so far that there isn't any doubt. Bitch! You'll never cuckold me again!"

"No, Clinton, no! Oh, God, I want to die. I never—I swear to you—"

"Swear away! I know what I know! Everything but their goddamn names!"

The roar of his own voice, the sob in hers, echoed and re-echoed. Past or present, Gervais could not say. Until he peered into Art Waldo's moon face, he could not tell whether they were only echoes—or whether he had really recreated the shocking scene aloud.

Waldo's whitened face gave him his answer. The mouth was round, a perfect "O."

"General, why are you telling me this?"

"I had to. So you'd see why Robin must win the contest, whatever it takes."

"The accident—I mean, the suicide?"

"We found her in her bathtub next morning. I'd come back to pack my bags. I had spent the night at the Officers' Club. As I walked in, Anna was screaming."

"Anna? Oh, yes. The maid."

"On that particular post, our only live-in servant. And you know what she told me, Waldo? She was hysterical, of course, or she'd not have dared admit it. But *she* was the one who'd used up that damned jelly!"

"How could that be?"

"When I was off on duty, Celeste sometimes took Robin and visited a few days with her mother. And Anna had a boy friend, this tech sergeant from the barracks. When she was alone, with a free run of the house, she'd take him on and help herself to my wife's . . . "

For once, the voice of command faltered. Gervais seemed unable to continue. He released his hold on Waldo's arm.

Observing him, Waldo felt the first faint stirring of pity for the man. Fiends were at work on him. And it was easy to understand why.

"I see now why Robin's winning is so important to you, sir. But General, she has an excellent chance of taking the crown on her own."

"Yes, I think she can win. But I've got to make sure, man. If SEARCH digs up a skeleton in the closet for even one of those judges—that's insurance. We need only one weak link."

Waldo's eyes brightened. *Insurance!* He snapped his fingers.

"I think that does it for us, General."

"What are you smiling about?"

"What you said about insurance just reminded me. While I was in Prescott's office yesterday, turning in some stories on Robin's luncheon, he was dictating to his secretary."

"What about it? What has that to do with Robin?"

"Nothing directly. It was a news release. A story on the insurance policies the Pageant has taken out on everyone connected with Princess America. They're all insured. Everyone listed in their roster. And whoever wins on Saturday will be covered for her year as Princess by a million-dollar policy. That's the peg for the story. This is the biggest policy ever taken out to cover a beauty queen."

"Robin's already insured. Since she was a baby. Why should I give a shit about their policies?"

"But you see, General, the judges have also been insured. They're covered against being sued for slander, or charged with unfair discrimination, or anything else that may arise out of their official functions."

Slowly, the general's eyes took on their usual knife-edge sharpness. "And?"

"I was in the Army with a guy who used to be a branch manager for Globe Insurance and Bonding, the outfit the Pageant gives their business to. He owes me a favor. If he's still there, I think he will get it for me."

"Get what?"

"The Social Security data you're after. It'll have to appear on the individual policies. I can get you every number you want, right up to Mr. Fleming's."

"Mr. Waldo," said the general earnestly, "I won't forget you for this. If we were together in combat, I'd award you a battlefield commission."

"Yes, sir. Thank you. Well, I'd better get in touch with Curt right away. If you'll excuse me?"

"Go on along. I'll just sit here a while longer, if I may. I'm . . . very tired."

"Of course, General. As long as you like. Just lock the door when you leave."

On his way out, it occurred to Waldo that General Clinton Gervais just had inducted him. Not, God be thanked, back into the Army. But into the ranks of the world's second oldest profession—spying.

26 · STEVE DORN

THE unshaded glare from a dangling bulb gave him all the light he needed to work by. Sleeves rolled up, denim shirt plastered to his spine in a dark sweat circle, Steve Dorn twisted a lag screw with the precision of a jeweler.

Tuning the *Nipper*'s balky old engine was an exercise in frustration. Jackknifed above the rear cylinders, he thought longingly of all those shiny late models on display at each spring's Motor Boat Show. His trek to the New York Coliseum for the exhibit was a high spot each year. But, short of winning that fifty-to-one shot in the chauffeurs' pool, he knew his cop's take-home pay could never afford a new boat.

So on free evenings like tonight, when Nancy attended classes in ceramic sculpture, he came here to the old police garage, hung up his uniform and gun belt on a wall peg and exchanged them for an old shirt and stained chinos.

The noise which alerted him was so slight it might have gone unnoticed by ears less trained to detect faint sounds. He instinctively ducked behind the engine for cover, peering across the cavern of the basement into shadows muffling the entrance stairs.

The intruder had padded down them silently. Now he was huddled against a grimy police emergency ambulance that stood mounted on blocks awaiting an overhaul job. Dorn was about to beeline it for his gun on the wall when the figure emerged from the darkness.

"Trick or treat, Stevie boy?"

Dorn groaned, his heart sinking. He recognized that teasing voice, all hot pants and ovaries.

"Utah! What the hell are you doing here?"

Lori stepped forward into the fan of light. She was wearing a man's pea jacket, turtle-neck sweater and ass-tight trousers. A black cap with a visor covered her hair.

"I'm the Pageant's resident call girl. I thought I'd pay you a house call." She removed the cap, threw it aside. "I know I don't turn you on in this Apache outfit. I borrowed it from Colorado so I could come here without being spotted. Flattered?"

"You little fool! If they find us here together, they'll slap the book at me and toss you in the Great Salt Lake. We'll be two lepers looking for a colony."

"Aren't you glad to see me, Steve?" The lips pouted. The eyes mocked. Dorn observed fleetingly that her generous bosom seemed surprisingly flat-chested.

"Hell, no. I could get busted. You could be kicked out of the Pageant on your can."

"So you've noticed my can? That's a move in the right direction. But there are other points of interest, Steve. Want to explore them? Let's play Columbus!"

"Look, Utah, make sense. It's real late. I'm about to shut up shop and get home to my wife. Whatever you came for—"

"I got bored studying my monologue from Shakespeare, so I came here to see how you look out of uniform."

Dorn took a short step under the bulb so that she could see his spattered chinos.

"Okay, Utah. Take a good look. These pants came off the rack at Brooks Brothers. Grease spots courtesy Hart, Schaffner and Marx. Now will you beat it?"

Lori moved closer, tossing her silky hair. "Not until we go some place where I can see you really out of uniform. If you know what I mean."

"I know what you mean, you little minx, and I'm not buying," he said harshly. Then, observing the predatory glint in her eyes, he shifted to the soft sell. His voice lowered. "After all, Utah, this is hardly the time or the place."

"It's always the time for some things, Steve. Remember what Brigham Young said to his wagon train of the Faithful, when he first sighted the Salt Lake basin? 'This is the place,' he said to them. Don't you want me, sweet Steve?"

The trouble was, it wouldn't be too hard for a guy to let himself want her. Sure, he was married. But he wasn't castrated.

But the risk, if he bounced her. He could be wrecking his career with the Department. He could even wind up in a jail cell, if she was young enough to be Sing Sing snatch. And there was Nancy . . .

"Why are you holding back, honey? Because you think I'm just some crazy kid? A virgin, even? Don't worry. I've been around the track a few times."

Lori edged toward him, swinging her hips. Dorn backed

away. But after two steps he found himself flush against Nipper's varnished hull and could retreat no farther.

"I feel overdressed," she said and began to unbutton the jacket.

"Now look here, Utah. This has gone far enough. Just you be a good kid and—"

The jacket slid off her like the skin from a banana, followed by her sweater. Now Dorn saw why she had looked flat chested. Under the sweater she was wearing a stocking tightly wrapped around her bosom.

"Now I'll show you how I can prove that the name of my home town is Bountiful, Utah."

Then, with a hungry little laugh, she unpopped a safety pin and let the restraining hose fall to the floor. She moved swiftly toward him like a carnivorous jungle creature, circled his waist with her arms. Her fingers began probing under his belt.

"Utah! Are you out of your bird?" He tried to push her away but it was useless. Her topless chest intercepted the command from his brain to his hands.

"Steve, darling, angel, sweetheart. Don't you know that the best part about sex is the loving before the loving. Let me work on you."

She thrust herself hard against him, exerting pressures that sensitized every erogenous zone of his body. Then she glued her lips to his mouth. *Christ,* he thought, *I'm getting a hard on! In spite of everything!*

He heard her giggle. The bitch was laughing at him. She knew she was getting through to him and that in moments he'd be on the ropes, wanting her as fiercely as she wanted him. Now he understood why men committed rape.

"All night, tiger. All night long. Give it to me!"

Dorn cursed inwardly at the rolling tide of desire that gripped him. Then he remembered. The holding pattern he relied on to prolong his bedtime bouts with Nancy. It consisted of mentally counting off the thirty-seven presidents. He began to concentrate. *Washington, Adams, Jefferson, Madison, Monroe, Adams, Jackson* . . . There was a shaky moment when he reached Fillmore, but he managed to hurdle it. He was almost up to Nixon before he could find himself complete master of body and soul again.

Not a man to handle women violently, now he used muscle. He forced the clinging girl away from him so roughly that she fell back toward the crude basement wall, stumbled, and went down on one knee. He knew he could never hit her. Her beauty was a magic shield.

"Listen to me, pussycat," he said. "The party's over. I'm a married man and a cop. Go play in somebody else's sandbox."

He picked up her jacket and shirt, tossed them at her. "Now go back to your room and brush up on your Shakespeare."

Lori looked at him, her face crestfallen, aware that the spell had been broken. A thin blue vein bulged on her neck like a delicate pencil mark.

"Twat-teaser!" She spat it out softly, smiling, as though it were an endearment.

She stood up slowly, the sweater and jacket in her left hand. It was this tactic gesture of defeat which threw him off guard. He turned around, went back to his boat, so that she could dress and clear out without the added shame of his gaze upon her. The beautiful Miss Utah had a problem in her head, a serious problem. It would be like gawking at a freak in a sideshow to watch her now, rejected.

That chivalrous impulse turned out to be his big mistake.

"Dorn!"

Steel in that single word. Purpose in that flat, cold voice. He veered around in response to it. And his jaw went lax in astonishment.

She was up against the rough masonry wall, back where he'd draped his gear on a peg. And in her unwavering right hand she held his police revolver. From the way she leveled it, from the thin smirk on those wet lips, there was no doubt in his mind that she was kookie enough to use it.

"Pussycat has claws," she said. It wasn't just another of her one-liners. It was a warning.

He tried to keep his voice steady. "Looks as if. But you won't shoot."

She released the safety catch. He could hear the click.

"Try me, lover. I had a Marine boy friend once. Great lay. He taught me how to hit tin cans in the air. So let's not waste valuable time. Strip for me, Stevie. First the shirt."

For a fragment of a moment longer, their eyes remained locked. What he read in hers was instant homicide. She wasn't kidding. She was going to have him. Or else.

His fingers traveled down the shirt buttons. He pulled out the denim tails and freed his arms from the sleeves with a shrug of rippling muscles. He cast the garment aside, not daring to look away from her for even a second. Their eyes always gave you first warning when they were ready to pull the trigger. You learned that fact early during the first week of police training.

"Listen, Utah—"

"Now the pants!"

There was nothing he could do about it, unless he chose to be the first cop in the annals of Surf City to get shot defending his honor. The faded chinos unzipped with a tiny metallic whisper, dropped down his legs to puddle at his ankles. When he stepped out of them, all that remained were his striped jockey shorts. And her glittering eyes were eating the bulge alive.

If he risked jumping her now ... But it would be hara-kari at this close range.

"Show me!" Where earlier had been her smile, he now saw teeth bared.

He hooked the waistband of his trunks, stretched it loose. And Adam stood without a fig leaf. He heard her gasp, a greedy sigh which became a moan of anticipation.

"My God, is all that hardware real?"

"You're looking at it. There's no way to pad it that I know."

"But I want it to stand up again, lover. When you go in, damn it, I want to feel it all the way up to my sinuses." She inched closer toward him. "Now, Romeo, play with my balcony."

Dorn followed orders. Although he could feel the cold nose of the gun jabbing his midriff, contact with her firm breasts recharged his battery.

She grabbed under his hips with her free hand, uttered a small, crowing laugh as she fondled him. "You don't want to use meat tenderizer on that, Stevie boy. I know a better way to make it soft."

His teeth parted in a disarming smile, like the flutter of a white flag. "All right, Annie Oakley. You play the organ beautifully. I surrender under protest."

"Where?" the demand exploded from her. "Where can we do it?"

He pretended to ponder this. In the past few moments a ploy had flashed through his mind. A gimmick not mentioned in the police instruction manual. But it would be tricky. He'd have to play her along as expertly as she'd just played with him.

"The housing situation's rough," he said. "Every joint is booked solid this week. I doubt there's an empty telephone booth in town."

She was breathing deeply. "Right now I'd trade the

crown for a mattress. Anyhow, I can't wait. On the floor?"

"We can do better than that." Dorn thumbed to his right. "That ambulance. It's fitted with a folding cot."

"Hey!" Her eyes lit up. "Just the spot for fun and games. Let's go."

She seemed convinced. But she was no fool. Wary, she still aimed the gun at him, watching every sector of his body in the dim light as he opened the vehicle's rear door, climbed up inside it. He could feel her eyes burning. So? Her looking didn't cost him a thing.

Dorn brushed past the pulmotor, oxygen tank, fire hose, acetylene torch and other emergency equipment lining the walls. Then he unhooked the collapsible cot from its recess in the partition behind the driver's seat, gave it a yank, and let it unfold into position for receiving a patient.

He turned around and extended his hand, eying her eagerly like an impatient bridegroom. In the moments while he had been fixing the cot, she had slipped out of the trousers that had defeminized her legs. They littered the floor a few steps away. She wasn't wearing anything now but the polished revolver. And that look of voracious want. Her palm felt hot as it grasped his so that he could pull her aboard.

Dorn stretched himself out on the pillowless cot, waiting for her to flop down beside him. Lori knelt down on her knees, semierect, examining the apparatus on the walls until she found what she was looking for. A long, slim flashlight.

With her free hand she slid forward the On button until it caught. Amazingly, its transistors still were juiced, and a spear of light flooded the scene. Then she forced the handle into the sagging nozzle of the coiled fire hose so that the flashlight hung like a lantern.

"I always like the lights on when I'm getting laid," she said huskily. "I love to see the expression on a man's face when he comes."

She unlimbered herself alongside him, straining against his torso so that she could feel his power and he could feel her breasts.

Dorn rolled her over tenderly, like a demolition expert handling a live bomb. He was still conscious of her dangerous trigger finger. Then, supporting his weight on one elbow, he swiftly reached up with his other hand and turned off the flashlight.

"Light and lust are deadly enemies," he said before she

could protest. "That's a line from Shakespeare's poem *The Rape of Lucrece*. Recognize it?"

Lori giggled in the darkness and squeezed his right buttock with her free hand. "I can't get over it. A cop who can quote the Old Bard."

"Utah . . . you've got me so worked up I could give you the screw of the century. But the gun. How the hell can I keep my mind on the job when I'm afraid you might shoot before I do?"

A sensuous sigh of victory escaped her lips. Dorn knew at once that his faked ardor, confirmed by the evidence of his night stick, had made her ego abandon all suspicion.

When she spoke, her voice was a mixture of gloat and concession.

"Okay, lover, it'll be farewell to arms. I knew you'd realize this is a fate far better than death." There was a pause, and in the faint light he saw her gun hand drop below the cot. Then a sliding sound as she skimmed the weapon across the floor.

She wiggled under him, a sheath searching for a sword. Both her hands were active now, kneading his buttocks. Supple, experienced fingers that volleyed quills of bliss up and down his spine.

He was tempted, God how he was tempted. He could always rationalize that it was a performance in the line of duty. But it was time now to go ahead with his original plan.

What a waste of body chemistry, he told himself sadly, as he steeled himself for his next move. He raised his right hand upward, fingered the wall until he encountered the object of his hunt. A pair of open handcuffs mounted on a hook. Then, grabbing her left wrist, he snapped one link around it. He had her shackled to the cot's headbar even before she could hear the double click.

Dorn fumbled around for the flashlight, expecting her to cut loose with a stream of profanity. But she was strangely quiet. When he finally found the flashlight and turned it on, he saw that her wide eyes were gaping at him in disbelief.

"What's the matter? Are you chicken? Don't you know what you're passing up?"

"Sure I know. Big-time trouble for both of us."

"But nobody'd even suspect. I can sneak back into my room through the terrace door without their ever finding I was gone. Oh, damn you. God damn you to hell!"

"Maybe He will. But not for a nympho who's sick in

her head." He retrieved his gun, hopped down to the garage floor and began to climb back into his uniform.

Her charm-school voice became a bullwhip. "Faggot!" she lashed at him. "Now I know why you copped out. You're a faggot without balls! You don't have a fuck in you!"

Steve grinned. "If it's any consolation to you, Utah, when I get home tonight I'm going to work it off on my wife. I'm going to wake her up and bang her like mad. But first, Miss Beauty Queen, we'll let you chill off that bountiful twat of yours for half an hour or so. Then I'm going to drive you back to your motel before they find you AWOL. And you'll be a good girl. There's a strait-jacket I can strap around you in that ambulance."

"Please, Steve. Please. I need it so bad. Do something to me. Anything. Or I'll be playing with myself all night. Steve . . . Steve . . . "

"Sorry, Utah, but I'm thinking of the driver's pool. You just might be in line for the crown this weekend, you dizzy little trollop. And I can't afford a two-thousand-dollar lay."

BOOK FIVE *Thursday*

27 · MISS UTAH

THURSDAY was the day for members of Lori's group to visit the Pageant's studio. Max Gerber—*the* Max Gerber, portraitist of the famous—was scheduled to take their official photographs. Lori's sitting had been set for eleven-thirty.

With his predictable punctuality, Steve Dorn drew up before the Imperial Hotel, where, dressed in a turquoise swimsuit, Lori stood waiting. Mrs. Burkenbuel was stationed beside her like a watchdog.

Lori had just spent a severe hour running the judges' gauntlet and was in little mood to accommodate the knot of teenagers who sought her signature in their autograph books. She had answered eight judges' questions indifferently, for once her wisecracks inhibited. The humiliating climax of last night's clandestine visit with Steve Dorn had broken her spirit.

Handsome in his police uniform, Dorn held open the door. His freshly shaved face was impassive, his eyes impersonal as he watched her and Mrs. Birkenbuel settle into the rear. Only a polite comment: "How'd it go?"

"Okay, I guess," Lori said listlessly. He was probably still thinking of the two-thousand-dollar prize in his lousy cops' pool.

In seconds he was at the wheel, spinning the car north.

Lori could feel the hot blood rush to her cheeks despite the cool ocean breeze kissing her face. With last night still branded in her memory, this present mission seemed meaningless. Steve's scornful rejection of her still burned like a live coal.

She felt cheapened, dirtied. And the worst of it was, she still wanted him. The steaming, almost scalding bath she had taken after he had helped her sneak back into her room had failed to dehydrate her pent-up passion. Afterward, with Barbara's Apache costume smuggled back to her closet, Lori had lain awake for hours. Counting "Lori's lambs" had failed her. Because Steve Dorn had blocked out the others.

Beside her, in the open convertible, Mrs. Birkenbuel kept gabbing enthusiastically about Lori's interview with the judges.

"I could tell that Dimitri Guitard and Adrian Koch were really impressed with you, dear. And so were most of the other judges."

"You really think I did okay? Some of their questions were lulus."

"I'm positive. I've been on the inside of enough Pageants to sense a winner. You've got the stuff, Lori. For first place."

"I hope you're right. I do want to be a credit to Utah." *Balls! I want that crown—for me! No man, not even Steve, would say no to Princess America!*

"You deserve it, Lori. Besides being a natural beauty, you're modest and sweet."

Modest and sweet! If Steve had overheard, he was laughing up to his armpits. She was as modest as a stripper, as sweet as Lucretia Borgia.

"Lori, dear," Mrs. Birkenbuel went on, "we'll have to park you at Gerber's. My bridge came loose at dinner last night. I'm borrowing Officer Dorn to run me over to my dentist. We'll be back to collect you in an hour. That's how long Gerber takes for a sitting."

She paused as Dorn eased the big car in front of an attractive brownstone. "You won't be unchaperoned, of course. Max qualifies as a member of the official Pageant family. Besides," she added, "he's old enough to be your father."

The studio was on the second floor of the brownstone. As Lori climbed the carpeted steps, Miss Vermont was coming down. She was followed by her chaperone, a short, plump Billikin. They nodded and exchanged insincere smiles. Moving aside to let them pass, Lori found her competitive urge rekindled enough to hope Vermont would trip down the stairs. Vermont, most likely, had similar thoughts about her.

"Miss Utah?" Gerber was waiting at the door.

"Present, Teach." She said it with charm, not impudence.

Gerber was of medium height and heavyset. His black hair was beginning to recede, leaving a shoreline of protuberant forehead to mark the ebb. Once, quite possibly, he had been mildly attractive. There was a spaniel sadness to his eyes. He looked like a man gnawed at by memories, private little foxes at work on private vines.

Gerber motioned to his left. "You'll find a dressing booth back there. And a rack of official Pageant gowns, all sizes. Pick one that fits you."

"I'm a quick-change artist," Lori said. "I won't keep you waiting."

Lori tried three gowns before finding one that fit her. It was a formal but flattering style, the accepted, demure uniform of a Pageant contender. It took her two minutes to slip out of her swimsuit and change into the satin dress. Then, reaching into her purse, she found her favorite pair of earrings. She slipped them on and was ready.

When she closed the door behind her, Gerber was in a corner of the long studio half hidden by a forest of tripods, lights and cameras. He was talking earnestly into a telephone, his back toward her.

While she waited, Lori surveyed the walls. They were decorated with framed portraits of the world-famous personalities who had sat before his lens. These pictures required no artful hanging, no trick lighting, no expensive frames to make them impressive. They spoke for themselves. They reminded her of the movie-star photographs she had seen in Dr. Lydecker's office.

Eleanor Roosevelt's difficult face had been caught sympathetically, the plainness many had called ugliness displaying a quiet nobility. And here was Cardinal Spellman, his face tranquil and saintly. And over here was Madam Chiang Kai-shek, regal, imperious, yet with a softness in her eyes that made her utterly feminine. And next to her, Churchill—already a sick man on that last American visit, as Max Gerber had caught him, indomitable.

Under a bank of high windows faced to catch north light stood a metal file cabinet, its top drawer protruding slightly. The upper part of a glossy print, showing only the head of a girl, stuck out and caught Lori's eye. Something familiar about the face prompted her to pull the photograph out. Bewilderment and shock stunned her as she examined it carefully.

It was Barbara Chrysler, all right. Modest Miss Colorado, who had visited Gerber's studio to sit for her official portrait just yesterday. As if the girl were repeating them in her ear, Lori could hear words from their first meeting: *"I used to wait until they were all asleep. Then I'd shower . . ."*

Times certainly had changed.

Here, without the slightest trace of self-consciousness in

her eyes, Colorado posed naked as a stag-party stripper. Her slim body was full face to the camera. Gerber's camera, without a doubt. The gentle delta where her thighs joined was shadowed with a triangle of curling down.

The setting was the interior of the same cramped cubicle Lori herself had just used. Dangling from one of the hooks she recognized the leopard-spotted swimsuit Colorado had put on before leaving for Gerber's studio. She pulled the drawer back a few more inches, rattled through the glossies lodged there. Examining them swiftly, she identified other members of Alpha Group. Florida, Maryland and Texas. All were in the nude.

"The creep!" she whispered to herself. "Why, that perverted—"

From behind she heard a breath, raggedly sucked in as if from an abyss. Still clutching Colorado's photograph, she whirled around.

"You get your high a stinking way, don't you, Mister?"

"I—I sometimes take unofficial art studies," he said lamely. "If a girl is willing to pose—"

Lori waved the picture under his nose.

"*This* girl never let you snap a skin shot of her. What's the gimmick? You've rigged the booth with some kind of hidden camera, right?"

Gerber nodded, his eyes almost shut, unable to meet hers.

"While their unsuspecting chaperones are sitting outside? While the girls themselves never dream you're a filthy peeping Tom? And you've gotten away with it because you're part of the holy Pageant family and everybody trusts you. Up until now!"

" 'Up until now?' What do you mean by that?" His voice trembled from fear.

"You don't for a minute think I'm going to let you get away with your sewer tricks? My God! No wonder you told me not to hurry. You took pictures of *me*, too, while I was bare ass in there!"

"Yes, I admit it." His lips twisted painfully.

"If there's any scabbier way for a middle-aged man to get his kicks—"

"You're shouting. Please don't shout. I haven't done anything, honest. I haven't hurt those girls. I never touched one of them, not one. I just couldn't help myself. They're all so young. So beautiful. And since my wife died—nothing, nothing . . . "

He stepped around her quickly, almost stumbling in his

haste. Before Lori could surmise his intention he was at the door and had shot home the bolt. Then he turned and faced her.

"I'll make you a bargain," he said. "If you'll promise not to tell—"

"Sorry, Buster. No deals. Now let me out of here."

"Listen, Utah. You want to be the thirteenth Princess, don't you?"

"That's obvious. And so is the dirty, perverted—"

"You can make a lot of trouble for me. We both know that. Ruin my professional reputation, after all these years. Even get me put in jail."

Lori laughed harshly. "That's your problem."

Gerber's eyes were filled with despair and terror. She could see cords working in the thick neck, and how a pulse in his temple was flickering like a distress signal. He moved toward the door, about to release the bolt, then paused.

"If you report me, Lori Macklin, you'll never have a ghost of a chance to win that shiny crown."

Lori snorted. "Why not?"

"The ugly publicity. A scandal always rubs off on a girl who's mixed up in it, no matter how clean she is. It's the old story. People always like to believe that where there's smoke there's fire."

"Your hidden candid camera is all the proof of my own innocence I'd need."

"There's something else to consider. You wouldn't have me helping you. You don't know it, but every year our judges get special instructions. They're told to award the girls secret points according to how well they photograph. We've estimated that our average Princess poses for commercial photographs more than twenty-four thousand times during her year's reign. So a winner who can't come out looking gorgeous in an ad is a definite liability. That's why the Eleventh Commandment of this whole Pageant show is: 'Thou shalt be photogenic.' "

Despite her contempt for the man, Lori had been listening with deep interest. Those secret points? How much weight *did* they carry in the final judging? What—as he seemed to be implying—could a cameraman do to improve a girl's chances?

"I know my business, Utah," Gerber went on, as though sensing her thoughts. "I could help you a lot. Light you flatteringly. Retouch the negative to eliminate some of the worry lines on your face. The way you'd come out, you'd have a big head start on Saturday."

"You'd do this for me? Just for my not blowing the whistle on you?"

Instead of replying, Gerber turned to the file cabinet and slid back one of the lower drawers. From it he scooped a handful of glossies and passed the top one over to her.

"All these girls made it to Surf City in past years. Beauties, each of them. But not one finished in the finals. Look at these pictures carefully and you'll discover why."

Lori studied the photo. Here was an extremely pretty blonde with a captivating smile. But her teeth, as captured by Gerber's merciless lens, seemed to jut out, as though they were buck.

Gerber passed her a second picture, a three-quarter profile of a comely girl with a graceful, swanlike neck.

"She looks terrific," said Lori. "But her left eye. It seems to have a slight cast."

"Correct," said Gerber. "This flaw was unnoticeable when you stood face to face with her. But my camera accented that particular defect. A Princess must be photogenic from all angles."

"Miss Oregon, three Pageants back," continued Gerber as he proffered another shot. "Her nose looked straight enough when you saw her. But on film? See for yourself."

Lori had been seeing. And thinking hard as she looked. *Thou shalt be photogenic.* It made sense. None of these other girls had won the crown.

"What about me?" she demanded. "You're the expert. What's wrong with me?"

"There wouldn't have to be anything wrong if . . ." Gerber hesitated, despising himself for having to ask mercy. "If . . ."

"If you get—what?"

She saw color beginning to rise in his face. It was a kind face, but ravaged now with anxiety. That broken line about a dead wife? He probably meant it. And he probably hadn't slept with a woman since the day he became a widower. He probably was so horny he had wet daydreams. Otherwise, why this sick underground hobby of his? Why those young bodies he must drool over through the long, lonely nights?

"I didn't mean . . . I wasn't trying to . . ." he stammered.

Scared, whimpering. Ready to burst into tears or panic or go down on his knees to her. Yet if the poor slob had fully realized it, he was the one in the catbird seat. She wanted that crown. She'd prefer it even if the consolation prize were life after death.

"Talk's cheap. How do I know you would deliver?"

"You'd always be able to make trouble for me later, wouldn't you? And I could help you. I really could. Look around you at the faces on these four walls, if you don't believe me. Just give me the chance to do my best and you'll get gold stars from every judge."

"Why only you? There must be other photographers who could replace you."

"There's only one Max Gerber." He said it simply, without vanity. Like a store clerk quoting the price from a catalogue.

"What could the great Gerber do for me that would be so unique?"

"First, I'd scrub that bright-orange lipstick off your mouth. It's murder in black and white. I'd put on blue-red. Then somehow I'd manage to relax you. Those tense lines around your mouth and at the corners of your eyes would ease up and disappear. I'd also have you kick off your shoes so you'd really be comfortable. And I'd yank off those rhinestone earrings so fast you'd holler. The razzle-dazzle reflected by them would fight the girl in the picture in any shot I took. Those are just a few of my professional tricks of the trade."

Lori thought for a moment, weighing his words. Then she made up her mind. She'd make a swap. Her pussy for his picture.

"What's that couch for?" she asked abruptly. "The one in the corner?"

His eyes widened. "I use it for naps. Between appointments. Sometimes I work so late—"

"Right now we're going to use it for something else, Max. Aren't we?"

"I don't know what you . . . I mean, I'm not trying to pressure you into—"

"You want it. You're desperate for it. I'll bet you haven't had it since coffee was a nickel. Well, Max, I hope your heart's in good condition, because I don't want to be arrested for manslaughter. I'm going to screw you to death. And then you'll take a picture of me that'll knock their eyeballs out. Right?"

The incredulous look on Gerber's face slowly changed to wondrous anticipation as Lori's beckoning eyes confirmed the trade. When she made her way through the thicket of equipment to the leather-cracked couch in the corner, he followed her hypnotically, like a lemming drawn to the sea.

She lay down, resting her head against the leatherette of the sloping couchhead, and pulled the white satin skirt back past her hips. Then she lifted her arms to him. How often had she made this same gesture, smiled this same invitation? *I'd need an adding machine to count the times,* she thought as Gerber flopped on top of her awkwardly. But this was different. This was to get her something she wanted, not for the pleasure of the moment itself. This was . . .

Am I really? Is that what I am? A whore?

The sound of his zipper was like the squeak of chalk on a blackboard. Then he was fumbling with candy-striped boxer shorts. Her thighs spread cooperatively as she felt his knees between her legs.

"We'll have to hurry," he whispered. "Mrs. Birkenbuel will be coming back soon."

"You locked the door, didn't you? Don't worry, live!"

He was trying. Jesus, how he was trying. The spirit was willing, but the flesh was weak. His penis was at half mast. He rubbed it back and forth against her crotch.

"I used to . . . " His voice was apologetic. "My wife and I—at least five times a week . . . "

Thou shalt be photogenic. Lori tried to spare him further humiliation. "You're just too tense, Max. Afraid we'll be caught. If you can't right now, is there any other way I can please you?"

"I like . . . I used to . . . You have such beautiful big breasts, Lori. Just like my wife."

"No problem. They're yours. And then we'll take that perfect photograph."

She arched to slip the gown's shoulder straps down her arms, with its built-in brassiere. Gerber stared tantalized at the splendid double feature.

"What are you waiting for, Max?" Lori said impatiently. "Don't you know that the bigger they are, the nicer they are?"

With a yearning moan, his face dipped into her cleavage. She felt the quick, starved lick of his tongue tip as it grazed her right nipple.

And then, hardly one second later, he stopped abruptly. "No," he said thickly. "No. I can't." It was almost a sob.

But his brief touch had already excited her. When you're dying of thirst, you'll drink from a mudhole.

"Do something to me, Max. *Anything."*

And then he was eating her, his tongue darting with the

swift shuttle movements of a waterbug on a pond's surface.

"Oh, my God! Oh, Max."

She found herself responding completely, to the flash and wet roughness of that probing tongue. She hadn't planned it this way. She had intended to lie quiet until he had satisfied himself, keeping her mind on what he could do for her with his camera skill once this was over. It would have been like paying a sales tax in advance.

But now—oh, Christ! Her lips began rising and falling, responding to him. Gerber raised his head to gulp in air. The moisture on his brow gleamed like varnish.

"Don't stop now! Please, Max, never stop. More, Steve, more!"

Max? Or Steve? Which name had she called him? It didn't matter, not now. Not while he was slowly lowering himself again between her thighs. Max Gerber was doing his real thing.

Her body throbbed down to her feet from the fury of his oral assault. And when she made it, it was like an Apollo rocket leaping into ignition. She screamed softly as the ball of fire inside her burned out like a falling star.

"I needed that, Lori," Gerber said. "You'll never be sorry. I'll take a picture of you—such a picture . . . "

"Who cares?" she moaned. "I read a book by some guy who said it takes seven minutes for a man to make a woman come. You owe me four more minutes, Max."

Mrs. Birkenbuel and Steve Dorn were patiently waiting at the curb when Lori finally appeared. Silent, impassive, Steve drove them back to the motel, where Lori was to change for the next event on her Pageant calendar.

"Max took such a long time with you, dear. He rarely runs over on a sitting."

"The gremlins were busy, Mrs. Birkenbuel. First he found he'd double-exposed the film. Then a fuse blew. He had to rearrange his lights."

"What did you think of him, Lori? Were you impressed?"

"It's hard to say," Lori said smoothly. "He seems like a very sad man. Somehow I feel sorry for him."

Mrs. Birkenbuel lurched against her as Dorn, passing a stalled trailer truck, zoomed the car with a hot-rod swerve and snaked ahead.

"Max Gerber had a very beautiful wife," she resumed when Dorn slowed to a normal pace. "He's never gotten over her death. She died of breast cancer."

They parted in the lobby and Lori hastened to her room. Easing out of her swimsuit, she stood before her mirror and studied the body with which she had bribed Max Gerber. The girl in the glass stared back.

Sick, Steve had called her. (But I want to win, Steve, and he could help me. So I gave him a box lunch.) *Sick.* (I didn't even like him, I certainly didn't want him. Yet at the end I was the one who was begging for it.) *Sick.* (Last night I was so hard up I tried to rape you. All within twelve hours!) *Sick, sick, sick ...*

She picked up a tissue and began to wipe off the red-blue grease on her lips. Then, with half an hour still to kill, she wandered back into the bedroom and picked up the dog-eared copy of *Hamlet.* Once holding the slim, morocco-bound volume, she couldn't imagine why she had bothered. She knew that damn Ophelia scene down to its final pitiful inflection. "Rosemary . . . that's for remembrance . . . " she began to quote.

She seated herself on the edge of the bed, the book opened flat on her lap, and idly turned the pages. She found herself staring down at an earlier episode in the drama. It was the scene between the gentle girl and her lover, the brooding Prince of Denmark, after Hamlet has come to realize that his real bag is avenging himself upon his incestuous uncle. One line rushed up at her: "Nymph, in thy orisons be all my sins remembered . . . "

Nymph.

The word stabbed her in the heart.

"Marge?" she whispered shakily. When they were children and she woke up in darkness and the shadows hunched along the ceiling seemed to menace her, it always had been Marge she cried for. "Help me, Marge!"

Somewhere in the motel corridor a maid was plying a vacuum cleaner. The whine of its motor sandpapered her nerves. A door slammed. From the far end of the terrace outside someone laughed. *Nymph.*

Lori's head slumped. The copy of *Hamlet* fell from her trembling fingers.

"Marge? What am I going to *do* about me?"

28 · ROGER MEGAN

THE last reserved spaces for rolling chairs along the Torchlight Parade's two-mile line of march had gone at scalper prices three days ago. There wasn't room in the bleachers for a shadow. Standees were jammed six ranks deep against the police barricades as though squeezed by hydraulic pressure.

Dead center of the route stood the reviewing grandstand, a huge double box rearing high above the scene like a military rampart. Its larger segment was occupied by the eight Pageant judges and official guests. The state's popular Governor and his young, second wife were being welcomed effusively by John Fleming. Three U.S. Senators sat lined up along the flag-draped railing.

Fleming's moist palms were the sole overt symptoms of how Thomas Worthington Walsh's threats had frazzled his nerves. The pulpy features kept serene. The milky eyes remained unvexed even though they spotted Walsh himself among the semicelebrities in the congested background, awaiting attention from the overworked ushers.

The smaller section of the box had been partitioned off as a bullpen for newspaper correspondents. Attached to the dividing railing between the two areas was a wireless intercom which emitted a low hum. Every minute or so it crackled with progress reports of the forming procession from Pageant men in the field. Both Roger Megan, on the press side, and Fleming in the hierarchial hive could keep an ear cocked for any announcement of trouble.

Two city blocks further up the boardwalk, on an elevated platform overlooking the crowd, a television crew was testing for color projection by focusing on the herd below. The results flashed spastically across a monitor screen in the press box, where Megan could keep a wary eye on it.

Bam! Pow! Rockets exploded in the sky, shedding brilliant golden petals of flame.

"Christ Jesus, make it work!" breathed Megan to himself.

Megan, who rarely appealed to divinity, was doing so now. Had he been alone, he might even have gone down on his knees—a position alien to him unless the dice were rolling or certain erotic calisthenics indulged in.

But he was far from being in private. He was right in the foreground of the public eye. Microphone adjusted, clever ad libs plotted, he was set to give America's viewers play-by-play details of Surf City's first nationallly telecast Pageant parade. Attired in white linen jacket, fawn slacks, flamingo shirt and Oleg Cassini necktie, he was the ever flip, eternally juvenile Mr. Pageant in person.

"Emergency . . . Emergency . . . Boardwalk at Virginia Avenue . . . "

Instantly, Fleming and Megan tensed perceptibly and tilted their heads from opposite directions toward the crucial squawk box.

"Trouble here with the North Dakota float. Still not set up. Difficulty in bolting on the superstructure."

Fleming barked back into the mechanism. "Will they be ready to fall into line in sequence?"

"They think so, sir. But it's already starting time."

"Tell whoever's working on it to shake the lead out, Eddie. If they miss, roll the next float. Work North Dakota into place where you can."

"Yes, sir!"

Fleming turned from the brief exchange to find his companion curious. "Mr. Fleming, what did your man mean about a superstructure? About bolting something on?"

"One of our many problems in float construction, Senator." To the casual eye, Fleming was once again his oleaginous self. "Highway tunnel clearance puts a height limit of thirteen feet on anything trucked through. So if a float is taller than that, the factory has to build it in sections. The upper parts are attached to the base after the truck arrives in Surf City."

"But thirteen feet? That gives enough headroom, surely?"

"This year, Miss North Dakota's float depicts a log fort. The young lady is representing a pioneer woman high up on the watch tower during an Indian raid."

"Fascinating!" observed the Senator. "You fellows really face some left-field problems, don't you?"

"A few, Senator. A few." Fleming could feel his heartbeat slowing back toward normal. The crisis, thank God, had not been Walsh and his damned threatened demonstration. Not the boardwalk arson that cannibal, Burrage, had hinted at.

Not this time.

Flashing his happy-go-lucky smile, waving to blurred faces below, answering a ticklish query from the UP man with a *double entendre*, Megan seemed insulated and secure as Fort Knox. But inside he was slowly dying from suspense.

Christ, how did a man ride out a ball-breaker like this one? How?

"Emergency . . . Emergency . . . "

Once again, the two men sucked in air and braced for Armageddon.

"Joe here, at the end of the boardwalk. There's a tugboat off the beach with her horn wide open. Blasting fit to kill, Mr. Fleming. The crowd's getting sore. They can't hear the music."

"Radio her to cut the comedy, damn it!"

"She can't, sir. Thing's stuck. She was signaling a freighter heading past, and now she can't close down again."

"Then send out the Beach Patrol. Tell them I want that horn silenced if they have to cut the tug down to her waterline."

"Yes, sir! Will do!"

The souvenir vendors were sprouting all over, hawking tiny stretch suits stamped "Future Princess America." Others rented "Bring-'em-up-closer" binoculars at three dollars a pair and ten dollars' deposit.

Far down the boardwalk, in the area where the parade was assembling, martial music lifted. Strains of the "Washington Post March" streamed down the long curve of the beach, drifted over the façades of luxury hotels and motor inns. The spectators stood on tiptoe, restless with anticipation.

"Hey, you see 'em?"

"Not yet. The music's just a warm-up."

The floats were lined up on side streets intersecting the beginning of the boardwalk planking, ready to fall in position like units of a planned invasion force. Each parade wagon would enter the course in sequence corresponding to the date of admission of its state into the Union.

None of these last moments before countdown was much different from the preceding twelve earlier parades. Each successive year, as the Pageant soared in acceptance as a national institution, the events had become more and more elaborate. But the basics remained the same. Only the scope increased. In the press box, ready to broadcast the spectacle in sync with the TV monitor, Megan could from past experience pretty well gauge the action in every sector.

With a single exception.

He would have traded a weekend date with the hottest piece in the Western Hemisphere for one scrap of knowledge. What was going on this minute inside a grimy brick warehouse on a certain shabby back street? His thoughts leaped six blocks inland from the human crush he now stood facing.

"Here they come!"

One voice yelled it.

A thousand throats echoed it.

And here they came. The open convertible bearing Surf City's mayor—as honorary parade marshal—crawled into sight at five miles per hour. Up until tonight, the car was to be shared by John Fleming. But at the last moment Fleming's mounting panic had caused him to alter his plans. The possibility of a black blitz by Walsh and Company had made him fearful of being out of instant communication with the field. Even in the time it took to measure off the boardwalk in a creeping car, all hell might burst loose.

Behind the mayor and a fleet of motorcycle police marched the famous Surf City Band, heavy with brass, drums pounding. And on the backlash of the Sousa music, coolly immune to the blare, rode Virginia Kerr, the reigning Princess America.

Ginny sat majestically on a throne built into the apex of an inverted cone striped in red, white and blue. At the four corners of her float, a soldier, a sailor, an Air Force cadet and a Marine stood solemnly as though they were on holy land.

Spotlights played over her, teasing sparks from the gems in her crown. A corsage of roses nestled over her bosom. Waving vivaciously, she greeted the exuberant crowd. On detail at one of the first side-street barricades she passed, Steve Dorn could scarcely recognize in this gracious goddess the inert doll he had dragged from the waves two nights earlier. Their eyes brushed and he fancied she blew a personal kiss to him. But it was hard to say. She was blowing them to everyone.

Long before the head of the parade rolled into his view, Roger Megan could tell by the swelling roar that it was coming. Suddenly he felt as if someone had looped his midsection with a wire lasso and was jerking the noose tight. Standing at the railing, he spotted Earl Burrage ambling insolently past the press box. Glancing up, Burrage deliberately slowed his pace. One black face among hundreds was all Megan could see. One grinning set of teeth. One pair of penetrating eyes, blazing with malice.

Burrage bowed with a mock humility, slapped his thigh as though it were a bongo drum.

"Big evening, Whitey!" The ambiguous greeting lifted quietly, iced with threat.

"Fuck you, Buster!" Megan's lips formed the syllables carefully. But he uttered no sound. The mike in his hand was open.

Burrage passed along, melting away with the last of the stragglers scurrying off the boardwalk seeking vantage points, a ledge, a railing or a car top they could stand on. And far up the promenade facing the surf, the red lights of the lead car and its motorcycle escort flickered like measle spots. More rockets tore at the sky, and Megan twisted his mike to pick up their shattering boom.

"With the lead units now rolling, folks, this annual feature of the Princess America Pageant is once again off and running," he reported. "A top-capacity crowd is on its feet and cheering . . . "

Descriptive, colorful words poured from Megan in a steady torrent, requiring no Teleprompter, no concentration. He could do the job blindfolded. The sweat coming out of his pores flowed just as easily. It trickled down his ribs and soaked his undershirt. Why the hell didn't Lou Cates get some word to him? Any of a dozen things could have gone wrong. A delayed plane. A blown bus tire. A suspicious cop too near a warehouse.

"And here's the parade marshal, folks," Megan's commentary continued. "His Honor is just passing our reviewing stand. There's a uniformed color guard on the float carrying Virginia Kerr. I've never seen America's Number One Valentine look more beautiful than—oops! Excuse me! Ginny just tossed a smile my way. I had to catch it!"

The next float came into view, evoking gasps of surprise from the mob. Eleven identical golden throne chairs circled its perimeter, facing outward from a mammoth, glittering replica of Princess America's crown.

"A surprise attraction," Megan spoke into the mike. "Have you ever wondered what happened to beauty Jane Ellis, the Pageant's very first Princess? She's riding before us now, on a spectacular float, together with all our previous beauty champs."

Eleven lovely women, a few of them now far from the first blush of girlhood, brandished scepters at the enthusiastic crowd. Across each of eleven chests ran a wide sash of crimson silk. On each was lettered, in gold numerals, a year from the past.

"Look, Junior! That's Dora Langley! She won the year Dad and I were married."

"Hey, Marilyn! Remember me? You gave me your autograph in the Armory right after they picked you, back in fifty-nine!"

"There's Sue Rossiter. Been with the Pageant ever since she won the title."

"Sally Thomas, sixty-two. She doesn't look one year older than when they crowned her."

"I bet that's a double chin starting on Hortense. And she's put on weight. Blondes fade early, huh?"

The catty cracks were definitely in the minority. Even the earliest years on the ribbons were drawing cheers, applause, and reviving nostalgic memories.

Eleven former Princess Americas, reunited for the first time in Pageant history and soon to be joined by a twelfth, rode glowingly up the boardwalk—back into their kingdom.

Behind them glided the first state float. It bore Miss Delaware clad in a gown of feathers to honor her state's poultry industry. She was reciting into an amplifier the saga of Ceasar Rodney's dramatic ride to Philadelphia—which had made him first signer of the Declaration of Independence and ranked his former colony Number One among the original thirteen.

Next came a detachment of Surf City's Veterans of Foreign Wars, then a second state float on which Miss Pennsylvania sat under an enormous, cracked Liberty Bell.

Considering the Pageant's firm rule that no float cost more than fifteen thousand dollars, some of the displays were marvels of ingenuity. In other years Megan had found it effortless to pay them homage. But not tonight. It was impossible to keep his mind on the Pageant caravan. His brain had been excised from his skull and was in a warehouse a quarter of a mile away.

Nevertheless, glib coverage kept spouting from his lips like water sluicing down a flume. "Here comes the Georgia float. As you folks at home can see, it's a revolving merry-go-round of flowers from our Peach Tree State.

Gorgeous Miss Georgia is sitting in that big magnolia blossom there at the top. Let me clue you in on a little secret . . . "

The Megan voice dipped to a whisper, creating an impression of an inside personal confidence about to be revealed. In a staggering number of homes families leaned toward their screens to catch the morsel.

"When you see one of these revolving displays on a Pageant float, can you guess what makes it turn? A motor? No, sir! A motor powerful enough to keep a wheel like this spinning would be so noisy it would be heard even above band music. No, friends, not a motor."

He paused coyly, allowing them time to make conjectures.

"Give up? Then—here's the secret. Boy power! There are kids there, in a pit under the float. Good, strong lads, pushing to keep it turning. It's the only way this effect can be managed on a moving vehicle. So next time you want to surprise a friend who isn't tuned in on us tonight—"

"Emergency! Emergency!" blatted the intercom. "Boardwalk at Wyoming!"

There was urgency in the voice this time. It carried the extra note of stress Megan had been waiting for. A nimble sidestep took him to the railing, even while his folksy chatter spun on. From across the barricade, Fleming cut in just as fast.

"Boardwalk at Wyoming! Demonstration group forming. Spade pickets with protest signs!"

Fleming's heart almost went into cardiac arrest. "Bastards!"

"That's not all, sir. There's an unauthorized float here. Just eased up from a side street. No credentials."

"What the hell does it look like, Eddie? Who is it?"

"I don't know, Mr. Fleming. Six pretty dinge broads dressed up like famous dames in history. They say if we don't let the float roll the demonstrators will bust through and take the parade over."

"What's the matter with our police? Can't Yoldring handle it?"

"Riot cars are pulling in now, sir. It's going to be a real Donnybrook."

Megan bent over to face Fleming. "Let the float through, JF. Tell whoever's in charge they can fall in right behind Hawaii."

Across the dividing fence, Fleming stared at Megan, bewildered. "Are you a raving lunatic, Roger? We can't let those hoodlums crash the parade. We're on television. Living color. It couldn't be hushed up."

"Who's hushing? Would you rather have our viewers see one float of black beauties or the kind of night-stick action they saw at the Democratic Convention in Chicago?" Megan watched the words hit home.

"This scum is not going to intimidate—"

"It's not intimidation," Megan rushed on. "Played right, it could be good for the Pageant." He paused expectantly. Where the hell was Walsh?

Thomas Walsh suddenly materialized at Fleming's elbow. "This is one of the little surprises we promised you the other morning," he said softly. "Openers."

Fleming glared at him. "Get your people off the boardwalk, or you'll regret it."

Walsh smiled mildly. "I think you'd regret it more than we. A riot? Innocent bystanders hurt? Police brutality well publicized? Is that what you want for the Pageant?"

"JF, they aren't kidding." Megan's voice was desperate. "Play it my way. Please."

Fleming's oyster eyes bulged in fury. His complexion was a lunar pallor. Finally, he dipped his head toward the intercom.

"Let the float in, Eddie. After Hawaii. Pass the word to Yoldring that I've okayed it."

"Yes—sir!" The low crackle of static cut off sharply.

With the self-protective instinct of an armadillo rolling up into a plated ball, Megan retreated from the railing before Fleming could question him any further, easing back into his live commentary.

"That, friends, was the All New Jersey Bagpipe Corps you've just been listening to." He had been holding a reversed mike at arm's length, picking up music to cover his hasty interchange with the Pageant's czar. Now he had yanked it back. "A magnificent sight, along with some first-rate piping. Not a swing of a kilt out of time."

Megan avoided looking at Fleming. He talked on hastily.

"And right behind them—here's Miss Louisiana. Doesn't she look like a real Creole heroine on that beautiful wrought-iron balcony? Ah, romantic old New Orleans! And next to pass us is—"

Now that the dreaded moment of confrontation lay behind him, Megan settled into an uneasy calm. Nothing more could happen now until almost the end of the parade. He would have to spend this next half hour in a kind of suspended animation.

If only, now, *this* cure would work!

Megan felt a tap on his shoulder. He turned to find Lou Cates standing behind him. Their eyes met significantly. Megan itched to ask a barrage of questions as he seldom itched even for a woman. But the queries remained unspoken. There was too much press in the box. Too many ears on the alert.

"A little dust-up outside the warehouse near Wyoming." Cates winked. "But it's settled now."

"So I heard." That was all.

Unit by unit, band by band, state by state, sponsor advertisement by sponsor advertisement, the gala march ran on. And Megan's voice kept pace with it, cracking the corny little witticisms, pointing out the items of interest, whipping up ersatz enthusiasm to cover a dull spot.

Only when the Hawaii float, constructed to resemble a volcano's peak, hove into view did he come tautly alive again.

From the papier-mâché cone flame-colored smoke was curling. The crowds at the barricades oohed and aahed at the vivid display, so imminent seemed an eruption. Megan pondered whether or not to tell them the flame glow was caused by a dozen red bulbs, battery-fed, and the smoke a product of fifty pounds of dry ice inside the cone. He decided against. His attention was elsewhere.

With Mepala Yates in a patterned sarong tossing vanda orchids right and left to spectators her myopic eyes could barely distinguish, the Hawaii float rumbled past.

And directly behind it rolled the float from which neither Roger Megan nor John Fleming could tear their eyes.

The basic structure was fairly simple. There had been less than forty-eight hours in which to locate a float and recondition it. What was in use here was a leftover ship from an old Columbus Day parade. The giant plaster-of-Paris waves which originally had lofted a *Santa Maria* and its Admiral of the Ocean Sea had been refurbished with gilt into a multitiered floodtide of gold. Out of each wave a colored girl bloomed like a black orchid. As Eddie had reported, they depicted "famous dames from history."

Famous beauties, to be more precise. Ladies who, because of their loveliness, had been the movers and shakers of myth, legend and history.

Eve, the premier siren of them all, held above her a huge red apple. Her unfettered hair fell free, half concealing gravity-defying breasts.

"How's *them* for watermelons?" the UP reporter gasped appreciatively.

Salome, stone-colored tan and lithe, was busy keeping her famous seven veils from unswirling about her.

Circe's diaphanous white robes flowed from chocolate-brown shoulders, revealing rounded arms cradling the symbolic lyre which had lured the crew from Ulysses' ship.

Cleopatra, her skin the gleaming ebon of cannel coal, seemed about to plunge a prop asp against her bosom. Catherine the Great, Empress of countless lovers, displayed a lovely mocha face under her powdered wig.

Atop the whole glittering pyramid, gazing down royally, rode Helen of Troy. The face that launched a thousand ships gave more than justice to Homer's description. The smooth skin drawn over a masterpiece of bone architecture was the gentle hue of pongee silk. The full lips were like poppy petals. And the body would have made a bull smash a pasture fence.

It all would have passed as a typical—and eye-filling—historical tableau. Except for one detail. Each of the girls held up a picket sign.

WE SHALL OVERCOME PAGEANT PREJUDICE, challenged one. Another pleaded: DON'T LET THEM BAN OUR BLACK BEAUTIES. A third proclaimed: NATURE KNOWS NO COLOR LINE, and a fourth: BLACK IS BEAUTIFUL.

Fleming spun around to Megan in an apoplectic rage, but Walsh grabbed his arm.

"Well, Mr. Fleming?"

A murmur like wind in trees swept down the boardwalk as astonished spectators reacted in unison to the Negro entry. The ominous sound reached the reviewing stand almost neck and neck with the float itself. The wind rose in volume. To Fleming, it was a cyclonic rush that chilled his blood.

"Well?" Walsh repeated.

With a mounting fury that destroyed his remaining composure, Fleming wrenched his arm away from Walsh, leaned within inches of the black man's face and sputtered: "Get . . . Get those damn signs out of my parade! Get them *out*! Now! *Immediately!"* The last word was a strident wail.

Walsh held his ground. "It's too late, Mr. Fleming. Unless, of course . . ." He finished the sentence with a smile.

Megan, his words skillfully pouring into the microphone, watched the exchange and timed his move to match the frustration he saw twisting Fleming's mouth into a grotesque, silent slash. "Now, let's hear more of this fine music," he said quickly, turning the microphone and leaning over to Fleming. "JF?"

Fleming seemed incapable of speech. He cast a furtive glance at the Negro float as it drew up to the reviewing stand, then looked to Megan with hurt eyes that said no explanation was needed.

"What the hell is it you people want?" Megan rasped to Walsh. "You've got your goddamned float."

"Not bad, those black girls," Walsh answered. "Or am I prejudiced?"

"They're beautiful," Megan said hastily. "But what do you want?"

"Which girl is the prettiest?" Walsh asked as though the seconds were not ticking off. "Pick one by the Pageant's standards."

Great, Megan told himself. Walsh was playing his part perfectly.

"JF? Your choice?"

Fleming, grateful that Megan had stepped in, swept the float with an anguished eye. He felt like the Pope being asked to vote for Margaret Sanger. "The one on the top, I guess," he stammered.

Of course the one on the top, Megan complimented his judgment. That was the design. The whole display played up Helen of Troy. "Who is she?" Megan demanded of Walsh. As if Hazel had never told him.

"Joyce Carrol," Walsh responded on cue. "She was voted Miss Washington, D.C., last month by the Negro Merchants Association."

Megan rubbed his face and closed his eyes as though deep in thought. He knew Fleming was hanging on every word, every motion. And now the whole charade depended on his final pitch. Let Fleming hang for a second or two. He had to be ripe for anything that sounded reasonable, any straw. Megan opened his eyes and saw the Negro float, bearing its inciting slogans and even more inciting flesh, move past the reviewing stand. It was less than a minute away from the television cameras. Now, thought Megan. It can't miss.

Megan waved Walsh away and put his arm around Fleming's shoulders and talked rapidly into the old man's ear. "I've got it, JF! If I read him right, Walsh will pull in his horns if we put one of his girls into the contest."

"Impossible," Fleming exploded, drawing from some inner well the strength to fight for his creation as it stood.

"But why?" Megan whispered.

"You know why. We've got one from each state ... fifty. That's—Good God, man, you know why."

"But you heard Walsh. She's Miss Washington, D.C. That's our answer! The fifty states *and* the District of Columbia. We come out smelling like a rose. Prescott will force-feed the media into eating out of our hand. And Walsh gets crap. She'll never win. And we avoid trouble."

Megan felt Fleming's body sag.

"Throw in the towel, JF," Megan said urgently. "Give him his moment. We'll land on our feet. Trust me. We have to realize even the Miss America Pageant has black representation now."

Fleming glanced at the TV monitor behind Megan and he knew what the next picture would be. He made a hopeless gesture of surrender and slumped into his chair.

Megan straightened and realized his shirt was soaking wet. But the plan had worked. A bloodless *coup d'état*. He waved Walsh over and said: "She's in." Walsh nodded slyly, pulled a plastic whistle from his pocket and blew a shrill note just as the front of the maverick float hit the left-hand edge of the TV monitor.

At the signal, every placard on the float dipped and vanished into the curlicues of the plaster waves. Radiant, poised, the six sepia lovelies broke into muscular smiles. That was how the TV cameras caught them as they sailed into range.

" . . . a surprise," Megan was announcing over the mike to the nation. "A historic first for the Princess America Pageant. Atop the District of Columbia float, Miss Washington, D.C., Joyce Carroll. For the first time in our history, our fifty-first entry. Fifty states *and* the District of Columbia. Just like in the electoral college."

Fleming, a monument toppled, gave Walsh a weary look. "So, Mr. Walsh. You outmaneuvered me. You win."

Then he pulled himself together and gave Walsh his most charming smile. He would make the best of the shotgun marriage. "See me after the parade and we'll work out the details."

"That will be a pleasure, Mr. Fleming," Walsh said, wondering if the old man would ever know he had been set up. "But we didn't win. *You* won. You won a very great deal for Princess America Pageants in years to come. And we'll all remember this day of the year for a long, long time." Play it cool, Megan had coached him. But Walsh couldn't resist a parting shot. "Yes, it will be remembered. The first time you let a nigger into the contest."

29 · SUE ROSSITER

MUCH to her chagrin, Sue Rossiter had witnessed no part of the climactic events of the Torchlight Parade. Missed the whole incredible business, from the spectacular intrusion of the NFL's piratical ship to the wild denouement that had legitimized it. All she had been aware of was that something extraordinary was going on somewhere behind her. Not until she came off her float at the Armory terminus did she hear the momentous news. It stunned her.

In previous years, Sue and Roger had traditionally flanked the reigning, soon-to-retire Princess, sharing with her the star vehicle at the heart of the grand cortege. But tonight, with the entire gaggle of past Princesses gathered for once, it had been decided that show-biz basics called for them to be enthroned on their own float. This deployment had necessarily resulted in reducing her from the unique Sue Rossiter to one of a group, and positioning her well in the vanguard of the parade.

Thus her float had long since passed the reviewing stands and was blocks away when the black girls suddenly materialized far down the line. From back there a tremendous roar had gone up, a human din that made the ocean inaudible.

Frightened at first, Sue had guessed correctly that Tom Walsh was keeping his promise to spring a surprise. But for all its clamor the fabric of the sound was affirmative. No screams, no panic, no police sirens. Instead, a thunderous eruption of cheers and applause.

And so, barricaded behind her smile, she rode on, waving left and right to people who, oblivious of her, looked only to where the action was. To where everything was, all behind her now. She regarded the ten Princesses riding with her down the boardwalk and wondered if they, too, hated being has-beens. By Saturday there would be one more.

Returning each year to the same enchanted sphere of Surf City, to the same season, the same people, the same round of duties, Sue had always felt a timeless, euphoric reassurance that nothing and no one had changed. But tonight she had been relegated to her venerable niche in history.

It had seemed to her then that with a little more encouragement from thoughts such as these, she might stop smiling long enough to throw up. And nobody would notice.

But the evening had scarcely begun.

The Armory was jumping with excitement. The parade kept spilling relentlessly into the receiving areas, and with every incoming float new arrivals added to the confusion. Inside the great auditorium hundreds milled about. Yard crews, riggers, contestants, chaperones, guards, mechanics, drivers moved from one knot of talkers to another. For a time they had been expecting the NFL contingent, but somewhere short of the Armory the blacks had left their float. It had sailed in manned only by police, like a seized contraband craft. Crowds clustered around TV monitors set up along the stage and runway, watching intently the last minutes of the telecast, as though hoping for an instant replay of the crisis, preferably in slow motion. It was too much to digest.

With one stroke the Pageant had been integrated, the NFL strife was over, and there was a Negro Miss Washington, D.C., in the contest. The air crackled with that special fearful thrill that pervades the scene of an accident.

Upstairs in the lofty recesses of the Armory, in the relative calm of her dressing room, Sue heard from Olga Loomis the scenario of the parade as it had unfolded on television. Sue sat in a robe before a huge mirror ringed with light, her eyes closed, while Toshio made dainty fluttering repairs to her makeup.

The usually contained Olga seemed unable to stop talking. How could it have happened? The *way* it happened! And what was going to happen now? Sue listened in silence, passively, a boulder parting the rapids, and Olga's chatter purled around her to Mrs. Baugh from Costume and Anton Sykes the hairdresser, who nodded at everything, statement, query, conjecture, and prediction, lost in his work.

The hell with it, Sue thought. It was impossible to cope with. She had problems enough. What she needed was a quiet interval, the phone remaining off the hook, a little time to find composure and the energy to make decisions. *Our life is frittered away by detail . . . simplify, simplify . . .* Thank you, H. D. Thoreau. That distant night (ten years ago!) when she had recited his lines, here in this building, Princess America the third, young and innocent. But, Princess, how did you fall from grace? You'd never believe it. I learned to make love in a shower. Simplify that.

"Sue, Mr. Ornadel phoned he'd be here any minute."

"Thank you, Olga."

The thing was, how was this brouhaha likely to affect her plans for the rest of the evening? Tentative plans to begin with, left up in the air by Roger the Rover. Come fly with me. Plans as clouded as her mood, so iffy that she'd had Mrs. Baugh bring three ensembles from her hotel, but choosing among them was still beyond her. A Geoffrey Beene red chiffon with delicate beading, originally destined for tonight's party, but perhaps too youthful; a black satin sheath, but perhaps too anxious; a Dior gray silk serge, but the silver slippers were not recommended for incognito stealth at four in the morning from Roger's suite.

"Will you be wearing the tiara, my dear?" Sykes asked.

She opened her eyes. Toshio had finished. He stood behind her, his head cocked, scrutinizing her mirror image. Their eyes met and both smiled. Toshio bowed and backed away. Sykes took his place, gliding into position.

"No tiara," Sue said. "Just comb it out a little."

"Spray?"

She sighed. "You mean I have a choice?"

"It's for your own protection, my dear. A chevelure like yours, well, thank God for it."

She watched him as he flourished to work. She thought of the parade again, of its amazing metamorphosis, with Roger in the middle of it, trapped, yet somehow, in Olga's vivid description, handling the situation masterfully. As he handled and survived every situation. Escaping sometimes without his skin, casting it off with serpentine ease. And staring at herself, but seeing only an abstraction of herself, of ten misused years of her life.

At this cheerless pass Mr. Basil Ornadel arrived, in very high spirits, with remarkable tidings, and everything changed. He was Sue's companion for the night. Sue had to be utterly prudent about her escorts, being, after all, as people occasionally remembered, a married woman. Men of rectitude, above suspicion as Caesar's wife, and about as manly; older men, prominently connected with the

Pageant, preferably feeblish. Or if young, then impossible.

Basil more than met the requirements—about forty, successful, amusing, a famous decorator, ultra-modish in fluffy sideburns, cross-grained silk tuxedo and mini-cape. And not gay, though sometimes, as now, in his great, almost girlish enthusiasm, he seemed it.

"Haven't you *heard* about Roger? The man of the evening! Maybe the man of the year! *Annus mirabilis!* It is possible you don't know?"

They goggled at him. Know what? Good heavens, Basil, man, know what?

"This fantastic compromise! This super-brilliant idea of a Miss Washington, D.C.! All Roger's doing! *Aurea mediocritas! Ex tempore! Suaviter in modo, fortiter in re!*"

Eventually, however, finding his way back to mostly English, Basil recounted for a fascinated group what none of the television audience had apprehended. John Fleming apoplectic with fury, helpless, locked in his wrath—and Roger quickly finessing an escape to lead them from chaos. Basil, near Roger in the stands, had been among the few who had been privy to the scene. And to JF's later effusions of gratitude to Roger, losing no face by the juxtaposition of their roles. For, as Basil perceived, Roger's genius had immediately become Fleming's.

"Roger, my boy," JF had said gallantly, "we have somehow engineered a triumph!"

To which Basil, grinning, appended, "So I should perhaps say that we have two heroes, since Mr. Fleming obviously believes *qui facit per alium facit per se,*" translating for once, "he who does something for another does it for himself."

Yes, thought Sue, she could understand that feeling. How often Roger's fortunes seemed to be so much her own. She was so thrilled she shook. She could hardly wait now to see Roger.

The party to which Basil escorted Sue was at the Pageant's Mayfair penthouse. It was an annual ritual, limited to the Pageant brass and a coterie of elite. Tonight, however, it had turned into something else.

It was all JF's doing. Shortly after coming out of shock, he had risen to the history-making occasion by declaring a jubilee and inviting guests from the NFL that included the beauties from the float and apparently numerous relatives and friends. Likewise welcomed was a swarm from the working press, who also had friends, and miscellaneous crashers, black and white, eager to make friends. It added up to an orgy of fellowship, a rollicking assemblage with the aspects of a revival meeting.

Shining, laughing black faces were everywhere—a little giddy perhaps at finding themselves within the enclave, but not nearly as giddy as JF was at the sight of it. Forgotten now were the four days of mounting anxiety, of threat and counter. All exorcised now by platitudes and beatitudes and consecrated with holy champagne. Over all this John Fleming presided with impartial grace, a nobleman every inch, a hypocrite supine on a field of clover.

Sue Rossiter had soon happily lost herself in the proceedings and, happier still, had lost Basil. She wandered about in a violet haze, drinking, meeting people, finding a lionized and exuberant Roger, congratulating him, then somehow separated again, to find him again and exchange a few lighthearted sentences.

Because how does a woman go about saying to a man, "Listen, you, will we be alone later or not?" A lovely young woman, eminently desirable, on all sides showered with compliments, ravished by looks? A woman of pride who has been in a love affair with the man for longer than she sometimes wants to remember?

Then it was time for the inevitable pictures, and there was Roger. But the photographers and their strobes never stopped, and things were too hectic to find time and place to talk. Flash: *Thomas Worthington Walsh flanked by Mayor Detzer and John Fleming in a three-way handshake, wreathed in smiles.* Here we have: *Sue Rossiter and Joyce Carrol, Miss District of Columbia, embracing as they plan to meet tomorrow.* In this next one: *Miss D. of C., Sue Rossiter and Mrs. Phoebe Lockwood, supervisor of chaperones, who will act as Miss D. of C.'s official chaperone.* One more, please: *Sue Rossiter, Miss D. of C., Thomas Worthington Walsh and Roger Megan.* And just another: *John Fleming, Chief of Police Yoldring, Thomas Worthington Walsh.*

Someone calculated that with the available cast of characters, the possible permutations for different poses numbered well over 75,000. When it seemed likely that these had all been exhausted, and a similar fate threatened Sue, she fled. Not so much looking for Roger, she told herself, as expecting to run into him. But he was not in the executive wing, in the glass-walled inner office that was the axis of the party, or in the library or reception room.

And now the party was beginning to wane. Returning to the inner office, she had a quick impression that several familiar faces were missing. Then Norm Prescott emerged from JF's own private eyrie, and, spying her, immediately beckoned.

She came to him, not liking the way he looked. "Yes?"

"Come inside," Norm said quietly. "It's not pleasant, but JF wants everybody in there."

"What's up?"

"An inquest," he said, opening the door.

She walked into JF's office and looked around, and her smile, forced into existence from habit, withered to a puzzled line. There were at least a dozen people standing about in various attitudes of tension, but no Roger. The ruling echelon of the Pageant in solemn array. JF sat in his upholstered armchair behind his massive desk, his expression icily satanic. Across the desk, Police Chief Yoldring, in a too tight gold-braided dress uniform, stood before him uncomfortably. Fleming nodded briefly to Sue, then turned his attention to Yoldring.

What was wrong? She could not imagine. Everything had gone marvelously—so well, in fact, it supported suspicion that the whole evening had been as carefully promoted and produced as the Pageant itself. Listening to Fleming, she thought at first this was what had set him off. But it was something quite different.

"We know it was staged," he addressed Yoldring. "But by whom? Walsh and his people? Absurd. This had the complicity of someone completely familiar with our operation, our facilities. Someone who knew about that float in storage, who knew how and when to get it on the boardwalk. With the whole goddam police force guarding the parade. All week we've been taking bows for doing such a great job of control with the pickets and demonstrators. Now we see why. They weren't out to make trouble. They behaved themselves and suckered you in—got you with your pants down. Got you looking every place but the right place. If it hadn't been for Megan," he sneered, "you might have had a real control job on your hands. A first-class riot, Mr. Yoldring."

The Mr. designation conveyed menacingly how close to civilian status Chief Yoldring now stood. Then, suddenly querulous, Fleming asked of no one in particular, "Where is Roger? Why isn't he here when I need him?"

Not a sound. Sweat continued to trickle down the Chief's neck to his stiff wet collar.

JF glared at him. "Don't you know *anything*!"

Yoldring said, "All we've been able to find out is that one of Walsh's assistants figured big in it—one of his organizers who's been here since May. A girl named Hazel Sanders, a top staff member."

"That's not important!" Fleming spat out. "Of course somebody on Walsh's staff was in on it. What I want to know is who on *your* staff was in on it!"

"If you mean the man I think you mean—"

"That nigger cop."

Yoldring flared briefly. "Impossible! Lt. Douglas was never out of my sight. I agree that it's an inside job, but I'll stake my badge that it's one of your people, not mine."

Fleming regarded him, then nodded. "That's fair enough." He took out his snuff box and fortified himself with a double pinch. "Perhaps tomorrow we'll be able to delve a little deeper," he said.

The snuff box clicked shut. The inquest was over. Tomorrow maybe there would be an autopsy. People began moving toward the door, unhurriedly, as though they might in this way become invisible when they left.

Sue, wondering whether she ought to stay, found Norm Prescott's eyes and suddenly realized he had been trying to get through to her. He motioned for her to wait.

She went to Fleming, made a few good-night comments about a wonderful party, and left. Outside only a handful of tail-enders and incapacitated remained. The waiters were clearing away the mountainous debris.

Sue lit a cigarette and paced, as though expecting someone to arrive with her wrap, trying to think what she was going to do, to fathom some possible reason for Roger's inexplicable disappearing act. Had he run out on her? It was inconceivable. But there had been nothing definite. On Wednesday night, just after the prelims, they had agreed their next practical chance would be tonight, after the parade. It had not been mentioned since, from which she had assumed—from their established way with each other—that it was set. What the hell did she need to go to bed with him—a notarized contract?

Presently Norm Prescott came out. Bad as he had looked before, he had now deteriorated to a pale positively lousy. "Are you alone?" he asked.

She smiled. "Yes. Basil always has my permission to find a live one." She added with a comic grimace, "I think he expected I'd be joining Roger, but—" shrugging—"no Roger either."

"Roger's at his hotel with Felix and some others. He asked me to tell you." Prescott sighed. "Listen, Sue, I've got to talk to you. It won't take long."

"You mean right now?"

"Yes, very much now. And very serious. In my office."

They walked to Prescott's office in the east wing. He let her in and locked the door. He motioned her to a chair, but she preferred to stand, tense now at Prescott's obvious discomfort. For a long minute, he simply looked at her. To Sue, the silence spelled disaster.

Prescott finally spoke in an ominous monotone. "I don't know how to tell you this, Sue, so I'll just say it straight out." He shook his head. "I hate this. But the fact is, Roger is in trouble. He's been tailed all week by private detectives. JF ordered it." Sue's hands curled into tight fists involuntarily. "I've been getting reports every day. I'm to pass them along to JF either tomorrow or Saturday." Prescott stopped, struggling for words. "Roger has to be warned. I naturally thought of you."

Sue felt very warm in the closed room. Private detectives? She tried to sound casual. "Norm, what is this all about and why me?" She thought it not impossible that she would quietly keel over.

"This will explain it." Prescott said as he unlocked his desk and removed a long green folder. He seemed to have taken on its color. He opened the folder and took out two stapled sheets of legal-sized stationery. "We're the old-timers, you, I and Roger. I suppose I should have warned him, but I didn't. You're as close to him as I am. At this stage of the game, I wouldn't know what to say. On the other hand, you can say you stumbled across this somehow." He held out the sheets to her.

Her hand was steady. The stationery said *The Carmody Investigative & Protective Agency*. She read everything Roger had done on Monday until she reached the point where Lou Cates drove him to 17 Tarpon Road, to a flat occupied by a Negro girl named Hazel Sanders. Here she paused, took out a cigarette, accepted a light, and resumed. The report took Roger to the Judah Cypress Funeral Chapel in Westbridge, in a car driven by Hazel Sanders. An hour and a half later the same driver, the same maroon Mustang, took him to where Lou Cates was waiting. They were then followed as they drove around until they came back to Surf City. A list of bars, and finally, at 1 A.M., Roger returned to the Hilton. And there the report ended.

She took a deep drag on her cigarette and reread parts of the report, fighting an inescapable conclusion that Prescott hadn't dreamed of. Had the report continued, he would have. But it didn't.

There was nothing in it about her, not a word. She could be thankful for small favors. She had been prepared, steeled and ready, for the paragraph that would read: *Upon Mr. Megan's return to the Hilton, he found Miss Sue Rossiter in his suite* ... But the final notation said: *Further activity terminated subsequent to Mr. Megan's return to the Hilton.*

With profound relief she realized what had happened. She was already in Roger's suite when he had returned—something the detective who had tailed him back to the Hilton couldn't know. Roger had not gone out again, and that had finished his Monday for the Carmody Agency. And, she thought, trembling, the secret of Rossiter and Megan was still safe. Only the indispensable Lou Cates had known.

Safe, safe, she kept repeating to herself, as though treading water, as though once she sank below the surface of this thought she would drown in a hundred others.

Sue looked up from the report and asked: "Is that all?"

Puzzled by the deadness of her response, for he was unaware of her affair with Megan, Prescott said, "Don't you see? Hazel Sanders. That's the name Yoldring mentioned to the old man. She's the assistant of Walsh's who figured big in this mess."

"I remember," Sue said.

"Then you must see the position Roger will be in when JF reads this."

"I do," Sue answered, her voice level and cold. "But this is rather gamey. It would certainly be easier coming from you. I wouldn't know what to say."

"Just tell him he was followed all week," Prescott explained. "He'll get the point. You must understand the spot I'm in. How can I explain why I didn't warn him? I wanted to, but JF trusts me. I'm legitimate with him. I like my job. I weighed the risk and didn't think it was worth it. After all, what could the report show? That Roger ran with women? We all know that. And when I read this on Tuesday, it didn't mean anything. I thought, well, he's seeing a Negro girl, so what? The circumstances were a little weird—a funeral chapel—but again, so what? It wasn't until I heard Yoldring mention this Sanders woman that I realized what a time bomb this is. The moment JF makes the connection he's sure to think Roger set up thc whole thing with the NFL."

Sue killed her cigarette in a desk ashtray and returned the report to Prescott. "Do you think it was Roger?"

"I don't know. All I know is that it doesn't look good.

Roger is a big hero with JF right now. But what do you think will happen if the old man thinks he's been had? Involved or not, Roger has to be warned. Will you do it, Sue?"

Sue almost smiled. If Norm only knew. But on what grounds could she refuse? This was a dear old friend in serious trouble. And there was no doubt in her mind that Roger had conspired with the NFL through Hazel Sanders. None at all. She would put nothing past Roger Megan. With one exception. He couldn't have . . .

"All right, Norm. I'll do it. Can you drop me at the Hilton?"

Leaving the penthouse with Prescott, she passed through the reception room again. She had been by there several times during the evening, hundreds through the years. This bloom-bedizened area, crammed with flowers and plants and bouquets, had often reminded her of a schlock florist shop. This time it made her think of a funeral chapel.

On the ride to the Hilton, she forced herself to make no judgment. This much she owed Roger and herself. Because if she accepted the ostensible evidence, she must come to either a logical or an emotional impasse. If she assumed that Roger was in collusion with the NFL and had manipulated Fleming, she could not fathom an explanation for it. But if this was not so, and Roger's association with this Hazel Sanders—this covert back-road liaison—had another reason, then it must be sex. But somehow this, too—because it involved Monday night—was completely unacceptable. Not with the way Monday night had been for her and Roger. On fire. He had almost torn her apart.

No, not Monday night. She put few things past Roger, but *this* was past Roger. She had understood him pretty well, right from the start. It had taken him three years to make his move—her third year with the Pageant as its Hostess. Vastly different though they were in many ways, they had by then achieved a great rapport, a frank and easy appreciation of each other. He was a darling, a prince, helpful at every turn, guiding, advising, admiring, an established star who was just another pro with her, capable of wonderful nonsense, with no put-ons. And no come-ons. Pro that he was at other things, like seduction (which it was not; infatuation was the truth), he had never shown his hand until he was ready to play for table stakes.

She saw in him something kindred, an allied spirit, as ambitious and talented and hard-working as she was. And as empty and confused. Full of dazzling hopes, but basically directionless, drifting.

Then one night during the week of the sixth Pageant, they were having coffee in the dining room of her hotel, and Roger said there was a great late late Bogart show that night. She had laughed and said, "Roger, is it possible you're contemplating making a pass at me?"

"All things are possible," he had said.

"And all women?"

"Almost all. If you want them badly enough."

"Even married women?" (She had been married a little over a year then, and it was already pretty well down the drain.)

"Yes, even. I'm married too. That's what makes it even."

"But why me? Haven't you got enough? Why me?"

He had grinned and answered, "I like a broad margin to my life."

"Great God A'mighty," she had said, "you quote Thoreau?"

"Not that much. I've only read two books of his."

"Why? To please *me?*"

"Yes. And to help me understand you and get at you."

She had been flattered and touched and impressed, and she had declined with thanks. But understanding him, she knew now that he had started moving, he would not stop.

A few months later, during one of her visits to Hollywood, they had met again. He dropped in on her one afternoon at the Marmont. They talked and played records, and Roger made stingers and they drank on the terrace and looked down across an expanse of pink and cream and blue. She had an appointment for cocktails later, and presently she had excused herself and gone inside to shower and get ready. Roger was stretched out on a chaise, enjoying the shade and sinking into mellow relaxation.

She had been in the shower perhaps two or three minutes—just beginning to soap herself—when the glass door slid open and without a word, his face as composed as if he were doing the most natural thing in the world, he stepped into the shower fully clothed and took her in his arms.

"Roger!" she cried. "What are you doing?"

"Oh, don't worry," he said, "this is all wash and wear."

It was the last casual sound that came out of him. There in the shower stall, still dressed, he made love to her with an urgency, with passion and imagination that she had never known. The nice refined girl who had been a virgin until she got engaged and who married the guy four years later. Fucking standing up, like horses. The nice girl who had never made it with anybody but her husband. The one who would after this gradually become the well-known Sue Rossiter of impeccable reputation. The regal Rossiter, whose marriage to a brilliant young corporation lawyer was a matter of public record and mystery, who shared a twelve-room duplex on Sutton Place with him but lived at opposite ends of their apartment when she was home. The gracious lady Rossiter who came out of the shower that day with bites on her shoulders, her breasts, livid marks on her thighs, filled and fulfilled with his love and love-making.

A long time later she had asked him, "How could you take such a chance with me? I might have screamed, fought. How could you do what you did?"

"Brinkmanship, my love," he had said. "I live very close to the brink."

And brinkmanship it had remained, for the both of them. She had long ago uprooted whatever small musing she might have entertained about marrying him. They played it by ear. They demanded nothing from each other. When chance or business brought them together, they made the most of it. There were gifts, flowers, occasional letters, phone calls. There were wonderful times in bed. The years went by, and she thought neither about the past or the future.

Tonight she was thinking about both.

It was almost midnight when she arrived at Roger's suite. Most of his company was leaving. They had all been watching the parade coverage on the late TV news. It had been a big story everywhere, all over the country, very gratifying. Roger was glad to see her, attentive, a drink, a light for her cigarette. But there was something strange about him. No, she wasn't imagining it. An odd mixture of remoteness and exhilaration and an effort to control showing either.

Presently only she and Felix and Roger remained. She had decided, out of kindness, to wait until she was alone with Roger before she spoke her little piece. Kindness to both of them—Felix could have convulsions at hearing one syllable of what she had to say. In fact, he seemed overwrought about something even now as he stood across the room with Roger, talking to him in a low agitated voice.

She gave them their privacy, poured herself a fresh

drink, and, sipping it, found herself wondering if Hazel Sanders had been at JF's party. And, if so, whether she had perhaps met this girl. What girl might she have been? Someone with Roger at some point? He had been so expansive, so delighted with everyone.

Suddenly Roger's voice rang out loudly. "All right, Felix, let's say I gambled it would work!" Not in anger, not even annoyed, but rather as though he didn't care whether Sue heard or not—as though he couldn't contain the feelings bursting out of him, good feelings, too powerful to hold back anymore.

"But what if it didn't?" Felix asked, shaking his head.

"The point is, it did. And I won! Big! Why can't you admit it was a sensational idea?"

"If it was so sensational, why didn't you go to Fleming and tell it to him and do it out in the open?"

"Because his mind was poisoned. He might easily have turned it down. He didn't want to find a way out anymore. He was going to fight. The only way I could be sure he didn't reject it was by not giving him the chance. And that meant doing it my way—presenting him with an untenable situation—the black float!"

Felix looked at Sue with a sad little smile. His shoulders came up and he made a mild, almost humorous gesture of despair, then turned back to Megan. "Obviously, I'm wrong," he said. "You think there's nothing to be said after you've won. Maybe so. Except this—and every gambler knows it; it's their own golden rule—never gamble for more than you can afford to lose. But not you, wonder boy. You gamble the way you live. You go for broke."

"Well, that's overdramatizing it a little," said Megan dryly, "but I like the picture. Very dashing. Cameo Kirby, the *Mississippi Rover* gamblin' fool. There's a character I could play to the hilt. Why don't you work on it?" He let a grin spread over his face. He wanted to mollify Felix; it made him guilty to watch him worry. "The truth is, Felix," he said, "I wasn't taking that big a chance. Even if it backfired and produced a bad scene, it couldn't have led back to me. There really was no way to connect me with it."

"Why? If you were involved, there are people who know it."

"Only one person knows, besides you and Lou Cates. I worked through one person."

"Only one. All right, only one. What if that one talked? Exposed you? Brought your name into it?"

"It could never happen. It's someone whose word is absolutely sacred with me. I'd bet my life on it."

"Hah!" Felix blurted, more of a bark than a laugh. "That's exactly what I said! You go for broke!" He threw his hands up in the air and called, "Good night, Sue, good night, Roger, good night, Chet, and good night, David. Let's hope that's what it is."

When the door closed, Roger went to the bar table, his eyes fastened on Sue. "I suppose you got the drift," he said. There was pride in his voice. His face seemed flushed. He grabbed a bottle of whiskey up to his lips and let the contents go gurgling down. When he had enough, he set the bottle down with elaborate care, returning his eyes to Sue. "You didn't answer me."

"Yes," said Sue. "I'm very good at getting the drift of things." Roger waited as though he expected her to say more, but she didn't. She would let the rooster crow.

"That's all you have to say?"

Sue raised her eyebrows to signify she thought it all had been said.

"Hmmmm," Roger said, his eyes sparkling with untold secrets. "Would you like to hear about it? About how Megan the Magnificent saved the day?" He strode regally across the room and threw his arms out, an actor calling for applause. She watched and said nothing. "The blacks love me and JF loves me—everybody loves me!" Megan spun around and almost lost his balance. He laughed. He was more than a little drunk.

"How does Hazel Sanders fit in?" Sue asked in even conversational tones.

"How do you . . . ? Aha! So you found out about her!" Megan did a time step on the rug. "A dear old friend. She will never tell. Her lips are sealed." He was compulsively acting the idiot, finally, as every lover who tells his old love about his new.

"You've been a busy little rabbit."

"That's me. Roger the Rabbit." He came toward her and reached out his arms. Sue moved back. "Hey . . ."

"Why don't you find Hazel and celebrate?" Sue said without emotion, an icy cold spreading in her stomach.

"I'm afraid that's over." Megan laughed. "A conflict of interests." He smiled expansively. "I gave her my farewell performance . . ."

"Monday night," Sue quietly prompted.

"Monday night," Megan concluded, still smiling. Then he added, "You know me too well. That's why we're so good together." He grabbed for her again, but Sue side-stepped and moved toward the door. Megan looked at her, confused.

Sue spit out the words. "You made love to me right after leaving her?"

Megan stopped smiling and tried to regain control of the conversation. "But Sue, we've never taken any vows of fidelity."

"Goodbye, Roger. The party's over. I don't drink from a public fountain."

Sue yanked open the door and slammed it behind her. In the hall she clasped a hand to her mouth and cried soundlessly. Then she wiped her eyes and walked to the elevator. Prescott would have to deliver his own message. The affair was over, done, finished. She pressed the down button and waited for the elevator to take her out of Roger Megan's life forever.

30 · GENERAL GERVAIS

THE sole feature which gave the building personality was that it had no personality.

It squatted among the skyscrapers of lower Manhattan like an ungainly toad among pond reeds. Its walls were gray concrete, stained by the city's poisoned air and defiled by pigeons. Its windows were spaced like punches in a time card, set so deep that the iron bars protecting them were all but invisible. Its door was so drab that nine out of ten pedestrians on the narrow downtown street were unaware of it as they passed.

General Clinton Gervais jabbed the white doorbell on the left and waited.

The man who opened the door was a Negro. A well-cut gray flannel suit matched the grizzle in his hair. The alert eyes were also gray, their paleness a contrast to cordovan skin.

Entering the vestibule, Gervais was conscious of the door closing behind him. The other man had not touched it. It operated by electric eye.

The gray eyes studied him sharply. The slight bulge of a revolver showed under the left breast pocket of the flannel suit.

"Clinton Gervais," the general said. He held out his identification card for inspection.

The colored man studied the photograph on the card carefully.

"Yes, General. We've been expecting you since your call this morning. Security clearance okay. I'm Claude Hayes."

"Then I can get right to work, Mr. Hayes?"

"Of course, General. SEARCH will be at your disposal for exactly fifty-five minutes. After your turn, we're stacked up with an admiral and a local representative from the Attorney General's office. I'm sorry."

"Fifty-five minutes should be sufficient, Mr. Hayes. My list is a modest one."

The colored man indicated a long corridor. Gervais followed him, their footfalls striking a subdued echo from the marble paving. Although the building seemed deserted, it teemed with activity.

Presently the corridor right-angled. Hayes made a turn, the general at his side.

"Here we are, sir." They had reached an unmarked door with two locks. Hayes took out a key ring, selected a long key and a short one, and opened the door.

Gervais preceded him into the room In the foreground, a small movie screen was set up against the wall. Prominent under the screen was a console-keyboard. Its four banks of buttons covered every letter of the alphabet, each numeral from 0 to 9. A fifth bank of buttons was inscribed with such words as *Repeat. Cancel. Clarify. Dig.*

Facing the screen, several leather-upholstered armchairs were ranged in a semicircle. Gervais selected the chair directly in front of the console.

"You know how to program SEARCH, sir? This is a brand-new model."

"I was in on the demonstration of the pilot, Mr. Hayes. If I have any difficulty, I'll call you. I can reach you on this phone, yes?" Gervais indicated a push-button model on a stand beside the console.

"Right. The number is three-two-four."

Left alone, Gervais consulted the list of Social Security numbers Waldo had obtained for him from his insurance contact, bent over the console, flipped the On lever, and punched out a series of letters and numbers.

Instantly, the screen before him lit up. For a fraction of a second, but no longer, its bright rectangle remained blank. Then the words began to flow across it, from right to left, like the symbols and figures on the Dow-Jones ticker tape.

WILLIAMS, LILY . . . FEDERAL JUDGE . . . APPOINTED IDAHO 1965 . . . TWO TERMS STATE LEGISLATURE, ONE TERM U.S. HOUSE OF REPRESENTATIVES . . . POLITICS, REPUBLICAN . . . NO RECORD OF ARRESTS . . . UNMARRIED . . . CREDIT RATING A . . . PRESENT RESIDENCE, BOISE . . .

The words, as Gervais well knew, were coming to him out of Fort Meade. The giant computer SEARCH was talking to him, spilling the information stored in its Leviathan bowels. There were half a dozen centers to which such data could be transmitted at lightning speed. Spofford had flown him to this one an hour ago.

DOWLING, GLENDA . . . COLUMNIST, U.S.A. SYNDICATE . . . RESIDENCE, HOLLYWOOD, CAL . . . SUED SLANDER 1962, ACTRESS CHARLENE LE MOYNE, JUDGMENT ENTERED, DISMISSED ON APPEAL . . . SUED LIBEL 1967, ACTORS RETT WEST AND BEAU MONTGOMERY, SODOMY ACCUSATION UNPROVEN, SETTLED OUT OF COURT . . . NO RECORD OF ARRESTS . . . CREDIT RATING A . . . DIVORCED 1952 FROM DIRECTOR JAY GARRET . . .

Gervais puffed thoughtfully, staring at the screen through a drift of smoke.

One by one, the names and dossiers of the eight judges streamed before him. Julius Laurel had trampled on many toes during his ruthless rise. But none of the trampling had been proved illegal. Bentley Eames had once been picked up by police for loitering in the men's toilet at Grand Central Terminal. But the charge had been dropped.

Otherwise, the computer's reports yielded not the faintest stigma concerning the private lives of any of the octet—unless one counted the frail fact that Athene Ciardi's credit rating was a mere "C." And this was typical of the casual attitude toward bill paying traditionally displayed by even prosperous opera divas.

When the eighth name had come and gone, however, the screen still pulsed with new information. Gervais felt a stirring of gratitude toward Art Waldo. As an extra dividend, Waldo had acquired the Social Security numbers of the entire Pageant personnel in addition to those of the judges.

MEGAN, ROGER . . . TELEVISION PERSONALITY . . . FORMERLY, STAR BROADWAY MUSICALS . . . FOUR FILMS, STAR OR FEATURED BILLING . . . ARREST, DRUNKEN DRIVING, 1961. DITTO, 1965 . . . ARREST, 1966, BRAWL IN CASINO, MIAMI BEACH, FLA . . . ALL SENTENCES SUSPENDED . . . MARRIED CLAIRE HOLLANDER, 1954, TWO CHILDREN . . . ASSOCIATED PRINCESS AMERICA PAGEANT AS M.C. SINCE 1957 . . .

The general was growing restive. He switched weight from buttock to buttock, grunting inaudibly around the wet end of his cigar.

Name after name, as he punched the console, the histories of each Pageant employee flashed before him. Megan's had been a disappointment. Although it contained discreditable material, each of these items had made headlines and was therefore general knowledge.

Norman Prescott was an ideal citizen. Susan Rossiter was the symbol of healthy, successful, intelligent young womanhood that her public image indicated. John Fleming had survived a few raunchy moments, but these were as well known as Megan's indiscretions.

It was almost forty-five minutes since Gervais had fingered the doorbell. And still nothing damning had appeared on the lighted oblong which could help him manipulate votes in Robin's favor. A heavy weight began to settle at the center of his stomach.

PETRIE, HAROLD . . . the moving letters on the screen spelled it out. Harold Petrie? Who the hell was Harold Petrie? Gervais glared at the unfamiliar name as if it had insulted him. Then he remembered. Petrie was the Pageant's chief auditor.

PETRIE, HAROLD . . . CERTIFIED PUBLIC ACCOUNTANT, EMPLOYED LAZARUS-STERN . . . GRADUATED KNICKERBOCKER SCHOOL OF BUSINESS ADMINISTRATION, 1957 . . . UNMARRIED . . . PRESENT JOB SINCE 1963, PREVIOUSLY SAME POSITION ALCORN & WHITTLEY . . . INDICTED 1959, CHARGES ARISING FROM—

The type on the viewing area continued gliding past. Gervais snapped forward in his seat toward the console. He punched two buttoms: *Repeat. Clarify.*

Then he settled back in his chair, for once forgetful of his cigar, and watched the screen anxiously. Instants later the computer oracle disgorged the details of Petrie's offense.

Damned clever racket, Gervais told himself as the words swam by. He glanced at his watch. He was six minutes under the deadline.

Gervais turned to the phone at his side, poked three digits on its base. Claude Hayes appeared a few moments later.

"Find what you wanted, General? Something to have made your trip worthwhile?"

General Gervais stood up and smiled. It was difficult for him to suppress a crow of triumph.

"Not a thing, Mr. Hayes. Not a thing. But thanks lots anyway."

The jet slid into Surf City's airport almost an hour before midnight. Gervais did not even wait for Spofford to attend to the necessary post-landing formalities. He took the car they had shared earlier on the drive out, leaving his subordinate to hunt a taxi.

Reaching his motel, he locked the door to his suite with an almost vicious click. Three strides carried him to the bedside telephone. He scanned the roster of Pageant personnel, looked up Harold Petrie's home telephone number, picked up the phone, and began to dial.

Midway he stopped and restored the instrument to its cradle. He reached for the box of Kleenex on the night table, pried out a tissue. He tore the sheet in half, rolled each part into a tiny wad. Then he inserted one wad far up into each of his nostrils. He resumed his dialing.

"Hello?" said a sleepy falsetto voice at the other end.

"Harold Petrie?" The general's words now had a strong adenoidal twang.

"Yes."

"You alone, Petrie?"

"Yeah, I'm . . . Say, what's it to you? Who are you, anyway?"

"Maybe a friend, Petrie. Maybe an enemy. That's really up to you."

"Wh-what are you talking about?"

"Suppose I mentioned the words 'jury summons?' Do they ring a bell, pal?"

For a second, there was silence. "I . . . why, I guess I've served on a couple of juries in my time. Never tried to duck it. Look here, friend—"

"Or enemy? I didn't ask about jury duty. I said 'jury summons.' "

"Oh, Jesus!" moaned Harold Petrie. He knew, by now, the name of the game.

"If you're lucky, Petrie, Jesus was looking the other way when you printed up those fake summons forms and sold them under the counter. Twenty bucks a form, wasn't it? Two hundred thousand and change, before the bubble popped?"

"Look, I don't know who you are or what you want, but—hell, guy, that was a long, long time ago, just after I got out of college. I've walked the chalk line ever since."

"Good for you, Hal. That's the American way."

"I—please—I can't afford trouble now. Not in a job like mine, with a firm like mine. I'm a married man with kids to raise. Give me a break."

"Don't play cute. You're a bachelor. No kids. We don't like guys who play cute."

"We?" Petrie's falsetto voice squeaked timorously. "More than one?"

"Hal, I'm calling you from Vegas. Our syndicate has a little favor to ask you."

"Why are you picking on me? *What do you want?*"

A short laugh answered him. "Sweat a little, pal. It's good for the complexion."

"You want money? I've got almost three thousand dollars. I'll give you every dime. Just lay off me."

"They'd certainly like to know the truth about you, your employers. A fine respectable firm like yours. How would it look if the papers carried a story on them entrusting the counting of Princess America votes to a forger?"

"I wasn't ever . . . really convicted. Just a fine."

"You were indicted for forging legal jury-summons forms. And for selling them to wise guys who would fill them out with their names. So that they could sneak two extra weeks' vacation with pay by showing the fake summonses to their bosses."

"I didn't really steal anything. I didn't go to jail."

"They let you off because they were afraid the publicity might give other guys the idea of pulling the same racket. Now listen, and listen sharp. The boys here are making book on the Pageant. There'll be a big bundle riding on Saturday night's winner. We want to know ahead of time who she'll be. So we can lay the odds in our favor."

"Yeah, but *nobody* knows that. Not even the judges. Each one only knows what scores he personally turns in on each girl. They all have to be correlated and tabulated before—"

"And who does this tabulation, pal?"

"Why . . . why . . . "

"*You*, buddy! Unless somebody's been lying to us. And smart people don't lie to us, Hal. They don't find it healthy."

"I'm not lying. I swear to you—"

"I know you're not lying, Hal. You're no chump. Are you?"

There was a moment's pause. "What do you want to know?"

"How are the fillies running in this race, pal? We want track positions."

"I—I have them here. But they're in sealed envelopes. I—I—"

"You got more envelopes handy, don't you? So unseal a few. You didn't get tongue-tied licking all that glue, boy?"

"Just a minute. Don't go away."

After a short wait, Petrie was back on the line again. "I—I have them."

"Shoot."

"In fifth place . . ." Petrie was unconsciously reading from the bottom up, in the same order the five finalists would be announced by Roger Megan on the Armory stage Saturday night. "In fifth place is Miss Alaska, Mildred Waxman."

"All right. In fourth place?"

"Miss Utah. That's Lori Macklin."

"Next?"

"Number three is California. Number two is New Jersey."

"So spring the big news. You're dragging your ass, Hal. Who's on top?"

"In first place is Miss Florida. Robin Gervais."

Robin! It was the general's turn to gulp. "By how strong a lead, Hal?"

"Four points. She's scored well with the judges all week, I see by the cards. But her answers in the judging interviews beat all the rest. That's what nailed down her lead."

"So it looks like Florida is the front-runner. Very interesting, Hal!"

"Look, mister, I told you everything. Now give me a break!"

"We aren't unreasonable, Hal. We scratch a back if the guy scratches ours."

"There's something else you should know, mister. I don't want you to think I loused you up. There's a third preliminary tomorrow night. A fluke could take place that could change the standings. I've seen it happen a few times."

"But you'll know if it does, won't you, Hal? I'll call again tomorrow night to see if there are any new developments. And you'll keep very close track for us, won't you—partner?"

"Partner? No."

"You're in it now, Hal. Right up to your ears. And don't forget it."

"I wish I could."

"Until tomorrow, Hal."

General Clinton Gervais nested the phone quietly. Robin! His Robin! Four points in the lead! But with New Jersey yelping at her heels!

BOOK SIX *Friday*

31 · MISS CALIFORNIA

THE DeGrays had just finished dressing for dinner when the closed-circuit speaker in the wall of their suite came on.

"Attention, all groups! Olga Loomis speaking for Sue Rossiter. Miss Washington, D.C., has this morning been validated as a Pageant contestant. She will participate in all three categories of competition in tonight's preliminary so that she can catch up on her points. She has already had her Q. and A. interview with the judges. We know you will welcome her warmly."

"Now I've got another girl to compete against!" Stacy exclaimed dolefully after the speaker went silent. "I saw her after the parade last night and she's wow!"

"I'll bet *she* doesn't have to worry about their damned no-repeat rule," Mrs. DeGray said bitterly.

"Mother, forget it. I've already given up hope of winning. If they guaranteed me second place this very minute, I'd grab it!"

"Well, I'm not going to settle for anything less than first." Mrs. DeGray's voice was filled with confidence. "Or there'll be the biggest stink since Pearl Harbor."

What old-time movie heavy is Mama playing now? Stacy wondered. Gail Patrick? Claire Dodd? She'd seen them both play bitchy parts in TV reruns.

"I told you they weren't going to cheat my baby of her fair chance at the crown," Mrs. DeGray went on. "I promised you that, didn't I? Well, dear, your mother is as good as her word."

"Mother, listen. I don't know what you've got in mind, but—"

"No, Stacy, *you* listen. We're going to Sue Rossiter's office together right now. Before this California-is-out-of-the-running business goes one hour further. And once Miss High and Mighty hears what I've got to say, there'll be some changes made."

Oh, Mama, Stacy wanted to say, the wind blows and the shit flows.

"Just like that, Mother?"

"Just like that!" Mrs. DeGray snapped her fingers, rage in her eyes. "Or the tip I'll pass along to Glenda Dowling will make the juiciest item since Jackie married Onassis. It's a powder keg that will wreck the Pageant!"

Stacy stared at her mother in puzzlement. "Wreck the Pageant?"

"They won't want the world to know, will they, that their darling Miss Rossiter is a common adulteress? Bedding down with that stallion Roger Megan? While he has a devoted wife and children waiting for him back home?" Her voice had the sting of a scorpion's tail.

"If we ever tried to cook up a story like that, Mother, we'd be sued for—"

"How can they sue when what we say is true? And we can prove it!"

Mrs. DeGray's eyes flared triumphantly. "I've got evidence, baby, evidence. Wait. I'll show you."

Mrs. DeGray stumped across the room to her bureau. She pulled back the center drawer, dipped into a pile of underthings. Buried under the heap was a leather camera case. She almost crowed with glee as she scooped it up, unsnapped the lid, and removed the camera.

Stacy's eyes widened. "Pictures? You have pictures of them in bed? I can't believe it!"

"Not pictures, dear. Trump cards." She placed the camera on the bureau, dug her fingers inside the case, and brought out a handkerchief.

"My first ace." she said. "One expensive handkerchief embroidered with the initials SR in the corner. Sue Rossiter's monogram. That's the hanky!"

Stacy studied the tiny square of lace, mystified.

Again her mother dipped into the empty case, groped for her second ace.

"And here's the panky!" She held up a small sheet of Hilton stationery. "Last Monday night I had one of my terrible migraines," she said. "I was all out of Excedrin, so I phoned the desk and asked them to get me a box. The hotel drugstore was closed, but the clerk was nice enough to call some all-night place and have them deliver it."

She paused to catch her breath, then continued.

"When the messenger arrived and I opened the door a crack to pay him, who did I see coming out of Roger Megan's suite but Sue Rossiter. At three in the A.M. I didn't believe my eyes. But the messenger recognized her, too. Because after she'd stepped into the elevator, he noticed that she'd dropped her hanky a few inches past Megan's door. 'I *thought* that was Sue Rossiter,' he told me when he picked it up and spotted her initials. I offered him fifty dollars to give me the hanky and write out a statement that he had practically seen her coming out of Megan's suite at three in the morning. He refused until I doubled the price."

Mrs. DeGray seemed crestfallen that Stacy hadn't applauded her brilliant summation.

"Now that you have this information—this evidence—what are you going to do with it, Mother?" Stacy asked.

"We're going to show it to Sue Rossiter and demand that she use her influence with Mr. Fleming to abolish their stupid rule. If Her Holiness doesn't agree, she can put it in her eggnog and smoke it. Then we'll hand it over to Glenda Dowling!"

Mrs. DeGray stormed into Sue Rossiter's office like a rhinoceros looking for something to gore. Stacy trailed behind her, her face apprehensive.

Olga Loomis looked up from her desk at the unexpected visitors. "Hello—Mrs. DeGray, isn't it? Can I help you?" There was mild surprise in her eyes.

"I've come to see Mrs. Rossiter on a personal matter. Very personal."

"I'm sorry. Miss Rossiter isn't in just now. She's meeting with Mr. Fleming on some Pageant business." Olga Loomis glanced at her watch. "She should be back very shortly."

"We'll wait," said Mrs. DeGray grimly. "We'll wait as long as may be necessary."

Olga Loomis made up her mind to be pleasant. Sue had warned her about Mrs. DeGray.

"Of course," she said. "You'll find that couch next to her desk very comfortable." Olga Loomis collected a stack of outgoing mail and rose. "Will you excuse me, please? I want to drop these off in time to catch the six-o'clock pickup." She smiled warmly at Stacy. "Good luck in the prelims tonight, just in case you're not here when I come back."

"Thanks, Miss Loomis," said Stacy. "I can use it."

Olga Loomis paused at the door. "I must tell you how much I enjoyed your mind-reading act the other night. Will you tell me how you did it after the contest is over?"

"After the contest is over," Stacy echoed.

The door shut, and Stacy coiled herself on the resilient

couch, grateful for the chance to relax. The imminent showdown Mama was about to force on Sue Rossiter had made her tense, tumbled her thoughts.

Oblivious to her daughter, Mrs. DeGray began to snoop around. A pile of opened letters in a wire basket on Sue Rossiter's desk caught her eye. She picked up the topmost one. There was a notation in the margin: "Mad Mail—send Xerox to Dr. Lydecker."

Mrs. DeGray read it swiftly. "Listen to this, Stacy. 'So I think it's my duty to tell you that this Maxine Howard who is now Miss North Carolina had two abortions and it's not fair for a bum like her should get to be a princess, as I know you folks will agree. I am not signing this letter as I wouldn't want my name on the same page with hers. Yours for a decent America, Anonymous.'

"Can you imagine, Stacy dear? In case this girl should beat you out, we could insist she be disqualified."

"M-mother . . . please, I don't think I can take any-more."

Mrs. DeGray whirled, dropped the letter back into the basket. She sat down on the couch beside her daughter. "Stacy? Baby—you're nervous, aren't you?"

"I'm so uptight I wish I could fall asleep and never wake up," Stacy sobbed. "I feel like over-all hell."

Instantly, Mama slipped a comforting arm around her shoulder. Her cloying perfume engulfed Stacy, inviting an attack of nausea.

Mama rocked her gently. "There, there, baby. Trust your mother. I can help."

"Nobody can help. Oh, I'm so tired of it all. If I just—if I could only—"

"You can," said the voice above her. "Here. Take it. Smoke it."

Freed of her mother's embrace, Stacy raised her head. She stared in amazement at the hand-rolled, crude cigarette held out to her between steady fingers. "You knew, Mother? You *knew?*"

"Of course I knew, child. Did you think the generation gap between us was so great I think pot is Tupperware? Baby, baby, we're so close. I've seen you through dolls, those awful tube things they put in your ears after the operation, braces on your teeth—everything. You should never be afraid to confide in your mother."

Stacy reached for the extended stick, a lifeline to sanity.

"But how could you make a connection here? We don't know a soul in Surf City."

"I didn't make a connection." Mrs. DeGray extracted a black-enameled cigarette case from her purse. She pressed it open, revealing a layer of joints.

"I found this in a corner of the living-room couch. I packed it in my luggage on a hunch."

"Charlie Walker's case! And he thought he'd lost it. Oh, Mother, you're wonderful!"

"Here, baby, I'll light it for you. Now, there you are . . . just puff in deep and pretty soon you won't be shaking so . . . that's my baby, puff again . . ."

Stacy dragged slowly, then greedily. A pungent smoke descended into her lungs. She let it linger there until she felt she would explode. Then, reluctantly, she let twin plumes escape from both her nostrils. Peace began to seep into her, the blissful, serene peace which had eluded her for the last four pressure-packed days.

"Of course I don't like it that you're on pot, Stacy. It's got to stop, once you're Princess America. You must promise me that."

"Anything, Mother. I'll never touch grass again. Just so there's something to help me through the crunch until Saturday night. I promise."

"Then, until you're Princess America all safe and sure, you just come to me when you feel the need for a little help. I'll have it ready, dear. Mother won't fail you. And once—"

Suddenly Mrs. DeGray snatched the half-smoked cigarette out of her daughter's hand and thrust it between her own thin lips. She had caught the tap of heels outside. The door opened and Sue Rossiter entered. As she shut it behind her, Mrs. DeGray took a short puff, then stubbed it in the nearby ashtray. Her excessive perfume hung heavy in the air, overpowering the acrid odor.

"Mrs. DeGray? Stacy? How nice to find you both here."

"Perhaps when you learn why we're here, Miss Sue Rossiter, you won't—"

"And what a coincidence! Because I was just about to call your suite and ask if you could visit me for a friendly little chat."

"A friendly little chat?"

"About that silly unwritten tradition of ours. The one against choosing a Princess from the same state two years in a row. Although we've never had occasion to enforce it, I know it's been troubling you. It's been troubling me, too. So entirely unfair for a lovely girl like Stacy, who's a top contender and deserves an even chance at the crown."

"Unfair, indeed. That's why we're here."

"I've just come from a meeting in Mr. Fleming's office, Mrs. DeGray, discussing the matter with our board of directors. And I'm so happy to tell you that we've changed the ground rules."

Mrs. DeGray seemed nonplussed. "I don't understand, Miss Rossiter . . ."

"We try to keep the Pageant honest, you know. The rumors about this 'unwritten tradition' have gotten out of hand. So today we've made it official. This year, and for every year from now on in, no girl is to be discriminated against if the previous winner came from her state. I give you my word that if Stacy scores highest, she's our next Princess. And a year from now—who knows? Still another Miss California may follow her."

A faint trail of smoke curled upward from the crushed cigarette, forming a vague question mark. Mrs. DeGray and Stacy sat stunned as Sue crossed the floor past them.

"If you'll give me just a moment to dash off a note for my assistant, asking her to notify the judges before tonight's preliminary . . ."

Reaching her desk, Sue stopped short abruptly.

"Oh, dear! When Olga spoke to the girls on our closed circuit a short while ago, she left the intercom key open."

Sue reached out and pushed a lever.

"How embarrassing!" She turned her head toward both DeGrays and smiled. "I do hope the two of you haven't been discussing family secrets. Because every word you said in here has gone out over our network. All the girls—and everyone in Mr. Fleming's office—overheard your entire conversation."

32 · GENERAL GERVAIS

SEATED inside the partioned flying office of his Army jet, General Clinton Gervais sat staring thoughtfully at the square of paper on his desk.

Five names were listed on its surface—the names of the contestants now holding the lead after the judges' scoring of this evening's preliminary, the last in the series. Gervais had obtained the updated list from Harold Petrie by calling the chief auditor from a telephone booth here at the airport, half an hour ago. Then he had scribbled down each name, together with accumulated points.

1.	Robin Gervais—Florida	284
2.	Darlene Bryant—New Jersey	281
3.	Lori Macklin—Utah	270
4.	Joyce Carrol—Washington, D.C.	268
5.	Mildred Waxman—Alaska	264

The big change since yesterday had been the abrupt elimination of Miss California. Petrie had explained that the management had discovered Stacy DeGray smoked pot. She had been immediately disqualified, all her points voided.

There were other revisions in the new ratings. Jersey had narrowed the gap between her and Robin by one point. Utah had advanced from fourth place to third. And Joyce Carrol, the black bombshell from the District of Columbia, had come on great in all three categories at tonight's preliminary and had crashed into fourth place.

If this voting pattern held constant tomorrow night, the contest would simmer down essentially to a race between his daughter and Miss New Jersey. Darlene Bryant was dangerously close to Robin. Too close.

Rapidly the general assessed the other contenders. Utah, fourteen points behind Robin, posed no problem. Waldo had caught her Ophelia scene and reported that the

Macklin girl had given a wooden performance. Miss D.C., however, was a literal dark horse not to be discounted. She could strike like a guerrilla from ambush; but that was a calculated risk he must take. Miss Alaska was no worry, no worry at all. From what Waldo had picked up, Mildred Waxman had collected a sympathy vote because she was Jewish.

No matter how he analyzed it, the real threat to Robin's winning the crown was Miss New Jersey. She had to be eliminated. Disqualified, like Miss California.

That was why he had phoned Dr. Lydecker from the airport a few minutes after he had spoken to Petrie.

That was why he had ordered Major Spofford to be ready to fly the jet at midnight on "official business."

And that was why he now carried fake documents in his briefcase and false credentials in his wallet.

Gervais reached for the copper grenade he had converted into a cigar lighter, held it over the ashtray, lit it, and fed the slip of paper into the flame, watched it shrivel into a patch of black cinder.

He picked up the phone that was his contact with the pilot.

"All set for take-off, Spofford?"

"We can go up as soon as he gets here, sir. Assuming the control towers clear us."

"Good. If you should have any occasion to speak to me while my party is here, Major, just call me general. Because of the Pageant, you know. He might link me with Robin. The security matter I'm discussing with him has no connection. But if he thought I was using my rank to impress him on her behalf—well, I wouldn't want that."

"I understand. I'll be careful, General."

"I'm General Simpson—Arthur Simpson. And I am with the Central Intelligence Agency," Gervais had said on the phone in the airport when he had called Dr. Lydecker earlier.

And the slightly accented, weary voice at the other end had responded with a polite "Yes, General?"

"I am calling about an extremely sensitive matter, Doctor. It involves national security. My talking to you in private is absolutely vital."

"What do you suggest, General?"

"My official plane is at the airport. If you could meet me there in an hour, we can be certain of strict privacy. Not even your superior, Mr. Fleming, must know of my mission."

"Unusual, most unusual."

"But necessary, I assure you. You will come?"
"In one hour? It is now ten-thirty. Where shall I look for you?"
"The plane will be on Runway Three, cleared and ready to take us up."
The minutes dragged by. General Gervais scowled. He was not a patient man. He began to worry when his watch indicated a quarter to twelve. Had something happened to Lydecker? Had he been sidetracked on an emergency call?
But, happily, his fears were groundless.
Outside the steel wire fence paralleling Runway Three, Gervais saw a modest sedan turn in from the service road and brake. Its headlights cut off. A man, almost sparrow-like in silhouette, climbed out of the car and began walking toward the Electra.
"Dr. Lydecker? Thank you for coming at this nasty hour. I'm General Simpson."
As Lydecker seated himself, Gervais signaled Spofford to take off. Then he turned to his guest.
"I do apologize, Doctor, for the aura of mystery about this meeting." He smiled. "You must be feeling like a character in a cloak-and-dagger melodrama."
"Frankly, General, I am more interested in explanations than in apologies."
"Of course. As soon as we're airborne. Will you please buckle your seat belt?"
The plane was already nosing smoothly down the runway. The roar of the jet motors discouraged conversation. Five minutes later, leveling off at the three-mile altitude the control tower had prescribed, they unfastened their seat belts.
"A cigar, Dr. Lydecker, before we begin?"
"I don't smoke, thanks. Not for a good many years now. But may I see your credentials?"
Behind tinted glasses worn for the occasion, General Gervais blinked. He had intended to display his forged card, but he resented the other man taking the initiative.
He brought out his wallet, passed it over to his visitor.
"Thank you, General." Lydecker studied it carefully, reading it line by line. Gervais stuck his hand out, waiting for the wallet to be returned, but Lydecker held on to it.
"Just a formality, General Simpson," the doctor said, "but will you please remove your glasses for a moment so that I can compare your face with the photograph on this card? You did say national security was involved."
Gervais cursed under his breath. The bastard. Was he suspicious, or had he read too many spy novels?

"Why, certainly, Doctor." He lifted his glasses while Lydecker scrutinized his features, then swiveled his eyes back to the card. "I'm glad to see you're a man of caution," Gervais added.

Lydecker nodded as he gave back the wallet, ignoring the flattery. "Now, then, General, what's this all about?"

Far below, the night city with its dimples of light had given way to darker coastline.

General Gervais leaned closer toward Lydecker, adopted a confidential tone.

"To explain this unfortunate crisis," he began. "We know, of course, that you are the official physician for the Princess America Pageant. You've held this position for many years. In this capacity you must know that it has been standard procedure for Mr. Fleming to submit a list of all state finalists to us for a clearance check. And that, over the years, we've been able to weed out several undesirables. Last season, for example, we discovered that one girl was strongly pro-Castro and had visited Cuba by way of a flight from Montreal."

Dr. Lydecker shook his head. "Yes. John told me about her. Miss Illinois, wasn't it?"

"Correct."

General Gervais was dealing from strength. And truth. The name General Arthur Simpson was not fictitious. Neither was his affiliation with the CIA. The two generals shared offices in the Pentagon.

It was because of his professional association and friendship with Simpson that Gervais had been able to construct a viable cover for tonight. Two weeks ago, Simpson had indeed checked out the annual list submitted by Fleming for the usual security check. Robin's name appeared on it along with the others. Simpson had joked about it, asking what his fellow officer would do if he had to report that Robin was a female Benedict Arnold.

Gervais had looked up the agency's Pageant file one day when Simpson had flown to Dallas and familiarized himself with the results of past years' investigations.

The file had sparked the genesis of his back-up plot to manipulate the contest in favor of Robin. High in a security branch of the government, Gervais had easy access to blank identification cards and stationery.

It was a thousand-to-one shot that his brief impersonation of General Simpson would be detected. The official plane with the Air Force insignia. His uniform with one silver star on each shoulder. His perfectly forged identity card. His inside knowledge of previous Pageant security check-ups. The package was foolproof, as official as a Presidential seal.

Lydecker would have to be clairvoyant to smell a rat.

The doctor's voice interrupted his musings.

"Thus far, General, I haven't heard anything I didn't already know."

Again Gervais leaned forward confidentially.

"This morning, Doctor, we learned that one of this year's contestants has extremely radical leanings. Many of her actions border on treason."

Lydecker played with the catch of his seat buckle. "I find that very difficult to believe, General. At any rate, you seem to have a security problem here, not a medical one."

"On the surface, yes. But bear with me a moment, Doctor. I phoned your chief auditor, Mr. Harold Petrie, as soon as this report came in. He told me the girl is so high in the standings she has an excellent chance to win tomorrow night. That must not happen. That is why I had to come here personally. There isn't time enough to proceed through the usual channels."

"Who is the girl, may I ask?"

"Her name is Darlene Bryant. Miss New Jersey."

Lydecker was silent for a moment, trying to recall the girl.

"Ah, yes. I place her now," he said. "Physically, sound as a dollar. And very pretty. But treason? She seemed neither neurotic nor compulsive."

"Treason may be too purple a word. Let's substitute subversive. Look here."

A carefully prepared document, typed earlier in the day on Waldo's borrowed portable, came out of the general's briefcase and was handed to Lydecker. The paper carried an impressive Central Intelligence Agency letterhead.

June 8, 1969—contributed $700 Soviet Cultural Society

Sept. 5, 1969—contributed $1,000 Black Panthers

Nov. 7, 1969—speaker at rally for Campus Disruptions Committee

Jan. 3, 1970—contributed $500 Friends of Social Reorientation

The list was considerably longer. It included a dozen underground newspapers and left-wing organizations which had benefitted from Darlene Bryant's cash contributions, or by her personal appearance at their secret meetings.

"You see our problem, Doctor? The girl can't be allowed to win. Can you imagine her traveling abroad as a Princess America—an unofficial ambassador for our country? Apt to embarrass our government by making irresponsible statements which our enemies could twist into anti-American propaganda? Free to make contacts with foreign agents!"

"What I don't understand," said Lydecker slowly, "is why a girl as rich as this one obviously is should follow the party line. Those contributions weren't jelly beans. Her father must be very wealthy."

"He's a millionaire a few times over. Operates a national construction-supply business. How to explain it? Who can? You know what kids are nowadays, Doctor. Kooks. Rebels. Anti-establishment."

"I've seen plenty of that. It's a—"

The plane lurched, chopping off Lydecker's words. Spofford had hit a storm. Lightning bolts blitzed the sky. The Electra leaped, then dropped thirty feet like an elevator whose cable had just snapped.

Lydecker felt the dormant hand inside his chest come to life, grab his arteries and begin to choke them. His fingers shook as they probed his jacket pocket for an ampule. He released the amyl nitrite under his nostrils, then let his head fall back against the seat cushion.

"Doctor?" General Gervais' face was grave. "What's wrong? Can you talk?"

"A chronic c-condition," Lydecker gasped. "Not serious. It will pass."

It passed. Gervais became genuinely alarmed. Christ! A heart condition! If he had so much as suspected that there was a chance the old medic might croak on him, up here in the clouds, and that there could be the aftermath of a corpse to explain away . . .

"You're feeling better? A glass of water? Would you like to lie down?"

"Thank you, General. I need nothing. It's over. Like the storm."

Sure enough, Spofford had fought them out of the squall. Light rain still splashed the windows, but the violence was behind.

"I apologize this time," said Lydecker, sitting upright as he spoke. "Let's return to Miss Bryant."

"Yes. Her winning this contest must be prevented."

"You said John Fleming wasn't to know. Surely he's the man to—"

Gervais had anticipated Lydecker's question. He had an answer ready. Would the doctor buy it?

"We have a delicate situation here," he said. "Mr. Fleming is a close friend of the Bryant girl's father. He owns a substantial number of shares in his company's stock. I'd be putting him on the spot. Out of loyalty to his friend, he could claim we were on a witch hunt, the old red-herring smear. After all, the girl hasn't done anything *illegal*. No, it would be best if we didn't stir up this hornets' nest."

The answer made sense, and Lydecker seemed to accept its validity. For a man who a few moments ago appeared to be on the brink of death, he was astoundingly sharp. Too sharp, as his next question indicated.

"If the girl is red-oriented as you say, General, and has so much money, surely she must have traveled abroad. If you could show Fleming that she visited Russia, or East Germany . . . or one of the Central American republics. That would convince him."

Again Gervais was able to supply a reasonable answer.

"She's made several attempts to visit abroad since we've had her under surveillance. But her passport applications have been denied on various technicalities. Her application is 'lost' in processing, or is 'incorrectly' filled out. The State Department has invented ingenious excuses to keep her on a leash. But now there's a new deal. She's pushing for Princess America. If she makes it, how will it look, our efforts to fence in the symbol of American womanhood?"

"The pinko press could have a field day, yes," Lydecker said. "Persecution. Denial of constitutional rights. The whole chant."

"In the end, we'd have to let her roam. And face international humiliation because our chosen flower is a crown-carrying Commie. So—we need you, Doctor."

"Me?"

"We thought it might be best for you to disqualify her on some medical pretext. You could claim you overlooked something when you examined her previously."

"How can I possibly do that? She is a strong, healthy girl. She does a sensational high-wire act, requiring perfect reflexes and stamina."

"How about a cardiac condition?"

"It would never stand up. I'd have to forbid her to perform her act tomorrow night. Ground her."

"Can't you report late lab findings? Something detected in her urine?"

Lydecker was by now almost restored to normal color, mulling the problem deeply.

"We can't do that either. In the old days we gave them all a urinalysis and a vaginal to test them for pregnancy. But then we were sandbagged by the father of one contestant, a prominent lawyer. He sued the Pageant for coercion and invasion of his daughter's privacy. When our legal department advised us that the courts would probably uphold him, we made a prompt settlement."

Lydecker smiled warmly. "I often wonder if our changed rule saved any poor little rabbits from dying."

Frustration began to shatter the general's confidence. It was the old jinx at work again. The Clinton Gervais jinx that seldom failed. He had painstakingly evolved a surefire way to eliminate Robin's closest rival. He had convinced Lydecker, who was far from being a fool. And now the whole house of cards was about to collapse.

"General Simpson?"

There was a bright nuance in the doctor's voice. The quality of Eureka. Gervais tensed.

"In our examinations this past week," Lydecker said, "I had to disqualify one girl for diabetes. I first suspected it while checking her eyes. Then her blood test confirmed it. Suppose I say my nurse made an error and recorded this case on the wrong card instead of on Jersey's? Suppose I report a correction? This girl who's actually a diabetic can't win anyhow. Worst talent I've ever seen. And we wrote her family doctor to break the news to her as soon as she gets home."

The general's eyes glinted with elation behind their glass mask.

"I think you've managed to fly us out of heavy weather, Doctor."

"I'll call Sue Rossiter tomorrow and instruct her to have our auditor disqualify Miss New Jersey. I'll play it typically routine. That way I'll bypass Fleming."

Fifteen minutes later, they were rolling to a standstill on Runway Three. The men shook hands. Gervais maintained a mien that was solemn and grateful. But he still felt sky-high, gravity free, even though he was now on solid ground.

BOOK SEVEN *Saturday*

33 · MISS ALASKA

MILDRED WAXMAN stood at the window and watched the early-morning haze that swathed Surf City gradually lift under the rising sun. She was fighting a case of creeping nerves. Behind her the breakfast cart was neat and untouched, the polished aluminum plate covers now cool. The thought of food nauseated her.

She breathed deeply and told herself there were no more days, just hours and minutes and seconds. She worked her fingers, which seemed suddenly arthritic and incapable of spanning an octave.

She was alone, her chaperone waiting in the lobby. She could be thankful for that. No need to pose, to smile. Ten blessed minutes alone before descending to the arena. How many reassuring, calming breaths was that? She drew more air into her lungs. From a short distance she heard muffled voices, Mepala's throaty laugh.

Mildred turned from the window and listened, directing an ear toward the half-open door that separated her suite from Miss Hawaii's.

" . . . you are, Dave." Mepala's voice.

Dave? Mildred walked softly across the room, still listening.

"I thought it was the least I could do."

Yes, Dave. In Mepala's room? Mildred stopped near the door and flushed a bit, feeling guilty for eavesdropping.

"You're a darling, Dave. An absolute darling."

"Your humble servant, Milady."

Mildred felt a slight chill. What were they talking about? And they sounded so chummy, so *friendly*. Suddenly, Mildred thought she would cry. She was jealous. Absolutely green-eyed!

"Screw the Princess!" A squawk. "Find the right hole!"

Mildred couldn't help herself. Her emotional balloon burst and she laughed uproariously.

"That you, Alaska?" Mepala called, pushing the door fully open. Mildred smiled and entered. Mepala's eyes twinkled and she held up a cage and turned to her bird. "See what effect you have on nice girls, King Kam?"

"Find the right hole!" said King Kam, tilting his head toward Mildred. "Screw nice girls!"

Mildred laughed until tears spilled down her face. She wiped her eyes with a handkerchief and saw Dave materialize next to Mepala through the mist. He was grinning.

". . . a present," Dave was saying. "You girls won't be back here until after the finals, so I thought I'd liberate King Kam from the storage room and let him wish Mepala luck. Besides, the porter was spoiling him. He was teaching him socially acceptable language."

"Isn't Dave an angel?" Mepala said to Mildred. "Win, lose or draw, I've got my fella back. Right, King Kam?"

"Get your clothes off. I'm horny!"

The three of them laughed.

"And to show I'm not playing favorites," Dave said between chuckles, "I've got a present for you, too, Alaska."

Mildred was pleased and not a little embarrassed that she could have thought whatever it was that she thought. But her reply was airy.

"Oh, Dave, it's not necessary. Really. After the wonderful way you helped me through my talent preliminary."

"But I insist."

"And I," said Mepala with a wink, "have to hide my bird and touch up my face. Thanks, Dave. And I'll see you downstairs in a few minutes, Mildred."

"Right," said Mildred, looking at Dave with what she hoped was a neutral expression. "About five minutes." Mepala backed into her room and closed the door.

"That gives me just enough time for my presentation," Dave said in overly formal tones. "Miss Alaska, darling Mildred, my gift to you, which I humbly present with my fondest wishes."

Mildred took the flat, oblong package he extended with a mock curtsy and said, "Miss Alaska accepts your humble offering, O lowly servant."

"There is one condition, O fair maid."

"And that is, pray tell?"

"That you won't open it until you return tonight after they crown the new Princess."

"Will you be here?"

Dave became serious. "No, I'm afraid I won't. I'm riding back to school with one of the guys from another hotel. We'll leave right from the Armory after they announce the winner."

"Oh." Mildred felt empty. She wanted to say it had been nice, that she was glad they had met, that he meant something more than a brief moment in her life. But all she said was "Oh, I see." She lowered her eyes and regarded the package in her hands. It had no meaning anymore.

"Hey," said Dave, stepping forward and lifting her chin with an open, gentle hand. "What's this? I bring a present and the queen is not joyous?"

Mildred searched his smiling face for a sign, a movement, *anything*. And again, emotions tumbling on each other, she thought she would cry. She spoke only with her eyes.

"Mildred . . . " Dave was serious again. "Mildred . . . "

Eli Waxman would not have recognized his shy daughter in the girl who moved without conscious thought, moved in response to an aching need. She kissed Dave hard and long and went limp in his arms, his gift dropping to the rug. And he held her, warm and gentle with arms of strength, this man who was safe and sure and who moved in her dreams. She felt his lips brush her car, felt his arms loosen and move her slowly away.

"You must go now," he said softly. "It's your day. You'll be wonderful."

"And our day?" Her voice was a plaintive whisper. "Will it ever be our day?"

Dave released her and smiled. "Stranger things have happened. I know where Juneau is and you know where I am. The mails move in both directions."

Mildred sniffed and brushed at her eyes and tried to smile with partial success. Then she bent and retrieved the package. "At least let me open this before you go."

"No, I'd rather you didn't."

"But why, Dave? I want . . ."

"Trust me." He paused. "Now promise you won't open it until the contest is over."

Mildred tried to find the answer in his eyes, but couldn't. His request was unreasonable. She couldn't go the day without knowing. But she said, "I promise."

Dave kissed her on the cheek and walked to the door. He opened it and turned. "*Mazeltov*, Millie. *Mazeltov*." He added softly, "Maybe when I see you next you'll be America's Princess. Or just my personal Princess." Then he was gone.

Mildred stood transfixed for a moment, unable to move

or think, the package still clutched in her hand. Then, without taking her eyes from the door, she tore open the wrapping and drew out the contents. And before she looked, she closed her eyes and prayed to God to forgive her for breaking her promise and to make whatever it was a beginning and not an end.

The note was clipped to a recent copy of the *Journal of the American Dermatology Association*. It read:

> MILLIE:
>
> I don't know if this is applicable in your case, but it might be. I hope it is. It starts on Page 105. In any case, please don't think of this as anything but an attempt to make you happy. I wouldn't hurt you for the world. All my love.
>
> DAVE

Mildred flipped through the magazine until she found the right page. She folded the journal open and read the title: "The Adjunctive Use of the Laser Beam in Cosmetic Surgery."

A cry caught in her throat. *My God! He knows! Somehow, he knows!*

With racing heart she read the brief article:

> Conventional plastic surgery to remove tattoos takes a long time and often leaves unsightly scars. But using laser beams, a team of University of Cincinnati doctors have developed a technique that literally explodes tattoo dyes out of the skin, vaporizing the particles. Preliminary results are so promising that the technique may shortly be used to treat soldiers who are literally tattooed when explosions implant tiny metallic fragments beneath their skins. . . .

Mildred let the magazine fall to the floor, dazed and feeling the great hope swell in her breast. He couldn't have known for sure the nature of her scar, but there it was. A possible cure for her albatross.

And I love you too, Dave. I love you with all my being. You silly fool. Why didn't you wait? Why? Did you think I wouldn't understand? Dave . . .

An urgent knock on the door shattered her thoughts.

"Mildred?" It was a breathless Mepala. "Mildred, what's holding you up? We're all ready to leave."

"Just a second," Mildred stammered, scooping up the

journal and stuffing it into a bureau drawer and dashing to the mirror to doctor her makeup. "One second."

And dabbing at her eyes and touching up her lipstick, Mildred Waxman, the fluke from Alaska, knew she was in the running for the top prize in Surf City and it had nothing to do with the selection of Princess America.

34 · DR. LYDECKER

FRANZ LYDECKER sat behind his desk and massaged his temples with the fingertips of both hands. He was not given to headaches, but he had one now, literally and figuratively. It has got to be reasonable and direct, he told himself. Routine. Above suspicion. An unfortunate error that merely needed correction. It occasionally happened.

Lydecker took a deep breath, reached for the telephone and dialed.

"Miss Rossiter's office. Miss Loomis speaking."

"Hello, Olga. This is Dr. Lydecker." Keep it simple. Nothing really amiss. "Is Sue there?"

"No, Dr. Lydecker. Can I help?"

"I don't think so, Olga. I wanted to talk directly to Sue. Nothing serious."

"Norm Prescott is just leaving. Want me to catch him?"

"Yes," said Lydecker, too quickly. "That is . . . yes, Norm would be fine. I just want to clarify something."

"Hold on."

Lydecker rubbed his forehead with his free hand and listened to Olga call out and tell Prescott he was on the telephone. He heard the footsteps approaching the other end of the line.

"Franz? What's up?"

"I'm afraid we've made a little booboo over here," Lydecker said, trying to keep the urgency out of his voice. "I wonder if you could get a message to our tally man. It's rather important."

"By all means, Franz. Shoot."

"Well, between Dr. Bernstein and myself we somehow missed out on Miss New Jersey," Lydecker said glibly. "I've just been checking the forms and it turns out she should have been black-marked for diabetes but wasn't. Will you get that through to the chief auditor so she is disqualified?"

"Certainly," said Prescott. "Glad you caught it."

"Fine," said Lydecker, convinced by Prescott's tone of voice that he suspected nothing. "Thank you, Norm."

Lydecker replaced the receiver, rose and walked to the filing cabinet in the empty examining room. He pulled out Miss New Jersey's form and returned to his desk. He glanced through the form, absently reading Maggie's scribbled notations and Bernstein's added comments in that fine accountant's hand. The handwriting wouldn't match, but that could be explained.

Childhood diseases: None. Scars: Small curved mark, lower right extremity, four inches above the knee. Healing vaccination, upper right arm, two inches below the shoulder. Operations: None. Allergies: None. Blood Tests: Normal.

Lydecker's head jerked involuntarily. An icy cold seemed to envelop his body. He stared at the form without moving a muscle, the blue ink rising from the page and burning acidlike into his brain. He sat that way for a long interval, the limited possibilities spinning through his mind, the one he feared the most rising above the others. He shuddered and dropped the form to the desk, bringing his hands to his face, rubbing, thinking—furiously thinking. And behind it all he could feel the pressure bands in his chest.

Finally, Lydecker moved. He grabbed the phone and dialed three short digits. "Miss New Jersey's number. Quickly." He didn't recognize his own voice. The pitch was much too high. He listened, jotted the number on a prescription pad and slammed the receiver down, retrieving it almost immediately to dial the number he had noted.

Lydecker drummed his fingers on the desk as the circuits rolled and clicked and a telephone rang somewhere out across Surf City. If only she were still in her room, taking her half-hour break after lunch.

"Miss New Jersey's suite," a voice answered after he had cleared himself with the operator. "This is Mrs. Martin."

"Mrs. Martin, this is Dr. Franz Lydecker. Is Miss . . ." Lydecker's eyes flew to the form on his desk. "Is Miss Bryant there? If she is, can you get her to my office immediately? It's extremely important."

"We were just leaving, but I guess . . ." Mrs. Martin's voice trailed off, obviously in confusion over the rush of Lydecker's words.

"This is absolutely necessary. Please. Right now."

Lydecker hung up, starved for breath, fighting the

bricks being piled onto his chest. He thrust a hand into his jacket pocket and pulled out another vial of amyl nitrite, crushed it and inhaled the fumes. He felt himself go limp for a moment. Then his lungs were free to expand. He loosened his shirt collar, then relaxed as the pressure eased off.

He leaned back in his chair and tried to assemble his thoughts. But there was still discomfort in his chest. He pressed his right hand against his breast bone and told himself to relax completely, his eyes closed, his thoughts swirling in eddies, going nowhere.

When Mrs. Martin arrived with Darlene Bryant, Lydecker was still resting in his chair.

"We came as fast as we could," said Mrs. Martin, a thin woman with pinched features. Both she and Darlene seemed troubled. "You sounded so . . ."

Lydecker came forward in his chair and waved the woman silent. "Just routine, I assure you," he said, picking up the medical form. "I can't read the writing here, something about a scar on your arm?"

"Oh," said Darlene with a sigh of relief. "It's nothing but a vaccination mark." She walked to the desk and extended her right arm. "See? It's practically healed."

Lydecker looked and saw and asked the question he wasn't sure he wanted answered. *"You see, Doctor, we can't possibly allow this young lady to leave the country."* He braced himself. "Why were you vaccinated at your age?"

"I had to," Darlene answered. "As a gift for winning the state title, my parents treated me to a week in Barbados. I had to get a smallpox shot."

"Her passport applications have been denied on various technicalities."

Lydecker knew his next question would be superfluous. "You have a passport, I take it?"

"Of course. I got it two years ago when we spent a summer in Switzerland."

"Thank you," Lydecker interrupted. "That will be all. Please close the door on your way out." The suspicion that had been dogging him for the past hour now swept over him as a tidal wave would swamp a small boat.

The two women stood motionless for a moment and then turned and left the office in utter confusion.

Lydecker shook himself and snatched up the phone the moment the door closed and dialed Fleming's number. The Old Man wasn't in. Sue was out. Prescott was gone. But the plane and the uniform and the documents . . .

How . . . ? Why . . . ? Lydecker feverishly dialed several other numbers. Everyone was out. Christ, are they all out walking the boardwalk? The Armory number was busy.

In desperation, Lydecker dialed Roger Megan's office suite.

"He's out, but he's due back any minute," answered Lou Cates. "Max Gerber is waiting for him with some publicity pictures he'd requested."

Lydecker was about to hang up when he caught himself. "By the way, do you know of any contestant who is in any way connected with the . . . military?"

"Offhand, no. No, wait a minute. Didn't Miss Florida fly here in an Army plane or something? I think I remember Prescott mentioning it the other day. Want me to check it out?"

Lydecker hung up without a word and almost ran to the cabinet, where he dug out Miss Florida's form. He began to sweat.

Father: Brigadier General Clinton Gervais! The form fluttered to the floor as Lydecker raced out of the office.

"I'm General Simpson—Arthur Simpson. And I am with the Central Intelligence Agency . . ."

"Sonofabitch!" Lydecker cursed as he flagged down a taxi and jumped in. "The dirty sonofabitch."

"How's that?" the driver said.

Lydecker had the cabbie take him to Megan's hotel and told the driver to wait. If Megan wasn't in, he'd go on to the Armory.

He climbed the stone steps leading to the lobby elevator, unmindful of his rapid heartbeat and the weight constricting his lungs.

Max Gerber opened the door for him.

"Hello, Franz. What are you . . . ?"

Gerber never finished the sentence. He saw Lydecker go completely white and stumble, one hand pressed to his chest. Gerber tried to catch him, but Lydecker wheeled and smashed into Megan's desk, knocking a typewriter case to the floor. Then he sank to the floor, pitching over flat on his back.

Gerber ran to Lydecker's side and loosened the stricken man's pants belt. Little bubbles of spittle were forming at the corners of Lydecker's bluish lips. Gerber turned toward Cates. "Man, don't just stand there? Call the police! Get an ambulance!" Cates stiffened, then headed for the extension on the coffee table.

Lydecker made a rattling sound and Gerber swung back to him, noticing as he did the typewriter case, which had sprung open when it fell. He saw the small tanks and the mask. *Oxygen?* He couldn't believe what he saw. He pulled the case over, tested the dials with the mask against his own mouth and nose until he felt the rush of pure oxygen, then held the mask over Lydecker's face.

"Breathe," Gerber coached. "Deep. An ambulance is on the way."

Lydecker stirred and twisted his face away from the hissing mask. Gerber tried to get it back in place, but the mouth was moving, forming words. Gerber leaned closer, his ear by Lydecker's lips.

"Tell Fleming . . . contest fixed . . . by General . . . for . . . Florida . . . Jersey already . . . disqualified . . . must . . . be . . . reinstated . . ."

Gerber lifted his head when the words stopped.

He looked directly into the wide-open, vacant eyes of a dead man.

Max Gerber was slumped in a chair facing Cates when they carried the body out. A volunteer fireman carrying a pulmotor stopped between them, not looking at either, and said: "We tried. It was just too late. Ain't none of us ever going to forget him. He saved a lot of our men in his day." Then he followed the others out of the suite, tears rolling down his cheek.

Gerber sat in his own insulated world, a world where death was no stranger. Some die young, he thought, like his wife. Others when they are old. Old is better. And the words. What did the words mean? Somehow, incredibly, the contest has been fixed. For Miss Florida? New Jersey, a top favorite, could win, but somehow she's been disqualified. General? What general? General what?

". . . to him."

Gerber looked up and realized Cates had been talking. "I'm sorry, Lou," he said. "You were saying?"

"I said I had just been talking to him. On the telephone. He seemed to want to see Megan very badly. Oh, my God! Roger's going to take this hard."

Gerber watched him closely. "Did Franz say what he wanted?"

"No. He just asked for Roger. That and about Miss Florida." He paused.

"Well, not really Miss Florida." Gerber's heart sank. "What he asked was if I knew of any contestant who was somehow connected with the military and the only one I could think of was Miss Florida. I think her father's a big-shot general."

General! Gerber leaned back and closed his eyes. It fit,

he thought. Miss Florida's father had somehow fixed the contest; he had somehow gotten Miss New Jersey disqualified. And Lydecker had somehow stumbled on the whole can of worms. Darlene Bryant was out.

Gerber rose from his chair and extended the eight-by-eleven manila envelope to Cates. "With all that's happened, I don't think I'll wait for Roger. He probably wouldn't be interested now in the pictures anyway. But I'll leave them with you, just in case."

"Thanks, Max. I'll have Roger call you if it's necessary."

Gerber took the elevator down and presently emerged into the sunshine of Surf City. The sun was warm. He decided to walk. Miss New Jersey figured to win, he thought. But now Lydecker was dead and so was she. He felt a warmth growing within that had nothing to do with the sun.

The front-runners were falling one by one. First Colorado, Hawaii, then California and now New Jersey. And Miss Florida is playing with a stacked deck. He smiled as he walked. Well, there is nothing to worry about there. Nothing at all.

35 · MISS UTAH

SINCE that unconsummated episode in the police garage, Lori had given Steve Dorn no trouble. He had dutifully chauffeured her about town on her various appointed rounds, but he had kept himself virtually incommunicado from her.

He had even avoided meeting her eyes in his windshield mirror. From his long experience as a cop, he well knew the fury of a woman scorned.

Mrs. Birkenbuel, honoring the tradition observed by all chaperones on the eve of the finals, had invited Lori home with her for a quiet family dinner. Dorn had dropped them off and sped back to Nancy to share a Chicken Delight meal she had ordered. When he returned an hour later, with the car's top up, he was surprised to see Lori coming out of the big Tudor house unescorted. She had climbed in behind him with the murmured explanation that Mrs. Birkenbuel was expecting an overseas call from her honeymooning daughter.

Dorn knew she was leaning against his headrest when he caught a whiff of the Arpege perfume she always used.

Her voice in his ear sounded like a child's. "Steve?"

He answered with a slight nod.

"Steve, I've waited for a chance ever since that night. A chance to tell you I'm sorry."

He kept his eyes on the wheel, his eyes forward.

"I know you think I'm a tramp. Maybe that's all I really am. But I don't mean to be. It's just that when something inside me gets going—"

"Sure," he countered dryly. "It's like a hiccup. You can't suppress it."

"Don't make fun—please. At least believe I'm trying to apologize. I don't know how I'll be able to face the audience tonight. I'm so ashamed of myself."

Dorn found himself half wanting to be convinced. He lit a cigarette to pollute the enticing scent of her perfume.

"I—I guess it's no use trying to make you understand," Lori went on. In his mirror, he could see her underlip twitch. "But it's always been this way. When Marge told me I was sick, I laughed at her. But now I realize it's true. Marge is my older sister."

Marge. What could she tell him about Marge that he didn't already know?

"Marge is so good to me. She's tried everything to help. She's spent hundreds—thousands—sending me to expensive psychiatrists."

The kid sounded worshipful. *My God, didn't she know?*

"And she's so fine herself, Steve. I never really appreciated her. I've hurt her, insulted her. Yet I know she'd give her right arm to see me straightened out. But I'm rotten clean through. I don't deserve a sister like her."

It was too much, that last line. Lori couldn't be making up anything so far out. It had to be for real. Dorn chanced another quick glance in his mirror. Gone was her invincible smile.

"How can I face her, Steve? When I've still got this dirty worm eating away inside me. I'd kill myself if she ever found out how I acted in that garage."

Dorn debated with himself. In his years as a cop, he often had to break the news to wives that their husbands were killers, narcotics pushers, rapists or bank robbers. They had reacted with tears, shock, hysteria and fainting spells. Some had cursed him, spit at him, and one dope-crazed woman had even tried to knife him. He remembered a high-society broad who had offered him a weekend on the Riviera, with her classy chassis thrown in. All she demanded was that he release her lover, whom he had picked up for a hit-and-run auto death, and give him twelve hours to fly to South America. When Dorn had responded by handcuffing the guy, she had tried to scratch his eyes out.

Now, as Dorn decided to tell the truth to Lori about her sister, he wondered which of these reactions he would be triggering.

He twisted his head obliquely and looked into her eyes.

"Lori, listen to Doctor Dorn. What's giving you your big hangup is that you've put your sister on a pedestal."

"Why not? Compared to a decent girl like Marge, I'm . . . filth."

Steve snorted. "I have news for you. Compared to Big Sister, you're Little Orphan Annie."

"What kind of a crack is that?" she bristled. "You've never even seen my sister."

"Oh, I've seen Marge. And a lot more like her."

"You couldn't have. You don't even know what she looks like."

"Don't I? Remember Thursday, when I drove you to the Torchlight Parade? You'd left your wallet in the back seat?"

"Yes, I remember. But what has my wallet to do with—"

"I examined it to see if it was yours or your chaperone's. It was yours, all right. And the snapshot in one of the plastic cases. The attractive blonde in the air-stewardess uniform who looks like you. She's your sister, right?"

"That's Marge. But why are you hinting—"

"Because I put in two years with our vice squad, Lori. Look, you can quit bugging yourself about disgracing a paragon. I recognized her right off. She's one of our convention regulars."

"What—what are you saying?"

"Just what you think. Your precious Marge—the idol you bleed for—is a call girl. A hotel hustler. A camp follower. This week she's playing Surf City. She takes dough, and big dough too, for what you've been hating yourself for giving out free."

"That's a lie. My sister's been an air stewardess for years!"

"She wears the uniform, sure. A lot of the smart pros do. It's the perfect cover. It gets them to whatever big city the current action's at. It gets them rooms in good hotels."

He waited nervously for her reaction. Claws? Curses? Shock?

It was neither. Lori leaned back against the upholstery and laughed. "For a moment I almost believed you," she said. "Until I realized it was a gag. Like my pulling that gun on you and pretending I'd shoot."

"You've got to learn the truth, Utah. So that you'll stop tormenting yourself. She's here in Surf City. Did you know that?"

"Of course I know. She came to my room the other night to wish me luck."

"And then went back to her own room to service any hard-up guy who will pay for a hot screw."

"That's a lie. You don't even know where Marge is staying."

"We know. Suite 2508 at the Regency Hotel. Putting

out for all comers at a C note a crack. Her room's a one-girl bordello."

"You're still kidding," Lori said. "Steve, please tell me it's a joke."

"Why would I kid you? I just don't want you to go into the finals feeling uptight, because you think you've let your sister down. Whatever you've done, she's done in spades. For a price. She's what we call a diaper-to-death whore. And the vice squad would have booked her if I hadn't begged Captain Boyd to look the other way. Because I was afraid she might be connected to you."

The disbelief in Lori's eyes changed to hate.

"Bastard. Lying bastard. You're making all this up because I told you I was feeling so ashamed of myself I couldn't face an audience tonight. You're still thinking of your lousy cops' pool. You're hoping I'll be your ticket to the jackpot."

Dorn could hear a door open, the sound of Mrs. Birkenbuel's heels as she hurried down the mansion's steps. He reached into his pocket and took out a key, then stretched his arm back over his seat and pressed it into Lori's hand. Before he could explain his action, Mrs. Birkenbuel was climbing in beside Lori with a breathless sigh.

"Thanks for waiting, both of you," she said. "But the Copenhagen circuits were busy and Irene had to reach me through London."

Steve turned on the ignition. The car started moving, smooth as a swan on a pond. But behind him he could feel the hate in Lori's eyes.

He couldn't do her much good after all. Not unless she believed him.

Out of a dimness, the downtown lights swam closer. The sound of the tires on paving a sanitation truck had just sprayed was an adder's hiss.

Lori sat motionless, watching the night flow past.

I won't think at all, and soon it will go away. It didn't really happen. He never said those things. He couldn't have said them, because we weren't alone together. Mrs. Birkenbuel was with us all the time.

Marge, Marge, but he had your hotel right. Even the suite number.

And how about your picture in my wallet, Marge?

The boardwalk ahead lay almost in view now. Crowds streamed toward it, faceless. Shadow crowds. The blades of giant searchlights dueled across the sky. Parry. Thrust. The car swerved, approaching the big ocean-front hotels.

Against the sky a huge sign divided the blackness into

furrows. HOTEL REGENCY. It blinked and vanished and was gone as though it never had been and blinked again. The car slowed at the entrance.

Mrs. Birkenbuel bent forward. "Why are we stopping here, Steve? This isn't—"

"Miss Macklin's sister is registered here for Pageant Week, ma'am."

"Oh! Lori, I didn't know. We should have had her join us for dinner."

It was Dorn again who answered. "She had another engagement, ma'am. But Miss Lori had promised to drop by and give her a ticket for the finals tonight. Besides, she's brought the family's good-luck juju with her from home. Miss Lori wants to pick it up before the show. She'll only be a few minutes."

Dorn was out of his driver's seat already, holding open the door for Lori.

"Twenty-fifth floor, Miss Utah," Dorn said in a low voice. "You know the room? It's next door to Miss Alaska's. Use the key I gave you."

"Do hurry, dear," urged Mrs. Birkenbuel. "We don't want to be late."

Lori ignored the hand Dorn held out to assist her, looking through him as though he were a phantom.

She glanced at the key still clutched in her palm. It wasn't a regular hotel key. There was no number on it, no tag. She never had seen one like it before, yet she sensed what this was. A police key. A master key. It would let in the law wherever they wanted to enter.

Vice squad . . . Vice raid . . . key . . . vice . . . key . . .

In past the uniformed doorman. Across a lobby where a few idlers recognized Miss Utah and whispered as she passed. Up in an elevator cage which was either crowded or empty, she didn't know which.

Here was floor twenty-five.

He thought I'd be afraid to call his bluff. Lying stinker. He just wants to win the pool, Marge. He'd arrest his own mother if there was a reward on her head.

The door was marked with metal numbers. Two and five and zero and eight.

Lori stared down at the key in her palm. It told her nothing. She'd open the door and Marge would tell her it was all a lie.

She was surprised when it fit the keyhole and turned easily.

The door swung open without a sound. There were three of them in the dimly lit room.

The two men were in their shorts. The one on the bed was obese and short. The other was muscular, with sparse red hair. His gaze riveted on the other two, he was masturbating.

The blonde was as naked as at the moment the obstetrician had delivered her.

She was on her knees in front of the fat man. Her head, bent forward, was bobbing up and down over him. His stumpy, thick legs were spread apart as he leaned back for support against the footboard of the double bed. He was breathing hard.

So was the one who watched him. His voyeur eyes were fever-bright. His busy hand kept up its greedy pace. Only when he sighted Lori did his fingers falter.

"Close the door, idiot!" he panted. "This isn't a peep show!"

"My sister, the hooker," Lori said as she pushed the door back. "Would you like me to pimp for you?"

The blonde came up off her knees in a streak of movement. "Lori!"

There was a soft thud and a softer latch click as the door closed behind her. Neither sound registered. Lori was staring fixedly at two crisp hundred-dollar bills lying like lovers, one atop the other, on Marge's dresser. They looked like the two bills Marge placed on her own bureau in the motel the other night.

Marge Macklin fumbled for words. "You don't understand, Lori. We're all old friends. We were having a little party. Billy here drank too much—passed out. So we took off his clothes—put him to bed. I was trying to help him."

"What were you doing, Marge? Giving him mouth-to-prick resuscitation?"

"Let me explain. I—I—"

"My perfect sister. The image I could never live up to! And you had the gall to yak at *me* for things I did!" Lori's words lashed out.

Marge had snatched up a dressing gown off her bed. She clutched it about her. "Lori, listen. I know this is a shock. But try to understand. I needed money for you. To keep you from growing up the way I did. To straighten out at least one of us. How else could I raise the money?"

"You could have written your memoirs. You'd have made more money than Christine Keeler," Lori said bitterly.

A hand fell imploringly on Lori's sleeve. It was shaking as if a motor vibrated it.

Lori jerked free of the clutching fingers. "Don't touch

me!" she cried. "You're lower than whale turd, Marge Macklin. And that's on the bottom of the ocean."

"Hey!" grunted the fat man still on the bed. "What the hell goes on? Who is this dizzy bitch, anyway?"

Lori's shrill voice took over. "I'm her little sister, fellows. Can't you tell? Don't you think we look alike?"

"Get out!" the fat man barked. "We didn't pay good money to watch some fucking family reunion bit. We paid this dame to give us the kind of scene we dig. And we're going to get it. Out of here, little sister!"

"I know what your scene is, boys. You like to watch each other getting it, don't you? Makes it twice as good to know the other one sees the whole routine?"

With a quick gesture, Lori pulled up her miniskirt over her head. Then she tugged down her panty girdle and tossed it onto a chair.

"You with the meat in your hand." She moved toward the redhead. He blinked back at her incredulously.

"I haven't seen cock like that since we bred bulls on the ranch. Let's give your buddy a circus. Let him watch you ramming me. And I'll give you a cut-rate. Only fifty bucks."

"No, Lori, no!" Marge was sobbing. "Please . . ."

"It's nothing you haven't done, is it? At least I'm taking it between the legs. Come on, big boy. Spread out on me and give your wrist a rest."

"Lori, your doctor said—"

"Screw my doctor. Hey, Big Red, aren't you man enough?"

She swayed against him, catching him off balance so that her weight sent them both sprawling across the bed. With a deft wriggle, she worked herself under him.

The fat man was watching them, goggle-eyed. Marge started toward her. But the fat man caught her and dragged her back.

"Please, Lori! Don't! If I've ever done anything for you, ever in our lives—"

"You've done a lot," a strange voice which seemed to have no source retorted. "A big, hairy lot, Marge."

"I love you, Lori. I've tried my best to protect you—even here. Those questionnaires they sent out—a fool could smell they were loaded. When I read yours—all those crazy answers—I switched them in the envelopes, just in case they were a trap. Lori, I love you!"

"And I love you, double dose. Hey, Red, it's waiting for you."

Marge struggled to escape the corpulent man's grasp.

She bit his hand savagely. He swore darkly, then struck her across the face with the flat of his hand. She staggered back, fell on the red carpet.

"Fuck the little cunt, Frank!" he exhorted. "Show her you're the last of the red-hot lovers. I'm watching, boy, I'm watching!"

Big Red entered her like a guided missile. Lori pressed against him, began to work her haunches violently.

The room spun. The gloating grin above her blurred and vanished. Presently she sensed Frank sliding off her, his passion drained. She must have climbed off the bed, for now she was standing. Burned out, bleak, like scorched earth after a napalm bomb. There was a distant little mewing sound in her ears.

Was she the one making it?

As if in a trance, she slipped back her girdle and put on her dress. Then she walked across to the dresser and picked up one of the new bills. Marge was still horizontal on the carpet, her face wet with tears.

"Here!" Lori heard a voice drift as if from an echo chamber. "Half of this is my fee. Keep it, Big Sister. It's a down payment on those psychiatrists' bills you paid for me. You've very, very welcome. And I'll pay it back as fast as I can earn it the way you do. With interest!"

"Lori. Forgive me. I'll go crazy without you."

"Cheer up, Big Sister. I'll send you a sympathy card."

A door slammed. What door? Who knew? Who cared? There was an elevator. There was a lobby. Lights and faces in the lobby. Voices. Eyes.

There was a revolving door. It turned heavily on its axis when she pushed against it. You could go round and round in the door, if you wanted to. No time for that, though. Have to hurry, Lori. Something important. Somewhere. Hurry.

Night air. A long white car at the curb. Waiting. People in the car. I belong with them.

I think I do.

An officer got out, very politely. He helped her into the back seat. Who?

"Was your sister in?" He looked at her intently.

"Guests," Lori said. Or somebody said. "Party."

"Rosemary . . . That's for remembrance . . ." Nothing, though, to remember.

"That's right, dear. Run through your talent spot one more time while we're on our way. Shakespeare should impress the judges. And you read so movingly."

"For . . . for remembrance . . ."

36 · THE THIRTEENTH PRINCESS

SHORTLY before twilight, the trailer truck hauling the huge searchlight came to a halt in front of the Surf City Armory. The driver and a young helper hopped to the sidewalk, then climbed onto the flat bed and cranked the housing of the great blank eye until it pointed into the azure sky. The driver threw a switch and the eye came alive and sent a barely visible shaft of blue-white light skyward.

The driver cut the switch and sat crosslegged next to the searchlight and lit a cigarette. He watched with detachment as the crowd behind the wooden barricades grew with each passing minute. They, in turn, watched him and the searchlight because there was nothing else to see.

In the gathering dusk there was the good-natured jockeying for position behind the barricades and the babble of voices excited by the Event of the Year. And the stage whisper of a ticket scalper as he moved through the crowd offering a pair of orchestra seats for $25.

At the immense oak doors that served as the main entrance to the Armory, Police Chief Yoldring talked quietly with Lieutenant Wesley Douglas. Yoldring pointed into the throng and gave a succinct order. The officer saluted, turned, ducked under one of the wooden horses, cut through the crowd and arrested the scalper, who called the cop a fascist as he was hauled away.

Yoldring waved an arm and the great searchlight crackled to life and buzzed contentedly, the shaft of light clearly visible now, seemingly reaching the darkening canopy of the sky itself. The crowd howled and cheered. There were about four hundred persons flanking the entrance to the Armory when the first car arrived, a black Lincoln with the familiar SC-1 license plate. Mayor Detzer stepped out and waved to the crowd.

Within the mammoth Armory the outside cheers were

faint, faraway sounds lost in the din and echo of furious, last-minute preparations for the climax of the annual Surf City spectacular. Dozens of Pageant officials and underlings scurried about, checking and rechecking.

And swarming around and through the Pageant family were some seventy television production people, some of them atop scaffolding at either side of the red-curtained stage where two of the four massive color cameras were positioned, high above the serpentine twists of a mile of camera, sound and light cables.

Norm Prescott had estimated there would be seventy-two tons of television equipment on hand. But now, as he stood to the right of the runway that jutted into the center of the audience, he thought the figure in his press release might be low. Around him, a score of reporters from the various media were already in their seats studying their press kits.

"Norm," said one, "it says here that three hundred and forty-one stations are carrying the telecast. I understand three Southern stations canceled out at the last minute."

"Right," said Prescott. "But twenty-four radio stations, all in the so-called 'Black Belt', are picking up the audio for the first time in our history."

Prescott left it there and turned to survey the Armory, which was now opening to the first arrivals. Everything was the same as last year. But above the balcony where the fifty state flags hung there was one conspicuous addition—the pennant of the City of Washington, D.C., with its prophetic motto: "Justice for All."

Looking at the flag of the Pageant's newest entry, Prescott thought they were lucky to lose only three stations. Inspirational seat juggling had enabled him to squeeze in reps of the Afro-American Press, New York's *Amsterdam News, Jet, Ebony* and other Negro publications. But what the hell, thought Prescott, it will add some color to the show. Besides, with the show being bounced off Telstar for the first time, it would give overseas viewers a better picture of American life. Equality abounds.

Behind the curtain, Roger Megan, resplendent in his hand-stitched blue-black tuxedo, went through his pre-finale backstage routine, which consisted of bad jokes and inane pattern. But it kept everybody loose. And the words were punctuated by that sparkling smile of reassurance.

It was an amazing performance because Megan was empty inside, drained of emotion, hollow and depressed. This had been a bad year for him, the worst of all. His life was a mess and going nowhere. Fleming had been impressed but had stopped trusting him. He and Sue were splitsville. And Hazel—dear, sweet Hazel, his black velvet mother earth—gone forever.

Fat, dowdy Mrs. Machans wandered by in a fog as she had for twelve years, the only chaperone who consistently went to pieces on the final night.

"Why aren't you wearing your evening gown?" Megan asked, mock concern shutting off the blazing smile. "Don't you know it's almost showtime?"

Mrs. Machans stopped and appeared bewildered. "Wha . . . ?"

"Oh, I am sorry." Megan laughed. "I thought you were one of the contestants."

Mrs. Machans floated away.

Megan moved on, stopping at each of the three dressing rooms, where he knocked and called out the same line: "Relax, girls, the Pageant has been canceled. World War Three has started and all the men in the Armory have been ordered to the front, which is now approximately three feet south of the boardwalk."

Stacy heard the muffled words and the laughter of the other girls in her group, but none of it really registered. She was in her own private world, a world created, for the most part, by the scheming gorgon called Elizabeth DeGray. *Mama. Mama. Why don't you go away forever and let me live, let me breathe?*

"Stacy, you look positively beautiful."

It was Miss North Carolina, whose reflection Stacy saw in her mirror. She didn't actually hear the words, but she saw the lips move and read them from force of habit. "You, too," she answered. They smiled at each other through the mirror, good losers exchanging nice words, fighting the numbing disappointment that clutched at them like a shroud.

Mama was gone now, off somewhere licking her wounds and creating the lies for those back home. She had been Camille all day, crying, swooning, dabbing the lace-fringed handkerchief to her mouth—a slightly seedy Greta Garbo. But it wouldn't work anymore.

On the plane. I'll tell her on the plane. It's over, Mama. All over. I'll run my life from now on. I can't fuck it up any worse than you have.

Stacy felt the tears well and wondered if she could say it when the time came. Maybe if she was high, she could. And Stacy DeGray, a beautiful also-ran in this dream world of Surf City, devoutly wished she was already high and out of the whole goddamned mess.

In the wings, Lou Cates intercepted Megan and told him it was ten minutes to curtain. Megan pulled Cates aside.

"Give me a drink," Megan said. "One for the road."

Cates took an ounce-and-a-half miniature from his pocket, checked around for wayward eyes, twisted off the top and handed it to Megan, who downed it in one gulp. Cates pocketed the empty and produced a small plastic spray bottle of Lavoris. Megan swished the red liquid around in his mouth and spit the residue against the back wall.

"Here we go, Lou," Megan said, the crinkle back around his eyes, the smile adjusted and set.

"Break a leg," Cates said in a ritualistic farewell and aimed Megan toward the stage with a pat on his rump.

A young man with a clipboard pointed to Megan and called out seven minutes.

"I'll need a little more time," Megan quipped. "After all there are fifty-one contestants this year and in the decking and dicking department I'm only up to Miss Texas."

The young man chuckled. No wonder everybody said Megan should be trustee of a sperm bank.

When he reached stage center, Megan checked the microphone, taking it from the stand and twisting the wire around behind him. Megan could hear the din of 8,000 voices, rustling programs, coughs and laughter, all muffled slightly by the heavy curtain.

He snapped the microphone back into the stand and spun around to check out the stage, all in white with scalloped platforms in the rear, four of them, four display shelves for the evening's stars. Two stagehands were tacking down a corner of one of the platforms that had warped under the extremely hot lights necessary for the live color telecast.

Megan felt the heat and pulled a handkerchief from his pocket to brush beads of sweat from his upper lip and forehead. He walked to the curtain, found the peephole and looked out, checking the house before they dimmed the lights. To the right of the runway, Megan picked out the judges in the first row and behind them the Pageant family—Fleming and Prescott and Littlefield and the others. And four rows back, Mayor Detzer and Carl Lindstrom and the rest of Surf City's dignitaries.

On the left from where he stood squinting through one eye, Megan found the press corps, sprinkled for the first time with black and brown faces. And Megan knew Hazel was out there someplace, but he couldn't spot her. If he could see her once more, just once more . . . Then what? Heartache? East is east and west is west and all that shit.

"Three minutes." It was the kid with the clipboard from the wings. Megan lifted an arm to signal he had heard. He dropped his eye and checked out the Teleprompter. It was his fail-safe. He knew the program by heart, but the Teleprompter was insurance and it would flash all the names. Megan saw the orchestra leader, Leo Bevacqua, check his watch.

Megan backed away from the curtain and did the same. Then he adjusted his bow tie, smoothed out his jacket and walked to the wings to await his entrance cue.

In "B" dressing room Lori Macklin mechanically touched up her lipstick and tried to recognize the face she saw in the mirror. She couldn't. The dull buzzing in her ears blocked out the other sounds in the room. She was isolated and cold and it was a dream, a nightmare over which she had no conscious control. She stood without knowing why and started for the door. Mrs. Birkenbuel stopped her.

"Whoa, there." she said. "I know you're anxious, but let's not jump the gun. We still have a minute or two. You are absolutely ravishing, my dear."

But Lori heard none of it, held there a few feet from the door by the gentle pressure of the older woman's hand on her arm, staring blankly at the door knob because it shined, waiting to be moved. And vaguely wondering if she would ever wake up from this strange dream.

Out front, Marge Macklin sat slumped in her chair twisting one white glove, praying to a God she didn't know, making promises she would never keep, waiting for the house lights to go down to make her invisible. She was poised at the end of her world and she didn't want to go over the edge. And, dear God, she didn't want to drag Lori with her!

Several rows back, an usher pointed to a single empty seat and accepted a quarter from the ramrod-straight man in the gabardine suit who excused himself as he moved down the row and took his seat.

General Clinton Gervais was more than satisfied. He was jubilant. Had Dr. Lydecker lived, he could not have risked being recognized. He would have had to watch it all on television. But Lydecker was dead—a shame, but people die every day—and he could be here when the objective was won. It was perfect. Planned and executed with military precision.

Lydecker's death had jarred him when Waldo had told

him about it earlier. The unexpected. But a hurried telephone call to Petrie had confirmed that Miss New Jersey had indeed been scratched. And there had been no further word on the subject. It had been Lydecker's last official act. Perfect. Robin was home clear and he was on hand to savor complete victory. Gervais allowed himself a small self-satisfied smile and studied his program.

At the same moment, Max Gerber, sitting with the official family two rows behind John Fleming, was biding his time, waiting for the exact moment to make his move. He was picking at a fingernail when the lights began to dim and the chatter of the audience diminished to a whisper.

On the bandstand, Leo Bevacqua raised his baton. When the house lights faded completely, he brought the stick down with a flourish and the orchestra struck up the overture.

When the applause stopped there was a sustained drum roll and an offstage voice announced: "And now, ladies and gentlemen, your host for the thirteenth annual Princess America Pageant . . . Roger Megan!"

The curtain parted to the strains of "Good Luck, Sweet Princess," and two beats after the curtain was fully open and the applause was at its height, Megan walked slowly onstage, nodding his head slightly to acknowledge the reception as he walked. He did not smile, which was surprising.

When he reached the microphone, Megan raised his arms for silence. The clapping trailed off.

Megan stood still for a moment, then spoke.

"Ladies and gentlemen, many of you may not be aware that the Princess America Pageant has suffered a death in the family." He paused dramatically. "Late this afternoon, hours before his retirement from the Pageant after twelve years of devoted service, Dr. Franz Lydecker, our medical genius, suffered a fatal heart attack."

Megan paused again until the whispers subsided.

"I know Dr. Lydecker would want the show to go on. But I think it would be appropriate at this time if we had a minute's silence for this wonderful man who was there at the beginning and did so much to make this Pageant the internationally renowned event that it is today. Will you join me, please."

Head bowed, Megan mentally began to count, one thousand and one, one thousand and two . . .

In the wings near the head of the line now forming for the first parade on stage, Mildred Waxman cried softly for the man who had given her the chance to scale the rarefied heights to the Princess America semifinals. She had not known. They had been rehearsing since nine that morning and there was little outside contact. Megan's words hit her hard. But she wiped away the tears and promised the little man with the kindly eyes that she would do her best to make him proud.

When Megan reached one thousand and sixty, he raised his head and said soberly, "Thank you, ladies and gentlemen. We will miss Dr. Franz Lydecker, but his memory will be with us always."

Again, Megan paused.

"And now, good people, on to the business of the evening, if I can have your undivided attention. I ask for that now because when the contestants come onstage, nobody pays any attention to me at all."

There was a ripple of laughter and Megan allowed himself his first smile. He pulled the microphone from the stand and began to move around the stage, playing to sections of the audience, getting close to the spectators, a Megan trademark.

Standing backstage with Olga Loomis, Sue Rossiter, already gowned and ready for the reunion sequence, marveled at Megan's ability to bounce back and bottle up his emotions. But that was part of his strength, his appeal, she thought. Roger Megan was a man who would not recognize defeat. But he would have to now. There was a time in everybody's life when he or she had to grow up. *Grow up, Roger. Be as gracious a loser as you are a winner.*

"And now . . ." Megan was saying, holding the second word for emphasis, "here are the flowers of our fifty states, plus a bonus—a representative of the District of Columbia, a first this year, but something the Pageant Planning Committee has been working on for some time."

In one of the back rows of the balcony, sitting between two of his woolen-haired allies, Earl Burrage hissed an audible "Sheeeeet" and shook his head.

Megan whipped the microphone cord behind him and walked to the far end of the stage. "And nooooow . . . the contestants. First, from the deep South, an example of what makes the Heart of Dixie throb, Miss Alabama, Terry Marshall!"

Terry Marshall, a vision in pink taffeta, walked into the spotlight to the strains of "Stars Fell on Alabama" and a deafening round of applause, radiating poise and hope, although she knew she was an also-ran.

As she approached, Megan admired the kid's guts and

turned his beam of a smile on her, then led her to her place on the third shelf.

"And from the far, *far* North where you can miss the summer if you blink your eyes at the wrong time, Miss Alaska, Mildred Waxman!"

Mildred, exquisite in her floor-length organdy gown, took several uncertain steps into the blinding spotlight, halted for a moment and was relieved to discover she could not see the audience at all. She felt as though she were alone on the stage, Megan and she, the same as at rehearsal.

She raised her chin, smiled the patented Pageant smile, daintily tucked up her full skirt slightly, and glided slowly across the stage to Megan, who took her hand and led her to the third tier next to Miss Alabama as a courtier would a queen. As Megan backed off with an exaggerated bow, Mildred became aware for the first time that the orchestra was playing "Alaska's Flag" and that there were cheers and thunderous applause. Won't Papa be proud, she thought. Papa and Mama and Dave.

He had followed her every move through the rented binoculars, his body half over the balcony railing. Now the twin lenses held on the face. That beautiful face! And there, with the din of the crowd pounding in his ears and her face close enough to touch, it seemed, Dave Lebow, nee Lebowitz, decided that Mildred Waxman would make a perfect doctor's wife, providing he was the doctor.

"There is more than cactus in the Southwest," Megan was saying, "and here to prove the point is Miss Arizona."

Pam Raleigh nimbly stepped out onto the stage to be enveloped in light and audience approval.

Four states back, Robin Gervais was beginning to feel a little numb. She wished she were on a jet winging for an island called Okinawa. *Paul, honey. What the hell am I going to do if I go down to the wire? What the hell am I going to do if I win?*

In the opposite wings, just behind where Megan stood, Ginny Kerr joined Sue Rossiter. Ginny wore the official Princess America gown, thirty-five pounds of white satin covered with sequins in the shape and color of fifty state flowers, plus the hastily added American beauty rose of Washington, D.C. Two wardrobe women had had to stand on chairs to lower it over her head.

"Megan is marvelous, isn't he?" Ginny said.

"Marvelous isn't the word," Sue answered without taking her eyes off the stage where Miss Arkansas was making her entrance. "He is incredible. Absolutely beyond belief." Sue smiled at her own little joke. Ginny just nodded naïvely.

"My man is out there," Ginny said. "In the fourteenth row. I told him to wear his kilts, but he chickened out. It was a great year, but I'm glad it's over."

"I know how you feel," said Sue, a little sadly. "It's something to treasure, but I wouldn't want to go through it all again. I don't think any of the girls would."

"Not me," reiterated Ginny. "I'm really glad it's over."

And Ian MacLaren was glad it was over. She had an entrance to make, a speech (short, he hoped), a crowning and an exit. Then he could get down to business. He took the small suede-covered box from his pocket for the nth time, snapped it open and watched the full-carat stone flicker even in the dim reflected light from the stage. He closed the box and returned it to his pocket. He smiled sheepishly at the woman in the next seat who had observed him.

Max Gerber wasn't even pretending to follow what was happening onstage. He repeatedly checked his watch and the brown envelope tucked into a folded copy of the Surf City *Press* resting on his lap. When he did return his gaze to the stage, Miss Florida was gracefully accepting an ovation and Megan was smiling, as always. Gerber allowed himself to smile, too. It was not a pleasant smile.

The smile on Art Waldo's face was genuine. He was sweating, but his ever-present handkerchief was on the floor where it had fallen when he half rose from his seat to lead the applause and cheers for Robin. He felt he was close to a winner and that made him perspire more profusely.

Onstage, the parade continued.

". . . a real Georgia peach . . ." Megan was saying.

Fleming was pleased with the proceedings. Everything was moving on schedule. Megan was having a good night, just cornball enough for the great American heartland but not enough to turn off the big-city sophisticates. Fleming had wanted to cut Megan's throat when he had read the detectives' report. But now that Fleming had taken all the bows for putting Miss Washington, D.C., into the contest, he couldn't reveal Megan had engineered the whole strategy even if he wanted to, and he wasn't sure he did. Megan had come up with another winner. He had taken an insane gamble, but it had worked. If only the man would keep his zipper up!

Fleming leaned forward and turned to his left.

"Norm?" he called.

Prescott, who sat three chairs down from Fleming on the side-aisle seat so he could move quickly should any emergencies arise, turned to Fleming and raised his eyebrows.

Fleming said: "Is everything under control?"

Prescott made a circle with his thumb and forefinger.

"Good," said Fleming, bobbing his head. He leaned back and saw Megan lead Miss Idaho to her place and then bring on Miss Illinois with a passable wisecrack about Chicago. The pace was good.

It was strange, thought Fleming, how a threatened catastrophe could be turned to good use. The reunion and the Pageant's first Negro were bound to boost the ratings, the rival station's blockbuster notwithstanding.

Onstage, Megan shot a quick glance at the Teleprompter and brought out Miss Kentucky. He was still sweating under the hot lights, but he was clicking. The drink had helped. The applause did the rest. He was on and here is where he belonged. This was the real Roger Megan.

In his seat at the corner of the runway and the stage, from where he could easily collect the judges' scorecards, Harold Petrie double-checked his tally sheet to make certain he had the fifteen disqualifications properly marked, plus the one he had received before entering the Armory from Norm Prescott. He had not had time to inform the judges, but it wasn't really necessary. It was his tally that counted. It gave him a certain Godlike feeling. It made up for the anonymity of the job.

A thunderous round of applause brought Petrie's head up with a jerk. He had missed the name, but the satin sash said "Miss New Jersey." A beautiful girl, thought Petrie. Obviously the favorite. But a case of tough titty, my dear. Harold Petrie must strike you down.

Robert Bryant watched his daughter with mixed emotions. He loved her and she was beautiful, but she had a lot to learn. Perhaps he had been too protective, too indulgent, but he had climbed out of the stink of Secaucus and battled his way to the top of the construction field so his children would never know the dire poverty of picking through the ashes for an unburned chunk of coal. Now he wondered if adversity wasn't a blessing, if having everything didn't stunt a person's growth.

"She's magnificent, Bob." His wife hugged his arm. She was crying. "Isn't she beautiful?" Bryant said she was and patted his wife's shoulder.

Darlene Bryant allowed Megan to lead her to her place on the second tier and tried to read his face. She saw nothing but a smiling mask, rigid and phony at close range. Well, my dear Megan, you have a surprise coming when I do my act!

Megan rejected an impulse to wink at the girl and wondered why the thought had crossed his mind. She was an imperious bitch, and if she won, she'd be unbearable. Still, she had something, a child-woman with innocent, yet knowing, eyes and a lush body. Perhaps . . .

Megan returned to the lip of the stage and plunged on, picking the names from the Teleprompter, working in the stale one-liners, leading them to their perches on the shelves bowing, humming off mike with the orchestra, pacing the action. It was Megan's annual shot of adrenalin that did little for his heart but wonders for his sagging ego. It was predictable but intoxicating, this kaleidoscopic rush of beauty and color and thousands of hands clapping until the sound filled every inch of the sprawling Armory.

"And here is one of Texas' brightest stars who will never be 'lone for long, Mary Sue Kincaid—Miss Texas!"

Bevacqua led his men into "Deep in the Heart of Texas," but they could have been playing a waltz for all anybody heard of the music above the crowd's outpouring of approval.

At the edge of the wings, Lori heard nothing, her mind locked away and safe from reality, hidden from the truth, protected. She was somewhere disembodied in a phantom zone. And it didn't seem to matter. Not at all.

She missed her cue.

In the wings, the young man with the clipboard said "Jesus Christ" and ran to Lori's side. "That's you," he almost shouted. "Get out there!"

Lori followed the order, moving mechanically into the bath of light, ignoring the applause, yet smiling in some automatic reflex to a situation she didn't quite understand. She would have walked clear into the far wings if Megan hadn't grabbed her hand and propelled her to the bottom tier.

Marge Macklin's heart had almost stopped when her sister didn't appear on cue. But now she was breathing again. *Dear God, help her. I'm the whore. Not her.*

At the end of the runway, in the section reserved for drivers, Steve Dorn turned to his wife and said, "Well, what do you think?"

"She's breath-taking. But she seems a little . . . wooden."

"She's far from wooden," Dorn said, immediately wishing he hadn't said it in quite that way. "I mean, she's probably nervous."

His wife gave him a sidelong glance, then smiled.

"Maybe I should keep you home next year. After all, the Pageant is where you found me—or did I find you?"

"That was different, Nancy. I wasn't your driver. Besides, why would I want to fool around with cheap prints when I have the original at home?"

"Flatterer."

"I'm only interested in the pool money," Dorn said. "If she wins, I'll take you down to the islands to prove it."

"You don't have to prove it, but I'll hold you to that trip to the islands. It's the least you can do for a broken-down ex-Miss Michigan."

"You got a deal, Mrs. Dorn."

They applauded for the next four girls.

"Easy on the hands, honey," Dorn said. "Save it for Utah the next time around. If we . . ."

"Hold it," said Nancy. "Here comes the added attraction."

There was a hush over the audience and Megan let it hover for a moment. Then he said: "And now, ladies and gentlemen, something new in the Princess America Pageant. We've been trying to figure out what to do about our nation's capital for some time. The Pageant just didn't seem to be complete without the District of Columbia. And here's our solution. And a lovely solution it is. Miss Washington, D. C., Joyce Carrol!"

The audience response was deafening.

Earl Burrage said "Sheeeeet" again.

John Fleming beamed like a proud father.

And Miss D.C. came on stage to the strains of "Washington Town," her white gown setting off the golden copper of her skin, her dark-brown eyes twinkling with the reflection of flash guns and strobe lights as photographers seemed to climb on one another's shoulders to get shots of the first black girl to grace the Surf City stage. Feet stamping and whistling augmented the applause.

Collapsed in a massive ball of wet flesh, Art Waldo was thinking evil thoughts. Had the general figured this? Had the general figured it might be love-a-nigger night?

General Gervais sat straight and still with his own private smile. Let them knock themselves out. She was too many points behind. It was the planning that counted. The strategy. He wished he could smoke a cigar.

Several rows behind the press section, Hazel Sanders was crying and laughing at the same time. Next to her,

Thomas Worthington Walsh glowed and clapped until his hands stung. Both had arrived late, but this was the moment they had come for. Hazel could hardly see the stage for her tears. She dug the fingers of her right hand into Walsh's arm and pressed the knuckles of her free hand to her mouth.

We made it! God, we made it! She blinked away the tears and watched Joyce move gracefully across the stage, pride and beauty intertwined in the exquisite moment. *Show them, honey. Show them all.*

Hazel followed the girl through misty eyes, followed her until Megan was there with outstretched hand.

Roger. Roger. Thank you for everything. Thank you and goodbye. Your hot chocolate loved you. You'll never know how much. But that's the way it's got to be with us. Maybe someday . . .

Walsh turned and grinned at her. "Black is beautiful, baby. Black is beautiful."

Hazel released her grip on his arm and let her hands drop limply into her lap. She took a deep breath and tried to smile. When she spoke, her voice was flat and empty. Without taking her eyes from Megan, she answered in the litany of her people: "Yes, Tommy. Black is beautiful."

Down front, Prescott was practically in Harry Chesleigh's lap trying to get Fleming's attention. When he caught the Old Man's eye, he said: "If this is any indication of the television draw, we'll pull our best rating ever."

"It's a winner," Fleming said. "When do we get the first figures?"

"I've got a phone open backstage," Prescott said. "A direct line. We should get a quickie report about thirty minutes into the show."

"Fine," said Fleming. "Where's the phone?"

"To the left of the dressing tooms. You can't miss it. Olga is standing by."

Megan now had Miss West Virginia in tow and deposited her in the proper niche, speeding up the pace because his showman's sense told him the final trip was anticlimactic. Misses Wisconsin and Wyoming seemed to be in place before the audience realized it.

"And there they are, ladies and gentlemen," Megan concluded, waving his free arm at the assembled contestants who stood unnaturally still, like a collection of dolls arranged in a glass display case. "The *fifty* fairest flowers . . ." He had used the line for years, but now he heard the start of a laugh and realized he had blown it, his nimble mind recovering in mid-sentence. ". . . of our sovereign states *and* our new entry from the District of Columbia."

The laugh died and Megan cast a glance at the audience as though he had no idea why it had started in the first place. Then he nodded to Bevacqua for the first note of "American Royalty" and went into his less than inspiring serenade to the contestants, a set piece for each Pageant.

"Goddam ham should be selling programs," Dowling hissed. Two seats down, Lois Smith made as though she hadn't heard the comment, but she had had enough. She resolved to herself that she would use all her contacts in the trade to get this power-mad bitch cut down to size. It would be a pleasure.

Megan's number drew limited applause.

"So I'm not Frank Sinatra," he quipped. "But it does give the judges time to mark their score cards."

It got a good laugh. It always did.

Megan continued his patter as the girls marched off to change into their swimsuits and then awarded prizes for the best parade floats to New York and Idaho, which was of little interest to anybody except as an indication that Miss New York and Miss Idaho were probably out of contention.

In the dressing room, Mepala Yates pulled up her bathing suit and addressed the room in general: "This is one grand waste of time. I've got a good mind to go out there with an orchid in my teeth and without the bathing suit. As King Kam would say: 'If you got it, baby, let it hang out.' Wouldn't that shake them up!"

They all laughed. The losers hardest of all.

Next door, Darlene Bryant kept tugging at the top of her straps, then muttered a curse because of the limited cleavage allowed by the white Pageant suit. What I need is a bikini, she thought. Not this suit of armor.

Mildred changed quickly and isolated herself in the ladies' room to touch up her neck.

A roar of laughter floated backstage.

"You people are marvelous," Megan was saying. "The best audience in the world." The audience applauded itself. And Megan was thinking he needed a drink. He was running down. Intermission was the oasis he was pointing for.

The parade of states began again, swimsuits replacing the gowns. When the contestants were in place, Megan turned to the audience with a helpless shrug. "I don't know how the judges can make a decision. I'd give up and wrap them and then take them all home." He paused. "Of course, my wife might object. She didn't even want me to come here this year, but I told her all the girls were heavily chaperoned and not to worry. And she said she wasn't worried about the girls. She was worried about the chaperones!"

And for the thirteenth year running, the line got the loudest guffaws of the night.

Max Gerber was halfway up the side aisle before the applause subsided, the folded Surf City *Press* clutched under his arm. He headed directly for the main Armory entrance and went out through the oak doors, his Pageant pass pinned to his jacket lapel.

Outside it was dark, but the huge searchlight lit up the area for almost a block, flies and specks of things swirling in the great beam of light that appeared focused on some star. The crowd behind the police barricade had thinned out, many of them going home or to a tavern to watch the rest of the festivities on TV. A few score still milled about in the cool night air listening to the proceedings over two loudspeakers.

Gerber nodded to a cop on duty and slipped around one of the wooden saw horses. He walked halfway up the block, stopped when he encountered a young boy wearing a Surf City T-shirt.

"Would you like to make five dollars?" Gerber asked.

"I sure would."

Gerber pulled a bill from his pocket. He slipped out a brown envelope from the folds of the newspaper. "I want you to take this envelope up to the barrier back there and give it to the police officer. Tell him it is extremely important that it gets to Mr. John Fleming as quickly as possible."

"Mr. John Fleming. Right."

Gerber glanced at the envelope and didn't recognize his own block printing, his left-handed letters that read: *Mr. John Fleming.*

And below that in large letters underlined twice: URGENT!

He gave the envelope and bill to the boy.

"Gee, thanks, Mister. Thanks very much."

The boy almost ran through the edge of the crowd to where the cop stood. Gerber saw the kid talking and then hand over the envelope. The cop looked at the envelope for a moment, turned and walked into the Armory. Gerber slipped back around the barricade and followed him in.

Gerber passed the cop, who was handing the envelope to an usher, without attracting attention. The house lights had dimmed again and the orchestra was doing a reprise of the overture.

Megan was well into his routine before Gerber saw the usher pass out of the corner of his eyes. He sighed in relief. It was rolling now, he thought. It was guaranteed. But had he been watching, Max Gerber would not have been so sure.

The usher stopped at Fleming's row and looked in.

"Yes?" said Prescott in half whisper.

"I have an envelope for Mr. Fleming."

"Give it here," said Prescott. "I'll get it to him."

"Right, Mr. Prescott." The usher handed over the envelope and retreated.

Prescott dropped the envelope into his lap to join in the applause for Miss Montana, his own personal favorite, but a loser, he knew. That was about all he knew. For the first time in his long tenure with the Pageant, Prescott could not pick the winner with any certainty. It had been a weird year. He would have bet on Miss New Jersey, but Lydecker had shot her down. It was strange. He had never known Lydecker to goof before. Maybe he was sicker than we knew, he thought. I wonder if this Bernstein is going to work out?

Prescott looked over his shoulder and picked out Dr. Scott Bernstein in the next row. That was Gerber sitting behind him, he noted. Two middle-aged men. They look as if they came out of the same mold. Prescott returned his gaze to the stage, where Miss Nevada was getting her last shot before the cameras.

He had completely forgotten about the envelope.

In his seat, Scott Bernstein was still upset by Lydecker's sudden death. He hadn't wanted to come, but Fleming had insisted. It seemed callous to him. The man was dead. A great man. What was all this nonsense compared to what had been lost? It was unfeeling. Now he seriously wondered if he wanted the job at all. He would think about it. Bernstein shifted uncomfortably in his chair.

Gerber had to lean to one side to keep Fleming in his line of sight. He couldn't figure what the hang-up was. Fleming didn't move. *Can't the stupid bastard read?* Gerber figured it might take until the next breakaway for a commercial. That would be all right. Still plenty of time.

On stage, Megan was in high gear—producers please note how this pro can keep things moving while never losing the audience's rapt attention. Megan was fortified because good old Lou Cates was always there. Warm inside and warm in the spotlight was the second best tonic in the world for Roger Megan.

John Fleming checked his watch. It was almost ten. He jumped up and started toward the side aisle.

Gerber saw Fleming's sudden move and misread it. He took a deep breath. This was it.

Prescott stood to allow Fleming to get into the aisle and the envelope slid silently from his lap and fell to the floor. "You want me to come along, JF?"

Fleming hesitated. "I don't think that's necessary, Norm. Keep an eye on things out here. I'll get word to you on how we're doing."

"Right. I've got my fingers crossed."

"We don't need fingers, we need numbers," Fleming said, moving down the aisle toward the backstage area.

"If it's anything less than a forty-five, I'll hand in my credit cards," Prescott called after him with a smile. He sat down, unmindful that his lap was empty.

"And now, ladies and gentlemen, the ten semifinalists as selected in secret ballot by our judges," Megan was saying. "We were going to have the ballots delivered by Wells Fargo, but they wanted too much to have them driven from the first row to the stage."

In the back tier, Mildred got ready to appear surprised. They had all known since early that morning. If you had to rehearse your talent number for the cameras, you were a semifinalist. And Mildred had rehearsed. So had Robin and Lori and Darlene and the cute colored girl. And Miss Texas and Miss Louisiana and Miss Nevada and Miss Montana and Miss Vermont. But they would all look surprised and squeal or giggle or put their hands to their mouths or let their jaws drop.

There was a drum roll. Megan said, "Miss Alaska!" Mildred put her hands to her mouth. Another drum roll. Megan announced, "Miss Florida!" Another drum roll.

General Gervais accepted Robin's openmouthed surprise as genuine. He was pleased she was surprised. He was pleased she had no idea that she was going to win. And pleased there was a place like Okinawa where you could exile interlopers. But most of all pleased with himself.

Five drum rolls later, Lori did not appear surprised at all. She did not move. She just stood there.

Dorn and his wife applauded wildly, standing and embracing each other and laughing. Maybe this *was* their year.

Marge Macklin bit her knuckles. Something was wrong.
And after two more drum rolls, Megan sang an abbreviated version of "American Royalty" and the curtain closed for another commercial.

"Joyce is in the semifinals," Hazel almost shouted at Tom Walsh, her eyes glazed with excitement. "Do you think she can win? I mean, is there any chance at all?"

"I doubt it," said Walsh. "But maybe we'll pick up the white man's guilt vote."

"But a black woman as Princess America?"

"They said we'd never get into the contest, no less to the semifinals," Walsh answered. "Who knows? In any case, we've waited one hundred years. We can wait a few more. We're very good at waiting."

Megan gulped another miniature and changed quickly into a dry shirt. "How's it going, Lou? Straight. No stories."

"Beautiful. I've never seen you carry it better. You've got them by the balls. If we don't get a firm offer out of this, nobody's watching the show."

"Good, good," Megan said, slipping into his jacket. The words, the whiskey, the footlights making him feel invincible. "Do me a favor, Lou?"

"Anything."

"Get me a broad for later."

"Anybody in particular?"

"I'll let you know."

When the curtain parted, Megan had returned the mike to its stand and was anchored behind it, the bright lights reflecting off his teeth.

"Before we get to our talented semifinalists," he said, "comes a chore I've always enjoyed. The Miss Personality award, which is the only award that's voted for by the girls themselves. Next to winning the crown, it's the most coveted award to be presented. And here is the winner—Miss Hawaii, Mepala Yates!"

When they had asked her to stand by in her gown, Mepala had been confused. Now she came onstage to what might be her last ovation, thankful she didn't have to climb any stairs because she couldn't see too clearly and it had nothing to do with being nearsighted.

Mepala accepted the trophy and looked questioningly at Megan. He motioned to the microphone.

"*Maholo nui loa,*" Mepala said. "*Aloha au ia oe.*" She crinkled her almond eyes and added, "That means in Hawaiian 'Thank you very much. I love you.' "

As Mepala moved off stage to a warm salute, Megan

ad-libbed: "I'm glad she translated that. I thought it was a recipe for three-fingered poi."

The applause trailed off into a wave of laughter and Megan savored it down to the last hand clap.

"And now, ladies and gentlemen, we move on to the talent portion of our elimination. I'm sure you will be thrilled, as I was, by the efforts of these young ladies." *If you buy that, you will buy anything.* "To start things off, here is our first semifinalist, Miss Alaska, to do a piano medley of—what else?—Gold Rush tunes!"

Fleming watched Mildred go into her number and marveled at her command of the piano. The talent was improving. He chuckled as he remembered some of the acts in previous years, like the idiot from Mississippi who recited Jack Sprat could eat no fat . . .

He was in good spirits. If the quick survey figures held, they had captured better than 51 percent of the viewing audience. The official figures would not be in for a week, but even if they lost a point or two, it would still be a record. Standing in the wings, Fleming felt very good indeed. He decided to stay where he was. He had never seen this part of the show from this particular vantage point. Besides, the rating service might come through with additional figures.

Max Gerber was concerned but not worried. They wouldn't move until after the talent portion. They couldn't. It would screw up the television show. Still, he began to sweat.

Megan introduced Miss Florida's gypsy number and withdrew to the wings. He, too, saw Fleming standing in the wings on the opposite side of the stage. He wondered what JF was doing there. Was something wrong? He decided he was just getting paranoid. The Old Man was smiling. Everything was all right.

Robin Gervais' gypsy fiddle number and her colorful costume brought down the house. The girl had style.

Megan hated this part of the show. All he did was walk on and off the stage lending a little professional gloss to the amateurs.

He sleep-walked through Miss Louisiana's unintentionally hilarious recitation of a twenty-second speech from an obscure Tennessee Williams play. Miss Nevada did a tap number that dated back to Ruby Keeler. Megan figured that if she had come in with a chance to win, she had just killed it.

"And here, for the first time on the Princess America stage," Megan announced after the applause had subsided, "a high-wire act—something I have been doing for years."

Megan gave the audience a broad wink. "Let's hear it for a brave little girl, Miss New Jersey!"

Darlene strutted out in the tightest leotard Megan had ever seen. He darted a look at Fleming, who was frowning.

Darlene climbed the ladder to the wire twenty feet above the stage. From her high perch she gave Megan a knowing look.

Then she pulled a black blindfold out from between her ample breasts and tied it around her eyes.

The miserable show-stealing, grandstanding bitch! Megan had an almost uncontrollable desire to get a gun and shoot her down, but he turned to the audience and said: "How about *that*, people?"

Darlene stepped confidently onto the wire and began to walk. She had taken eight steps when she suddenly lost her balance and fell into the net. Gasps and moans from the audience followed her down.

Megan moved to the net as Darlene rolled out and swung to the floor. He grabbed her hand and smiled, happy in the thought that the brassy cunt had finally done herself in. "A big hand for this game little girl!" he shouted to the crowd. He wanted to add, "Across her mouth."

Mrs. Bryant buried her head in her husband's shoulder. He patted her arm and said, "It's all right, dear. She didn't hurt herself." And Robert Bryant said to himself: Maybe this is what she needed. To make an ass of herself in front of sixty million people. If she can live with this, she'll be better for it. God, I hope so.

Megan saw the shine of tears in Darlene's eyes and found himself troubled that he cared. He led her off and wondered if she would attend the traditional "Losers' Party," where the five also-rans in the semi-finals got together and drank away their miseries to the strains of "It Only Hurts for a Lifetime." If she did . . .

Lori waited in a trance through Miss Texas' routine. She did not return Fleming's encouraging smile. She didn't see it. She wore a diaphanous, soiled white gown and clutched some dying daisies to her bosom. Her hair was disheveled.

". . . an abridged version of Ophelia's mad scene from *Hamlet*. Miss Utah!"

She had not heard Megan's introduction, but somehow the final two words broke through to her clouded mind and she moved by rote to the microphone. She began in a barely audible voice, her head slightly bowed, her body slack.

"There's Rosemary, that's for remembrance . . ."
There was absolute quiet in the Armory.

" . . . Pray you, love, remember. And there is pansies, that's for thoughts . . ."

The words came in a curious singsong of the mad.

". . . There's fennel for you, and columbines. There's rue for you, and here's some for me. We may call it herb or grace o' Sundays. O, you must wear your rue with a difference! There's a daisy. I would give you some violets, but they withered all when my father died. They say he made a good end . . ."

Steve Dorn was wide-eyed with disbelief. I'll be a sonofabitch, she's dynamite! They're hanging on every word!

". . . His beard was as white as snow, all flaxen was his poll. He is gone, he is gone, and we cast away moan. God 'a' mercy on his soul! And all of you Christian souls, pray God. God be wi' you . . ."

Transfixed, Megan saw it but didn't believe it. She wasn't just saying the words, she was *living* them. She is Ophelia! Right down to the clouded eyes.

". . . We must be patient; but I cannot choose but weep to think they would lay him i' the cold ground. My brother shall know of it; and so I thank you for your good counsel. Come, my coach! Good night, ladies. Good night, sweet ladies. Good night, good night."

The last word was a whisper but it was heard in the far reaches and the balcony, such was the attentive silence. And Lori stood in the deepening quiet without moving.

Then it came, scattered at first, but building to an incredible roar of hands and of cheers, echoing and re-echoing around the cavernous Armory. And they stood, eight thousand of them, not a few with tears in their eyes, and beat their hands red.

But Marge Macklin didn't stand. She slumped in her chair and wept for joy.

Dorn shouted to his wife above the noise, "Pack your bags!"

General Gervais stood because he didn't want to appear conspicuous. He conceded she'd be first runner-up. It really didn't matter. Robin had wowed the audience, too. And she had scored highest in the interview session. She had to be the winner.

Megan allowed Lori as much of the accolade as the tight television schedule permitted, then led her off so he could bring on Miss Vermont, whose misfortune it was to follow Lori.

Eames Bentley in the judges' row saw nothing of Miss

Vermont's turn on roller skates. He was busy with his score and making notes to several top movie directors, suggesting screen tests for one Lori Macklin.

"... Miss Washington, D.C., ladies and gentlemen, to sing 'Somewhere'! Maestro, if you please."

Joyce Carrol waited for the audience to settle down and began her number in a throaty, gospel voice.

"There's a place for us, somewhere, a place for us.*
Peace and quiet and open air
Waits for us, somewhere.
There's a time for us,
Someday, a time for us.
Time together with time to spare
Time to learn, time to care.
Someday, somewhere.
We'll find a new way of living,
We'll find a way of forgiving, somewhere ..."

And as the orchestra played the bridge softly, Joyce recited: "Yes, there's a place for each of us. Where love is like a passion and burns like a fire. Let our efforts be as that of Dr. Martin Luther King, who had a dream that all God's children—black men, white men, Jews, Gentiles, Protestants and Catholics—could join hands and say that spiritual of old: 'Free at last, Free at last. Thank God almighty, free at last!' "

Bevacqua pulled the orchestra to its full volume for the final chorus, cymbals and drums booming.

"Hold my hand and we're halfway there,
Hold my hand and I'll take you there,
Somehow.
Someday.
Somewhere ..."

Her head thrown back, Joyce held the last note until the muscles rippled in her neck, her eyes closed, arms outstretched as though to pull the entire audience to her breast. Then she cut the note in perfect timing with the orchestra, dropped her head forward and let her arms fall limply to her sides. For a moment there wasn't a sound, and then the audience broke loose with its second standing ovation of the night.

Megan came on beaming, thinking to himself that he had been only half right about this girl. She could not only sing, she could act as well. Could a minor miracle be happening right before his eyes? Megan's Miracle. A black Princess America! Fleming would have his head sent up by room service.

"Thank you, ladies and gentlemen. And now, another commercial message. You know what a commercial is. That's something the program is always interrupting."

Lou Cates materialized as soon as Megan hit the wings. He mopped Megan's forehead and held a mirror while Megan brushed and patted his hair. "You're killing them," he said.

"Lou," Megan said, smoothing down a stray hair, "get me Miss New Jersey."

"That bitch?"

"Just do it, Lou, you'll probably find her at the Losers' Table. Promise her anything. Hollywood. Glamour. You know how to work it."

"I'll try."

"If I read her right, you won't have to try too hard."

Harry Chesleigh twisted in his seat to get at a cough drop and his foot brushed something on the floor. He bent over and picked up an envelope and read the front.

"You drop this, Norm? It's addressed to JF."

"Oh, Jesus. I'd forgotten it." Prescott took the envelope and stood for a moment searching for Fleming. He caught Max Gerber's eye and waved his free hand.

Gerber thought his heart had stopped, but returned the wave. He saw that Prescott had the envelope and, judging from his actions, it hadn't been opened yet. God damn it! What had gone wrong? Prescott must have shortstopped it when the usher delivered it. And where was Fleming? What the hell did he bolt backstage for? Open the goddam thing, Norm!

Gerber saw Prescott sit down again and died a little. That fucking idiot! Open the envelope!

Megan waited for his cue, then picked up the tally from Petrie in full view of the camera. He returned to the microphone. "I don't know how they did it, but the judges have selected the five finalists. And here they are, in alphabetical order:

"Miss Alaska . . ."

Mildred thought for a moment that she would faint.

"Miss Florida . . ."

It can't be, Robin thought in confusion. *Paul, Paul! I need you!*

"Miss New Jersey . . ."

Darlene stepped forward. *They are throwing me a bone.*

But it was Megan's turn to be surprised. To get to the finals she must have had enough points locked up before she blew her wire act. The idiot could have recited "Humpty Dumpty" and placed. She could still win the crown.

Darlene saw Megan smile and wink and wondered if he knew something she didn't.

"Miss Utah . . ."

Miss Montana had to push Lori forward and Lori turned to her with a blank look on her face.

"And Miss Washington, D.C."

Walsh said to Hazel, "You see that, baby. Never underestimate the white man's guilt."

From the other side of the Armory, General Gervais surveyed the five finalists and congratulated himself again. Clockwork. Precision. The points told the story. Maybe it hadn't been necessary to go through all that planning, but who could anticipate she would fall from the wire. Certainty was all that mattered and he was certain. Robin could not lose.

". . . something you followers of the Pageant have been waiting for," Megan was saying. "So, without further ado, here are all our former winners with their families. First, Miss . . ."

Megan rattled off the names and the years and saw all of them smiling and radiant, the older ones showing their age, most of them fucked up in one way or another. Princess 1958 had four children in tow from four marriages; Princess 1962 was notorious for her drinking escapades and probably had to be dried out to make the show; Princess 1965 had recently been featured in a nudie movie; Princess 1967 was doing television commercials for the Georgia Pecan Growers Association. And Princess 1960 got mixed up with a guy named Roger Megan but had kissed him off.

Sue Rossiter gave Megan a cold smile and looked quickly away.

". . . and the current Princess America, Virginia Kerr!"

Ginny stepped out of the reunion line wearing her crown and velvet cloak with ermine tails and wielding her scepter. She approached the microphone.

"It has been a wonderful, wonderful year . . ."

Gerber could feel his hands shaking. Prescott hadn't

moved. He had to do something. But what? Think, damn it, think!

"... the scholarships and the marvelous people I've met. I just wish it could go on forever, but ..."

Gerber wiped the sweat from his palms, rose and moved out to the side aisle. It was risky, but he had to try. He walked down and knelt in the aisle next to Prescott's seat.

"Norm? Did you want me for something a while back?"

"Huh? Oh, Max. No, no. I was just waving hello. Great show, isn't it."

"Yes, it is," Gerber said through a mouth that seemed void of saliva. *Make it casual.* "What's the envelope?"

"Oh, this? It came for JF."

"Where is the Old Man?"

"Backstage. He's watching from the wings. By the way, we got a fifty-five rating. Isn't that great?"

"Wonderful," said Gerber, trying to put excitement in his voice. "What's with the big red urgent?"

"I haven't the foggiest."

"Well," said Gerber, "I'll see you after the show."

"Right," said Prescott.

When Gerber returned to his seat, Prescott studied the envelope with renewed interest. The printing looked like the work of a child. He turned it over. No return address. Urgent?

"... and I know to whomever I pass on my scepter, cloak and crown, these traditions will be carried forward so that all America can be proud of their new Princess. Thank you."

Ian McLaren glowed with pride and checked his little box again.

Megan gave Ginny one of his minted smiles and silently thanked her for making her speech mercifully short.

"Now for a short commercial message, after which we'll all find out who will be our new Princess America." Megan nodded to the five finalists who sat in chairs to Ginny Kerr's left, the former Princesses lined up in a semicircle in the background. He covered the microphone and said, "Sixty seconds to launching. Start the countdown."

Prescott thought of going backstage to find Fleming but decided an interruption at this time, unless absolutely vital, would not make him any points with the Old Man. Still, it said "Urgent." And underlined twice.

There was a drum roll.

Prescott flipped the envelope over and pried loose the flap.

The drum roll ended and Megan announced from the stage: "This is the moment we've all been waiting for and the moment these girls have been working toward for six months. The chief auditor will give me the final tally, please . . ."

Prescott slipped the contents of the envelope into his lap and looked. The blood drained out of his face.

"The third runner-up—Miss Alaska!"

Prescott couldn't move. He was frozen to his seat. The crowd's sudden explosion into applause brought him to life. He grabbed the material in his lap, jumped up and started down the aisle, his face white, his hands trembling.

"The second runner-up—Miss Washington, D.C.!"

Prescott stopped short, abreast of the judges in the first row. He couldn't get backstage! There wasn't enough time! He stopped and ran along in front of the judges until he reached the corner where the runway met the stage.

"The first runner-up—Miss Utah!"

Prescott stuck his head over the stage. "Megan. Megan!" But the applause drowned him out. "*Megan!*"

Megan led Lori to her place at the right hand of the throne, then nodded to Bevacqua for a drum roll. In that fraction of a second, he thought he heard someone call his name. It would have to wait.

Bevacqua cut the drum roll.

"*Roger!*" Prescott's voice was a wail of anguish.

Megan shot a glance to the edge of the stage and caught a glimpse of Prescott's distorted features. What the hell? He quickly turned to the wings to catch Fleming's eye. JF was smiling and nodding. Christ, that's a relief.

"And now, ladies and gentlemen, the winner of this year's Pageant and the new Princess America . . . Robin Gervais—Miss Florida!"

The Armory went wild.

Prescott tried to climb onto the stage.

Megan ran forward, covering the microphone, stooping to meet Prescott. "Norm. What the hell are you . . .?" Prescott thrust the envelope and its contents into Megan's face. Megan took one look, grabbed the material, stood up and shouted into the microphone.

"Ladies and gentlemen. Ladies and gentlemen. *Please!* There has been a terrible mistake. A mistake in the scoring. *Please!* Your attention, please! A mistake has been discovered in the scoring . . ."

Fleming's face went beet red. He appeared to be choking.

". . . the official winner is not Miss Florida . . ."

Thank God, thought Robin.

In his seat, General Gervais sat incredibly still. The only movement was a twitch in his left cheek.

". . . the new Princess America is Lori Macklin—Miss Utah!"

There was pandemonium in the Armory.

Marge Macklin cheered at the top of her lungs, tears streaming down her face. Dorn grabbed his wife and did an impromptu dance on the top of his seat. Fleming's body sagged and a stagehand moved in to support him. Prescott fell back in a heap and wiped the sweat from his face.

Bevacqua, as confused as anybody, led the orchestra into "Good Luck, Sweet Princess." Dumbfounded, each of the eight judges was standing.

Megan, moving quickly, folded the envelope in half and tucked it under his arm, then grabbed Lori's hand and brought her forward, shouting over the crowd and the orchestra, "Here she is! The thirteenth Princess America . . . Lori Macklin—Miss Utah!" He said it again so there would be no mistake. "Miss Utah!"

Walsh threw his arms around Hazel and yelled, "We came in second! Second! That isn't bad for the first time around."

Robin Gervais ran to Lori, threw her arms around her and kissed her. The audience roared its approval.

"You'll make a wonderful Princess," Robin whispered. "I'm so glad you won." She smiled and faded into the background, waiting for her chance to slip offstage.

Lori tried to understand it all—the voices, the noise, the music, the lights. And wasn't that Robin who kissed her? If this is a dream, why can't I wake up? Marge . . . something about Marge . . .

Lori was seated on the throne now and Ginny Kerr had placed the crown on her head and handed her the scepter. Ginny then slipped out of the white ermine-tipped cloak and paused for a moment to allow the photographers to set up for her last official act.

Robin slipped off in the confusion, went quickly to the dressing room, dug some change from her pocketbook and used the pay telephone. "Information? I'd like the telephone number of whatever airline has connecting flights to Okinawa from Surf City. That's right. Okinawa."

Megan was at Fleming's side.

"Megan . . ." Fleming's voice was a whip. "How the hell could you make such a mistake?"

Megan shoved the folded envelope into Fleming's rigid fingers and ran back onstage in time to start singing "Good Luck, Sweet Princess" as Lori started for the runway amid flashing cameras.

Fleming unfolded the envelope and could not stifle a shocked "Oh, my God!"

On top was a photograph of Robin Gervais, completely nude and apparently massaging her crotch in some obscene sex gesture. A second photograph showed her with bare breasts. And attached to the lewd photographs the actual negatives, proving the pictures were not faked.

Fleming began to breathe again. We would have been ruined, he thought. This last-minute chaos would be difficult to explain, but it could be done. Prescott was a master at explaining ticklish situations. We could come out smelling like a rose yet. And Megan. That s.o.b. did it again. I suppose it wouldn't be the Pageant without him.

Megan was on his second chorus of "Good Luck, Sweet Princess," the smile as broad and as sparkling as ever, his body putting English into the higher notes he couldn't quite reach. He had saved everybody's bacon. And he had done it because this was *his* show. The girls came and went. Fleming was fat and rich. Only Roger Megan was as constant as a star. This was his show and they could make all the snide remarks they wanted. Long after the flashes were gone and forgotten, they would remember Roger Megan, consort Prince to each Princess.

Lori was halfway down the runway when the haze began to lift, when the random thoughts began to settle into a pattern of thought, when the light and sound began to make sense. It was far from a dream, all of it. It was reality. The cruel reality of Marge. Oh, what a bad joke! Selling herself to try and keep me from giving it away for nothing. Shoveling shit against the tide!

And the marvelous reality of this. The dream wasn't a dream at all. I *am* Princess America, chaste and pure by edict. Marge could have saved all that money. Here I am pure as the driven snow and Marge has calluses on her back.

At the end of the runway, Lori turned and started her royal march back toward the stage, the emerging thoughts masked by the official Pageant smile, first turned this way, then that way for the Brownie cameras and to share the glorious moment with them all.

Near the stage, Lori caught a glimpse of Max Gerber, a

little roach of a man lost in a herd of unimportant people. She saw him wink at her and shake his clasped hands like a winning fighter.

Back on stage, Lori turned to the audience and drank in the applause, a thunderous ovation for the new Princess America. And she wondered what little Max expected for making sure she photographed well. And she wondered what it was that had held Steve back when she threw it out for him. And she wondered what they all would think if they knew what Steve and Max knew.

That the Princess was a whore.